GW00492919

Sally Aviss

The Girl in Jack's Portrait

The Girl in Jack's Portrait
by Sally Aviss

Text © Sally Aviss, 2018
Front cover from an original painting by Iveta Kasiliauskaite
(Website: www.ivetakart.com Facebook: Iveta.K.Art)

This is a work of fiction. Names, characters, businesses, places, events and incidents are either the products of the author's imagination or used in a fictitious manner. Any resemblance to actual persons, living or dead, or actual events is purely coincidental.

The right of Sally Aviss to be identified as the author of this work has been asserted by her in accordance with the Copyright, Designs and Patents Act 1988.

All rights reserved. No part of this document may be reproduced, copied, distributed, transferred, modified, or transmitted, in any form or by any means, electronic or mechanical, including photocopying, recording, or by any information storage or retrieval system, without the prior written permission of the copyright owner; nor can it be circulated in any form of binding or cover other than that in which it is published and without similar conditions including this condition being imposed on a subsequent purchaser. In no event shall the author or publisher be liable for any damages caused in any way by use of this document.

Published by Ōzaru Books, an imprint of BJ Translations Ltd
Street Acre, Shuart Lane, St Nicholas-at-Wade,
BIRCHINGTON, CT7 0NG, U.K.
www.ozaru.net

First edition published 27 January 2018
Printed by Lightning Source
ISBN: 978-0-9931587-6-6

The vagaries of life can take people in all sorts of unexpected directions. Take barrister Callie Martin, for example, struggling to cope with a vocation she doesn't fully understand or enjoy. Or Edie Paignton, about to lose the one thing that is closest to her heart. Or soldier Jamie Rutherford who encounters the girl of his dreams only to see her disappear into the crowd. Not to mention architect Ben Rutherford, still coming to terms with the loss of his wife or businessman Erik van der Waals, whose studied sophistication hides deep-seated resentment. And what about mental health nurse Sarah Adhabi who finds hidden strengths when confronted by emotional turmoil?

Six people seeking an escape from their pasts; six people seeking redemption in the present; six people who find their lives interwoven and their secrets revealed.

But just who is The Girl in Jack's Portrait?

*For my family
with love*

Also by Sally Aviss, published by Ōzaru Books

The Cairnmor Trilogy:

The Call of Cairnmor

Changing Tides, Changing Times

Where Gloom and Brightness Meet

Message from Captivity

Acknowledgements

I am, as ever, indebted to my family Peter, Timothy and Elizabeth Aviss and to the many friends I have made through my writing for their unstinting support and encouragement. And also to Ben Jones at Ozaru Books for his continued willingness to publish my books.

Contents

Horse Guards Arch
London

Eyes forward. Look neither left nor right. Remain still.

A party of Japanese tourists crowds round the soldier with excited exclamations and clicking cameras. They stay for several minutes before moving on.

Great. Thanks. Now I can't see anything except flashing lights.

Eyes forward. Look neither left nor right. Remain still.

A family stop and stare: a little boy and girl with their parents.

"Why's he wearing those funny clothes?" the boy asks.

"That's his uniform."

"Those boots must be uncomfortable. They go right over his knees and stick out at the side."

"They're very shiny," observes the girl as they walk away. "So's his sword."

Eyes forward. Look neither left nor right. Remain still.

Everything that's shiny takes hours to polish. Days if we've something special coming up.

A group of giggling schoolgirls arrives.

"Go on. I dare you," says one of them. "Kiss 'im on the cheek."

"Don't knock his helmet off," says another. "Here Miss," and she addresses the teacher, "wot's his hat called?"

"Er, I'm not sure but it's definitely made from silver and the plume is white horse-hair, I think."

"I wouldn't fancy getting that in me eyes. What happens if you have a bad helmet day?" They snigger.

"Come along, now," says the teacher wearily and the group move off with the exception of the two girls.

"Go on then. Now's your chance. Quick, before Miss sees."

"I don't know…" says her friend.

"Chicken are you?"

"You do it then."

She does. A quick peck on the cheek.

"Look, I made him blush!"

And they run off to tell their classmates of their daring.

Eyes forward. Look neither left nor right. Remain still.

Stupid girls.

A mother and daughter walk by.

"Do you want to take a photo?" asks the mother.

"No," replies the daughter. "I'd be much too embarrassed. I wonder if the soldiers ever feel embarrassed? Imagine just having to stand there while people do all sorts of silly things around you. It must take an awful lot of self-discipline not to move or react at all."

"I know. I'd hate it."

"Me too."

1

"Their uniforms are amazing, aren't they? The Household Cavalry always look so smart, especially when they're on horseback. Shall we walk or get the bus?"

"The bus."

Thank you. We always take great pride in our appearance so we look our best in public.

Eyes forward. Look neither left nor right. Remain still.

"Where shall we meet after work?"

Two young women walk under the archway on their way from Horse Guards Parade to Whitehall.

"How about Counter Coffee in Piccadilly? You know, the one just up from Riverstones."

"Fine. What time?"

"Five-ish?"

"Great. See you then."

One of the women walks away and the other's phone rings. She juggles mobile, handbag, small suitcase on wheels and brief-case, dropping the latter in the process. It springs open, spilling the contents onto the flagstones. She moves to gather up her documents, stamping on papers that escape from their pink ribbons and which threaten to blow away in a sudden gust of wind that whips without warning through the archway.

The young woman looks up at the soldier and smiles, shaking her head and biting her bottom lip, feeling like a complete idiot.

Eyes forward. Look neither left nor right...

I can't.

The soldier smiles back and for a moment time stands still.

The young woman moves on, dealing with her phone call but all the while looking back at the soldier.

Eyes forward. Look neither left nor right. Remain still.

I can't.

He turns his head briefly in her direction.

What if I never see her again?

The thought fills him with alarm and he considers possibilities.

After we've changed guard, I'm off duty. If I'm quick at grooming Lysander and clean everything thoroughly and efficiently when I'm back in barracks, I could easily get to Counter Coffee by five.

His heart pounds with hope and nervousness.

Eyes forward. Look neither left nor right. Remain still.

A sad-looking, middle-aged woman walks slowly by; shoulders hunched, eyes cast downwards, seemingly weighed down by the cares of the whole world. As she passes, she glances briefly at the soldier before returning to stare unseeing into the middle distance, oblivious to everything and everyone.

She looks lonely. She should go for a coffee somewhere. Try and cheer herself up a bit. She could go to Counter Coffee.

What shall I do if the girl's not there? Or I'm too late and miss her?

I have to see her.

He wonders who she is; where she's going, where she works, what her name is. He suppresses the urge to run into Whitehall to see if she might still be there.

What if she doesn't go to the coffee shop at all? I might never find her again. If she is there, what shall I say? I could always go down on one knee and ask her to marry me. I want to ask her to marry me. But that's ridiculous, I've only seen her once. I don't know anything about her. In any case, she'd run a mile if I did that.

A well-dressed man speaking to someone on his mobile approaches the soldier and stops in front of him.

"Yes, Judith? New clients? I see – they came in this morning after I'd left the office? A house just on the market, you say. Where? U-uh."

He winks at the soldier and pulls a comical face.

Eyes forward. Look neither left nor right. Remain still.

I'm going to laugh in a minute. Go away.

"What's my diary like for tomorrow? Stupidly, I brought the wrong phone with me, didn't I? The other one's got everything in it, appointments the lot."

Duh.

"Is it a big project? I see. Can't Matt handle it? My portfolio's fuller than I'd like at the moment. Oh, of course, I'd forgotten. He's on his way up north, isn't he? Okay then. What time?" He extracts a note book from his overcoat pocket and writes something down. "Yep. Got that. Ten o'clock tomorrow. Thanks, Judith. Tell them they might have to wait a while before I can start, though. Cheers."

He ends the call and smiles at the soldier.

"I wondered if you'd be here today."

Eyes forward. Look neither left nor right. Remain still.

The soldier smiles with his eyes.

It's good to see you, Dad.

"Counter Coffee in Piccadilly? Five-ish?" asks his father. "Any possibility?"

Imperceptibly, the soldier inclines his head. It's enough.

Pleased, the man gives him a thumbs-up and moves away.

The soldier is pleased too. Perfect.

No, it's not! The girl!

Eyes forward. Look neither left nor right. Remain still.

Will his dad melt into the background if the girl is there?

He's like that, his dad; tactful and astute. Not a drag like some parents who sound dreadful. But will the situation be a bit much even for his own father?

The soldier wonders if he really wants his dad around while he walks up to a strange girl and asks her to marry him. Or even just out on a date?

A date sounds terribly old-fashioned. He hopes the girl is. The soldier knows he's an old-fashioned kind of fellow. In any case, he'd curl up with embarrassment if his dad was around.

I'll text him later. Tell him something's cropped up. He'll understand. Best Dad in the world. We'd planned to see each other at the weekend, anyway. So if we don't manage this, it'll be okay.

Eyes forward. Look neither left nor right. Remain still.

CHAPTER 1

Edie was a dinosaur.

Well, she wasn't really a dinosaur but that's what her ex-husband had called her the day he walked out on her to start a new life with a woman half his age.

Edie had been distraught, furious, bereft. Relieved.

"The children are all independent, now," he'd said to her. "You can have the house. I don't want it. I've always hated its depressing Victoriana anyway."

Ah, but that's what Edie had always loved – its character, its charm, its sense of history. After all, wasn't that what they'd both loved when they'd found it forlorn and derelict during the heady, idealistic start to their marriage? And hadn't they joyfully renovated the house together – sweeping and cleaning, painting and decorating?

Or had it all been an illusion? Perhaps she'd looked at everything through rose-tinted glasses. Perhaps she was the one who'd loved it and he never had. Perhaps, because she was already pregnant and filled with the nesting instinct, she hadn't noticed that her husband was less enthusiastic than she.

He'd wanted to knock down walls and make it into some modernist statement. But Edie had resisted him; summoning up every ounce of persuasive argument she could muster until, eventually, he'd shrugged his shoulders and relented before going off to the pub for a drink with some colleagues from work, coming home tipsy and amorous.

She'd always loved the original period features of her house – the ceiling roses, the decorative cornicing; the inlaid, colourful fireplaces with their pretty patterned tiles on the hearth. And it had always been *her* house: the place where she had spent so much of her life – cooking, cleaning, gardening, decorating; raising their three children (with precious little help from her stockbroker husband), safe within its friendly, familiar walls and generous outside space.

She had never found it depressing. It had been her sanctuary during the difficult times; her place of refuge from the outside world.

She was very much like her mother, she supposed, but her mother had always been serenely happy and content wherever her home had been as long as she was with Edie's father.

Edie had never been like that. She needed her beloved Victorian house to provide the emotional stability and comfort lacking in her marriage; a marriage that hadn't lasted; a marriage that hadn't really been a marriage at all.

She could see that now, now that it was all over. In fact, if she dared look even further, she could see that it was a union (or rather dis-union) that should never have happened in the first place; one that took place for all the wrong reasons; one that her parents had advised her against and said, in their generous, caring way, while hiding the disappointment she knew they must have felt, that having a baby outside of marriage was not such a terrible thing and that they would look after the child while she continued her studies by going to university.

That was the most important thing, they'd said, to carry on with her education while she had the chance.

4

Edie knew they must have been equally upset when she'd accepted Trevor's proposal and made the move to London but she was in love and her boyfriend was standing by her (albeit reluctantly, she realized now) and that was all that had mattered to her then.

She wished now she'd listened to her parents' advice.

So, here she was, a year to the day after her divorce had been finalized – alone, walking through Horse Guards Arch; mentally removed from the hustle and bustle of traffic on the busy road ahead of her and gawping tourists crowding the pavements.

A dinosaur. A fuddy-duddy. A stay-at-home. A throwback to a bygone age.

Her children didn't really need her; her ex-husband certainly didn't need her. Her parents were long gone; her brothers and sisters (all older than she) scattered up and down the far reaches of the country, absorbed and fulfilled in their own lives.

As she passed through Horse Guards Arch into the quadrangle, Edie glanced briefly at the Household Cavalry soldier standing so still and expressionless in all his splendid regalia. She wondered what he was thinking; whether he thought anything at all during the time he was on ceremonial duty guarding The Queen. She wished she could stand as he did without thinking; without *having* to think.

She wished her problems would all go away so she could just focus on her own simple, everyday needs.

"You should get out and about a bit, Mum," her daughter Victoria, newly married and genuinely happy, had said. "Meet some different people. Try an internet dating agency. Stop moping around. After all, it's been more than two years now since Dad left. I know that he hurt you, but let's face it, you and he never did get on very well, did you?"

Hadn't they? She supposed not. They were always arguing about this or that and when he eventually did come home from work, there was always an atmosphere to spoil the contentment of her day. Still, by making compromises and hiding things from her children (mostly by maintaining a cheerful demeanour in front of them) she'd managed to cope for the thirty-eight years she was with Trevor.

Her off-spring had turned out well on the whole, apart from David, the middle child, who'd been a bit of a handful as a teenager; bunking off school and getting in with the wrong crowd; failing his exams; drifting from one dead-end job to another while working his way through a string of unsuitable girlfriends.

She worried about him still, even though a few months ago he'd unexpectedly fallen head-over-heels in love with a nice girl who from the start, seemed to be a stabilizing influence on him and was gradually turning his life around. Renovating the little run-down cottage they had bought in Cornwall had given him focus and purpose and he'd even begun to think about enrolling in evening classes. It wasn't through lack of ability that he'd failed his exams, he said, but lack of effort and application.

However, Edie remained anxious about him and she wasn't particularly happy about Daniel, her eldest, either. He was a stockbroker like his father: gregarious and party-loving, riding out the current economic roller-coaster with skilled and calculated deviousness. His somewhat dubious successes didn't endear him to Edie, especially as he was also arrogant and opinionated, again like his father.

She had to admit that it had been something of a relief when, belatedly, at the age of thirty, having saved up a vast fortune, he had finally moved out of the family home into an outrageously expensive, open-plan penthouse flat in a converted warehouse overlooking the Thames.

Edie envied him his view, but not his life-style – he was far too busy socializing and playing the field. He couldn't understand it when she expressed a desire to see him settled.

"Why on earth do I need to do that, Mum," he'd asked, genuinely mystified, "when I'm happy the way I am?"

For herself, Edie had always dreamed of having the fairy-tale marriage she presumed her parents had shared and who, even in old age, had been a devoted couple, passing away within a few short months of each other; the one who was left unable to survive without the other.

Instead, she had had an errant husband who throughout their life together, had been a good provider but who had always made her feel as though she was an embarrassment, a frump; someone to be treated like a door-mat.

Not once in the whole of their marriage had he ever taken her to his firm's lavish Christmas dinners or social occasions; not once had she gone with him on his frequent trips abroad. He had always fobbed her off with excuses and protestations, saying that she wouldn't enjoy it.

"It'll be all money-talk, Edie," he'd said. "You know, stockbroker stuff. You'd be bored stiff."

And she'd swallowed his reasoning, convincing herself that it was for the best; that she wouldn't enjoy going out for an evening to some swanky restaurant where she'd feel out of her depth; that what she needed most of all was to be at home for her family.

Apart from her children, well, Vicky and latterly David, and her house, her life had been an emotional wasteland, an arid desert. She supposed she'd had moments of joy and wonderment but these were so few and far between that they'd become blurred forever with the indistinct texture of the past.

Edie wondered how she'd endured it for the thirty-eight years until her husband had walked out on her.

Then, to make matters worse (as if leaving her wasn't enough) a couple of months ago, she'd received a letter from his solicitor to say that Trevor intended to stop paying her alimony, citing that he was struggling financially and couldn't afford to support her any more.

She didn't understand. He was a stockbroker and stockbrokers made pots of money, didn't they? Edie had spent sleepless nights railing at the unfairness and injustice of it all, in the end taking him to court to try and protect her rights. But it had been all to no avail.

Her barrister niece, young and inexperienced, taking on her first solo case after completing her training, had been terribly upset at the verdict as she knew that Trevor (whom she'd met only once even though he was her uncle) was lying through his teeth. She could find nothing with which to counter the opposing counsel who produced all kinds of financial evidence to support his client's case;

nor was she able to convince the judge of Edie's rights and Trevor's moral obligation.

Outside the courtroom at the end of the hearing, Callie had burst into tears, convinced that her aunt would never want to speak to her again; distraught that she hadn't been able to do better and worried as to how Edie would manage. Perhaps her own father could help out financially, Callie had suggested.

"It's alright," Edie had said bravely, putting her arms around her niece's shoulders and consoling her in a motherly way. "Don't worry. I'll get by," while wondering exactly how she would.

She was too proud to ask for money from her family and in order to survive, she knew she would either have to find a job (at her age in the middle of a recession?) or sell her house, the merest thought of which filled her with terrible fear and anxiety.

However, left without a choice she had, early that morning, come to a heart-rending decision. Bravely and without giving herself the chance to consider the matter further, she had put her house on the market. The estate agent who came around half-an-hour later to assess the property said it was rare to find such a perfect example of a Victorian house in its original condition and that it was absolutely ripe for development.

How could a perfectly preserved house be ripe for development? It didn't make any sense. Edie had felt as though her world was about to end.

After the man had gone, restless and unsettled, she'd come into town, hoping to escape from the heartache of having to leave her home and the terrible fate that might befall it; a heartache even greater and infinitely more painful than when Trevor had left her.

She wandered aimlessly around the centre of London – staring at paintings she didn't see; going in and out of shops with no idea what they sold; ordering a lunch she couldn't finish – putting off the terrible moment before she returned home to stab her beloved house in the back.

CHAPTER 2

Callie's feet were aching. She wished now she'd worn her other shoes.

The high heels had looked so elegant with her gown when she'd tried them on in front of the mirror and she'd thought that as this was her first trial at the Royal Courts of Justice, even though she was only the supporting junior in the case, she ought to look smart.

She wished she hadn't chosen the shoes now. "Comfort over elegance" her grandmother had always told her, and Callie knew that she was right. The long corridors and stairs were taking their toll on her back as well as her feet.

She looked at her watch. The session was running over time – surely the judge must adjourn the proceedings soon? She was due back in chambers at three-thirty to see a new client and his solicitor. She hoped they didn't take up more than their allotted time as she was meeting Amy in Counter Coffee at five. It looked like being a complicated case and she would be on her own again for this latest foray into the world of law, something that filled her with trepidation.

She knew she was not exactly fulfilling expectations with her success rate (or rather, lack of it) and the head of chambers had called her into his room the previous day and told her in no uncertain terms that her "batting average was below par" and that she needed "to pull her socks up".

Callie thought of Auntie Edie and knew that he was right despite his prolific use of metaphors – something she'd been told to avoid during her training.

Under cover of the table at which she was seated, Callie released her aching feet from their stylish prison, stretching out her toes rather in the manner of a contented cat that had just awoken from a deep sleep.

Idly, she admired the polished wood-panelling that lined the room and studied the shelves filled with law books. She wondered whether they were used for reference during court cases anymore. Even if they weren't, she liked to see them arranged like that; they made the room feel civilized and learned.

She thought about the Household Cavalry soldier she'd seen that morning and who had had such expressive, intelligent eyes. She hadn't been able to stop staring at him after he'd smiled at her. He had looked so smart and proud in his ceremonial uniform.

She regretted now not saying anything to him but she presumed he wouldn't have been able to respond anyway.

Callie wondered what his name was and where he came from; what he was like as a person. She rather liked him. Especially his eyes.

Perhaps she would come to work that way tomorrow. He might be there again.

The barrister next to her surreptitiously nudged her with his elbow.

"You're on," he whispered in her ear.

"Oh God," muttered Callie, rising to her feet.

She had absolutely no idea what the prosecution had just said or where they'd got to in the proceedings.

"My Lord," she began and stopped, swallowing hard.

The judge looked at her enquiringly. He wondered why she looked so much smaller than she had earlier.

"Yes?" he said, raising bushy, benevolent eyebrows in her direction.

"My Friend," she said, thinking quickly on her stockinged feet, "has made his case very succinctly. Too succinctly. He has tried to bring before the court a certain emphasis in building the case for the Prosecution by omitting important details that were previously outlined by the Defence and which are vital to our client's... defence and the eventual successful outcome, from our client's perspective at least, of this hearing."

Callie knew she was speaking a load of waffle, but what else could she do? With her heart pounding, she cast around in her mind for further, suitably plausible, ambivalent phrases.

"It is on those details that the case for the Defence rests. That is not to say..." she added hastily, "that the Defence rests its case," this was becoming ridiculous, "but merely that my colleagues and I have presented our case in great... detail and this, as in any case brought before the court, is vitally important if the truth in its entirety is to be established."

Callie sat down, her cheeks red with embarrassment.

"Thank you, Miss Martin," said the judge, his eyes twinkling with amusement, "that was most... erudite. And, what's more, I am inclined to agree with you that truth in its entirety should be established. So, on that profound note, therefore, as we have exceeded our time today, this court is adjourned until ten o'clock tomorrow morning and please, ladies and gentlemen," he added wearily, regarding the assembled lawyers over the rim of his glasses, "I do hope that we shall be able to close the proceedings by the end of the day."

"All rise," intoned the clerk and everyone stood up.

The judge retired to his chambers.

"You didn't have any idea where we were just then, did you? They warned me you were clueless," said her colleague, as they gathered up their papers. "You were lucky we had old Wainwright. Anyone else would've had your guts for garters."

Stung by his words, Callie wondered why everyone was talking in metaphors.

Maybe I'm not cut out to be a barrister, after all, she thought. *Too much stress. Too many tedious late nights preparing for court. I just want to be free to go and have a coffee with Amy whenever I like.*

Perhaps, like Amy, she should have become a literary agent instead of a lawyer. Then she would at least have the satisfaction of one day finding a talented, unknown author and nurturing their career.

But she'd probably be useless at that as well – after all, what did she know about anything?

With a sigh, Callie took off her wig, gown and white neckbands, packing them away in her suitcase. She collected her papers together, gathered up all her belongings and left the building.

She crossed the Strand and walked down Middle Temple Lane to Royal Court Chambers where she went into her room, dumped everything except her documents case on the floor and began to study the brief for her next client and his solicitor who both arrived late.

The meeting took an inordinate amount of time and Callie texted Amy to cancel their coffee.

How about tomorrow instead? :-)

No problem. I'm a bit tied up at work as well :-(

Jamie left Hyde Park Barracks as soon as he was free and jumped onto a bus, alighting opposite Green Park and manoeuvring his way along the crowded rush-hour pavements, arriving at Counter Coffee in burst of expectant energy.

Having first checked that she was not downstairs, he ordered coffee and cake and positioned himself by the door. Here he'd have the perfect view as his perfect girl came into the building. He hoped her friend would melt into the background, just as he knew his dad would have done had he been here.

His dad had been fine about not meeting him and had texted back to say that he was looking forward to their weekend together. He suggested they drove across to the house in Maybury and took the boat out on the Thames.

Jamie always enjoyed going out in the motorboat. It had once belonged to his great-grandparents and had a rather distinguished history. After his dad had taken over the vessel when Jamie was little, he'd brought it down to Maybury on a low-loader all the way from Scotland. After that, the two of them had had enormous fun in the school holidays motoring to different destinations along the interconnected network of waterways that radiated across the country.

Jamie's mother had died when he was twelve and from that time on, it had always been just him and his dad. They had gone everywhere together, done everything together – his dad doing his utmost to compensate for the loss of Jamie's mother who, because she worked abroad most of the time, had never been at home much anyway. In fact, thought Jamie, it had always been the best when it was just him and his dad.

The bell pinged and Jamie looked up at the door.

A mother and daughter came in and ordered two complicated coffees, apportioning between them tray, haversack and plastic bags bulging with books from Riverstones before taking everything downstairs.

Didn't they walk by me earlier this morning? thought Jamie.

When he'd asked his dad why his mother wasn't at home much, his dad had said that she was doing important and necessary work abroad and that although he missed her terribly and knew that Jamie did as well, it was right that she followed her heart and her vocation.

However, Jamie had felt far too guilty and embarrassed to say that he actually preferred it when she wasn't at home. Things seemed so much more settled and less disrupted; he and his dad could do the things they liked doing without having to make compromises.

The door opened again and a couple of American tourists came in, closely followed by the sad-looking woman.

I definitely saw her this morning. She still looks just as unhappy.

Jamie finished his coffee and ordered another.

His dad had been so proud when Jamie had got a place at university and said that his great-grandma would have been delighted to think that he was doing a history degree, as that's what she had done many, many years previously at Edinburgh.

Jamie remembered his great-grandmother. She had been warm and kind and still beautiful, even in old age. When he was little, he could remember sitting on a stool at her feet as she sat in the easy chair by the kitchen range, gazing up at her as she read to him or told him stories about when she was young.

Sometimes, though, a deep sadness would come over her and tears would fill her eyes. His dad told him that was because she missed Greatgramps terribly. After that, whenever he saw that she was upset, Jamie would bring her something to look at or tell her about what he had been doing. He had liked being able to make her smile again.

Jamie looked at his watch and checked his phone for messages. He could go on social media to pass the time, but he didn't want to miss his girl when she came through the door.

If she came through the door.

The seconds ticked by… then the minutes… then an hour.

He asked for another coffee and chose a chocolate muffin.

I shan't sleep tonight at this rate, he thought.

The mother and daughter left, smiling their thanks to the hard-pressed people serving behind the counter.

The sad-looking woman went out of the door.

Reluctantly, at seven o'clock, Jamie decided his girl wasn't coming.

Disappointed and frustrated, he made his way back to barracks. There was nothing he could do to find his girl and he felt as despondent as the sad-looking woman.

Then, to cap it all, as he waited for the bus, it began to rain.

CHAPTER 3

Edie spent a restless night, alternately tossing and turning, woken up by dreams of a vaguely disturbing nature, the details of which she couldn't remember.

She had arrived home the previous evening to find a message on the answerphone from the estate agent to say that they had secured a viewing for ten o'clock the following day. Edie thought that was ultra-efficient especially as her house had only just gone on the market. They hadn't even had time to send along the promised photographer to take pictures.

Despite her lack of sleep, Edie was up early, hoovering and cleaning to make her house look at its very best. The thought occurred to her that perhaps she ought to un-tidy it and move the furniture around into awkward positions so that it looked crowded and no one would want to buy it. But, she supposed, people would see through the mess and cluttered appearance anyway.

At ten o'clock precisely, the doorbell rang and with some trepidation, Edie answered the door.

"Mrs Paignton?"

"Yes?"

After the couple had introduced themselves, the husband said to Edie, "The estate agent sends his apologies – detained by some last-minute panic with another client. We were so anxious to see the house before anyone else that we've come without him and brought our architect along as well. I hope you don't mind."

Architect? Edie felt a momentary panic. Why did they need an architect?

"No-o, of course not," and she stepped back to allow the couple into the hall, who immediately looked at the floor tiles.

"What do you think? Green oak throughout?" said the wife. "Those tiles won't fit in with my vision of what we want, will they, darling?"

"Absolutely not."

Edie felt sick. Her beautiful patterned, original tiles, lovingly cleaned and maintained, to be desecrated by a plain, boring wooden floor, even if it was oak.

The architect, who had not been introduced and who had been quietly observing Edie, extended his hand.

"I'm Ben, by the way," he said, his manner kind. "Ben Rutherford."

Edie shook his hand and her eyes filled with tears. She blinked hastily, trying not to embarrass herself. This viewing was going to be harder than she had imagined.

"Hello," she managed to say.

The architect didn't accompany his clients directly as they went from room to room discussing which walls they wanted to take down; how they wanted to "bring the garden into the house" by building into the side-return and adding a kitchen extension to create a vast dining-living area complete with skylights and bi-fold doors.

Instead, the architect chose to remain at Edie's side as she showed the couple into each room in turn, observing her increasingly horrified reactions as his prospective clients discussed re-plastering the walls and ceilings; removing picture

12

and dado rails; taking out the fitted bookshelves and cupboards either side of the chimney breasts.

He listened carefully to what was being said, without making comment, as the couple voiced their preferences without tact or consideration for their hostess or even being aware of how much pain they were inflicting.

The architect began to develop an increasing antipathy towards them while Edie could see her beloved home being ruthlessly ripped apart.

She felt like crying out in anguish.

The couple looked at the fire surrounds in the sitting and dining rooms.

"We can get a good price for those at... what's that scruffy place called just around the corner from here, you know, the one that has all the junk out the front?"

"John's Emporium."

"That's the one. It would help off-set the cost of the renovations."

"Hardly. But I don't like them anyway. Much too dark and dingy."

Dark and dingy? thought Edie. *They're beautiful!*

"Can we see upstairs?"

Silently and in despair, Edie led the way.

"We'll have those fireplaces out. Perhaps the chimney breasts can be removed as well. They take up too much room and spoil the nice smooth lines of the walls. That'll create greater openness. And we must put in a loft extension. Harry needs his own space. And those wooden sashes will have to go. So inefficient. And as for the window on the landing – such a peculiar pattern in the glass. All those colours. Like on the front door. That'll have to be replaced. Ugh."

Edie thought of the multi-coloured sunlight that streamed in through the large oval-topped landing window first thing in the morning as well as through the stained-glass downstairs in the evening. She loved to see the intricate patterns reflected on the walls and the floor tiles.

How could anyone not appreciate its beauty? Were these people complete Philistines?

"I'll get Honey to design a stair carpet for us. Thin, bright, multi-coloured stripes would look very stylish and contrast well with the oak floors. What do you think?" The wife turned to the architect, who remained impassive. "Have you been writing everything down? I do hope so, because when I look at any house, my immediate instincts are always my best ideas."

This woman is insufferable, thought Edie. *I don't want to sell my house to these people. If they want to make all these alterations because it's not what they want, why don't they build their own house?*

"I have made mental notes," replied the architect.

The wife looked at him. "Well, I hope you have a good memory."

This woman is insufferable, thought Ben. *They ought to build their own house instead of wrecking this one.* "I'm renowned for it," he said equably.

Edie couldn't help smiling.

The architect smiled back, thinking that she ought to smile more often as it was a very attractive smile and made her look twenty years younger. Judging by the habitual sadness in her expression, apart from her obvious distress at what was being suggested, he guessed that her smile was a bit rusty.

13

The woman turned to her husband. "Well, darling, I think we've seen just about everything that we need to. An offer is definitely on the cards, Mrs Paignton. This house is just what we've been looking for. A blank canvas onto which we can put our own stamp. We need to go home and do some sums and," she turned to the architect, "if you could have the plans drawn up pronto, we'll get our builders over here to estimate the costs. We'll contact our solicitor and you'll hear from him in due course, Mrs Paignton."

Edie didn't reply.

Nor did the architect.

She showed the three of them out of the door and shut it behind them, remaining motionless in the hall, fighting back the tears.

I can't do this, she thought. *I can't go through with this.*

She jumped as the doorbell rang.

On the doorstep stood the architect.

"Forgive me," he said, "but I don't think you should sell your house to that couple."

"Really?"

"They were hideous."

"They were, weren't they?" she said gratefully.

"In fact, I don't think you should sell your house at all."

"You don't? Why not?"

"Because it will break your heart."

Edie's bottom lip trembled and the tears spilled over. "You're very perceptive."

"It's my middle name." He offered her his handkerchief. "It is clean."

He seemed to hesitate on the doorstep.

Edie didn't want him to go. She really didn't want to be alone at that moment.

"Would you like a cup of tea?"

He was a stranger. Edie knew you should never invite strangers into your house when you were on your own. Yet she just had.

"Thank you. I'd like that very much. Prospective clients like those two are thirsty work. And here's my business card, so that you know that everything's legit." Ben handed her an embossed white rectangle.

Edie smiled and led the way into the kitchen.

"Will you take them on?" she asked.

The architect shook his head. "No. And you must withdraw this house from the market. There are too many people out there who want to do the same things as those two barracudas. Although the tide is gradually turning, there are too many magazines, too many property programmes that see that sort of thing as 'improvement' and 'desirable'. Makes me want to shout at estate agents and the television sometimes. Sorry. I'm up on my soapbox."

"I feel exactly the same," said Edie.

He looked around the kitchen while she prepared their tea.

"I've never seen such a perfect example of an original Victorian house. If such things were possible, it ought to have listed status or a preservation order on it at the very least. Those fireplaces in the reception rooms are magnificent and as for

14

that range and bread oven in here… it's a historian's dream! To find it all in situ as well. Is it original? Does it work?"

"Yes and it does, but I can quite see why they lost their popularity when other means of cooking food came in. It's a devil of a job to prime and keep the temperature constant. And as for cleaning – it's a nightmare. But whenever there are power cuts, it's a God-send. It was worth every ounce of effort during the miner's strike in the seventies."

"Yesterday."

Edie laughed. "It was, wasn't it? However, let me show you my concession to so-called modern living."

Edie took Ben out to what would have been the scullery.

"There was nothing in here, I'm afraid, when we first moved in. The brick housing for the copper had already been demolished and the sink was damaged beyond repair, so I decided to use it to hide away all the modern stuff – kitchen units, gas hob, electric oven, washing machine, tumble dryer, dishwasher; all the usual appliances. With three children to raise, I had to be practical, but I tried to do it in such a way as to keep all that modernity hidden away and not disturb the character in the rest of the house. Then I've been able to update over the years to my heart's content without worrying about whether it's authentic or not."

"Clever. Your idea?"

"Yes. This house is my creation. Well, it's someone else's creation, but I've always felt as though I'm the custodian. I know that might sound a bit pretentious, and Trevor always told me I was pretentious where this house was concerned…"

"Trevor?"

"My ex-husband."

"Ah."

"But I've always felt that this house was a piece of living history. And to be a part of that is a great privilege." She stopped and bit her lip. "Sorry. I'm talking too much."

"No, you're not. Was it like this when you first moved in?"

"No, it was in a terrible state. All the original features were intact fortunately, although hidden behind Sixties hardboard, but the whole place was full of grime and sadly neglected."

"How long have you lived here?"

"Thirty-eight years."

"Wow." He wondered how old she was.

"I was eighteen and newly married when we bought the house," continued Edie, unable to stop, needing to talk to someone. Anyone. "And pregnant. And then penniless after we'd bought it. I'd seen it in an estate agent's window and fortunately, we got it really cheaply. No one else wanted it and it seemed to call out to me. So, I set about restoring it."

"What about your husband? Did he help?"

Edie laughed harshly. "Trevor? No. He wasn't a bit interested and only went through the motions. Too career-orientated." She took a deep breath and made the tea, pouring it out into two mugs. "So, I went to Westminster library, the Victoria and Albert museum and did my research. I learnt all sorts of things – the correct way to restore and maintain floor-tiles; how to clean layers of paint off cornicing; how to restore fireplaces to their original glory and so on. I worked on the sash-windows myself, re-aligning and re-hanging, even managing to keep the original glass as I love the way the reflections shimmer in the light. And along the way, by doing all these things, I developed an enthusiasm for internal and external architectural history. Not just Victorian but other periods too." Edie looked at Ben earnestly. "My bookshelves are full of books I've collected over the years and these days, the internet is a wonderful resource."

"And London is full of living examples."

Edie smiled. "Isn't it just? Although I feel as though I want to buy up all the houses that still have their original features intact and preserve them before it's too late and their originality disappears forever."

"How right you are," he said, looking at his watch and finishing his tea. "Much as I'd like to continue our conversation, I'm afraid I have to go as I have another appointment shortly."

"I'm so sorry," she apologized. "I've talked too much."

Edie was afraid she'd made herself seem like an idiot: one of these lonely, middle-aged women so desperate for company that they become overwhelming and irritating.

"You haven't, honestly." Ben saw her anxious expression and fearing that he might have been a bit abrupt, added hastily, "In fact, I would like to see you again."

He bit his lip. He hadn't meant it to sound quite like that.

See me again? Edie was concerned. She'd only asked him in for a cup of tea not a date.

"I mean…" he added, seeing her confusion. "Look, how about lunch? What about meeting me in town?"

Lunch? It was becoming worse by the minute.

"You need to talk to someone about what to do with your house. I'm very well qualified in that sort of thing."

That was true. He seemed genuine. *But you can never tell these days*, thought Edie.

"Alright," she agreed cautiously. "When?"

"How about today."

"Today!"

"Yes. Today." He could get it over and done with. "Do you like Thai-Chinese?" Did she? "I don't know."

"Live dangerously! Try it. I'll meet you outside Riverstones in Piccadilly about one. The place I have mind is in Great Windmill Street. Not far away." He smiled. "It's only lunch."

Why did Edie feel disappointed? "Of course."

"Until one o'clock, then."

"Yes."

Edie stood on the doorstep watching shyly as the architect got into his car and drove away.

Somewhere underneath that downtrodden exterior beats the heart of a neglected, loving woman, thought Ben, as he glanced at her through the driver's side-view mirror.

And perhaps, if only he dared admit it to himself, he was actually as lonely as the woman whose house he had just left.

Callie walked through Horse Guards Arch, hoping that her soldier might be on duty.

He wasn't, unfortunately; at least, she assumed that the Life Guard who stood there on foot wasn't him. It was hard to tell with the ornate strap covering his chin and a helmet that came down low over his eyes.

She tried her best to peer beneath its concealing decorativeness but she hadn't wanted to make what she was doing too obvious in case she was mistaken for some kind of nut-case. Besides, it was a ridiculous thing to do – peering up some strange soldier's nose in case he turned out to be the man of her dreams.

She felt too awkward to ask the other soldier standing at the nearby entrance to the Guard's Museum deep in conversation with a member of the public if he knew the name of the soldier who had been on guard duty in the quadrangle the previous morning.

Becoming anxious in case she was late, Callie walked away into Whitehall and caught a taxi to the Royal Courts of Justice.

Jamie, seated astride his horse facing Whitehall, saw Callie go by. Unable to call out to her or chase after her, he could only watch with a desperate, sinking feeling in his heart as she walked past, without looking up or back, and hailed a taxi. Try as he might, he couldn't discern what she said to the driver as there was too much extraneous noise from the street.

He wondered if she had come by the Arch specially to see if he was there. He told himself not to be so ridiculously fanciful.

CHAPTER 4

Edie was early.

She was always early. Even as a child, she was the one who was ready first. Her own offspring had always been organized and on time for everything. They were never late for school or for school trips or concerts. She had never wanted to be one of those mums who arrived at the last moment, harassed and out-of-breath, with disorientated children in tow.

Even though she had had any number of rows with David if she tried to persuade him to do his homework, at least when he was younger, he always arrived at school on time looking reasonably smart. Of course, as all three of her children grew older, it became their own responsibility to get to school, but Edie had always prided herself on giving them a head start. She was pleased that Vicky had followed her example and was well prepared with her own children.

Edie hoped she looked alright. Her combination of jeans, jacket and favourite patterned blue top (which her father always said perfectly matched the colour of her eyes that were so like her mother's) weren't exactly fashionable, but she felt comfortable in them.

Edie hadn't minded him saying that, about being like her mother. She had had beautifully expressive eyes, although Edie had always loved the warmth in her father's as well.

She still missed her parents. Even now, just thinking about them, she could feel the pain of their loss, all too aware of the great gaping void in her life that their absence created. She remembered their generosity, their mutual happiness in each other; the happiness they gave to others.

Edie looked inside the door of Riverstones and then at her watch.

She hoped the architect wouldn't turn up. It was ridiculous to have lunch with a man she'd only just met. The thought of spending time with a virtual stranger made her feel nervous yet at the same time, if she dared to admit it, it was quite exciting.

Edie hoped she wouldn't be a liability and do or say things that would make her squirm with embarrassment or shame when she later recalled her lunch-time adventure. Always with Trevor she'd had to tread on eggshells in case he snapped at her or slammed out of the house saying he couldn't stand her inane, boring conversation.

He would come home eventually but it was always later, much later. Sometimes not until two or three o'clock in the morning. After a while, she got to the stage of wondering why he bothered to come back at all.

Then one day, he hadn't and that was that.

She wondered how many affairs he'd had over the years and now, looking back, she realized what an idiot she'd been to put up with his infidelities for so long. She should have just walked out on him as soon as she realized what was going on – especially after that first devastating discovery – and told him to get lost.

But, there had been the house to consider, hadn't there? And the children. Also, she had no qualifications, no career and no way of supporting her family. It had been a difficult choice and rightly or wrongly, she had chosen to ignore the times he'd come home exhausted, smelling of someone else's perfume; coping with the situation by taking herself off into the spare room and making that into her private domain, her sanctuary.

She said nothing to her parents, of course, who would have been only too willing to accommodate both her and her young family in the rambling farmhouse where she had grown up. But they lived too far away and the children were settled in their schools. Besides, Edie hadn't wanted to leave her house behind and was too proud to admit that she had made a colossal mistake with her marriage.

So, instead, for the sake of her own sanity, Edie had compromised and taken the children to spend every Christmas, Easter and the long, blissful summer holidays with her parents. If they asked where Trevor was, she always said that he was incredibly busy at the moment because the stock market was at a crucial stage and he was unable to leave his clients. She always added that he sent his love and apologies.

If her parents saw through her white lies, they chose not to remark upon the fact, expressing genuine delight and joy in seeing their youngest daughter and their rapidly growing-up grandchildren so frequently.

Edie's own brothers and sisters just accepted without comment that Trevor never came to stay or even visit and the younger generation, her own children's cousins, grew up not knowing him at all. Especially Callie, who was the youngest.

"Hello."

A voice behind her made her jump. She turned and there he was, the architect.

"I'm sorry to have startled you."

"No, no. It's my fault. I was miles away."

Oh dear, should she have said that? She could feel her cheeks begin to redden. That was something else Trevor had disliked about her. He said that everyone could see her coming a mile off; that she was like some kind of warning beacon.

Edie put her hands up to her cheeks to hide their colour.

Ben smiled. "I'm glad the weather's fine. The sky was looking a bit overcast earlier but I think we're going to be lucky. Now, how about our lunch? I have exactly an hour until I have to be back in the office. Shall we go?"

Edie smiled. "Yes, why not?"

They circumvented the people on the pavement, crossed the road, wound a circuitous route past Eros, remarked upon the bustling souvenir shops and stands before arriving in Great Windmill Street where they sat down in a compact but pleasant buffet-style eatery.

"It's not posh," he said, "but the food is tasty and hot. And the selection process immediate, so it's ideal if one hasn't a great deal of time. I often come here if I'm in the centre of town and it's a good place to meet clients informally."

I'm talking too much, thought Ben. *Just as I always do these days when I'm with a woman on my own in a social setting. I should never have invited her.*

He hadn't been out with anyone in years. Not since his wife had died. He'd concentrated on bringing up Jamie and building up his architectural restoration practice. Even after Jamie had gone to university and then joined the army, Ben still hadn't met anyone whom he wanted to ask out, resisting all attempts by friends to set him up with blind dates or introduce him to single acquaintances, by insisting his world was full enough with his son and his work.

But this lunch with Edie was not a date, he reminded himself. It was merely a discussion.

He knew that no one would ever be able to take the place of his wife, whose memory he still cherished and whose love he still remembered – each homecoming she made from the far-flung reaches of the world a special and wonderful reunion. While he was all too aware that the vividness of their relationship and the emotional impact of its subsequent loss were gradually fading with time, he still tried desperately to keep her alive in his memory and hold onto her with his mind.

"It looks very nice," said Edie. *And I like the way his words come so easily*, she thought. *It's reassuring and companionable*.

They were handed plates and cutlery and their order for drinks taken.

They made their selection and sat down and for a moment they were both at a loss for words.

Ben was the first to speak. "So, why are you selling your house?" He thought his question sounded sudden and abrupt.

"Because I can't afford to live there anymore."

He looked enquiringly at her. "Oh?"

"My ex-husband has stopped my alimony payments," she said quietly, not wishing to reveal to the whole restaurant (could something this small be called a restaurant?) her private business.

"Can't you take him to court?"

"I did."

"And?"

"I lost."

"I see. Do you have a job?"

"No."

"Ah. That's difficult then."

"Yes."

"What about trying to find one?"

"At my age? In the middle of a recession?"

"I take your point. Qualifications?"

"None. I was pregnant and we had to get married."

Edie looked down at her plate, feeling ashamed.

The architect was silent. "'A' Levels?" he ventured after a while.

"Three. French, German and History."

"Grades?"

Edie toyed with her food. "Terrible. I passed but only just. I'd met Trevor, you see."

Ben did. He sighed, thinking of his own Highers and First-Class honours. He remembered how proud his family had been at his graduation ceremony from Edinburgh University.

"Where would you have gone had everything… turned out okay?" he asked.

"Cambridge."

"To read what?"

20

"Then, modern languages. Now, if I had a choice, history."

Ben looked at her afresh. "You could always try again."

Edie shook her head. "I haven't done anything remotely academic in years, except help with homework. And besides which, how would I live?"

"You mustn't sell your house."

Her eyes filled with tears. Hastily, she wiped them away with her serviette.

"I have to."

"Don't. For your own sake. As I said to you earlier, it will break your heart."

Edie knew that was true, but while she was grateful once again for his perspicacity, she couldn't fathom why a virtual stranger, a man she had met only once, was trying to persuade her not to sell her house.

For his part, Ben couldn't understand why he was urging some strange woman in dire financial straits not to sell her house.

Suddenly, an idea occurred to him.

"It's a large house, why don't you let out one of the rooms?"

Edie was horrified. "To some stranger? He might turn out to be an axe-murderer!" she exclaimed, her voice louder than she had intended.

At that moment, the restaurant fell silent.

Edie didn't know where to look. She wanted to hide herself under the table or to wake up and find that the moment was the only bad part in a wonderfully pleasant dream.

Ben laughed and Edie's bottom lip began to tremble.

"I'm sorry. I wasn't laughing at you, honestly. It's just that when I was about twelve, I came home from school one day to find that we had a stranger staying in our spare room. What you said just now is exactly what I said then when I found out. Except that with me, the emphasis was one of relish rather than fear."

He smiled at her and struck by his openness, Edie began to feel better.

"Besides, 'he' might turn out to be a 'she'," said Ben. "There are plenty of young women professionals out there looking for a central location but can't afford the exorbitant rent that landlords are charging these days, even for a studio flat. You wouldn't be able to specify male or female in your adverts but when it comes down to the wire in the interviews, see who you prefer. In any case, you would need to ask for references."

"But where would I put her. Or him?" added Edie, trying to be fair.

"Well, it wouldn't take much to convert one of the upstairs rooms into some sort of studio apartment. That would mean your lodger could be independent. You could even take in two and that should cover your living costs easily, even after tax and the usual expenses for utilities and so on."

Edie looked at him intently; her food untouched, her mind racing.

"I hadn't even considered that. I had wondered about renting the whole house but I'd discounted that idea as I didn't want anyone else using my things or having to sell most of my furniture. But individual rooms? I hadn't thought of that at all." She smiled. "Thank you," she added quietly.

"No problem. Now, do eat up because I want to go back for seconds."

They chatted in general terms for a while and after finishing and paying (which Ben insisted on doing as it was he who had asked Edie – at least, that's what he told her) for their meal, they went out into the crowded street.

"Okay?" he asked her, as he turned to leave.

"I think so," she replied.

"Good."

Edie didn't want him to go.

"I know this might sound odd," she said hesitantly, "but would you like to come to supper one evening next week and we could discuss your suggestion in more detail and have a look at the house? At the rooms and so on? Possibilities?"

It took a lot of courage for her to say that. Once again, she hoped she didn't sound like some desperately lonely, middle-aged woman.

Undecided for a moment, Ben looked at her, his gaze open and direct.

"If you don't want to it's alright. I mean, I wasn't…" and Edie blushed a very deep red.

"I didn't think that for one minute." He smiled at her embarrassment and feeling vaguely sorry for her, put aside his doubts and accepted. "Thank you for asking and I'd like to come for supper." He checked his phone. "I'm away this weekend and I've got a meeting on Monday. How about Tuesday? Around seven?"

"That's fine. I'm not doing anything."

"Good. Now, I'm afraid I must dash."

"Of course." She understood. "Thank you for suggesting lunch. Till Tuesday, then," she called after him as he disappeared into the crowd.

"Tuesday!" he called back with a wave of his hand, not sure what had prompted him to accept.

I could always cancel, he thought.

Edie suddenly felt foolish. Why had she invited him to supper on the spur of the moment?

I could always cancel, she thought.

But some mutual spark of curiosity told each of them that they would not.

On Monday, Callie returned home at the end of her day via Horse Guards Arch.

As she turned towards the quadrangle from Whitehall, one of the horses in its guard box moved towards her, gently nudging her, causing her to look up in surprise. From this angle, she could see right up inside the helmet of its rider.

She gasped. It was him. Her soldier. Briefly, he glanced at her and Callie could see both pleasure and frustration in his eyes.

What should she do?

Write down her mobile number? Email? Say her name and where she worked out loud?

There were any number of ways to be in contact with someone but what was one to do when the person you were trying to give information to could neither talk nor respond to you in any way whatsoever? And you didn't want your personal details broadcast to all and sundry?

After dithering around for a few moments, Callie opened her brief-case and took out her notebook, scribbling down her name and mobile number and tearing out the page.

The whole thing was crazy and she wondered what to do next.

The place was seething with rush-hour pedestrians hurrying to catch their homeward trains and also full of tourists, all standing around admiring the novelty of the mounted ceremonial guard or busily taking photographs, taking advantage of the sunny weather.

She looked at the horse with its sheepskin saddle and bridle; she looked at the soldier with his boots and sword. There were plenty of places in which to tuck a piece of paper but everywhere was far too public for her to carry out the action subtly and surreptitiously. She didn't want to get him into trouble either.

His horse moved and nudged her again.

Hurriedly, she tucked the piece of paper under the sheepskin. The soldier moved his horse away again and Callie, feeling slightly stupid, smiled self-consciously and after a moment, went on her way.

But as she disappeared through the arch, the paper slipped to the ground and Jamie could only watch in horror as a rogue gust of wind sent the precious information rolling and tumbling away from him along the pavement.

CHAPTER 5

The following Tuesday, Ben arrived soon after seven.

He stood uncertainly on the doorstep after ringing the bell, wondering what on earth he was doing having supper with a lonely, middle-aged woman whom he scarcely knew and who might turn out to be some kind of frustrated female predator.

Yet why should he be so suspicious? He had seen nothing in her manner when they had had lunch together that would seem to indicate any of those things. She had seemed perfectly normal: a pleasant, slightly shy lady who, he guessed, had been treated badly by her ex-husband.

He had nothing to fear yet irrationally, Ben was reluctant to step over the threshold. Perhaps he should run away now while he still had the chance.

When Edie opened the door, she seemed genuinely pleased to see him without being overly effusive when thanking him for the flowers he had brought, and he couldn't help but smile with relief.

However, it still felt like one of those awful so-called reality television programmes where strangers visit each other's houses, cook a meal, play the host and receive a mark out of ten for their efforts. He had once received a telephone invitation to take part in such a programme but after enduring an episode in order to see whether it was something he might like to do. He discovered it was not, so he had politely declined.

Inside the hallway, delicious smells emanated from the direction of the kitchen and his glimpse at the dining room table was enough to reveal that Edie had gone to a great deal of trouble to prepare for the evening.

Once again, he hoped she didn't think it was a date.

For her part, because he had brought her flowers, Edie hoped he didn't regard the evening as a date.

Nervously, she led him to the kitchen where she found a vase, filled it with water, deftly arranged the blooms and placed the whole thing on the windowsill where it added a distinctive perfume to the aroma of supper.

Ben was struck once again by the generous proportions of the room and remarked upon that fact.

"Yes," replied Edie, "I was told by the estate agent when we bought the house that the large size of kitchen in this particular design of building is rather unusual. And the scullery also provides enough additional space for me to have my compact modern kitchen, of course. This one is really just a novelty in which to eat breakfast. Mum's 'folly' the children always called it. Although I do spend a great deal of time in here," she added.

"I'm not surprised. But the house doesn't strike me as being a museum piece."

"It's not. It's a functional family home. But it also offers a glimpse into the past: a potent reminder of bygone days without the practicalities of the present intruding on its character. At least, that's how I've always regarded it," she added, feeling her cheeks redden. (Why, oh why, had I inherited that particular trait from her mother?). "I must admit I've only used the lighter Victorian wallpaper designs and avoided authentic-coloured paint which, like the wallpapers, tended to be rather dark and oppressive."

"As well as, in those days, containing arsenic and lead."

Edie looked at him. "You know about that?"

Ben smiled. "I'm an architect, remember? It's my job. My firm specializes in period restoration of old buildings. That's why I wouldn't work for those obnoxious people who came here that day."

"They were after complete renovation not restoration," said Edie.

"Wanton destruction, more like."

They both laughed.

"No wonder the Victorians were ill all the time," observed Edie. "Noxious atmosphere in the home, pollution outside from chimneys and factories."

"Not to mention contaminated water from lead pipes and open sewers," added Ben.

"And if you include the hideously restrictive corsets that women wore, it's hardly surprising upper and middle-class ladies were always in need of smelling salts and working-class women died young."

"Overworked…"

"Numerous children…"

"Washing, cooking, cleaning. Drudgery."

"High infant mortality rate. Incurable diseases."

"New inventions that were unreliable and had a propensity to blow up."

"Not much of a life really when you look at it that way, was it? Even if you were lucky enough to have servants," said Edie with a smile.

"But for all its shortcomings," said Ben, "what an innovative and amazing time of industrial advance and excellence it was. We still live today with the legacy of what the Victorians achieved."

"I agree. It can't have been all bad though, can it? I'd love to have been there and actually experienced it. Do you know, I think if I could wish for anything, it would be to go back in time."

"Could be dangerous. What happens if you do something that affects the time-line?"

"Oh, in my version, you wouldn't be able to do that! You'd be able to be a part of what was going on – smell the smells, feel the atmosphere, witness the sights and sounds in reality. But you would be physically unable to interact with anyone or catch some nasty illness. Just think of all the things you could see and learn. It would be genuine first-hand knowledge."

"Which period would you go back to?" asked Ben thoughtfully.

"Peri*ods*. Victorian, Edwardian certainly and perhaps the Thirties and Forties and into the Fifties."

"Sixties and beyond?"

"No, thank you very much. I remember that time for real and wouldn't want to go through it all again, whereas my memory of the Fifties is only partial." Edie looked at him. "What about you?"

"The same actually. I find those periods of history fascinating, hence my architectural specialism. For example, I'd love to have experienced what my grandparents saw and knew during the war, not to mention my father."

"I know exactly what you mean. I'd love to have been part of what my parents went through as well. But it's not just that. No matter how much detail history books go into or how vivid first-hand accounts are, it's always one step removed from the reality of what it must have *felt* like to experience it, to actually live it."

"Old films and television series can play their part."

"Yes, but it's rare that you get the true feeling and it wouldn't be *you*. The closest I've come to the Fifties, for example, is through watching the entire BBC live broadcast of the Coronation together with the processions to and from the Abbey. And because it was the live broadcast in its entirety without being edited or having a modern perspective imposed upon it, it really did capture a moment in time. Not just the Coronation itself, which was both profound and beautiful, but the appearance and reactions of the people that lined the route and also the standard of excellence the organizers and the commentators sought to achieve."

Edie's eyes sparkled as she became lost in her words and Ben found himself unavoidably drawn in by her increasing vivacity and obvious passion.

"…not to mention the pride and effort that went into every aspect of it," she continued not noticing his preoccupation. "I mean, the absolute precision of the armed forces as they marched in the procession and Richard Dimbleby's wonderful commentary in the Abbey. The whole thing is something that could never be done again in the same way and I'm close enough to that time for the sights and sounds to be somehow familiar and implanted within my living memory." Suddenly, Edie stopped, becoming aware of his scrutiny of her. "I'm sorry. I'm talking too much. Again."

"No, you're not. I admire your enthusiasm," he replied honestly. "And I share it absolutely. I watched that same broadcast."

"You did? You do?" Edie looked at him.

She had thought she was an oddity, a one-off. After the loss of her parents, no one else in her family really understood her attachment to the past. So over the years, she'd kept quiet; maintained her interests and absorbed herself in them, using them as yet another escape when things became difficult in her own domestic life.

"Yes."

The smell of the cooking was becoming mouth-watering and Edie looked at the clock.

"Excuse me, I must check on our supper."

She opened the door of the black-leaded range.

"You've prepared supper using that?" he remarked in surprise.

Edie smiled. "Yes. I've been battling its foibles all day!"

Ben looked at her quizzically.

"It's alright," she reassured him, "I've got the measure of it after all these years and with modern adjustments, it's perfectly safe. It can still a bit of a beastie but it does the job."

Ben offered to put the finishing touches to the meal by tossing the salad in vinaigrette and slicing the home-made bread which he said smelt delicious.

"Wow!" he said, tasting a bit.

"Cooked in the little bread-oven. If I use the electric one, it doesn't taste anything like the same."

"They knew what they were about these people from the past."

"Oh yes. We could learn a thing or two from them."

They took the dishes and plates into the dining room and as they sat down, Ben admired the gas mantles on either side of the fire-place.

"Yes, they certainly have character," said Edie. "Unfortunately, I had to have new fittings made when North Sea gas came in, as the pressure was greater than the old town gas and would have been dangerous to use. However, I've kept the originals and had exact replicas made."

"And you have gas lights in the ceiling rose as well."

"Yes, I had to hang onto those, didn't I?" she smiled. "So, I had the same thing done. They have such lovely ornate brackets and shades. My concession to modernity in here and the sitting room is with the electric table lamps which, of course, are portable."

"The lighting makes the room seem very cosy."

"I'm glad you think so."

"I don't suppose the gas pipes are the originals by any chance?"

Edie smiled again. "Yes, believe it or not. I can show them to you down in the cellar, if you like. It's quite remarkable that they survived the onslaught of modernization, let alone to still be in a usable condition. I had them checked out again by the gas people just recently and they're fine. An extension of the pipes also supplies my modern gas hob in the scullery." Edie couldn't keep the pride out of her voice.

Ben smiled, enjoying the conversation and the meal she had prepared. In all the years since he had been living in London, he had not tasted home-made food as delicious as this. And he said so.

"That's range cooking for you," she replied.

"My grandmother used to swear by hers."

"They are the best."

They cleared away the dishes and while Edie was preparing dessert, Ben wandered back into the dining room and studied the books on the shelves.

She was a copious reader and her books were certainly not showy coffee-table fodder. He recognized several architectural guides that he also possessed and wondered just how much Edie actually knew. More than she would ever reveal, he guessed.

She brought in their dessert and afterwards, they took their coffee into the sitting room where more books lined the walls. Ben could see that Edie had managed to achieve that rarity – a perfect balance between space and comfort, tradition and practicality.

He appreciated why she loved her house so much and he wondered what its history was.

"When did you buy it?" he asked.

"1975. I was nearly nineteen."

"We're the same age, then."

"Really?"

For a brief moment, they held each other's gaze.

"What state was it in?"

"Filthy dirty, neglected. Fireplaces boarded over, including the one in the kitchen, banisters and doors boxed in. The usual Sixties refurb job."

"But infinitely preferable to what's happening now," observed Ben.

"Oh yes. At least the original features were preserved behind their coverings. Now, Victorian houses are being changed beyond all recognition and what was once there can never be recovered. I hate the way everyone has to follow the trend and go for this open-plan minimalist, uniform look that takes the heart out of period houses and erases the history of the people who've lived there. People are so busy trying to put 'their own stamp' on houses that I think sensitivity to the past and adapting to one's surroundings are becoming a lost art," said Edie.

"A bit like losing touch with the land, do you mean?"

"Yes. Now there's a subject," she remarked.

"It certainly is," agreed Ben.

They looked at each other again.

"Every house is different, isn't it?" he said, after a moment or two. "Some houses feel warm and welcoming while others are not. I've always thought that houses reflect the things that have happened in them over the years as well as the personality of the builder."

"I agree absolutely. My uncle tells the true story of the day he, my aunt and my then little cousin went into a house they were thinking of buying. As soon as they went upstairs, everywhere suddenly went icy cold and my uncle felt the hairs rise on the back of his neck. My cousin started to scream and they left that house as fast as they could. As soon they were outside again, Reuben immediately stopped crying and became his usual, sunny self. To this day, my uncle thinks that something bad must have happened there."

Ben could believe it. He said that he had once sensed something sinister the moment he went through the front door of a house he'd been contracted to restore. He took the job but it had not exactly been a pleasant few months, neither had he managed to change the atmosphere.

"Definitely spooky!" said Edie. "Shall we go upstairs?" she suggested. "I have a few ideas I'd like to hear your opinion on. I promise you, it's completely ghost free!" she added with an impish smile.

They went up to the top floor and Edie showed him what she had in mind.

"These two bedrooms both share that bathroom, which is quite large and also has a new shower over the bath. My guests could be tucked up here out of the way and there's a little box room in between with a wash basin. I could convert that into a sort of kitchenette as the plumbing's already there. I was wondering about installing a few things like a fridge-freezer, microwave as well as tea and coffee-making facilities. I don't really want to have a completely fitted kitchen up here yet as I'm not sure I want masses of food-preparation going on by other people in my house. If they turn out to be nice lodgers and are desperate for a proper evening meal, I thought I could cook for them on the odd occasion."

"And charge them. You wouldn't want to be out of pocket."

"Of course not."

Ben's admiration for Edie began to grow. Overcoming her initial uncertainty, she seemed to be embracing the idea of letting rooms with increasing confidence. Her cheeks, putting aside her tendency to blush, seemed to be losing their pallor and her demeanour was showing signs of being less defeated.

"What do you think?" she asked anxiously.

"I think it's a splendid idea. How much do you know about the legal side of things?"

"I've looked it up on the internet and it seems fairly straightforward. I might need some help filling in tax returns, though."

"I'm sure my firm's accountant would be able to advise you," said Ben, without any hesitation.

Edie looked at him gratefully, touched by his kindness.

"Thank you," she said.

It was getting late but Ben was reluctant to leave.

"More coffee?" suggested Edie.

"I'd like that very much," he said, warmed and comforted in a way that he had not felt for many, many years.

With a lightness of step, he followed Edie back downstairs to the kitchen where he helped her to clear away the dishes and load the dishwasher.

After which they sat at the kitchen table and drank their coffee and chatted amicably in the radiant glow of the venerable range.

CHAPTER 6

For a fortnight after she had tucked her name and mobile number under the horse's saddle, Callie waited patiently for a response, going through all kinds of speculation as to why her soldier hadn't rung her immediately.

Perhaps he'd left for a posting abroad. Perhaps he'd found himself on ceremonial duty somewhere else in the country (she certainly hadn't seen him on Horse Guards). Perhaps he'd lost the piece of paper with the number on it or maybe he just didn't care and she'd misread his expression. When she became wrapped up in her own thoughts, she often missed things about people, which was a distinct disadvantage given her profession.

At that moment, her phone rang. 'Caller unknown' read the display. Callie's heart beat faster. At last, this might be her soldier who had been so strangely silent!

For a brief moment, indignation crept into her mind and she wondered whether or not to answer. If it was him, he really couldn't be that interested if he'd waited so long before contacting her. On the other hand, there might a legitimate reason for the delay.

Without further hesitation, she answered the call, wanting to speak to him; knowing she could do nothing else but be in contact with the unknown soldier who had occupied so many of her recent thought processes.

"Hello?"

"Callie Martin?"

"Speaking. Who is this?"

"My name is Erik."

"Who?" Her soldier hadn't looked like an Eric. "I don't know anyone called Eric."

"You do now," said the voice effortlessly.

The caller didn't sound as she had imagined her soldier would.

"How did you get my name and number?" she asked suspiciously.

"It fell like manna from heaven and I picked it up," he replied disarmingly.

"Are you my soldier?" She had to know for certain.

"Ah, if only I were, fair lady, then I could impress you with my chivalry and daring."

Oh, thought Callie, disappointed. Perhaps the contact details she had tucked underneath the saddle had somehow become lost and this strange man, whoever he was, had found them.

"I'm afraid I don't believe you."

"You do not think that I am bold and tenacious?"

"No, that my name and telephone number fell from heaven."

She found herself engaging in conversation with a stranger when she knew she shouldn't be.

"It is true."

"I still don't believe you."

"Alright, I will confess. The piece of paper arrived at my feet, blown along the pavement in the wind, leading me to you. I see now it was meant for someone else.

However, that is irrelevant. I was the one who found it and from this unexpected beginning, I have resolved that we should meet."

"Ah."

Callie wondered how the piece of paper had gone astray. Had the soldier discarded it? Or had it somehow fallen from beneath the saddle?

She pictured her soldier sitting astride his horse, upset and frustrated by seeing his chance to contact Callie slipping away from him, unable to do anything about it; seeing some random stranger walk away with his only means of contacting – Callie wondered how her soldier regarded her – the girl of his dreams? (That was in *her* dreams, most likely).

Anyway, because of that, she was now talking to this unknown caller with a rather seductive voice.

"I found the manner in which this information came to me intriguing," he continued, "and knew immediately that we must meet because of it. It is our destiny. Do you not agree?"

"No, I don't.

"That is a shame, because I feel the strength of its possibility. Just as you will come to do so."

Sensing the danger of being drawn in by his smooth self-assurance, Callie immediately terminated the call.

When she went to work the next day, just as it had been for the previous couple of weeks, the soldier was not there, not on horse-back or on foot. Similarly, when she came home.

Where was he?

'Eric' phoned again that evening. Callie jumped when she saw 'caller unknown' once more on the display.

"You have no right to do this. I don't know you," she said, her palms damp with sweat and her heart racing as she heard his voice again.

"But you do know me. We have spoken to each other on the phone. My voice and our conversation are inside your head, just as your name and my desire to meet you are inside mine. If I took you out to dinner, you could get to know me properly. We could get to know each other. And who knows where it might lead?"

"But I don't want to know you or for you to know me."

"That's what you say. But deep inside, you know that having discovered each other in this rather unusual, deeply personal way you find the thought of me irresistible," he added persuasively, leaving her feeling naked and vulnerable at the other end of the phone. "It would be so easy for you to say yes. I should like it very much if you did say yes. You know you want to, you know you want to give in to my suggestion."

Callie hesitated, her heart pounding, rendered susceptible by the tone of his voice and tempted by the surprising truth in his words.

"Are you not just a tiny bit curious?" he continued, as though he was reading her mind. "Does the thought of our being together not excite you?"

Callie found herself drifting towards acceptance.

Suddenly, common sense replaced dreamy acquiescence. She thought of her soldier again. She had to find him. He was real and *safe*. This man clearly was not.

"No, thank you," she said firmly and decisively. "I have no wish to know you. Not now, not ever. Please do not call me again."

Thoroughly rattled, the next morning, Callie went straight to the nearest mobile shop and bought a new simcard and then notified her phone company. There was nothing they could do, of course, and suggested that she went to the police. Which she did.

However, although the police were sympathetic, there was not much for them to go on and as the man had been neither offensive nor threatening, there was no action they could take, especially as he had withheld his number. But they suggested, kindly, that she should come and see them again if she had any further trouble. They said she was acting sensibly by changing her phone number.

When Callie got home, she cut the old simcard into tiny pieces and spent the evening going through the laborious process of notifying officialdom, her friends, family and work colleagues of her new number. By midnight, she had still not finished and fell asleep before she had completed her extensive list. By doing so, she omitted several important contacts, including her aunt, whom she never got around to notifying.

The next morning, even after taking these measures, Callie remained in a state of insecurity especially after searching for herself on the internet and finding that the area of London in which she lived was readily identifiable – her name linked to electoral roll records, not to mention Royal Court Chambers.

Each day, she went to work constantly looking over her shoulder; afraid, yet at the same time perversely curious as she recalled her conversation with 'Eric', wondering who he might be and what he looked like.

However, as time went on, when she saw no one following her or loitering suspiciously outside her flat, Callie began to put him out of her mind and relax, able to tell herself that she was being ridiculous and paranoid. To meet with him would be both stupid and dangerous. Besides, this Eric person might not have sufficient *nous* to go to that much trouble and actually try to find her once he found her phone number had been discontinued. In that case, she wasn't interested anyway.

Relieved and feeling stronger, Callie walked to and from work via Horse Guards Parade, alert and watchful. Fortunately, her imagined pursuer was nowhere to be seen, but then, neither was her soldier.

Chosen for special duties, Jamie was unable to complete his statutory month at Horse Guards, which meant he had no chance of encountering his mysterious and elusive girl again.

While undertaking his allotted task of training an unexpectedly skittish new horse to cope with crowds and ceremony, he wondered whether his girl (he had come to think of her like that) was still walking to and from work via the arch (at least, he assumed that was what she had been doing on the three occasions he had seen her).

He tried to imagine the conversations they might have in the unlikely event they should ever meet again, but this was unrealistic as Jamie knew nothing about her.

It didn't stop him creating different scenarios, though, in which they might find each other again and what would happen when they did.

He wondered what she was interested in. Did she share his interest in history, horses, science fiction and art? What would he do if they discovered they had nothing in common other than a mutual attraction? (He hoped it had been mutual – yes, it must have been for her to write down her contact details and 'give' them to him, even if they had gone astray almost immediately. That wasn't her fault).

There was no harm in imagining what he might bring her on their first date.

He could buy her flowers, that was certainly romantic, but what if she suffered from hay-fever? It would be embarrassing for her and awkward for him if their first romantic rendezvous was interrupted by constant sneezing. That wouldn't exactly be the best way of getting to know each other, would it?

He could always buy her chocolates. Most girls liked that. But what if she was a chocaholic trying to resist the lure of sweet things? He wouldn't want to be responsible for her backsliding and resenting him for being inconsiderate. Or what if she had a severe nut allergy and reacted to one of the chocolates? The last thing he would want to do on their first date would be to stab an emergency EpiPen into her thigh because she had gone into anaphylactic shock.

Jamie chuckled to himself at these unlikely scenarios as he quietly and skilfully guided the horse he was training through the summer greenery of Hyde Park, trying to keep his thoughts cheerful and relaxed so that the animal beneath him did not pick up any tension or disquiet from its rider; making sure the inexperienced horse moved calmly and confidently alongside the after-work picnickers and energetic frisbee throwers.

Well, he reasoned, suppressing his usual impetuous desire to act upon a situation immediately (in his private life, that was; he was patient and watchful when on duty), maybe the opportunity to find this girl of his dreams would present itself to him again and soon.

He certainly hoped so. A lot of thought processes had been invested in her and that had to be worth something, didn't it?

CHAPTER 7

A fortnight after their evening together, Edie had not heard anything from Ben.

Not that she had expected to, of course, but somewhere, deep inside her innermost self, she had *hoped*.

They had parted in good spirits after the meal but neither of them had suggested that they meet up again. It was his turn, really, thought Edie. She didn't want to appear as though she was chasing after him.

On the other hand, it didn't really matter as neither of their meals together had been dates.

It's just that it had sort of felt like that.

The day after their dinner, Edie had followed Ben's advice and removed her house from the market (much to the barely concealed displeasure of the estate agent who had spotted a potential percentage earner) and had instead placed advertisements for lodgers in the appropriate newspapers.

She protected her privacy by using a P.O. box number – the setting up of which had been an unexpected added expense, especially after taking up the facility to have the post forwarded to her home address – as well as putting advertising cards in local shop windows and on reputable internet sites.

After a week, replies began to arrive with increasing rapidity and Edie spent several days sifting through the letters that dropped through her letter box or arrived in the separate e-mail address that she had created.

Once the closing date had passed, she whittled the applicants down to a shortlist of six, one of whom she puzzled over as she knew the name but where nothing else seemed to tally to confirm the person's identity.

Edie contacted the selected people and arranged for them to meet her (as they were strangers) on neutral territory – a pleasant café in the High Street where she was a regular customer and where she had developed something of a friendship with the owners who on this occasion, were willing hosts for her endeavour.

The prospective lodgers arrived at their appointed times, each bringing their references as Edie had requested. She had never done anything remotely like this before and when she said as much to Bartosz (known to all and sundry as Baz), he'd replied, "Ah, Edie, sweetheart, you just go with your gut. It's what I do when I hire the staff for my little café. It works always the best."

She mentally rejected the first two candidates straight away as she felt uncomfortable in their presence but was surprised when the third arrived, slightly late and somewhat out of breath.

They stared at each other in surprise and mutual recognition.

"Goodness me!" exclaimed Edie.

"No!" exclaimed Callie, with complete disbelief.

And they hugged each other in amazement.

"I'd have that one," said Baz, leaning across the counter. "She looks nice girl. And you know her."

"More than that," said Edie. "She's family!"

"Family is good," said Baz. "I have big family and lovely wife. All British citizens now."

Callie smiled at him. "You must be very proud."

"I am. We come from Poland. Make better life here."

Suddenly, Callie felt safe. Instinctively she sensed that this was one of those London communities where everyone knew each other.

"Can I come and stay with you?"

Edie sensed a certain anxiousness in her voice. "Of course you can."

"I'll pay rent."

"Of course you won't. I wouldn't dream of taking a penny."

"You take her rent, Edie sweetheart. You need the money so you don't have to sell house. She good girl. She won't do you out of what she should pay."

"There speaks the hard-headed business man!" said Edie with a good-natured smile.

"The only way, my friend. The only way," and Baz turned to serve a customer who had just come in.

"So it really is you. I couldn't believe it when I saw your name among the applications," said Edie to Callie, "but the phone number was different and so was the address, which totally confused me. Even though your profession was the same, I couldn't be absolutely certain. So I chose you anyway, just in case."

"I've been staying with a friend. It's a long story."

"Well, you must tell me later."

"I will. Oh, Auntie, I can't tell you how glad I am that it's you," she said effusively.

Edie wondered why Callie seemed so relieved to see her, over and above the obvious family connection.

"Why didn't you just ring me up and ask to stay with me?" she said kindly. "You didn't have to do it by answering my advert if you needed a bolt-hole."

Embarrassed, Callie said, "I hadn't wanted to be a nuisance and just dump myself on you. Also, I wasn't sure if I was welcome after the debacle of, you know, the court case."

"Oh, Callie, don't be silly. Of course you're welcome!"

"Thank you," replied her niece, genuinely grateful. "You see, it was your advert that gave me the idea of renting a room rather than trying to find another flat, so I answered the advert and replied to the mysterious mrsep45@me-mail.com."

Edie chuckled. "Yes, I wanted to preserve my anonymity just in case any of the applicants turned out to be undesirables."

"You can have no idea how wise that was," said Callie, thinking of 'Eric'. "Anyway, if I hadn't heard back from you after the closing date, I would've bitten the bullet and phoned you up!"

"Look, why don't you come to supper this evening. Stay the night if you want to. Try out your new room. And tell me why you're giving up your lovely spacious apartment."

"Oh, I shall."

And after saying goodbye, Callie went away relieved but still nervous, Edie thought. However, there was no time for further reflection as the next candidates appeared at their allotted times, both of which Edie deemed not suitable. Tactfully, she promised to let them know in due course.

The last applicant appeared to be a sensible, level-headed young woman in her early to mid-twenties called Sarah Adhabi, who had just secured a job as a mental health nurse at the Queen Elizabeth Hospital in Woolwich.

She told Edie that she was looking for a safe, comfortable place to stay because her parents back home were worried about her being in London by herself and didn't want her to be living on her own, even though they knew that she was more than capable of looking out for herself. She wasn't eligible for hospital accommodation, she said, couldn't afford a flat on her pitiful wages and hated the cheap hotel where she was currently living. Renting a room in a location like Carlton was the ideal solution for her.

Liking her no-nonsense attitude and warm-hearted personality, Edie accepted her on the spot and they made arrangements for her to come and see the room the following day, with a view to moving in on Sunday if she was happy. The pleasure in Sarah's face was palpable as she left.

"Two happy customers, Edie," said Baz. "Their rent sort out your money problems. Then you keep house."

"I think that I shall be keeping house in more ways than one with those two," observed Edie, thinking that Callie seemed emotionally rather needy and Sarah would be working long hours in her profession.

"Keep you busy," said Baz. "Stop you thinking about the Prize Rat. I never like him, even when he live here. Edie too good for him, I always say to my dearest Halka."

Edie laughed and not sure how to respond, she patted his arm and said, "Thank you, Baz. That's a really nice thing to say. And thank you for letting me use your café."

"It my pleasure. Send your girls along to Baz if they want nice meal at end of day. Halka and I look after them for you. Treat them like family."

"Oh, I shall."

And with a grateful wave, Edie went out of the café.

She called in at John's Emporium, a sprawling antiques-cum-second-hand-books-cum-furniture shop where she had spent many pleasant hours trawling the book shelves for her own amusement and cluttered interior in search of authentic items for the house.

"Afternoon, Edie," said John Fisher, the owner, always pleased to see her as she was one of his favourite and most regular customers. "What can I do for you today? Or are you just browsing?"

"Just browsing, thank you, John."

Edie looked along the book shelves, glancing beyond the lines of dog-eared novels where, occasionally, she found an absolute gem for a pound, to see what there was among the old guide books in the travel section.

As an extension of her interest in architectural history, she also enjoyed reading about places as they once had been. She loved old photographs and descriptions of rural and urban life; of traditional crafts and tight-knit communities.

Life had often been difficult and poverty-stricken then, she knew that, but these hamlets, villages and towns from earlier times seemed full of character and like the countryside itself, abundant with trees and hedgerows and overgrown grass verges where nothing spoiled the imagined rustic idyll or urban charm.

Together with this and her interest in old houses, Edie decided that she was definitely living in the wrong era.

There were one or two books on John's shelves that she hadn't seen before, but none that caught her eye and as the light began to fade, Edie bade farewell to the proprietor and made her way home.

As she stepped over the threshold, the telephone rang and quickly, she closed the front door behind her, flicked on the light and went to answer it.

"Hello?"

"Hello," said the voice. "Edie?"

"Speaking."

"It's Ben Rutherford here."

She heard him take a deep breath and for some reason, her heart beat faster.

"My partner…"

Edie experienced a moment of panic. Male or female? Business or domestic?

"…and I are entertaining some new clients. I was wondering if you'd like to come as my guest? Your knowledge and outlook may prove invaluable."

Edie was so shocked, she had to sit down on the chair next to the hall table where the phone was kept.

Doubts assailed her. Surely there was nothing she could add to the professional expertise he and his partner would have? Surely he didn't need her to add her observations to the discussion?

Then a thought occurred to her. Perhaps this was his way of obliquely asking her out on a date.

No, she told herself, it couldn't possibly be that.

"Thank you," she heard her voice replying as though from a great distance. "I'd like that. When?"

"Next Thursday. I'll pick you up at five."

Five o'clock? That seemed rather early. Perhaps the restaurant was a long way away.

"That's fine. What should I wear?"

There was silence at the other end of the phone. Edie wondered if she'd said the wrong thing.

"Smart casual. Okay?"

"Yes." What did he mean by 'smart casual'? She didn't dare ask.

"See you then."

"Yes."

And before Edie could say anything else, he rang off.

She sat there feeling stunned. She knew she should ring him back and say that she couldn't go after all; that her diary was full, that she had an important engagement that she couldn't miss.

But she knew she wouldn't do that and no matter how much of an ordeal it might be to forsake her quiet existence for a meal with someone who was entertaining his important clients, Edie knew she couldn't let Ben down.

He had been kind to her and the least she could do was to repay that kindness.

CHAPTER 8

Jamie was in a state of complete frustration.

His earlier forbearance and optimism had evaporated and he was now impatient to find the girl of his dreams. Losing the only means of contacting her when the piece of paper blew away, tumbling and rolling down the street, had been a catastrophe. Even now, he could recall his total despair as he saw it disappear, knowing he could do nothing to retrieve the situation. He'd become increasingly morose and taciturn with his friends ever since and what was more, his month on duty at Horse Guards had passed, cut short by having to settle and train the new horse.

He thought back to the first day he had seen his girl and wondered whether there was any significance in the pink ribbons that had bound her documents when they fell out of her briefcase.

Mentally, he kicked himself. Why hadn't he thought of that before? In the absence of any positive identification after the loss of her name and telephone number, it was the only thing he had to work on and Jamie resolved to do some detective work on the internet. Even if a few (wasted) weeks had gone by since he first encountered her, at least he now had a pointer and it was better to do something than nothing.

Later, after he had finished his duties for the day, Jamie typed 'pink ribbon round documents' into his laptop and there it was, the first entry: a barrister's blog.

She was a barrister.

Jamie sat back in his chair, experiencing an unaccustomed sense of inferiority. Well, at least he had a university degree but he was only a trooper not an officer. What might she think of him when she discovered that?

If she ever did. If they ever managed to meet up.

Jamie read on.

He learned how barristers worked out of chambers sharing costs and resources and how they co-operated together, even though they might find themselves in opposition to each other in court.

He discovered there were four Inns of Court, one of which each barrister had to belong, as well as innumerable chambers in London.

It would be like looking for a needle in a legal haystack.

He took a deep breath and rolled up his shirt sleeves. If it took every moment of his spare time, Jamie knew he had to try to find her.

Edie was in state of complete panic.

She had no idea what she should wear.

"What's smart casual?" she asked of Callie as they sat in the kitchen eating supper that evening.

"Something that looks great but isn't too formal. Do you have any idea which restaurant you're going to?"

"No. I was so taken aback by the invitation, that I forgot to ask."

"How well do you know this guy?" Callie thought it was quite exciting that her auntie had been asked out but mindful of her own fears and concerns, was being cautious.

"Well enough to trust him, if that's what you're saying," replied Edie, her cheeks reddening.

Callie smiled, observing her aunt. She was glad she hadn't inherited that particular characteristic from her grandmother.

She wondered who this man was. She hoped he was nicer than her little-known uncle, who'd been a right so and so.

"But you say it isn't a date?" said Callie.

"No. Just business."

"But you like him?"

Edie blushed again. "I hadn't really thought about it," she said.

Callie smiled again. Of course she had, but her aunt was probably avoiding the issue – to herself as well as everyone else.

"Would you like me to help you?" she asked.

"With what?" asked Edie, wondering what her niece meant.

"Buying a whole new outfit for the occasion."

"Ye-es," replied Edie. "But I wouldn't want to be a nuisance."

"You're never that, Auntie. How about this Saturday? We could go to Oxford Street. Make a day of it. Go out to lunch as well. My treat."

"I don't want to have one of these make-overs though," said Edie.

"Don't worry. We'll just buy clothes!"

"I can't afford it."

"Yes you can. You've got two lodgers now, remember? We'll transform your life, Auntie Edie! For the first time, you'll have your *own* money to spend, rather than relying on Uncle Trevor. You'll be independent."

Edie hadn't thought of it like that. It might actually be fun now that Callie was in the house. She had to admit that she had been rather lonely.

"But won't you want to pack up your flat and then settle in on Saturday?"

"I'm packed already, Auntie. I can move in on Friday evening and I'll have masses of time to get things sorted out on Sunday."

"But what about your furniture?"

"It wasn't ever mine. It belonged to the flat. So there was only my own personal stuff to box up and bring. My friend Amy and her boyfriend have offered to do that in their car as I don't drive."

"Surely you'll be helping them?"

Callie looked down at her plate and shook her head.

Edie regarded her niece closely and said gently, "So, what's all this about?"

Callie took a deep breath and blushed.

"It's a bit silly really."

"Go on."

"Several weeks ago, I was walking under Horse Guards Arch and some of my papers fell out of my brief-case. As I bent to pick them up, the Life Guard on foot duty smiled at me. There was some kind of connection, I suppose, because I haven't been able to stop thinking about him ever since."

"And of course, he didn't know who you were."

"No. Anyway, a couple of days later, I wrote down my name and mobile number and tucked it under his saddle."

Edie looked puzzled. "His saddle?"

Callie laughed. "He was on his horse this time, Auntie!"

"Oh. Right."

"Anyway, I didn't hear from him so I presumed that either he wasn't interested or something must have happened. But then I got this phone call from some creep who called himself Eric, so I guessed that the sheet of paper must have somehow got lost."

"You're sure it wasn't the soldier ringing up?"

"Oh no. He looked really nice. Normal. Sane. Even with his face half-hidden by his helmet, I could tell," she added, blushing.

"Yes, I'm sure you could."

"Anyway, I had a second call from this guy called Eric and it rattled me so much that I changed my simcard and moved in with my friend Amy. I was getting paranoid that somehow he might find out where I lived and start stalking me."

"That's understandable."

"I told the phone company and the police but there was nothing they could do. So when I read your advert, it was just what I was looking for. I couldn't stay with Amy and her boyfriend indefinitely, that would have been unfair. So, here I am."

"Well, I think you've done absolutely the right thing. I'm sure you have nothing to worry about."

"I know. That's what I keep trying to tell myself. But it's a bit like someone having an irrational fear of spiders lurking under the bed. And to make things worse, I sort of feel as though he has some kind of power over me and is out there waiting to pounce. Which is ridiculous."

"Well, you've done everything you can. At least there's always going to be someone in the house. Sarah moves in on Sunday."

"Yes."

"What about the soldier? Have you not seen him since?" asked Edie.

"No. I keep walking to and from work via Horse Guards, but he's not been there. I suppose he's doing something else with his regiment. Am I being silly?"

Edie smiled. "No, not at all. He obviously made a big impression on you," remembering how her parents had first met and the profound effect they had had on each other.

Try as she might, Edie couldn't remember how she had felt when she was first introduced to Trevor at a friend's eighteenth birthday party. She did recall that he'd been a persistent young man and had managed to persuade her into bed almost as soon as they started going out, something she had regretted ever since. She hoped Callie was more sensible than she had been.

"He did," said Callie, blushing. "A huge impression."

A thought struck Edie. "Have you asked who was on duty the days you actually saw him?"

Callie stared at her aunt. "I never thought of that! Do you think they'd tell me?"

"I have no idea. We can ask at the museum on Saturday. They'd be able to at least tell us if it was possible or not."

"Or if it breaches confidentiality."

"Yes."

While modern life, thought Edie, had gained so much freedom, in many ways, it had also lost simplicity and trust in the process.

"So, let's clear up these dishes and we'll go and have a look at your room."

On Saturday, Edie and Callie headed straight for Horse Guards Museum.

There was no one who could help them at that moment, but they were told apologetically that it was unlikely that they would be able to obtain that sort of information as it was confidential. However, they did learn that the troopers' turn of duty at Horse Guards consisted of a month on and a month off and that each 'shift' lasted for twenty-four hours.

"Well, at least we've found that much out," said Callie, as they went on their way.

"You'll just have to resume your route to and from work through Horse Guards and see when he's there again. Though it'll be a bit out of your way now as you'll be coming in from the other side of London."

"Am I being silly?" she asked again.

Edie thought of all the things that she had put aside in case someone thought she was being silly, some of which were no more than a whim, a passing fancy; others that had held greater significance. In total, however, they added up to a lifetime of disappointment and missed opportunities, large and small.

"No. You'll only regret it if you don't look for him and then you'd spend the rest of your life thinking 'if only'."

"Yes. I feel that too."

"Now, shall we take the tube or bus to Oxford Street?"

"Taxi."

"Quicker on the Tube."

"More walking though."

Edie looked Callie up and down and said good-naturedly, "You've got legs."

"I know. But they're more used to being under a desk or standing up in court."

"All the more reason to get them moving then, isn't it?"

And the two women smiled at each other.

Yes, thought Edie, *it's going to be good having Callie around.*

Ben drew up outside the house promptly at five o'clock for their evening out.

"Your chariot awaits, madame," he said expansively, as she opened the door.

"Why thank you, kind sir," replied Edie, her mouth dry with nervousness.

They got into the car and in silence, set off on their journey.

"Where are we going?" she asked after a while.

"Oxfordshire," he said.

"Oxfordshire!"

"There's a restaurant I know that does the most marvellous food. We're meeting the clients there at seven-thirty but before that, you and I are going to have a look at the house in question so that you will have an accurate picture of what I'm trying to preserve when they outline their open-plan, destructive 'vision'." He grimaced. "I want to hear your opinion."

"My opinion?"

"Aye." He smiled. "My partner and I are wining and dining our new clients in the hope that we'll be able to dissuade them from creating a monstrosity out of a beautiful old house."

"Why don't you just walk away like you did with the couple that wanted to buy my house?"

"For two reasons. Firstly, because they'll just get someone else to do it and re-apply for planning permission. Secondly, because it's not far from where I have a house myself. I don't want to see the area spoilt by a precedent being set should they succeed in getting my meticulous plans scrapped."

"You have a house in the country?"

This man must be *very* successful. Edie felt even more intimidated.

Ben looked at her briefly. "I do. But it's inherited and not the result of my own labours. I must admit that I came close to selling it some years ago when life became financially precarious."

She wondered what had happened but refrained for the moment from asking. "So, you need me as reinforcement for your side of things."

"Exactly. Your support will be invaluable. I'll pay you a fee, of course."

Edie was taken aback. "I – I wouldn't dream of taking a penny. I'm only too glad to be of help."

Ben smiled. "I know that. But look upon yourself as a freelance consultant, which is how I shall introduce you. We're going to need all the persuasive powers we can muster."

"Alright," said Edie, feeling her cheeks grow warm. "I'll do it. But you still don't have to pay me."

"You could always regard it as the start of a whole new career."

"A one-off, more like."

Ben didn't respond to this and Edie cast him a sideways glance.

They travelled on in silence for several minutes; Edie not quite knowing what to say, Ben concentrating on the rush-hour traffic. She thought that he obviously knew London well, as he circumvented the most congested routes and soon, they were driving along the motorway heading west.

"Do you have family?" she asked, once she could see he had relaxed again.

During their time together, they had talked about Edie and her immediate family. Ben had not said anything about his.

"Yes, a son, Jamie."

"How old?"

"Twenty-four."

"What does he do?"

"He's in the army. Soon to be deployed in Afghanistan."

"Goodness. That must cause you some sleepless nights."

He glanced at her. "Yes."

"How long will he be out there for?"

"Six months. But he's lucky. After this, many of them will have to be out there for eight or nine months. The British Army is being withdrawn in a year or so and the government is gradually increasing the amount of time the combat troops are out there rather than training up new battalions for only a couple of months deployment."

"I see. And what about your wife?" Edie assumed he was married, although he had not mentioned her either.

"I'm a widower."

"Oh. I am so sorry." She looked at him with genuine sympathy. "How long?"

"Twelve years."

"A long time." She didn't like to enquire.

Ben sensed the unasked question and said, "She was a photographer, working for a large charity that did a lot of stuff abroad. Foolishly, and despite my best efforts to dissuade her, she volunteered to go to Africa. She was out in some remote village when she went down with some nasty fever and they couldn't get her to a hospital in time."

"I'm so sorry."

"It was a long time ago."

But you still bear the scars, thought Edie. "How did you manage?" she said.

"Picked myself up and focused on Jamie first and building up my business second, which I'd only just started up."

"What had you been doing before that?"

"I worked for a high-powered architectural firm in the City that was more interested in making money than ethics and aesthetics, shall we say."

"So you left."

"Yes, along with my partner. We sank every penny we'd ever earned into establishing the new business. Our wives, who were reasonably well-paid fortunately, supported us at the outset."

"And then…"

"Yes."

"And you nearly had to sell your house in the country."

"Yes."

"It must have been a difficult time."

"Aye. But Jamie and I came through it."

Edie felt guilty. On the three occasions that they'd met, she'd spent the time rattling on about her family woes, which paled into insignificance besides all that Ben had gone through. What must he think of her?

"Did you not ask your family for help?" she asked, assuming he had family.

Ben chuckled. "Like you, I was too proud. Still am."

They smiled at each other.

"I can understand that," said Edie.

They left the motorway and drove on towards their destination.

Edie smiled as she saw the signposts to Maybury. Here she was on home territory. She had spent many summer holidays at her grandparents' country house when she was little, enjoying the freedom of the large grounds with her brothers and sisters;

fishing in the Thames while sitting on the jetty at the bottom of the terraced garden reading a book and dabbling her feet in the river.

As they turned slowly into a sweeping gravelled driveway, Edie gave a gasp of shocked recognition and her eyes filled with tears as her grandparents' house came into view. There it was – as majestic as ever, its red-brick as vibrant as ever but its once immaculate lawns sadly neglected, its beautiful grounds overgrown and dilapidated.

"Well, this is it," said Ben. "The house. The clients want to convert my carefully planned layout of the new flats into open-plan disasters."

"They can't," said Edie, in distress. "They absolutely can't."

Ben smiled, relieved. "I knew you'd feel that way. That's one of the reasons why I asked you to come."

"No, it's more than that. Much more than that. This house used to belong to my grandparents!"

CHAPTER 9

"Your grandparents!" Ben was stunned.

"Yes."

"What happened?" He knew something of its history but here with Edie was accuracy and authenticity.

"My uncle inherited it from them but it was much too large for him and his wife and family and he didn't want to keep it. My mother couldn't afford to buy it from him, even with her inheritance, so Uncle Richard sold it. And kept the proceeds. It made him a millionaire, even after paying capital gains tax and death duties."

"I'm not surprised. It's a fine house. How did your mother feel about that?"

"She didn't say much, though I know that she was very upset at the time. But, my grandparents had willed it to Uncle Richard as the eldest child and as Mum was set to inherit the farm on St Nicolas where we lived, she and my father were actually quite content with that."

"You grew up in the Channel Islands?" asked Ben in surprise.

"Yes."

"So you're an island lass?"

"Yes."

"Island life is unique, isn't it?" said Ben, thinking of his own upbringing.

"It is indeed."

"Are your parents still alive?"

"No, they died some years ago."

He sensed the regret in her voice. "And you still miss them?"

"Yes. They were remarkable people."

"Who inherited the farm from your mother?"

"My eldest brother. He's a farmer through and through, as is his eldest son, and they continue to make a success of the land, even in these topsy-turvy times."

"What did you get?"

"A small inheritance from my parents who had literally ploughed everything they had into keeping the farm and the stables going. Over the years, I've used up most of the capital on my house and in just trying to live since Trevor stopped my alimony payments."

"Well, I've no doubt you'll soon recover the money."

Ben parked the car and they got out and stood before the house in all its Edwardian splendour.

He thought that this was turning out to be better than anything he could have hoped for. Apart from being intrigued by the coincidence of her connection to the building, Edie's passion for her subject would be fuelled by a real personal knowledge, thus rendering her arguments stronger and more convincing.

At least, he hoped that would be the case.

"Shall we go in?" he said.

They stood on the threshold together and Edie looked once again upon the elegant, sweeping staircase and black and white patterned tiles of the hallway, their familiarity redolent of childhood; echoes of the past finding their way into the present.

She remembered her beloved father reprimanding her two brothers for sliding down the bannisters; her lovely mother imploring them to be careful yet laughing at their antics; her grandfather, who always smelt of expensive cigars, lifting Edie high into the air and her grandmother – warm, welcoming and pleasantly bossy – ushering everyone into the sitting room.

Edie's eyes filled with tears again; the loss of her happy, carefree childhood gripping her chest, even after all this time. Hastily, she wiped the tell-tale droplets away with the back of her hand.

And all the while Ben observed her quietly.

Together, they explored the house, Edie commenting on its run-down state.

"When was it sold originally?" asked Ben, as they stood in one of the bedrooms on the first floor.

"In 1976 after my grandmother passed away. She had stayed on here after my grandfather died, with a live-in helper and cook and a close friend of hers, a widow who had no family to turn to. My grandmother refused to move out and remained determinedly active right up until the end of her life. She was quite a character."

"I can imagine."

"After my uncle sold the house, I have no idea what happened to it."

"Well," said Ben, "as far as I can gather, it changed hands again in the nineties but it's been unoccupied for the past ten years and beginning to decay. My clients bought it at auction."

"How much?"

"Eight hundred and fifty thousand pounds."

"That's a lot of money to pay at auction."

"But not a great deal for a house like this. I think they saw a huge profit margin."

Edie sighed. Why was everything about money these days?

"This was my mother's room when she was young," she said, after they had gone upstairs. "Those shelves used to be filled with books."

"Where are they now?"

"When she and my father married, she took them with her to the farmhouse and I have some of her vast collection in my dining room. The rest are boxed up in the attic." Edie looked at Ben apologetically. "Like my mother before me, I love books, you see."

"I can tell." He smiled. "Do you ever read the ones in the attic?"

Edie laughed. "Actually, I do. I have this sort of rota system where I dust them off and they take their turn on the shelves."

As they turned to leave the room, Edie remained behind and took one last look round. Her parents also had always slept in this room whenever they stayed at the house, even though there were larger, grander guest rooms.

"It's very special to us," they'd told Edie when she'd asked them why.

The restaurant was in the centre of Maybury, which itself was slightly busier but largely unaltered since the time that Edie had known it and they chatted about the town and how it had looked years ago.

"There must have been occasions when we were both here at the same time," said Edie in amazement. "Supposing we played together as children in the park and never knew it!"

"It's certainly an interesting thought," said Ben regarding her, his gaze open and direct.

They recalled the ruined mill which had been demolished in the late sixties and the little boathouse nearby which was still there, now reincarnated and restored. They talked about the old bargeman with his horse, plodding along the tow-path. They remembered the play-park as it used to be, with its swings, slide and roundabout now replaced by modern interpretations.

"Not the same as when we were young," remarked Edie.

"Nothing is, is it?" replied Ben. "Was it really better back then, or are we looking at it through rose coloured spectacles?"

"Both. If your childhood seemed idyllic and your adult life not so good, then of course it's going to be better. It probably is by comparison and possibly so in reality. But in general, for all the technological advances that we've gained in the present day, I do think that we've lost an awful lot of what was good in the fifties and early sixties."

"Simplicity and trust for one thing."

"And certain freedoms. Everything's so complicated these days."

"Is it that we are on the cusp of getting old?"

Edie laughed. "Probably. Trevor used to say that I was a dinosaur."

"That you are not," said Ben, with feeling. "But even if you were, then I am one also," and he smiled at her.

Jamie was spending every moment he was not on duty working at his laptop.

Methodically, on the internet, he began to trawl through lists of barrister's chambers in London looking at photographs of lawyers. However, not all of them had pictures. Most of them just had names.

He had nothing to go on, no means of identification. But he did learn a great deal and found some interesting films following barristers as they went through the qualifying process before being called to the Bar.

Like the army, barristers seemed to work very long hours. At least he and the girl he wanted to marry had that in common.

Eventually, bleary-eyed, Jamie gave up the unequal task. It was hopeless. In any case, after his next leave, he was off to Windsor to join his armoured unit ready for deployment.

Perhaps he'd be able to do something before then. What though, he couldn't imagine. Maybe he could spend every morning and evening at Horse Guards in case she walked that way to and from work.

Now he really was being ridiculous. What a waste of a leave.

On the other hand, it might be the only solution. Besides, he had nothing else to do. He would be with his dad at weekends and evenings and could try to find his girl during the day.

Why not? At least he'd go to Afghanistan knowing he'd done everything that he possibly could.

After the meal was over; after the clients and Ben's partner had gone, they lingered at the table, even though it was getting late and they had a long drive back into London.

"You were fantastic!" said Ben. "Thank you."

Edie blushed. "I don't know that I did much."

"You did enough. It was your arguments that turned the tide. That was very clever to tell them that they ought to buck the current fashion in house renovation. It appealed to their vanity when you told them that they would be seen as trend-setters if they marketed the flats as being full of *real* character and not some pseudo modern idea of it where most of the existing features had been stripped away or changed in some way. Telling them to create a building that was not just good to live in but was a whole Edwardian experience without compromising modern luxury was a stroke of genius!"

Edie shrugged. "It just seemed the right thing to say. I meant every word of it too."

"I know. And it was your sincerity that made it convincing!"

"I nearly fell off my chair when they asked if I was going to act with your firm as a consultant on the project and you said that I was." Edie felt anxious. "Ben, I know nothing! And they'll find that out when I run out of emotion and words."

"No, they won't and neither will you. Whenever we go on site, you'll always be with me. I wouldn't subject you to that kind of pressure on your own." He smiled apologetically. "I hope you didn't mind my committing you in that way? You can always back out if you feel it's too much."

"I don't mind at all, actually." Edie blushed. "While we were all talking, I was sort of hoping something like that would happen but I didn't think for a moment that it would."

Ben smiled. "Well, it has and I'm really pleased you feel like that. Look, why don't you come by the office on Monday and we'll go over my drawings. See what you think."

"I'm hardly qualified to do that."

"I'll explain them to you. It's the overall concept I'd like you to see. The finer details are complicated, but that's for me to worry about."

"Alright. What time?"

"About ten?"

"Okay."

"We'll talk about your expenses."

"Expenses?" Edie smiled mischievously. "You couldn't afford me."

Ben laughed. "Probably not but I'm not paying. The clients are and they are rich beyond the dreams of avarice."

"That sounds like a line from a well-known science fiction film!"

"Yep."

"Are you a fan then?" Edie's lips twitched as she asked the question.

"No, I just enjoy watching them. But my son is. He loves the whole lot," said Ben, almost apologetically.

"So does my niece. When she was little and used to stay with me, we had to watch at least one episode or one film every day, so I had to make sure I had all the films and all the series on DVD."

"Didn't she have them at her home?"

"No, she said they were her holiday treat. Vicky, my daughter, loved them too, so they used to sit down and watch them together. My niece used to dream of marrying the captain when she grew up."

"Not the alien with the pointed ears?" Ben smiled.

"No, though she quite likes him in his latest incarnation."

"Well, how was it?" asked Callie, coming down the stairs as soon as she heard the front door click.

"I think I'm in shock," said Edie and explained everything that had happened.

"Well, good for you, Auntie!" said Callie once her aunt had finished. "That's fantastic! A whole new career as a freelance consultant."

"Hardly."

"This Ben sounds nice."

"He is," and Edie blushed.

Callie laughed. "Auntie!"

"It's not like that in the least. We're friends, that's all."

"That's what they always say."

"Yes, well. Anyway, it's getting late and I need my bed." She smiled at Callie. "Thank you for waiting up. It's lovely to have someone to talk to."

"Night-night, Auntie."

"Good-night my dear."

And the two women exchanged a hug.

That night, Edie lay in bed tossing and turning unable to sleep; her mind over-active; her digestive system dealing with unaccustomed food; her heart soaring with long-forgotten freedom.

The evening kept going round in her mind: what everyone said, how she had enjoyed herself; how much she liked being with Ben, the way he looked at her.

How much she looked forward to seeing him again.

Jamie greeted his father as he came through the door of their house in Cornwallis Gardens.

"Hi Dad! Did you have a good evening, wherever it was that you went?"

"Yes, it was very good, actually. Matt and I were entertaining some new clients in Maybury."

"Successful?"

"Definitely. We managed to dissuade them from wrecking that wonderful old house on the Shiplake Road."

"Good for you. It has such character. Especially when you see it from the river."

It was too late and too complicated to say that the house had belonged to Edie's grandparents and that Edie would be working with him. It was too personal as yet to say that he liked being with Edie; that he enjoyed her company, that he liked talking to her. That he wanted to go on talking to her and to be with her forever.

So instead he remarked: "I met someone whose niece shares your passion for a certain science-fiction series."

Jamie laughed, "Really? That's nice. Anyway, I'm glad you had a good evening. I've only just come in myself."

"Shall we do anything tomorrow?"

"As it's Saturday and my first day on leave, I intend having a lie-in," said Jamie with definite emphasis. "It'll make a change from being up at five-thirty every morning. After that, I'm having a seriously lazy day. Do you mind? We can do something the next day."

"Not at all. I could do with one of those myself!"

"How about a superhero DVD fest in the evening?"

"Sounds good to me."

As Ben climbed the stairs to his room, he thought about his evening. Of Edie; of the clients; of this, his latest project – an endeavour that filled him with an unexpected surge of anticipation, of delight even; something he hadn't felt in a long, long time.

And he realized that the more he thought about it, the more obvious it seemed that the prospect of working with Edie was an intrinsic and vital part of that feeling.

CHAPTER 10

Callie decided that it would be too much to go to Horse Guards Parade at the beginning of each day because it was essential that she arrive at work fresh, ready to go straight into a court case or to a meeting in her room at Royal Court Chambers. She would go there after she'd finished.

She had to admit that even though her journey time to and from work was rather longer, being able to stay with Edie in Carlton was as though a weight had been lifted from her shoulders. She was able, at long last, to put the phone calls from Eric and his possible pursuance of her to the back of her mind.

Callie had given notice to the landlord of her old flat and now that the statutory month was up, she was finally free of that financial commitment and connection. She had grown fond of her top-floor apartment but if she were honest, she preferred Edie's house. It was warmer, cosier and, of course, full of the character that her aunt so loved.

There was something to be said for this character business, Callie decided. She hadn't been sure at first but after Edie had shown her round the house and told her about all the things she had done over the years to maintain its fabric and condition, Callie had begun to appreciate its considerable attractions.

It had a depth to its soul in the way that newly-built or updated older houses did not. It was criminal, Edie said, that in the rush to refurbish older houses, the heart was being ripped out of them. Under the influence of her aunt's enthusiasm, Callie found herself a willing convert to Edie's philosophy.

After this, with her new insight, Callie had spent several lazy Sunday mornings with her aunt watching property programmes. All too often, buildings crying out for love and careful restoration were ruthlessly denuded of all the features that gave them the characteristic charm that the new owners had originally purported to like – a contradiction that both Callie and Edie found difficult to comprehend – and all in the name of either a quick profit or wanting to follow a particular trend. She had agreed with her aunt when Edie declared that there was "far too much emphasis on making money these days" and that "greed in the modern world is a terrible thing."

Callie smiled as she turned under Horse Guards Arch at the end of a particularly gruelling day in court, about a month following her move, thinking about Auntie Edie's gentle soap-box philosophies and how true they were. How often had she come across court cases that resulted from greed or unscrupulous lawyers who were in it just to milk the opposition on behalf of their clients?

Despite a greater feeling of security in her home life, things at work were still no better. That very morning, Callie had lost yet another case, thus compounding her reputation for lack of success. She knew that if it continued, she could find herself side-lined and not given as many advocacy cases by the clerk at her chambers; if she was given any at all.

What was it that she was doing wrong? She believed in her clients; she did her research; she was conscientious in her approach; she had all the facts at her fingertips.

So why did she not manage to win over the judge in court?

Before being called to the Bar, while still a student, she had impressed everyone with her verbal dexterity and skill both in practice cases and numerous moots and debates. But as soon as she had qualified, had served her apprenticeship and been accepted into chambers, it was as though all her confidence and skill had suddenly disappeared.

Callie was beginning to wonder whether attaining the goal of becoming a fully-fledged barrister, while still cocooned within the safer haven of university or mentoring, had been of greater interest to her than the actual job itself. Especially as her father had chosen law as a career for her.

Perhaps that was it. Perhaps she enjoyed the security of studying more than the competitiveness of the real world; perhaps she didn't see being a barrister as the vocation it ought to be and therefore she lacked the competitive edge, only wanting a quieter, less stressful life where she had the freedom to be herself.

As she emerged onto Horse Guards Parade, Callie realized that she had been so deep in her thoughts that she had forgotten to look at the soldiers on duty and also that she didn't need to go right through the arch and across the parade ground anymore because the train station that led to her new home was in the opposite direction.

Feeling like an idiot, she retraced her steps.

Jamie saw his girl emerge onto Horse Guards and then turn back under the arch.

He identified her instantly because of the brief-case in her hand and the small suitcase on wheels. After that, he recognized the colour of her hair and finally, once she emerged from the crowd, he could see her face.

Surreptitiously, his heart pounding, he peered round the edge of the building and saw her pause briefly to study the soldier on foot duty outside the museum, before moving on towards Whitehall. He saw her stand still next to the soldiers on horseback and was just about to go after her when an unruly crowd of schoolchildren converged under the arch, blocking his path and keeping him pinned against the entrance of the building. Unable to move and expecting her to retrace her steps in his direction, as that was the way she had originally been heading, Jamie could do nothing but wait for her to come back.

The moments ticked by and when she didn't return, he braved any future ribbing he might receive from his comrades by sprinting through the arch and out into Whitehall, looking frantically up and down the street among the throng of rush-hour travellers.

She was nowhere to be seen.

In utter frustration, Jamie thumped his fist against the iron railings and after once more searching fruitlessly and pointlessly along the street, he gave up and walked, furious with himself, down Villiers Street to Embankment Underground Station, where he caught the Tube to South Kensington and home.

Jamie consoled himself with the fact that at least he had seen her again. And, unless it was his imagination, she seemed to be looking closely at the soldiers on duty.

Perhaps she hadn't given up on him after all.

Revived by this thought, Jamie knew that he would resume his vigil for as long as it took in the time that he had before his leave was over.

It was nearly seven o'clock and they were still at the house in Maybury.

Under Ben's clear guidance, the flats were beginning to take shape. Edie could now visualize how the house would look when divided up into spacious apartments.

His original drawings, as passed by the planning office, had always kept the fabric of the building intact and the installation of additional kitchens and bathrooms necessitated by the conversion would be in keeping with the era and would even enhance the building, thought Edie. It was better this way than to see it going to rack and ruin through neglect.

She liked what he had done and could see the care and attention to detail in his ideas and his complete understanding of the period within which he was working.

"Well," said Ben, "I think that's as much as we can do today. The carpenters are arriving tomorrow and like our builders, they are renovation specialists who do a fantastic job. I've worked with them before and know they'll make sure that everything is preserved in the way that it should be. They're all under orders, as it were, to take instruction only from me as project manager which should safeguard any sudden whims that the clients might have."

Edie smiled. "I think this is going to look wonderful when it's done. I'm actually looking forward to seeing the finished product."

"It gets like that. It's one of the reasons I enjoy my job. A project like this that preserves an old building virtually intact while being able to give it a new lease of life, is an absolute joy. It's one of the reasons I set up my own firm." He hesitated briefly. "Shall we drive back to London now or have supper at my house here in Maybury?"

The invitation was given casually, almost as an afterthought, but its effect on Edie and the expression she saw in his eyes was unexpected and overwhelming. The romantic thoughts that she had been entertaining for the past month but had resolutely pushed to the back of her mind, flooded into her consciousness.

What if Ben had been thinking along similar lines? She felt her cheeks go warm at the possibility, hardly daring to believe it to be true, yet knowing that having spent the time working together every day, travelling home on the train or by car, they had become close, both of them consciously extending the time they spent in each other's company.

When at the house, Ben involved her in every aspect of the conversion, over and above what she was actually needed for. Edie was all too aware that he could have done this project by himself but he seemed happy with her company and acted upon her comments and suggestions. They also made each other laugh and Edie had never felt so joyously happy.

She didn't want this to end. Ever.

"Supper, please. I'd like to see your house," she replied, feeling her cheeks become an even deeper shade of red.

Seeing her blushes grow, Ben felt his inner self respond to her, just as he did every morning and frequently during the day whenever they were together. The unexpected intensity of his feelings for her sometimes threatened to overwhelm him, especially as she sat beside him in the car or on the train or while they were working.

His reaction to her was especially potent when they had lunch together – which they did every day – finding some quiet, secluded spot under the trees when the weather was fine, sitting on the grass to eat the delicious picnic lunch which Edie invariably prepared; both of them deliberately delaying their return to work for as long as possible; Ben exerting all his self-control not to take her in his arms and kiss her.

Of course, he could have done this project by himself but he'd come to realize that he relied on her opinions and wanted her working alongside him. He sought out Edie at every available opportunity, not only professionally but in order to hear her voice and watch her expressive eyes; becoming increasingly unwilling to relinquish her company.

He realized that miraculously, he was beginning to crave again the particular closeness and intimacy that only a woman could give.

That only Edie could give.

Quickly, Ben brushed the feeling aside and led the way out to his car. This was business, strictly business, he told himself. And, of course, friendship.

He hoped that Edie wasn't becoming too fond of him. That would be disastrous because Ben knew that he was becoming much too fond of her. For them to have any other kind of relationship would make him disloyal to his wife – something that he knew must never happen.

Ever.

When they arrived at Ben's house, Edie was most complimentary about the beautiful brick and flint building.

"It has a lovely feeling about it," she said as they went inside, admiring the stylish Thirties décor.

"It's always been a happy home," replied Ben, "at least, I've always known it to be so."

"Who did it belong to before it was yours?"

"My great-grandfather and grandmother. I inherited it from them."

"Did you grow up here?"

"No."

"Where were you born?"

"London but I grew up on Cairnmor."

"Cairnmor!" Edie turned to him with a smile. "So you're an island laddie as well then? I thought I could hear the tiny trace of a Scottish accent in your voice."

"Aye, it peeks out sometimes."

He regarded her with such an open direct gaze that Edie felt a tremor go through her.

"That makes us both island people," he said.

She smiled at him. "Something else to add to the long list of things we have in common."

"Yes." He regarded her again. "Would you like to see round the house?"

"I'd love to!"

Joyfully, she followed him as he showed her the kitchen, study and the sitting room.

"This was my er... grandparent's bedroom," said Ben, after they had gone upstairs. "Katherine, my grandmother, loved the view of the Thames from here and that window seat was her favourite place in which to sit."

"My mother had a similar view from her bedroom, although, as you saw, she didn't have a window seat." Edie thought for a moment. "I wonder if our relatives ever came across each other? I mean they might have done. Maybury is not a large place."

"It's an incredible thought, isn't it?"

They concluded their tour in the second reception room with its grand piano and elegant French windows leading onto the garden. Edie admired the photographs on the piano.

"My great-aunts did this as well," she said. "Theirs was only a baby grand, not like this one, and no one played it so they put a chenille cover over it and used it to display photos."

She picked up a picture of a good-looking man and rather lovely young woman; he older than she, but nevertheless to Edie, it was obvious how much they were in love.

"This is my father and step-mother."

"Are they still alive?"

"Yes. Dad's ninety-one now and still going strong. Grace says that..."

"Grace?"

"My step-mother. She says that Cairnmor holds the elixir of life as most residents seem to live to an extraordinary age."

"What about your real mother? Is she still alive? Do you have a photograph of her?"

"As far as I know she is, and no, I don't have a photo of her."

The tone of his voice left much unsaid and Edie realized she had stumbled onto a sensitive area.

"I'm sorry, I didn't mean to pry."

"I know. It was a natural question. I'll tell you sometime." He smiled again. "We both have lots of stories to tell."

Edie looked at him gratefully, knowing that this was a statement of genuine curiosity, and not something made out of politeness, creating a natural extension for them into the future.

"Now, how about supper?" said Ben.

"Sounds good. What do you have? I'm quite good at rustling something out of nothing."

"I know."

They went into the kitchen and Ben opened the door to the walk-in pantry which held nothing but unpromising tins and packets of pasta.

"Well," he said after a few moments, "there's always the fridge, though I think I may have cleared that out too within living memory. I haven't had time to do any shopping. It might end up being a take-away. Do you mind?"

"Not at all. That would be a novelty for me. Why don't we do that anyway?"

"How do you feel about an Indian?"

"I've no idea. I've never had one."

"Never had one!" exclaimed Ben.

"No, I've always avoided eating other people," she said impishly.

Ben laughed. "Well, Edie Paignton, or rather… what was your maiden name?"

"Anderson." It seemed odd but rather nice after thirty-eight years to hear her old name again.

"Well, Edie Anderson, let me initiate you in the wonders of Maybury's finest, and only, take-away."

After the meal, with the dishes cleared and put away, they brought their coffee back into the sitting room and Ben drew the curtains and put on the table lamps.

On opposite sides of the hearth, they sat in silence for a while before Edie said, "I'm becoming quite adventurous these days – new clothes, a new job, eating exotic food. Unheard of!"

"It's good for you."

Ben could see the change in her: the new brightness in her manner; the liveliness in her conversation; her whole demeanour younger and more energetic. Just as he felt, also.

Instinctively, he knew what else would be good for her; what else would be good for both of them.

"And it's all thanks to you," she said. "You've been a catalyst in my life."

She had been a catalyst for him too. Ben sat on the edge of his chair, regarding her; long-suppressed, deep-seated desires rising to the surface. He knew he could not fight them anymore.

He continued to look at her, his expression troubled, and Edie, bravely reassuring, trying to read his expression, said, "We are friends, I hope, so there's no pressure on either of us to instigate anything else, is there?"

"But what happens if we want to instigate something else?" he said ardently.

Edie stared at him, her world somersaulting. "I don't know," she said.

"And what if we actually do?"

Edie hesitated for a moment; her heart pounding, her mouth dry. "I don't know."

"I do."

Putting his cup down on the coffee table, Ben went across to her and turning Edie towards him he put his lips to hers, his lengthy abstinence from intimate physical contact driving him on quickly and urgently, giving neither of them time to draw breath.

"Wow!" said Edie, when eventually they did pause.

"I need you," he murmured. "We need each other."

"We do?"

"Oh yes."

Dare she?

Doubts assailed her. Trevor's jibe that she was useless in bed; her own lack of interest and responsiveness after she had discovered his affairs; the relatively short time she had known Ben.

"We hardly know each other."

"We know enough," said Ben. "It's been almost two months since we first met."

He kissed her again and she found herself responding to his impassioned embrace with growing excitement.

Was it right to allow it to happen like this so quickly and easily after the first kiss? Should she? Dare she?

"It's been a long time," she said.

"For both of us."

He began to undo her blouse.

What about contraception? thought Edie as she lay back on the sofa. How many years was it since her last period? Two years, maybe three?

"Ah!" His touch on her skin was gentle and spine-tingling. *I shouldn't be doing this*, she thought.

"Come to bed with me," he urged. "Spend the night with me. Please."

Why not? Why not give in to her feelings? she thought. It was what she wanted more than anything and would make her new life complete.

"Oh yes," she said, throwing caution to the wind as he took her hand and led her upstairs to his bedroom.

CHAPTER 11

Things were not going well for Callie.

That morning, the senior barrister of Royal Court Chambers had summoned her into his room as soon as she had arrived and told her that she would be shadowing an experienced colleague for the next six weeks as she obviously needed further training in how to conduct herself in court and win cases.

Her success rate was pitiful, he said.

She was also instructed to return to Chambers at the end of the day if she had been in court or remain in her office after her research and meetings were completed, in order to study the technique of persuasive argument and transcripts of cases until she was regarded as being thoroughly competent in the subject.

Callie's immediate reaction to this insult was not to feel the understandable mortification and inevitable public humiliation this would bring upon her or even resentment of the manner in which her sentence had been delivered.

No.

Her first thought was that she wouldn't be able to look for her soldier at the end of each day. That seemed to be more important than her career at this particular moment.

Or was it just displacement thinking in order to deny her own embarrassment and shame?

Callie stood silently as the senior partner continued to outline the things she needed to learn; the ways in which she needed to improve herself; the standards she needed to achieve.

She remained silent until she could no longer do so.

"This is all very kind of you," said Callie, hiding growing impatience behind politeness, "and I appreciate your willingness to help me."

"It's not for your benefit," he replied testily, "but for the good of Royal Court Chambers and your colleagues. You damage not only your own but our collective reputation each time you lose."

"I see," she said, beginning to understand his motivation. "Would you rather I left and went elsewhere?"

He had looked at her impassively. "Yes, Miss Martin, I would. I'm sure that there are any number of chambers more suited to your, er… particular talents. I will, of course, be happy to give you an excellent reference."

"Thank you. If you do not wish me to serve any notice, then I'll be out of here by the end of today."

So Callie had left his room, sorted and handed her current case notes to the clerk for him to apportion out to other barristers; found suitable cardboard boxes and spent the rest of the day packing up her books and files, professional and personal paraphernalia. There was too much to take in a taxi or on the train, so she told the clerk she would make arrangements to collect it all first thing in the morning.

As she stood outside in the sunlit grounds of Middle Temple, Callie fought to suppress the tears that threatened to overwhelm her and turned instead towards the

Strand where she headed for Whitehall, passing the patient sentries sitting quietly on horseback or on foot at Horse Guards.

Her soldier was not there.

Disappointed, Callie went under the arch and out into the parade ground.

"Hello."

She screamed, her thoughts racing wildly.

It must be Eric. Somehow, he must have found out where she worked and followed her, seizing his opportunity to pounce on her; waiting for weeks until she had forgotten all about him so he could catch her at her most vulnerable.

Without looking round, Callie ran across the parade ground as fast as she could in the direction of St James's Park, leaving Jamie to stand open-mouthed with shock at her reaction to his simple and friendly greeting.

When Edie put the key in the lock and opened the door, the house was quiet.

She guessed that neither of the girls were home just yet and for this she was immensely grateful. They were unobtrusive yet friendly lodgers and her relationship with Callie was blossoming into something special but now, at this moment, she wanted to be on her own.

She had come home from Maybury alone; the short train journey interminable; her life and self-esteem in tatters.

Just when it seemed as though everything was perfect, it had all gone horribly and inexplicably wrong.

After the wonderful intimacy she had shared with Ben, Edie had awoken to find that he was not lying beside her. She had left the bed and padded over to the window from where she could see him by the river, already dressed, sitting on the grass beside the little jetty at the bottom of the garden.

She put on her skirt and an ancient jumper she discovered in the chest of drawers and found her way out into the garden.

Wordlessly, she sat down beside him, willing him to take her in his arms again.

But he remained silent, impassive.

"We shouldn't have done what we did last night," he said after a long while, his voice full of agitation.

"Why not?"

Had it been so terrible for him? thought Edie. Had she misinterpreted his passion? Was she so useless at making love that he was now regretting it?

Suddenly, all her old doubts and anxieties came crowding in on her.

Had he seen her as some kind of easy conquest – a lonely, middle-aged woman desperate for affection, of whom he had taken advantage (no, that wasn't true as she'd been a willing accomplice) and now, having had his way with her, was no longer interested? Was he afraid in case she became too attached to him and clung on in desperation?

Edie looked at him aghast. He couldn't be thinking like that, surely?

Or, was it that he had lost all respect for her because she'd been so eager and responsive? *Nice girls don't*, Trevor's mother had once remarked while looking disdainfully at her obviously pregnant, future daughter-in-law.

60

But she had done – willingly with a man whom she'd met only relatively recently and in the past, of course, with Trevor. And look what happened there. Perhaps she wasn't a *nice* girl after all and Ben sensed that.

Yet none of this seemed to matter last night when everything they did had seemed so very *right*. She thought that he had felt the same.

"It's all my fault," he'd said morosely.

"How is it your fault?" Edie had asked as gently as she could, trying to hide her anxiety and hurt.

"Because it is."

"Did I do anything wrong?"

He'd turned to her then and taken both her hands in his.

"Oh no, Edie. It's not you. Please believe me when I say that." He kissed her fingers. "You were wonderful. No," he continued, "it's me. Just me."

"I don't understand."

"By doing what we did, it means I've been unfaithful to my wife."

Edie was confused. "But I thought you said that you were a widower."

Had he been lying to her? She looked at him, her face pale with shock. She would hate to be the 'other' woman. She knew only too well what it was like to be on the receiving end.

"I am but…" He dropped her hands and turned away, looking out across the river. "When my wife died, I made a vow that I would never be with another woman as long as I lived."

"But that's…" She was about to say daft, stupid, but stopped herself. "Wouldn't she have wanted you to be happy, even if it meant leaving her behind?"

It was twelve years since he had lost his wife. Surely, thought Edie, he was over her by now and a promise like that could no longer hold sway?

She could understand it if, like her, he had been hurt and unwilling to take the chance with another relationship. She could understand it if, also like her, he doubted whether he could ever trust anyone again. No one had been hurt more than she over the years and yet with Ben, even she had allowed herself to take that chance.

"You see," he continued, "it's not just my vow. We made that pact together when we first married and I am the one left who has to fulfil it."

"But that's all wrong. For your own sake, you have to move on."

I have, she thought, *or at least, I thought I was moving on. Until now.*

"I have moved on, believe me, but I also have to live with my conscience. You see, I am not a man to break my promises."

Edie was silent. He was obviously in some emotional distress. What could she say?

"I'm sorry," he muttered, ashamed to look at her, his expression full of guilt and pain.

They sat in unbearable silence for what seemed like an eternity.

"I think it best of we don't see each other again" he said at length.

Edie swallowed hard, feeling sick.

"But what about the house? What about our project?"

"I should never have involved you," he said. "I'll pay you the full fee in lieu, of course, for your services."

His words cut through her like a knife. At last, Edie was roused to anger.

"I don't want your money!" she exclaimed. "What we've had since we've known each other has been special, good, wonderful. Even I can tell that – me, with my limited and jaundiced experience! And you mean to tell me that you can just sit there and say that you're about to give it all up for some... some ludicrous agreement you made years ago?"

"My wife and I were very happy."

Edie sensed a defensiveness in his statement, as though he was trying to justify it to himself.

"I'm sure you were. But you could be just as happy again. With me. With us. Why can't you see that? Please don't throw your chance for happiness away, Ben. Or mine."

"I'm so sorry, Edie."

And with that final, shattering apology, she had walked up the path away from him, fighting back her tears. Blindly, she had dressed, collected her things and left, stumbling to the station and catching the first train that came along.

Maybury would never seem the same again.

She had ended up in some remote rural location that had somehow managed to escape Dr Beeching's disastrous railway axe fifty years previously, walking aimlessly along country lanes until, exhausted and foot-sore, she had caught the train back to London and home.

Edie dumped her bag in the hall and ran upstairs to her bedroom where she shut the door and flung herself on the bed reflecting on the fact that she had lived with a man for thirty-eight years who had been incapable of being faithful to her, only to fall in love with someone else who was so determinedly faithful to his dead wife, that he felt he couldn't let go.

She wept at the irony of it and ultimately, bravely, came to the conclusion that perhaps she wasn't enough for Ben and that one day, he would find someone for whom he couldn't help but abandon his ridiculous vow.

The thought of someone else being with him filled her with a pain and grief that was far, far greater than anything she had felt when Trevor had left or even when she had decided to sell her house.

Callie was fast, but Jamie was faster.

He was determined not to lose her.

"Go away, Eric! Don't touch me!" she shouted, as he drew nearer. "Get away from me!"

"Wait! Please stop!" he called out to her, mindful of passers-by turning to stare at them as they raced by.

It would be just his luck if some zealous, law-abiding citizen grabbed hold of him and stopped him from pursuing Callie in the mistaken belief that he was about to do her harm. Fortunately, his pursuit happened too fast for anyone to react except with stunned observation as the two of them progressed rapidly along the Mall.

He caught up with her just before the Victoria Memorial and seized her by the arms.

"Let go of me, you brute!"

She squirmed and writhed and kicked him on the shins with such force that he cried out in agony and had to let go. She ran off across the road to stand by the gates of Buckingham Palace trying to regain her breath, hoping the busy traffic would give her sufficient time to do so, enabling her to escape before he was able to cross the road.

But Jamie went after her immediately, dodging the cars that blared furiously at him as he cut recklessly across their path.

Transfixed, Callie watched his tortuous progress towards her. He arrived very out of breath, to stand beside her, his hands on the Palace railings, leaning over trying to put some air into his lungs.

"My name... isn't... Eric," he gasped.

Seeing him close up like this, Callie realized she'd made a terrible mistake.

"It isn't?" she said meekly and nervously.

"No," he said, recovering. "It's Jamie."

"Oh," she replied. "Oh God, I'm so sorry. And I kicked you like that. I thought you were... someone else."

"That much is obvious," he replied without resentment. "Though I hope you don't mete out that sort of treatment to everyone you know."

Callie smiled and shook her head. Jamie placed his hand on her upper arm.

"So," he said, "just in case you attempt to run away again and I lose you, which I don't want to do ever again, please tell me your name."

"It's Callie. Callie Martin. And I promise not to run away any more."

She held out her hand which he took in his.

"I'm glad to hear that." He smiled at her. "I'm Jamie Rutherford."

"It's good to meet you, Jamie," she said, warmed by his smile and not wanting to let go of his hand.

She liked his surname. Callie Rutherford had a lovely ring to it.

Mentally, she shook herself. What on earth had made that thought come into her mind?

They began to walk on slowly, following the line of the black and gold palace railings.

"You're my soldier, aren't you?" she said, looking up at him.

He nodded. "Yes, and you are my girl from under the Arch."

"Of course I am. Why didn't you phone me?"

"Your piece of paper blew away."

"I did wonder. Someone else picked it up."

"The guy called Eric?"

Callie nodded.

"And I presume he made a nuisance of himself."

"Yes. He only contacted me twice but it was enough to persuade me change my phone number and make me generally nervous. I kept thinking that he might find out where I lived or worked and begin stalking me. So I moved out of my flat and in with a friend. I'm living with my aunt now, so I feel much safer."

"Until today."

Callie laughed. "Until today." She blushed. "I'm so sorry about kicking you."

"It's alright. You were under a misapprehension. I'll survive. It was worth every bruise."

"What do you mean?"

"That I've found you at last."

"Have you been searching long?"

"Every day that I could after I first saw you. Twice a day since I've been on leave."

"Really? And I've been coming to Horse Guards as often as I could after work."

They smiled at each other.

"I'm glad that you didn't give up on me," said Callie.

"Likewise," replied Jamie.

In a speculative silence filled with anticipation, their pace slowed.

"When does your leave finish?"

"In a couple of weeks. I'm off to Afghanistan soon after that."

Callie's heart began to race. "But you can't be. We've only just met!"

"But we have met and that's what matters." He turned towards her. "Look, why don't we go and find a coffee somewhere."

"How about Counter Coffee?" suggested Callie.

"Perfect," said Jamie, smiling at her.

They turned and began to walk in the direction of Green Park.

"That first day I saw you," he said, taking her hand again as they crossed the road, "I overheard you arranging to meet your friend there. I got special permission to leave barracks and sat in Counter Coffee for hours in the hope of seeing you."

"You did?" replied Callie, affected by his admission. "And I never came. I had to work late so I cancelled." She touched his arm. "I'm so sorry."

Jamie chuckled. "It wasn't your fault. You weren't to know."

He kept hold of her hand. It felt soft and warm as though it belonged in his. He wondered if she felt as comfortable with him as he did with her. She certainly seemed relaxed. Suddenly, Jamie had the urge to share with her everything about the day they met.

"Did you know that the first time I saw you when your brief-case sprang open and we smiled at each other, I wanted to ask you to marry me."

He wondered what her reaction would be. Would she try and escape again?

"Really?" she said, her heart skipping a beat.

"Yes, really. Ridiculous isn't it?" He smiled.

"No, it's not in the slightest! I think it's rather romantic actually."

"You do? Even though I didn't know you?"

"Yes."

"You're not going to run away again because I told you?"

"Of course not! Why would I do that? Anyway, I gave up my position in Royal Court Chambers because I didn't want to miss the chance of finding you," said Callie, hoping Jamie wouldn't think her irresponsible and stupid.

"You did?"

"Yes. I'm a barrister, you see."

"I know."

"How?"

"You had a pink ribbon around your documents in the brief case. I looked up what it means on the internet and found out what you did. I then tried to discover which chambers you were in. I must have trawled through Lord knows how many but in the end, the sheer number of barristers defeated me."

"That must have taken a lot of patience."

She pictured him sitting at his computer for hours. He must really have wanted to find her, just as she had him. She liked the thought of that. It gave her a warm glow inside. Not like the thought of Eric trying to find her, which filled her with dread.

"Along the way, I learnt all sorts of things about being a barrister but, without knowing your name, it was an impossible task to find you." Jamie smiled apologetically. "So, tell me what happened that made you have to choose between finding me or staying at your chambers?"

"Am I a total idiot for leaving a secure, highly-paid job?" she asked when she'd finished recounting the story.

"Not in the least. If you were unhappy, there was no point in staying. In that situation, you wouldn't have been true to yourself. Besides, it sounds to me as though the head of your chambers is a pompous prick."

Callie laughed. "He is. That sums him up perfectly. No one likes him."

He looked at her. "What will you do now?"

"Marry you?" she said pertly.

Jamie chuckled and put his arm round her shoulders making Callie feel safe and secure. She responded by putting her arm round his waist.

Was this really happening to her, she wondered or would she wake up in the cold light of day to discover that Jamie was all just a dream and Eric the unpleasant reality?

They sauntered through the spacious leafiness of the park until they reached the bustling pavements of Piccadilly, going into Counter Coffee.

"Where do you live?" he asked after they had found somewhere to sit down with their drinks.

"With my aunt in Carlton. I rent a room from her. What about you?"

"Hyde Park Barracks. We can go and see it if you like. It's a bit of a monstrosity architecturally speaking – my dad hates it – but it's functional and conveniently situated next to the park for when we exercise the horses or rehearse for special occasions." He hesitated for a moment and then said, "How do you feel about horses?"

"Oh," responded Callie immediately. "I love them! My grandparents bred horses on their farm and as I lived with them during school and university holidays, I more or less grew up with them. Granddad taught me how to ride."

Jamie felt a tremor of connection go through him. He wondered what else they had in common, what else they would find out about each other.

CHAPTER 12

"You are sad today, Edie, my friend," said Baz, as his favourite customer sat at a table in his café morosely stirring her coffee, her expression blank and unseeing. "No project again today, then? How long is it now? One week? Two? Three? The architect not want our Edie anymore?"

"No." *Just as well he doesn't know the half of it*, she thought.

"He want sense knocking into his head, that one. Expert like you on old buildings – he don't know what he's missing, does he, John?" he said to the antiques shop owner who had just walked in.

"What's that?"

"Edie not do project any more. The architect is an Idiot Rat."

"Well, you could always come and work in my shop," said John. "I could do with some extra help. With all these antique programmes on the television, I seem to be more inundated than ever. There's only me, so it's a bit tough going sometimes."

"There you are," said Baz. "Right up your street. At least John here appreciates your worth."

Edie smiled. She didn't like to refuse (as she knew she would) there and then and hurt John's feelings publicly so she said, "Thank you, that's so kind. May I think about it?"

"Take your time, Edie. There's no rush. You know where to find me." He turned to Baz, "Anyway, I mustn't stay. I've left one of the customers guarding the shop. Cup of your special coffee, please, Baz, to take away."

"One coffee coming right up. That one pound twenty, please."

"You should charge more. Can't get coffee anywhere like yours."

"At my prices, I sell more. Therefore, profit margin greater. See you, John."

"Yep."

"He nice man," said Baz to Edie. "You go work for him. Do you good."

"Perhaps," she replied, thinking of Ben.

He was a nice man too. Really nice. Wonderful, in fact. And, like Trevor, he had let her down.

A few weeks after he had messed things up so completely with Edie, as soon as he was able to leave the project in the hands of his trusted foreman from the specialist builders, Ben flew from Gatwick to Glasgow and took a train to Oban from where he boarded the childhood-familiar ferry to the port of Lochaberdale on the isle of Cairnmor.

He needed to breathe the clear, invigorating air of the place in which he had grown up to try and make some sense out of his thoughts away from the confines of London and work.

Jamie had been content for him to go, preferring, without stating why, to stay at home on his own. He sent love to the family and said he would try to visit them before he went to Afghanistan.

Secretly, Ben had been relieved, even though it was only a week before Jamie was due to rejoin his regiment. He suspected that his son had acquired a girlfriend, although nothing had been said, but he had been out all day, every day, returning home at a surprisingly reasonable hour, happy and buoyant.

Ben had not enquired further. Jamie was his own man and would tell him when he was ready.

Lochaberdale had changed a great deal since Ben's childhood but he could feel his spirits lift as soon as he left the ferry, walking around the bustling harbour and up the hill towards the farmhouse, his former home.

His step-mother greeted him at the door with affection.

"It's so good to see you, again," she said.

"And you, Grace. How's Dad?"

"Looking forward to seeing you. I'll go and wake him in a moment. He's been having his afternoon nap on the bed. I'll make some tea. I expect you're thirsty after all that travelling."

Edie would enjoy that range, thought Ben, as Grace turned to put the kettle on the hot-plate, lifting the heavy lid with care.

"How are you?" she said. "Working hard?"

He nodded. "What about you?"

"Aye, I'm fine. Not doing quite so much these days. Mike's taken over the reins now up here on the farm."

"Yes, you said in your last letter. How's Sandy coping?"

"She's doing really well, considering the short time she's been looking after her side of things. Mike says she's thinking of bringing in the BBC to do another wildlife programme here – says it's important to keep Cairnmor in the public eye. And, as you know, Charlie is involved up at the school and Marie's as busy as ever with her art work and the B&B, so all four of your half-siblings are doing well. Likewise, all your nieces and nephews."

From overhead, they heard the steady thump, thump of footsteps and shortly, Jack came into the kitchen.

Ben went to greet him. "Hello, Dad. You look well."

The two men hugged each other.

"Mustn't complain. Grace here keeps me on my toes." He smiled at his wife. "Fantastic woman that she is."

"You sit down there and stop your nonsense," said Grace, kissing his forehead. "Good sleep?"

"Yes. Sufficient for Ben and I to go out for a walk after we've finished these necessary refreshments. Is there any of that cake left?"

"'Fraid not. Our ravenous grandchildren finished it off this morning."

She smiled and poignantly, with her striking similarity to her mother, Ben was reminded of Katherine, his beloved grandmother.

"But I've made a fresh batch since."

Jack and Grace looked at each other and smiled and for Ben, the years fell away as he felt the comfort of his younger days.

"So, my son, to what do we owe this brief, unscheduled and very welcome visit?"

The two men were strolling along the beautiful white-gold sands of South Lochaberdale where unusually benevolent Atlantic waves washed placidly against the shore.

Ben sighed. "I needed to ask you something."

"Fire away."

"When I was growing up, I seem to remember some talk or other about you and my real mother; how you had some kind of agreement that you wouldn't marry anyone else after you separated. Is that true?"

Jack raised his eyebrows. He hadn't realized that Ben knew about that. He thought carefully before replying.

"It wasn't so much an agreement as a long-held conviction but yes, much to my regret, in essence, I'm afraid that is so."

"Why?"

"Because for many years, stupidly, we both of us clung onto the notion that we would never find anyone else who could match up to what we had once shared; that we might one day at some unknown future time, get back together. Which was ridiculous, not only considering the acrimonious circumstances that led to our break-up but most of all, because it delayed my being with Grace. I was blinded by my stupidity in not letting go of the past and failing to see the beauty that had been under my nose all along."

Ben was silent. Was he being equally obtuse? But wasn't his a different situation?

"My mother came here once when I was about twelve, didn't she?" said Ben, after a while.

"Yes. And she never came back after that. You were staying at a friend's house on Cairnbeg at the time so you never saw her, fortunately."

"Why fortunately?"

"Because it would only have... confused you."

"Because she didn't really want anything to do with me, you mean, and it would all have been a pretence?"

"Partly. You were happy and settled here with Katherine and Alastair while I was away at sea. And with Grace, although she was much younger. You always maintained that you didn't need another mother."

"I remember. And it was absolutely true."

Ben thought back to his happy and settled childhood and how fortunate he had been; how he had been surrounded by loving, caring adults and had not missed his mother at all. He'd wondered about her, of course, but he had never dwelt upon it. There had been no need.

"So, what made you think of Anna and I having that understanding?" asked Jack. "How did you find out about it, by the way?"

"I accidentally overheard Grandma and Granddad discussing it once."

Jack raised his eyebrows again. "I see. Well, Anna and I clung onto that ridiculous notion for far too long. Way beyond anything that was reasonable and sensible. Fortunately, that last time she came here we realized we were no longer

68

in love and would never get back together. We agreed to divorce and I was free at last to marry Grace."

"Is my mother still alive?"

"As far as I know." Jack regarded his son astutely. "Why? Are you thinking of getting in touch?"

"No, not again." He had tried, disastrously, when he was in his twenties. "Once was enough."

"I'm sorry that she still didn't want to know you. That must have hurt."

"I got over it."

"So, what was it you wanted to tell me?"

"When I first married Dana, we made a pact that if one of us died before the other then whoever was left wouldn't marry anyone else but would keep the spirit of the marriage alive."

"And now you've met someone who you want to be with?"

Ben flushed a dull red under his father's open and direct gaze, knowing there was no hiding place from his astute parent.

"Already got the T-shirt, Dad."

Jack laughed. "Well, good for you! It's about time."

"But I ended it before it had really begun. I felt I'd been unfaithful to Dana."

"And the pact that you'd made."

Jack sighed. He understood. Ben was so like him. And Anna, but only in that one respect.

"Yes."

"How did you meet her?"

"I was taken to her house by some prospective clients." And Ben went onto explain.

"How old is she?"

"Same age as me."

Jack was silent for a moment. "Do you love her?"

"I was beginning to love her, I think."

"You think! Surely you know?"

"It isn't that simple, Dad. At least, not for me."

"No, I'm aware of that. Well, if you want my advice, dear boy, just follow your heart. Let that be your guide and whatever happens as a result will be what you really need and also what is right for you. Try to balance the past and present and see which is more vital and alive. Then, having made your decision, stick to it and don't look back or regret a thing."

"I'll try. Thanks, Dad."

Jack smiled. "Any time. Now tomorrow, if the weather's fine, how about a spot of fishing?"

"Fishing sounds great!"

Full of emotion and gratitude, Ben hugged his father and the two men headed back to the farmhouse.

Even so, while accepting his father's sensible words, Ben knew he had not yet erased his guilt for breaking the bond with his wife and because of this, he could not be certain whether he was ready as yet to commit his heart to Edie.

CHAPTER 13

"You haven't told me yet why you wanted to join the Household Cavalry," said Callie, as she sat next to Jamie in the little bistro in South Kensington which, along with Counter Coffee, had become one of their favourite haunts during the past week. Now they were spending their last few precious moments quietly together before the dreaded separation necessitated by Jamie's return to duty.

In all the time they had spent together since that fateful day outside Buckingham Palace – and by mutual joyous consent it had been all day, every day – Callie had not asked about his army career, the very thing that had brought them together and the very thing that would take Jamie away from her.

They had met each morning by the Admiralty building on Horse Guards Parade, preferring to avoid the complicated family explanations which would inevitably follow if they went to each other's houses and restrict the time when they could be alone; spending long, carefree days filled with laughter and fun and a growing companionship.

On fine days, they took sun-baked trips to the coast, where they paddled in the sea and built sandcastles, ate ice-creams and spent bags of pennies and two-pence pieces playing on the old-fashioned slot machines on the pier; giggling with laughter and jubilant exclamations when they won small amounts of money; groaning with good-natured anguish and frustration when they lost it all again.

They had visited just about all the art galleries they could find in central London because Callie had told Jamie that she loved art. Standing close together, they admired portraits and landscapes; marvelled at the vibrant colours and skill of Titian and Vermeer; the gentle landscapes of Constable and sheer range and scope of Turner. They studied the Impressionists and weird and wonderful examples of contemporary art in large buildings and tiny galleries discovered by chance in spacious parkland.

"My grandfather does the odd picture or two," Jamie had hinted as they looked at several examples of his work in passing – Callie unknowingly, Jamie keeping the detail of his connection quiet; immensely proud of, but not wishing to boast about, his distinguished relative.

"I've always wished I could paint," Callie had replied, "but I'm useless at it."

"So am I," Jamie had confessed, remembering how his grandfather had tried to teach him and given it up as a hopeless task. "I still love it though."

"I love *you*," said Callie.

And, taken by surprise, Jamie had held her close, mindful of the people around them, discreetly telling her with quiet intensity that he felt the same.

They drove west into the countryside for a picnic, spreading out the car blanket on the bank of the Thames, holding hands while they watched the water flowing through the reeds.

"It's so peaceful here," said Callie, lying back and looking up at the sky, her hands behind her head.

Jamie had kissed her then, unable to resist any longer; her lips responsive, his heart beating fast at her delicious closeness; while Callie trembled under the gentle tenderness and promise of his embrace.

"When I come back…" he'd whispered.

"Yes," she had replied dreamily before their growing passion was interrupted by the arrival of walkers further along the river bank.

"However, as we have unwelcome company," he said, sitting up and smiling at her, "we should eat our food before the ants do."

"You've thought of everything," said Callie, impressed by his organizational skills as he produced plates, glasses and serviettes from the wicker basket. "I'd have forgotten something vital like the bread or the filling for the sandwiches."

"That's why I bought pasties. Much easier," he'd replied.

"That's cheating!"

Playfully, she had tickled him and he had kissed her again.

On their final day together, Jamie arranged for them to go riding on Wimbledon Common; hiring horses from a riding school nearby; the owner content to allow them to go out without a member of her staff after assessing both his and Callie's expertise in the ménage and discovering that Jamie was in the Household Cavalry.

"You ride well," said Jamie admiringly as they set off across the open spaces of the Common.

"So do you," said Callie.

"Thank you, ma'am."

They had ridden for miles and it had been a glorious day of warm, summer sunshine and freedom which inevitably had to come to an end all too soon.

Now, it was their last evening together, a time to share their final few precious hours before Jamie's leave was over, before he had to report back to his regiment.

With his departure so imminent, Callie gave in to her curiosity as to why someone like Jamie had decided upon a career in the army.

"To answer your question," said Jamie, "when I was little, my Dad took me to see Trooping the Colour every year and after I was old enough, I used to head off to watch the Changing of the Guard and every Royal event that I possibly could. I loved the uniform of the Life Guards with their bright red jackets, shining swords and breastplates and the sound of the horses as they trotted along The Mall. I couldn't wait to grow up and be part of the whole spectacle."

"Yet you went to university first."

"Yes. I was persuaded to finish my education and then join up."

"So, if you have a degree, why didn't you become an officer?" she asked, a question that had been in her mind for a while.

"As a trooper, I'm out there on ceremonial duty more often than I would be as an officer, so I decided to follow that particular path, even if it is pretty mind-numbing at times. However," Jamie took Callie's hand in his and kissed it meaningfully, "perhaps sometime in the not-to-distant future, as I may have greater domestic responsibilities," and he smiled at her, "I should apply for officer training."

Callie looked at him in amazement.

"Are you… are you in an oblique, roundabout way, actually asking me to marry you even though we've only known each other a week?"

"Will you?" he said tenderly.

Callie smiled. "Yes."

Jamie kissed her hand again.

"When I get back from Afghanistan…" he said.

"…in six long months," said Callie. "A lifetime of waiting."

"It will pass."

"Yes, but so many things could happen in the meantime." She felt a rising sense of panic as long-held doubts about her steadfastness in that kind of situation assailed her.

"Don't think about it. Think about the kind of spectacular wedding that every girl dreams of. Guard of honour – on horseback, no less – splendid uniforms, impressive surroundings, the lot. Because you could have that, you know."

"Wow!" said Callie, a vivid picture already in her mind. Then an additional thought occurred to her. "How long would officer training last, Jamie?"

"Forty-four weeks at Sandhurst."

"Forty-four weeks?" Callie was thinking. "What if we delayed the wedding until you've become an officer? Just think how proud our children would be to see you in an officer's uniform when we look at the wedding photos."

And her parents, thought Callie. Better than just being an ordinary trooper which in the Household Cavalry was the equivalent of a private in the rest of the army.

Jamie regarded her carefully for a moment and asked quietly, "Is that what you'd prefer? To wait nearly a year for our wedding for the sake of one day's photographs?"

Callie blushed. "Well, not exactly."

"Does it bother you that I'm only a trooper?"

His heart began to beat faster. Was this lovely girl turning out to be a bit of a snob?

"No, not exactly."

"What then?"

"I'm worried about what my parents will think," answered Callie honestly.

"Why?"

"I guess that because my grandfather had such a distinguished war record and my great-grandfather was a knighted British ambassador they might think I'm…"

"What? Setting your sights too low?" Rankled, Jamie was fired to indignation. "Look, if they want *rank*, my great-great grandfather was a Commodore in the Royal Navy and my great-grandmother a Chief Officer in the Wrens during World War Two. My grandfather was a Captain in the Royal Navy and my great-uncle is a Baronet. Is that enough *rank* for you?"

Callie was chagrined by his outburst.

"I'm sorry," she said.

For a moment, an uneasy silence existed between them after this, their first altercation.

Jamie took some deep breaths and regarded his fiancée again, more calmly this time.

"Look, as I said to you just now, I am a trooper because I want to do the ceremonial stuff. I love being out there in uniform on horse-back at Royal occasions. It's a real honour and a privilege."

Callie bit her bottom lip. She knew she'd upset him and for the most stupid of reasons – snobbery.

"What have you taken part in?" she asked.

"I've done Trooping the Colour, took part in the Queen's Diamond Jubilee celebrations, did a mounted display at the London Olympics, as well as all the other regular duties, like the Major-General's inspection on Horse Guards, the State Opening of Parliament and accompanying visiting dignitaries and foreign Heads of State. And the Royal Windsor Horse Show."

"Oh."

"Now do you see? Being a trooper, I get to do all the ceremonial stuff regularly. As an officer, I'd only be doing some of them as there are more troopers needed than officers in each parade."

"I'm sorry," said Callie again, beginning to understand.

"It's alright," said Jamie. "But I don't want to delay our wedding any more than we have to. It's going to be a long enough wait as it is."

"I know."

With a sigh, Jamie looked at his watch and then at Callie. They ought to leave soon yet their disagreement still hung in the air. This was not how their final few moments together should have been.

"I need to take you home before it gets too late," he said, before paying the bill.

"I'm glad we've had this week with each other," said Callie almost apologetically, their evening tarnished by her stupidity.

He squeezed her hand as they walked down the steps into the Tube station.

"So am I. And as soon as I get back, we'll set a date and start planning our wedding. How does that sound?"

"Wonderful! But in the meantime, it'll be our secret?"

"If that's what you would prefer."

Jamie wondered whether Callie was still ashamed of him in some way.

"It's for no other reason than I want it to be just us," she said earnestly. "We've only known each other for a short time and I don't want relatives fawning all over us…"

"Or putting up social barriers…" teased Jamie.

"Beast," said Callie, blushing shamefacedly.

"Sorry." He grinned at her. "Couldn't resist that."

"I deserved it."

Jamie held her to him and kissed her lightly on the lips.

"At least we're able to talk about it," he said.

"Yes."

Callie tucked her arm into his as they stepped onto the train which hurtled them rapidly towards the inevitable moment of parting.

"You see, I sort of feel that our relationship is at a tender stage. It's probably the reason why we haven't said anything much about our families, if that makes any sense."

"It makes perfect sense and I agree, although my family is rather nice. As I'm sure yours is," he added hastily. "But I have loved having you to myself in our own private world."

"Perhaps that's what marriage will be like. Our own private world."

"Until we have children." Jamie made a wry face.

"It'll still be our world, though."

"True."

"In the meantime," and Callie tried not to think about being alone while he was away in Afghanistan, "I've got to find myself another job. I've rather put it off since we've been together."

"I'm so glad you did."

"Yes."

"Well, I can support you if you struggle."

Callie laid her head on his shoulder. "Thank you. That's a gentlemanly thing to say."

She liked the old-fashioned courtesy and respect that he showed towards her. It was refreshing in an age of instant gratification and transient relationships. Callie was glad she had never particularly subscribed to all of that although, with two previous boyfriends, she wasn't exactly innocent.

But then who was, these days?

She wondered how many girls Jamie had slept with. They hadn't broached that particular subject and now was not the time to raise it. He certainly knew what he was doing when they were alone together but in a careful, considerate, measured sort of way as though he was holding back, waiting until they could be together properly. It certainly made the prospect of his return all the more exciting.

They sat in silence as the train drew nearer to Carlton, dreading the parting that was to come; holding onto the last few precious moments as best they could.

"You've got all my contact details safe, haven't you?" said Jamie, as they reached Edie's house, using practicalities to stem the surge of painful emotion he felt.

Callie nodded, unable to speak; afraid of their parting; afraid that she might not live up to his expectations.

"And I have yours." He touched her cheek. "It'll be alright, you'll see."

He took her in his arms and after one final, lingering kiss, they parted with Callie standing on the door-step watching Jamie walk down the road until he had turned the corner and disappeared out of sight after one final wave.

Lonely and assailed by self-doubt, she let herself into the darkened house.

CHAPTER 14

"Right," said John, "these go here, those go over there and this lot stack up behind here."

It was Edie's first day working at John's Emporium.

After travelling to St Nicolas for a week's holiday and then moping at home for several days, she had decided not to sit around any longer feeling sorry for herself. So, despite her initial reservations, Edie came to the conclusion that it was better to be out and about meeting people and earning some money if it stopped her thinking of Ben.

And Trevor. Although she had to admit, she scarcely gave him a thought these days.

So, she decided to take the plunge and work for John. They agreed that she would do three days a week plus any extras if he had to go on one of his foraging trips.

The premises were a bewildering hotchpotch of second-hand books, antiques and out in the covered back yard a fascinating, to Edie at any rate, collection of Victorian and Edwardian fireplaces, baths, large items of furniture as well as Art Deco paraphernalia – bureaus, wireless sets and table lamps.

Customers came a long way to see John, who was an expert on just about everything. If he hadn't got what they wanted in the shop, he would try his best to get it for them, travelling all over the country in search of rare and valuable items. He charged them a high premium for his efforts but it was a price his clients were more than willing to pay in their quest for authenticity.

He sold to private collectors as well as hiring out items to film companies and television production teams doing period dramas, he told Edie, as he showed her round after she had come into the shop and told him that she'd like to take up his offer and work for him.

"You'll have to hold the fort during the times I'm away," he said. "If you don't know how to deal with something, phone me. My mobile's always on and I'll always answer it. You'll also be able to put your conservation skills to good use as I often have people coming into the shop to ask how much I will give them for the fireplace they're ripping out of the terraced house they're renovating. You could persuade them not to and leave it in situ."

"Won't that do you out of business?" asked Edie.

"Maybe some, but I'd rather see the traditional features remain in the houses into which they were built. I do this job for the money, certainly – it's my living – but I also see my shop as a means of making sure historical things don't just disappear onto the scrap heap."

Surprisingly, Edie found John to be a person after her own heart.

However, not in the romantic sense. That part of her was broken beyond repair.

Ben stood in the house that had belonged to Edie's grandparents and surveyed his handiwork – well, not just *his* handiwork – but the conception had been his and the realization of it should have engendered the satisfaction he usually experienced when a project was well on the way to a successful conclusion.

However, this time, he felt nothing but regret.

Despite his efforts to the contrary, the character of the house was changing. It was no longer as it had been. It was as if its soul had fled in the face of all the re-plastering and re-ordering, even though the latter had been kept to a minimum and the original interior features, such as the fireplaces, over-mantel and folding shutters, had been retained.

The tiles in the communal entrance hallway were now immaculate, shining and clean; the bannisters polished to perfection. Outside, the sash and dormer windows had been cleaned and re-hung; the pediment over the newly-painted front door and the cornice below the roof repaired or replaced. Every detail that he and Edie had been so keen on had been kept.

But still this fine Edwardian, three-storey house had somehow lost its heart. Or was it that he had lost heart because Edie was no longer working beside him?

Since returning from Cairnmor, Ben had pondered long and hard as to what he should do.

He had broken his promise to his wife, that much was a given, and there could be no going back. He had to wrestle with his conscience because of that but, if he approached Edie again, it would have to be knowing he was prepared to make a commitment to her. He had too much respect for her not to do so and too much knowledge of how she had been hurt in the past to suggest that theirs should be an intimate but casual relationship.

Ben needed her closeness again. He longed to feel the softness of her body as she yielded to him, so different from the angular limbs of his lost wife, and he ached for Edie with a yearning that he had forgotten existed.

His father had asked him if he loved her. Was what he felt love or were his feelings merely intense physical needs re-awakened and masquerading as love – that elusive emotion chased and agonized over by poets, novelists and lesser mortals like himself?

Ben stood alone in the hallway, wondering about all these things but, unable to reach a conclusion or allow his thoughts to go the extra dimension, he closed and locked the door behind him and walked to his car, driving slowly back to the office where Judith, his P.A., greeted him with a sunny smile and made him a cup of tea.

As time went by, Edie discovered that three days at the Emporium were enough for her, even though each day held variety and each person's requirements differed.

Putting Ben aside, she knew she preferred the consultancy role that she had tasted so briefly – somehow it was more intellectually satisfying – but she was grateful for the income, especially as the money John paid her was generous.

They chatted companionably as they discussed, catalogued, dated and valued each item that came into the shop while John kept her amused over numerous cups of tea with funny stories as he recounted his exploits up and down the country. It was all very friendly and very undemanding.

Her days passed pleasantly enough but at night, Edie thought about Ben constantly and her body, even after just one encounter, longed for him. Having tasted such intimacy after so long, she found it difficult to sublimate her needs and longed for his caress and the deep satisfaction his embrace had afforded her. He was a kind and passionate man and she had truly loved every moment.

Her sex life with Trevor had been a series of stops and starts in between his affairs until, at Edie's instigation when she could stand his capricious behaviour no longer, it had ceased altogether.

In the intervening years, her body had gone to sleep and, to have her natural desires re-awoken with such joy only for it all to be snatched away from her almost immediately, was intolerably cruel and she found herself once more in the position of having her battered emotions caught in an erratic situation.

She wondered if it would be wrong to contact Ben. It wouldn't be *wrong*, she concluded, but if she did so, she would run the risk of rejection once again and Edie knew she hadn't the emotional reserves to cope with that any more.

"Do you know why Edie looks so sad much of the time, Baz?" asked John of his friend, one day, as he came into the café to buy a couple of take-away coffees for himself and Edie. "I haven't liked to ask."

"Ah, well," said Baz, lowering his voice confidentially, "her husband was a Prize Rat and a while ago, she landed good job with an architect – I not know his name – who promise much and who turns out to be different kind of rat, an Idiot Rat. Edie not say great deal but she think about him a lot and still mope around, so says my beloved Halka. But this moping, it is not good." His expression brightened as he snapped on the lids and handed John the polystyrene cups. "But it is good that she work for you now. Be kind to her. She nice woman."

"I know that," said John, who paid for the coffees and turned to go out of the shop. "Thanks, Baz."

"You welcome."

Yes, thought John, Edie was a nice woman. He decided to keep a weather eye out for her well-being. Besides, there was something he liked about her.

Very much.

The next day, as they price-tagged a consignment of knives, forks and spoons that had just arrived, John asked conversationally, "What's Edie short for?" He handed her some more labels. "Edna? Edith?"

"Neither." Edie made a wry face. "It's Eden."

John raised an eyebrow. "That's an unusual name."

"My parents felt that 'Eden' would be rather appropriate as I was conceived," Edie blushed, "on a private, secluded beach that belonged to the farmhouse where they lived and which they considered to be their own personal paradise."

John smiled and raised his eyebrows. "I presume they were married at the time and their reckless abandonment didn't result in a fall of biblical proportions for your mother?"

"Given what happened in the original Garden of Eden, you mean?"

"Something like that."

Edie laughed. "No, they were safely and happily married and had been for ten years. I'm the youngest of five."

A wonderful, unanticipated afterthought, her mother, Sophie, had always told her; *the precious gift of a bonus baby,* her father, Robert, had added.

But, of course, Edie said none of this to John.

He wondered if beneath her quiet, self-possessed exterior, Edie could be as bold and spontaneous as her parents had obviously been.

John began to look at her in a different way. He had probably done so, if he thought about it, even if the relationship with his long-term, occasional girlfriend (whom he had visited every time he went up north on business) hadn't reached its inevitable, protracted demise two weeks previously. Perhaps he had taken a subconscious interest in Edie even when she had been just a customer. Perhaps that was why he'd offered her the job in the first place.

He knew they were rarely short of conversation; that they worked amicably together and even though John was a few years younger than she, it was nothing in the overall scheme of things. He had no desire for any more children – his two teenage offspring who lived with their mother were enough – and, if he thought about it, he actually quite *fancied* Edie.

The realization surprised him.

John wondered whether she would be responsive to something outside of work, but mindful of her lack of flirtatiousness towards him as well as Baz's observations, he guessed she wasn't in that frame of mind. He knew she wasn't seeing anyone else, but there was something the café owner had said about some architect that made him wonder if Edie's affections were elsewhere.

Perhaps he would suggest that she accompany him on one of his periodic antique foraging expeditions. He was going to Shropshire next week. She could come with him then. She might let her guard down enough to allow him to get to know her better. They were becoming friends, so why not add companionship into the mix? John knew he made her laugh and that was as good a starting point as any.

He made them a pot of tea and began to be more attentive towards her before putting to her the idea of a trip across country.

Callie was not having much success in finding another place to work. No chambers seemed willing to accept her or to have room to take on another barrister. Over the past month or so since parting from Jamie, she had made many enquiries without success and her internet searches had proved equally fruitless.

She had begun to wonder whether she should try outside London, something she was reluctant to do.

She had just about given up, when she had a phone call from Amy, her literary agent friend.

"Hi, Callie."

"Amy! How are you?"

"Fine, thanks. Any luck with the job hunt yet?"

"No, nothing. It's like a desert out there. I'm beginning to regret my hasty exit from Royal Court."

"Don't do that. Look, I may have found you something. It's a one-off but you never know where it might lead. A publishing house we work with is having legal problems with one of our authors – something to do with intellectual copyright – and the guy I spoke to on the phone who was telling me all the gory details, happened to mention in passing that they'll need a barrister. So, I recommended you. Interested? They'll pay you, of course."

"Interested! Just try and keep me away!"

"Look here's the name of the firm and their telephone number. I've told them about you and they're expecting your call."

"Thanks, Amy. I really appreciate this."

"No problem. Are you free tomorrow evening, by any chance? It's been ages since we've been out together. George is away at the moment so it'll just be us two. Which will be good as you've been more than secretive recently. In fact, you've been positively recluse-like."

"I know I have, I'm sorry. And I am free then. How about sixish at our usual place?"

"Brilliant. See you then then, and we can catch up on all the latest. Good luck with the publishing firm."

"Thank you, Amy. I owe you one!"

"Nah. What are friends for?"

The next day, having made her appointment, Callie presented herself at a towering, brand-new, industrial-type building just south of the river. After reporting to reception, she was shown into a sleek, glass-walled office.

Behind the desk sat an attractive, bespectacled man who said, as he stood up and approached her, "Ah, Miss Martin, do come in. I'm Erik van der Waals. Your friend Amy at Merediths has told me a great deal about you and I've been looking forward to meeting you properly at last."

"Are you free next Thursday?" asked Judith.

Ben was caught by surprise. He was just about to leave the office at the end of the day.

"Why?" he asked cautiously. He hoped that his P.A. hadn't set him up with some kind of blind date.

"Well, my friends Tom and Laura are having a dinner party that evening…"

Here we go, thought Ben.

"…and my date for the evening has cancelled out on me. I've got a baby-sitter all arranged and I didn't really want to let my friends down, so I was wondering," she looked up at him with one of her ready smiles, "if you would like to come along in his place."

Caught by surprise, Ben remained silent for several moments. He was flattered, of course, but he wondered whether the whole 'cancelled date' scenario was just a ruse to ask him out. He didn't want to offend her by refusing but neither did he want to go out for the evening to a dinner party with people he'd never met with a woman for whom he held not the slightest interest outside the workplace even though she had occasionally tried to exert her charms in his direction.

"Do come, Ben." She smiled at him again with just the smallest amount of flirtatiousness. "It'll do you good. You've been so preoccupied and down-in-the-mouth recently, that it's been like working with a block of stone."

"Has it? I'm sorry." Had he really been that bad?

"No strings, I promise." Judith smiled sweetly at him.

For a moment, Ben believed her and foolishly, persuading himself that it would be good to go out for a change, he agreed.

"That's wonderful!" she replied, surprised despite her aspirations.

Was it? He swallowed hard, the fight or flight instinct making him want to run away.

"What time shall I pick you up?" he heard himself say.

"Don't worry. I'll collect you. It's easier if I drive rather than trying to explain how to get there on the way. I'm hopeless at giving directions."

Ben felt uneasy. This was not the sort of thing he had planned for himself.

CHAPTER 15

On Monday morning, John collected Edie from her front door and helped put her suitcase into the back of the van.

"All set?"

Edie nodded. Was she doing the right thing? she wondered, as John held the door open for her and she climbed into the passenger seat. She watched him as he went round to the driver's side. He started the engine and they set off on their first joint trip.

"It'll be fun," he'd said, after he had persuaded her to accompany him on this, his latest foray. "We'll see some of the countryside on the journey, go out to some nice restaurants and bring back some useful new stuff for the Emporium. It won't hurt to shut up shop for a couple of days. We both deserve a break."

She couldn't argue with that. They had been busier than ever and deciding he was right, had agreed to go with him.

They were heading for Ludlow in Shropshire, a town with numerous antique and vintage shops, that held an enormous fair on the racecourse each year.

"I know that five o'clock in the morning is an early start," he said, "but I reckon we'll beat the rush-hour and arrive in time to book into our hotel and head straight for the race-course to spend a glorious day at the Fair. There's plenty of places for food, so we won't starve."

The three-and-a-half-hour journey passed pleasantly enough and they arrived, without having been stressed by delays on the way, in a town full of wonderful historical buildings.

"Edie paradise!" quipped John.

However, there was no time for more than a cursory look around as, having booked into their rooms, they travelled to the racecourse where John managed to find a parking space in the car park.

"There you go, Edie," he said, as they got out of the car, "go lose yourself. We'll catch up later. Browse to your heart's content. If you see anything along the way that might suit the shop, give us a buzz and I shall come galloping to your side. I'll do the bargaining – you're far too nice to go cut-throating with the stall-holders." He gave her a quick peck on the cheek. "Ta-ta. See you later."

Edie smiled as he went whistling on his way. She liked his cheerfulness and she had to admit that he had been amusing company on the journey.

The antiques fair was huge – the biggest she'd ever seen. There was just about anything anyone could wish for and methodically, she set about going up and down the aisles of stalls, looking at the wares – some of it tat, some of it good quality.

She came across a beautiful Victorian register grate, complete with cast-iron hood and tiled surround. It was in excellent condition and she phoned John who appeared by her side a minute or so later.

"Wow!" he exclaimed, as he looked it over. "We'll have that. Those companion sets look good too. We'll take those." He looked at the stall holder. "Any more fireplaces like this tucked away?"

"A few."

The man took them to his van, where he had three more stacked up ready to be displayed.

"I've got some original fender tiles as well if you're interested," and he opened a box and showed Edie and John.

"Yep, we'll have those as well." He turned to Edie. "Well done, you! Fantastic. Now, off you go and see what else you can find. I'll stay here and do the haggling."

Edie was vaguely irritated. She didn't want to be sent away like some child excluded from grown-up conversation (not that her parents had ever done that to her). She had wanted to see what price John managed to get for her lucky find and whether he got the bargain she knew he would be after.

She looked back and saw him deep in conversation with the stall holder. Twice he pretended to walk away; twice the stall holder called him back. Eventually, both satisfied, they shook hands, and she saw John produce a wodge of cash from his wallet and give it to the stall holder who wrote out a receipt. Then the two men carried the weighty purchases to John's van.

Edie continued on her wanderings. She looked at various items without particular interest until she came to an enormous second-hand book stall. Taking her time, she browsed through the usual rejected novels and ancient encyclopaedias until she came to the travel section. Carefully, she perused the layers of books but found nothing to tempt her and was just about to move on, when she caught sight of the word 'Cairnmor'. Moving some of the other books out of the way, she picked up three books tied together with a piece of string.

She looked at the titles and stared at them open-mouthed.

My Travels Round Cairnmor and Cairnbeg (*1898*) by George Fergus Mayhew; *Mrs Gilgarry's Herbal Recipes for Health* by Katherine Stewart and Marcus Kendrick, with illustrations and photographs by Jack Rutherford; *A Traveller's Guide to Cairnmor* by Grace Rutherford and Alastair Stewart.

Edie didn't care how much they cost. She gave the stall holder the full price for them, aware that even if they'd been twice as expensive, she would have paid whatever it took to secure them.

Jack and Grace. Ben had talked about someone called Grace as being his step-mother. It had to be the same person. And Jack must be his father. There couldn't be that many people with the surname of Rutherford on Cairnmor, surely?

Edie knew she now had a bona-fide excuse to contact Ben and her heart beat faster at the possibility of seeing him again.

Even so, she wondered if she had the courage to do so.

Of course she had, she told herself sternly. Besides, it would be unfair not to tell him of her find. He could take it or leave it as he wished she thought boldly, trying to convince herself that she could cope with yet more personal rejection. But if Jack Rutherford was his father and Katherine and Alastair or Marcus his relatives, then it was only right and proper that he should know about the books. He might have copies already but on the other hand, he may not.

Edie placed the books safely in her bag. She decided not to tell John, as she had no wish to share this with him. Besides, he'd probably be disappointed in her for not securing a bargain.

Happily, she thanked the stall holder and went on her way. She made a few other discoveries which John purchased with enthusiasm and at the end of the day, footsore but flushed with success, they ate a celebratory meal in an old-fashioned restaurant tucked away in Ludlow town centre before retiring to their hotel for the night.

John behaved like a perfect gentleman and Edie was very relieved.

"So what did you do when he said his name was Erik?" asked Amy, after they had ordered their food.

"I wanted to scream and run out of the door," replied Callie. "But I didn't. I listened to what he had to say and when he didn't seem to make any move or give any indication that he had already had contact with me, I began to relax and just got on with the job. I mean, no one asked for me by name did they?"

"Not as far as I know. Besides, it was me that suggested you. I could have said anyone."

"Exactly. I also thought that it would be too much of a coincidence for it to be the same guy who phoned me up."

"Unless he's playing a clever game of double-bluff or double-think or whatever they call it in thrillers." Amy thought for a moment. "Clever subterfuge I think is what might be the term."

"Anyway, Erik and the author's solicitor seemed most grateful that I'd agreed to take on the case."

"So," said Amy, after they had discreetly discussed the author's legal difficulties for a few moments, "he didn't look at you in a funny way or ask you to meet him in some obscure place once you'd finished all the formal stuff?"

"No, he seemed perfectly pleasant and rational."

And very charming. And very attractive in a compelling sort of way, though she kept both of those things to herself – there was no point in making her friend jump to the wrong conclusion.

Amy laughed. "That's not good."

"What isn't?" (Had Amy read her mind?)

"Because he's a publisher. No publisher is normal. They're all as mad as hatters. Goes with the territory."

Callie laughed. "And of course, as a literary agent, you'd recognize the type?"

"Naturally. I'm dealing with them all the time. And I live with one." Amy took a sip of wine. "So what have you been up to?"

"I have a new boyfriend."

Callie knew that she and Jamie had agreed to keep their engagement secret but she saw no reason not tell Amy, who was her closest friend and had been since before university, that she had met someone. Besides, she was desperate to talk about him; to keep him real in her mind.

"Really? I thought you were done and dusted for life after the last one."

"That was then, this is now. He's really nice, Amy, and we're serious about each other."

"So, what's he like in bed?"

Callie smiled and shook her head. "I have no idea."

"You mean you haven't slept with him yet?" Amy was shocked. "Is there something wrong with him?"

"No. He's just gentlemanly and sort of old-fashioned, that's all. Which I happen to like. And besides, we've sort of only been with each other for a couple of weeks."

"George and I slept together after our second date. Why wait?"

"I don't know. It just sort of never happened."

"I presume he's a normal full-blooded male?"

"Of course he is!" Callie smiled, recalling random intimate moments. "Very normal."

"So when do I get to meet him?"

"In about five months."

"Five months!" Amy frowned and looked at her friend quizzically. "Why?"

"Because he's in the army out in Afghanistan."

"Really?"

"He's in the Household Cavalry."

"Don't they do Trooping the Colour and all that stuff and wear those silver helmets with the plumes?"

"Yes. But they have a dual role and are combat soldiers as well as doing ceremonial duty."

"So, what's his name?"

"Jamie."

Amy regarded her friend carefully. "You really like him, don't you?"

Callie blushed. "Yes, I think I do," she replied, wanting to confide in her friend so that she could check she was doing the right thing in becoming engaged but holding back from doing so because of her promise to Jamie.

Sensing a slight hesitation in her manner, Amy remarked, "Well, I hope you're not making the same mistake of being dragged into having yet another relationship on the back of someone else's desires rather than your own, like you did with those two guys you went out with at uni, unable to make up your mind between them. Don't forget, I know you well. Especially as I had to pick up the pieces afterwards."

Amy remembered all too clearly the emotional hoops her friend had put herself through.

Callie blushed again and shook her head. "Not this time."

"Well, if that's the case, I'm really pleased for you and wish you all the luck in the world." Amy raised her glass. "Well, here's to you and Jamie."

"Thank you."

Watching them from a quiet, hidden corner, Erik van der Waals poured himself another brandy and regarded Callie with undisguised admiration as he studied the contours of her body and the way she moved. He could see she had the potential to match his needs perfectly. She was just the type of woman he found desirable and, what's more, she had come along at exactly the right time. He was about to put an end his current conquest, with whom he was now bored, and without a twinge of conscience, he decided to make Callie Martin his next acquisition.

Erik took a sip from his glass and, warmed by the liquid as it slipped down his throat, he contemplated the best way to pursue her.

CHAPTER 16

A couple of days later, Callie was asked to pay a second visit to Erik van der Waals.

He said there was a further legal point to clarify and happy to earn yet more money, Callie returned to the glass building in the City that she had visited before.

"Our mutual friend Amy at Merediths tells me you are looking for a permanent position?" he asked smoothly, offering her coffee from the hi-tech, expensive-looking chrome machine across the room from his desk.

"Yes, that's right, I am."

"Do you take milk? Sugar?"

"Milk, no sugar."

"It just so happens that there is an opening in the legal department that oversees my various business interests, of which the publishing house is but one. I already employ a small team of solicitors and I need a barrister to add to the fold. You fit the bill perfectly and would be required to give legal advice on commercial and corporate issues, intellectual copyright, new acquisitions and so on. The work will be mainly research and points of law but may well involve some advocacy. Our overheads…" he handed Callie her coffee cup, "…are astronomical and naturally, we command a premium from our clients."

"I can understand that."

"Therefore, we offset our costs and make a nice profit. If you are interested in money, it is a good place in which to work."

Was she that interested in money? Not really. She only needed enough to live on. But Callie liked the sound of the job.

"Okay," she said cautiously.

"You could obtain a reference?"

"Yes. That wouldn't be a problem."

"Are you good at your work?"

Callie blushed.

"Of course, I see you are far too modest to say." He smiled at her. "More to the point, do other people think you are good at your work?"

"Of course," she said, blushing at the lie.

Erik looked at her sharply. "Why did you leave Royal Court Chambers?"

Callie thought it best not to say, thinking of Jamie's description – 'because the head of chambers was a pompous prick' – and replied instead, "Sir Alan and I never quite got along with each other."

"Ah, I see." He took a sip of his coffee. "Yet he will give you a reference?"

"Yes. He said he would give me an excellent reference."

At least that was true.

Erik raised an eyebrow. "What would you say are your strengths?"

"Research, points of law, cross-referencing, memory for detail, instinctive understanding of what's required and the knowledge to validate it."

"And your weaknesses?"

Callie took a deep breath. "Reading people. I don't always get it right if they're being deceptive. And advocacy. I don't like standing up in court."

There she had said it all. That was it – her reputation sunk forever. He would undoubtedly rescind the job offer and probably have a good laugh with his colleagues at her expense.

However, Erik seemed unfazed by her statements, nor did he show any amusement.

"These present no problems, Miss Martin, or may I call you Callie?"

"Of course."

"In fact, what I have in mind for you will suit both of us as you will rarely have to deal with clients on your own or have to stand up in court. I prefer to settle any er... disputes before they reach that stage." He smiled disarmingly. "I shall take great pleasure in guiding you in all your work and I thank you for your honesty. Now," he put down his cup and pressed a bell on his desk, "subject to a satisfactory reference and completion of the appropriate forms, we shall begin our new association on Monday." He shook Callie's hand in a business-like way, yet with the subtlest hint of prolonged contact. "My P.A. will supply you with details and all other necessary information concerning your application."

"Thank you, Mr van der Waals," replied Callie.

"Please, my name is Erik."

Did she recognize the inflection in his voice, she wondered? Did she detect the slightest trace of an accent she had heard before?

Callie told herself not to be so ridiculous. She was onto a good thing in working here. Besides, she couldn't really remember what her mysterious caller sounded like now; it was too long ago and anyway, she had put him out of her mind.

As soon as she got home that evening, Callie wrote a long letter to Jamie. She wrote in great detail, having learned from him that even with mass communication technology, one of the things that British troops serving abroad prized the most were letters from home.

Despite his initial reluctance at the beginning of the evening, Ben had to admit that he had enjoyed himself, despite finding himself in an unaccustomed social circle. Tom and Laura turned out to be good company, as did Judith, and the meal was felt by everyone to be a success.

Secretly, however, he was glad when it came to an end. He had a full day of meetings coming up and was itching to get on with an intriguing design for his latest clients.

Judith stopped the car outside his house.

"Thank you," he said. "It's been a good evening."

"I'm so glad."

Without preamble, she pulled him towards her and kissed him on the lips.

"That was just to say thank you for this evening."

"Ah." Ben put his hand on the handle, preparing to open the door and escape. "Well, goodnight. Thank you for the lift."

"Aren't you going to invite me in?" she said provocatively, slowly running her hand along the inside of his thigh.

"I wasn't, no." He swallowed hard, caught unawares, feeling his body respond to her audacious caress.

He ought to stop her, she was his employee; he was her boss…

"Are you sure?" she said, allowing her hand to remain where it was.

She kissed him again and despite his best intentions, Ben found himself increasingly and confusingly caught up in her intimate advances by responding in kind; his recently re-awakened but quickly suppressed sexuality threatening to overwhelm his common sense and all thoughts of loyalty to his wife.

After a while, Judith lay back in her seat and gave him a knowing look.

"Well!" she exclaimed, "I think we definitely need to go inside, don't you? We can't go any further out here. Whatever would the neighbours say!"

Foolishly, chastising himself for his weakness, Ben got out of the car and she followed him into the house.

It was nearly midnight when John stopped the van as near to Edie's house as he could, having found difficulty in locating an available space, and extracted her suitcase from the boot.

"Are you sure you don't want me to carry this to your house for you?"

She smiled. "No thanks, John. I can manage. It's not heavy."

"Okay."

He handed the case to her and kissed her on the cheek.

"Thank you, my dear," he said, putting his hand on her shoulder. "We must do this again. I think I shall take you with me every time I go up country! We've done well and I'm grateful to you."

"I've enjoyed it too. Thank you, John," she replied.

Edie stood on the pavement and waved to him as he drove away.

She turned and walked towards her house. As it came into view, sitting hunched on the doorstep looking haggard and drawn, was Ben.

"Hello," he said, looking up at her, his expression troubled, his eyes full of pain. "I think I may have done something really stupid."

"Well," said Edie matter-of-factly, "perhaps you'd better come inside and tell me about it."

Ben stood up, took her suitcase from her and followed her indoors.

He sat at the kitchen table while Edie, even though it was now early in the morning, made them a pot of tea.

"So what is it you've done that's so terrible that it brings you rushing to my door?"

Ben sensed a reprimand in her voice. He deserved it. More than Edie could possibly know.

"You probably won't want anything to do with me ever again," he began.

"I wasn't aware that we'd had anything to do with each other for quite a while," she replied tersely.

The truth of her words stung him.

"I got carried away," he blurted out.

"Carried away?"

"With another woman."

"Another woman?"

Edie looked at him. He sounded like the proverbial guilty husband confessing to his wife.

But Edie wasn't Ben's wife. She had been Trevor's wife and he'd never confessed. He had felt no guilt whatsoever.

"What do you mean 'got carried away'?" she said. "That you couldn't help yourself and ended up in bed with her?"

Ashamed, Ben looked down at the table. "Not exactly, but something like that."

"What then? Why should you want to tell me this anyway? What's it to me?" Anger and jealousy made her voice harsh.

"I thought of you."

"While you were having sex?"

"In a manner of speaking."

"That's disgusting."

"I'm sorry. That's not how it was nor how I meant it to sound."

"I'm sure it wasn't."

Ben knew this was going from bad to worse. He sighed and pressed the palms of his hands against his eyes.

"What I meant was that I didn't feel guilty because I'd been unfaithful to my wife. I felt guilty because I knew I was being unfaithful to you."

Edie stared at him.

"I wasn't aware that we were a couple," she said. *Despite our coupling*, she thought.

"We could have been."

"Yes, and you stopped it happening."

"I know and I regret that too."

Edie glared at him, her habitual reticence cast aside in a tide of righteous indignation and anger. "Your life just seems to be one regret after another, doesn't it?"

Ben winced as her words struck home.

"Isn't yours?" he retorted gently.

"Yes," answered Edie honestly, "but nothing like this. And in your haste to confess, you've just added another regret to my list."

"How?"

"That I ever allowed you to make love to me in the first place."

Chagrined, Ben stood up. "Perhaps I ought to leave."

Edie stared angrily at him, the inner hurt she had nursed ever since their separation rising to the surface.

"Why not? It's what you're good at."

"What do you mean?"

"Don't be obtuse."

Aggrieved, Ben moved towards the door.

The kettle boiled.

"I don't want to go," he said quietly, turning back towards her.

She looked at him for a moment, her anger dissipating as quickly as it had arisen.

"Then don't," said Edie, throwing them both a lifeline. "Stay for tea, at least."

Ben sat down again and watched her with a rapidly beating heart and a sense of inner relief as she lifted the kettle off the range and made the tea.

Perhaps there was hope for him after all.

CHAPTER 17

"Will you have supper with me this evening, Callie?" said Erik, as they walked to the lift at the end of another working day. "I always like to take a new employee out for a meal. I find it helps them to settle in and for me to get to know them better."

They had spent many hours during her first week ensconced in his office where Erik had, in great detail, given the low-down of each company he ran and its legal requirements – with Callie amazed by just how extensive her work was going to be as his business interests were multifarious and complex.

Erik had taken great pains to explain to her how each individual company operated; what her role would be within the overall corporate structure and what would be expected of her. He said that he would play to her strengths and guide her closely through the whole process so that she became accustomed to his way of operating.

Callie felt excited by the prospect of what she would be doing and the help she would receive. This job was just what she needed and she couldn't believe her luck in landing a position like this. She could see that working here would go a long way to restoring her battered professional self-esteem.

But supper? She hesitated. Should she? There could be no harm in it, surely?

"I saw you and our mutual friend Amy some time ago in that restaurant near Hyde Park Corner. I was having a meal with some clients," Erik said smoothly.

Surprised, Callie said, "You should have come over to say hello."

"Ah, you were deep in conversation. I didn't like to disturb you. But I enjoyed observing you."

Callie looked at him in surprise.

"You should take that as a compliment."

She blushed. "Thank you."

"We could go to the same place for our evening out, if you wish."

It was a statement rather than a question.

Callie found herself accepting, suppressing her inner voice which told her to steer clear. "Yes, alright," she said.

"I shall collect you from your home at seven."

"Thank you."

"I am looking forward to our evening together immensely."

"Yes," replied Callie, with more conviction than she actually felt.

After avoiding the inevitable embarrassment of face to face contact with his PA and working from home for a week, Ben knew he had to bite the bullet and go into the office. He couldn't run away and hide forever. There were clients to see and business to attend to.

However, he refused to look at Judith as he walked past her desk.

They would have to speak eventually but Ben skirted round it for as long as possible. He closed the door to his office and worked steadily at his drawings and plans throughout the morning, avoiding seeing anyone.

He wondered if Judith had said anything to the other girls in the office – especially his partner's secretary as he knew they were close – or to the girl in finance with whom she often enjoyed a good gossip.

As lunchtime drew near, there was a brisk knock on his door and Judith walked in, standing hesitantly on the threshold of his room.

"Hello?" she said uncertainly.

Ben looked up at her but didn't respond.

"I'm sorry about what happened last week."

"So am I," he said unapologetically, regret colouring his voice.

"I shouldn't have come onto you like that."

"No. You shouldn't."

"I ought to have waited until we'd got to know each other first."

He looked at her sharply, unable to believe what he was hearing.

"I realize that you weren't all that keen to start with... but you made up for it later," she added quickly and defensively, smiling at him a little too brightly.

Had he? Ben was puzzled. It hadn't felt like that, especially as he'd stopped her from going any further virtually as soon as they'd gone into the house.

"It wasn't a spur of the moment thing for me," she continued blithely. "Well," she corrected herself, hastily, "it was, but it wasn't, if you see what I mean."

He didn't, nor did he try.

"But perhaps we can put this all behind us and get to know each other better outside of work. You know – go on a couple of dates and stuff. I really like you, Ben. I have done for a long time."

He looked up at her and heaved a deep sigh, his eyes troubled.

"I know," he said quietly. "I'm all too aware of that."

"I did enjoy it."

"Really?"

As far as he was concerned, there'd been nothing to enjoy. It was the most embarrassing encounter he'd ever had. Not that he was vastly experienced, of course.

His wife and Edie. That was it. And both of them had been wonderful. Especially Edie who was sublime.

His distasteful fumblings with Judith in the car were something he would prefer to forget. It was certainly something he had no desire to repeat.

"How about starting over?" she asked, her manner animated by hope. "Get things established properly, you know. My children stay with their father each Wednesday. I'm free then."

"I'm sorry, Judith, but I'm busy."

"How about the weekend? On Sunday. The children are with my ex every other weekend. As you know, we have joint custody."

"I already have plans, I'm afraid," he said with deliberate care.

He had no wish to be unkind but he had to be clear. There would be no repetition of anything.

"How about next Wednesday?"

Couldn't this woman take a hint?

"No," said Ben firmly and decisively.

Even Judith couldn't mistake the tone of his voice.

"You don't want to see me again? Ever?"

Ben shook his head apologetically. "Not in that way."

"But you have no one. You're not attached to anyone. You're not seeing anyone."

"I am."

"Since when?"

He now knew without a shadow of doubt that he wanted to be with Edie. Permanently.

To follow his heart.

"It's none of your business, Judith," he said.

"It is my business. I don't go encouraging every man I fancy, you know." She was becoming huffy. "Only those I really like."

Ben took a mental note of 'only those'. He wondered how many men she had been with since her divorce. Quite a few, he imagined. She was that type. He remembered her gleeful declaration of freedom after her *decree absolute* and the succession of different men who collected her after work each Wednesday.

Flinching inwardly, he recalled her words the moment they had walked through the front door of his house: "I never take any risks," she'd told him proudly and confidently. "I'd hate to catch anything nasty. So, I always make sure the bloke is well-kitted out."

Ben remembered his involuntary shudder of distaste as she then moved towards him with the intention of completing what she had begun in the car.

In those critical moments, he knew with absolute certainty that, should he allow Judith to continue, he would be unfaithful to the woman he truly loved and in those critical, vital moments, he yearned with all his heart and soul for the safety of Edie.

The intensity of this realization had made him push Judith away from him, who reacted with shock, disbelief then anger.

Even so, after declining her advances, he had tried to be polite towards her (she was after all a very good PA) and eventually she went on her way with a philosophical shrug of her shoulders hiding the disappointment and frustration he knew she must have felt.

Her departure left Ben feeling ashamed and embarrassed by the whole scenario. His need to tell Edie how he felt and to clear his conscience overrode his chagrin at what had nearly taken place, even though he knew he could draw comfort from the fact that he had seen sense before it was too late; that he had asked Judith to leave before things really had gone too far.

With this salve to his conscience, late as it was, he had driven to Edie's house and sat on the doorstep, waiting for her to come home.

And what followed had been worth every moment of that anxious and lengthy wait.

Jamie was sitting on a wooden chair outside the mess tent of Camp Bastion brushing the all-pervasive sand off Callie's letter.

It was a long one, full of the little details he prized so much. He loved the way that she wrote: the way she phrased things, the pictures of London and home it created in his mind.

She wrote of the Life Guards on duty; of how she loved her new job; of the new challenges she faced within it. She wrote of how considerate and helpful the chief executive was towards her; how often he called upon her services; how lucky she was to find work like this after her humiliation at Royal Court Chambers.

She said how much she longed to see Jamie again; how their time together now seemed like a distant dream; how frustrating it was to be separated from someone who, despite their commitment, she felt as though she hardly knew.

But I know you, thought Jamie, concerned that she felt she didn't know him.

Sometime ago, he'd asked for a photograph of her as the guys in his quarters all had photos of wives, fiancées and girlfriends pinned up beside them on make-shift, bedside lockers constructed from old wooden crates that had once housed ammunition or food supplies.

Finding that she had enclosed a photo with this particular letter, he extracted it, fashioned a photo-frame of sorts out of scraps of wood and proudly put it on display next to his bed.

Its appearance aroused considerable interest from his fellow soldiers in his tent and he told them that she was his fiancée – it didn't seem to matter anymore that people knew, especially this far away from home. In fact, he *wanted* everyone to know that he was engaged.

It was as though by reiterating the fact, it made it more real, lending a substance and solidity to his connection with Callie that time and distance might render ephemeral. Besides, Jamie felt proud that he was going to get married because having a loyal partner was admired and respected out here as many relationships didn't survive the long periods of separation.

His comrades were amazed when he said he and Callie had got engaged after only a week.

"Are you sure she'll wait for you?" said one of his friends, someone who had been badly let down by his girlfriend and therefore held something of a jaundiced point of view. "After all, you hardly know her."

"Of course she will," Jamie replied equably. "How long we've actually been together is irrelevant."

"Well, I only hope you're right, mate. Romances that begin that quick never last, especially when you're on a six-month tour of duty. And I'm not the only one it's happened to. There's lots of the lads who've arrived with a long-standing girlfriend, let alone a new one, only to return to England to find they haven't got one anymore."

"Well, it won't happen to me," said Jamie defiantly, trying to keep his annoyance in check. "Tell me something I haven't already heard, why don't you?"

"Just saying it the way it is, mate."

As time went on, his friend's sobering words kept returning to Jamie and in his replies to Callie's letters, he made sure he filled them with thoughts about their future together: how much he loved her; how special she was; how he couldn't bear to be without her – as though by doing so, he could ward off the feeling of insecurity engendered by his friend's observations.

He began to wish he'd never told anyone about Callie now. Perhaps the first, shared instinct that their relationship should remain concealed from prying eyes because it was in a most tender and delicate state was correct.

He hoped he wouldn't lose her because they hadn't had time to establish things properly first.

CHAPTER 18

That first, enjoyable meal with Erik quickly became a regular occurrence after work – once a week, twice a week, then every weekday night.

He proved to be good company and Callie found him to be the kind of man that, if she hadn't been engaged to Jamie (from whom she hadn't heard in a while, something that made her feel neglected and anxious) she would have liked to go out with, had he asked her.

She admired Erik's strength and purpose. He was attentive and charming and she found herself drawn in by his maturity and charismatic presence. He was thirty-six, he told her; had studied law at university but decided to go into business rather than become a barrister as he didn't enjoy standing up in court.

"We have that in common," he said, "but with me, I just found the whole process tedious not nerve-racking." He smiled at her disarmingly. "I knew I'd enjoy the cut and thrust of the business world more than that of the courtroom, and my ability to make deals has been helped by my knowledge of the law."

He told her that he had been born in Amsterdam but his parents had moved to England when he was ten years old after his father was offered a top job as an executive with an oil company involved in North Sea exploration. He spoke Dutch and Flemish, he said, but he preferred English as he felt it was less harsh and guttural.

Erik didn't just talk about himself. He asked about her family and her friends; about her likes and dislikes; her favourite films and types of music. He was relaxed and genial and made Callie laugh with amusing tales of his travels and the people he encountered in the boardroom.

She put off writing to Jamie (whom she had heard from at last) telling herself that she would do it later, salving her conscience with her busyness at work and social preoccupations afterwards.

There was nothing wrong in the growing closeness of her association with Erik, she persuaded herself. He was her boss, after all, and wasn't it perfectly natural for him to take her out?

One evening, after working late in the office, he said he would be going on a five-day international business convention to be held in Copenhagen in a couple of weeks, and asked her to accompany him.

"It's a rather important conference and highly prestigious. I need to have someone by my side who understands the way I work as it is essential if I am to make the right impression," he said, his manner effortlessly persuasive as he took both her hands in his. "Besides, I enjoy your company and you know how compatible we are."

Callie couldn't deny that everything he had said was true. Mentally, she tried to persuade herself that there was no harm in it, that it would be an exciting adventure; an opportunity she would be silly to refuse. Yet she hesitated, overwhelmed by indecision, uncertainty and unease at the back of her mind.

"My suggestion is all above board – I swear," he added, with an appealing smile, still holding onto her hands.

"I've never been to Denmark," ventured Callie.

"Well, then, it's about time you did. We shall travel by car and leave five days before the conference begins and see the sights along the way. We'll make a holiday if it."

She took a deep breath and against her better judgement, agreed to go.

He lifted her hands to his lips. "Excellent. You won't regret it."

Callie looked at the expression in his eyes and hoped that she wouldn't.

John smiled at Edie when she came into the Emporium.

"You're looking cheerful today," he remarked, as she poked her nose into the little cubbyhole he called his office to deliver her customary good morning.

"Am I?" she said, with an enigmatic smile.

"Good weekend?"

"Wonderful thanks," she said.

Edie hung up her coat on the stand in the corner, trying to hide her flushed cheeks within the shelter of its Victorian arms.

She'd found it in a skip a few weeks previously and she and John had gone along in the early morning just before it became light and quietly removed it.

"I hope there are no security cameras around," she'd said to John as they walked along the road supporting it between them, keeping to the shadows like furtive criminals.

"Nah. Not in this neck of the woods," he'd said. "You only get them in rough areas to catch the drunks and the murderers and in the posh areas so rich people can protect their property. This is a nice, safe, middle-class London street and paranoia hasn't reached here yet, so no one will worry. Besides Nineteen Eighty-Four isn't quite with us," he'd quipped, "so don't worry about it."

Now, as she stood in the doorway of his little office, he perceived a difference in her manner.

"So where did you go?"

"What do you mean, where did I go?"

"For your lovely weekend."

He should have offered to take her somewhere. He'd had nothing to do.

"Oxfordshire. Maybury."

"Nice place, Maybury. I went there once. Got a particularly fine antique shop."

He looked at her vital, alive expression; her new clothes, her neatly trimmed hair.

"Did you go alone?" he ventured.

Edie blushed.

Dammit, thought John, *I've been so busy playing Mr Nice Guy that I've gone and missed the boat.*

He thought of the rather attractive-looking blonde he'd met last Wednesday at a party. She'd seemed nice and they'd got on well and chatted on about this and that. Perhaps he'd ask her out on a date. She'd given him her mobile number. He might give her a call sometime. He'd wanted to after the party but had hung back in case things developed between himself and Edie.

"Anyone I know?"

Edie shook her head.

"Not Trevor?" He asked but he couldn't quite believe she'd allow the Prize Rat back into her life.

She looked shocked. "Good grief! I wouldn't spend the weekend with him if he was the last man on earth."

"What if I were the last man?" asked John, unable to resist asking the question.

"Then I'd be with a good friend and an incredibly kind and considerate man."

He inclined his head. "Why thank you, dear lady. I take that as a great compliment."

"You should."

"I'd take you to bed with me if you were the last woman."

"Only then, huh?" retorted Edie.

John chuckled. "You know that's not what I mean."

"I know." She patted him on the shoulder. "And that's nice."

"So, on a scale of one to ten, how serious was your weekend?"

"Eleven."

"Serious, then."

"Absolutely."

"I hope he treats you well," he said, "otherwise he'll have me to answer for."

Edie laughed. "Thank you, O Gallant Knight."

With a tinge of regret, John realized that anything he might have vaguely hoped for with Edie was now out of the question.

I'll definitely give that blonde a ring, he thought. *But maybe not quite yet.*

Edie took a deep breath. "Well, come on then, let's get moving," she said. "Can't stand around here all day when there's work to be done."

"No, ma'am."

They began to sort through some old magazines someone had brought in.

"So who is he, this man who makes our Edie so happy?" said John, consigning several torn and crumpled sheets of paper to the recycling bin, having first established their unworthiness.

"Nosey-parker."

"Are you sure I don't know him?"

"No."

"Will I ever get to meet him? After all, if it's the same bloke, you've been seeing him for a while now."

"You might, one day."

"Will you invite me to your wedding?"

"Not if you carry on asking me so many questions."

"Meanie."

"It's my middle name."

"No, it's not. Unless you were lying when you completed your application form."

Edie laughed. "What application form was that?"

"Ah. The one I forgot to give you. A serious technical oversight on my part."

"Besides," she said, "no one's said anything about a wedding."

"But you'd like one," said John.

Edie blushed. "One day perhaps. But for now, we're happy as we are, thank you very much."

Before John could reply, the doorbell pinged and a customer came into the shop and he went to see if they needed any assistance.

Glad to be left on her own, Edie continued to sort through the magazines thinking about Ben; once more going over in her mind the sequence of events that led up to her present joy and contentment.

Ben had appeared on her doorstep again on the evening following his confession, armed with a huge bouquet of flowers and Edie had been unable to conceal her delight at seeing him.

"Will you be my only love and go out with me properly this time?" he'd implored her, his expression genuine and heart-felt. "Will you let me make love to you again?"

"Yes," she'd replied unhesitatingly. "To everything."

And Edie, blushing furiously and telling him to keep his voice down in case the neighbours heard, had brought him into her house and back into her life.

"You're sure you forgive me?" he'd asked once again.

"As I said to you after your unexpected appearance on my doorstep yesterday, there's really nothing to forgive," she'd told him. "You were a free agent at the time and in the end nothing drastic happened."

"I still shouldn't have done what I did."

"Maybe not, but the most important thing was that your moment of indiscretion made you feel as though you had been unfaithful to *me*."

"Oh yes," he'd said ardently, "and it made me realize that you and I should be together."

"I know and I'm so, so glad."

He'd looked at her in such a way that her heart beat quickly with the bold and wonderful significance of what was happening to them.

"I think I love you," he'd said.

"I *know* I love you," she'd replied.

So, after seeing each other platonically for a short while, they'd travelled to Maybury for their first, wonderful weekend together and in the cosy lamplight of the sitting room, after they had made love, Edie had shown Ben the books she'd found in Ludlow. She had been delighted by his enthusiastic reaction as he turned over the pages: each one a vivid reminder of his childhood on Cairnmor.

"I don't have these in my possession, so it's a real find, especially as they're all first editions. Dad will be delighted."

"Your dad – Jack."

"Yes. He's an artist."

"And a highly talented one as well judging by the illustrations."

"That he most certainly is. And to think these books turned up in Ludlow of all places!" Ben could still scarcely believe it.

"John says that things like that happen all the time in the antiques business."

"Well, when the weather improves, I'll take you to Cairnmor and you can meet my folks and see where I grew up. And experience what the guide books say for real."

"And as soon as we can, we must go to St Nicolas and I can show you where *I* grew up."

"And the beach where you were conceived."

Edie chuckled. "Trust you to remember that."

"I'd like to have had children with you." Ben's voice held a touch of regret.

"I know what you mean and I feel the same, but just think of the freedom we can enjoy without having any of the anxiety? Between us we have four offspring and that's plenty by anyone's standards." She kissed him. "I'm just glad we found our way back to each other."

"So am I."

In Helmand Province, Jamie was out on night-time patrol with his unit; accompanying a convoy of trucks and armoured vehicles travelling along the infamous and vitally important Highway One – the life-line for the British Army in Afghanistan and which served to keep the vitally important Afghan economy moving.

It stretched for two thousand miles, winding its way throughout the country, linking towns, villages and patrol bases. It was notoriously difficult to defend in its entirety and littered with improvised explosive devices, known to all as IEDs.

Jamie was well aware that according to intelligence reports, the insurgents had recently been laying some of these booby-trap bombs along this particular stretch of road and in the light of this, everyone was justifiably nervous but none more so than the Afghan security forces who now worked alongside the British and other NATO troops.

Cautiously, the convoy inched forward, the dust and darkness making conditions unpleasant and difficult. Jamie's vehicle was well-armoured and well-armed but everyone remained apprehensive and cautious until they reached the safety of the camp.

Suddenly, the convoy came to a halt and word spread that an IED had been uncovered up ahead by the soldiers with specially-adapted metal detectors patrolling on foot either side of and in front of the convoy. A general air of controlled concern pervaded the men and women as their vehicles waited for the all clear before being re-routed along a hastily constructed roadway at a safe distance from the mine.

Jamie's personnel carrier was one of the last to reach the new route when suddenly, just as he approached the diversion, a huge explosion threw the armoured truck behind him sideways, sending shards of burning debris down onto his vehicle.

"IED! IED!"

Without thinking or waiting for orders, Jamie leapt onto the road and immediately went to the aid of his brothers-in-arms.

Fighting off the encroaching flames and ignoring the dangerous possibility of further explosions, he wrenched open the door and managed to pull one of the soldiers to safety, his bravery noted by an officer just arriving at the scene, bringing with him more men who rescued the remaining soldiers from inside the cab and extinguished the fire.

"Is anyone hurt badly?" asked the officer, expecting horrendous injuries to life and limb.

"Don't know yet, sir," replied Jamie, squatting down beside the three shocked soldiers sprawled out on the ground.

The officer went over to them. "Everyone alright?"

"Yes, sir."

"Just stunned, sir."

"You guys are bloody lucky!" he said, feeling extraordinary relief that no one had gone down, knowing how unusual it was for no one to be seriously or fatally injured after an IED explosion.

So did his men.

"Yes, sir."

"Take a moment or two and then we must get back on the road," said the officer. "Trooper, stay with them, make sure they're okay. Thank God they're not seriously hurt. We'll have to wait until we reach camp to get them checked over at the hospital. We need to get out of here as quickly as we can. They can travel in your vehicle when you're ready to move."

"Yes, sir."

"And Rutherford, you did well here. It's not the first time I've seen you react instinctively to help your comrades in a dangerous situation. Well done."

"Thank you, sir,"

"Come and see me when we get back to base."

"Yes, sir."

Jamie wondered what that was all about.

In the darkness, he kept a watch over his companions, listening out above the idling engine noise of the halted convoy for any sign of an impending ambush.

Once the remnants of the damaged vehicle had been made safe and any sensitive equipment and electronics removed, they climbed into Jamie's personnel carrier and the convoy proceeded on its way.

As dawn came, they reached the camp and everyone breathed a sigh of relief, mentally free now to look forward to some 'down time' after being away from Musa Qal'ah for several weeks.

Jamie allowed himself to think of Callie, knowing that his tour of duty would be over one day soon.

One day soon. He had to hold onto that.

He was conscious of the fact that after all this time, they would need to get to know each other again but the prospect of doing so and being with Callie filled him with a keen sense of anticipation and excitement. Their re-connection would have the same freshness, the same beauty and charm as the two exquisite weeks they had spent together but this time it would be without the spectre of separation hanging over them.

He knew that what he had with Callie was something rare and precious: a fragile connection to be nurtured and cherished; a natural affinity to be expanded and enhanced into a mutual devotion that would set the foundations for a lifetime. He wanted to take his time, to savour and experience every moment with Callie to its fullest extent.

Jamie tried hard not to let his thoughts dwell on the fact that he had not heard from her in a while. Perhaps she was busy, perhaps work was taking up most of her time. Perhaps her letters had not reached him yet, especially as he'd been out on patrol. He would hear from her when they returned to Camp Bastion, of that he was certain, and then one day in the not too distant future, he would be able to go home to her.

He reminded himself that he would have to be patient as there was still a long way to go before this particular tour of duty was over – a sensible thought but one that could not conceal or diminish his awareness of the gaping chasm caused by their separation in which anything could happen.

Throughout the detailed preparations for their trip, Callie relied on Erik to deal with their travel arrangements and accommodation; revelling in the luxury of not having to say or do anything towards the organization as she could see he knew exactly what he was doing.

From the outset, their pace of travel was leisurely – eating meals in wayside cafes, staying overnight in tiny candle-lit *auberges* – with Erik becoming ever bolder in his manner towards her, drawing her to him with compelling ease.

After spending every minute of every day in constant contact with him, Callie found herself so absorbed by the power of his personality and so distracted by their close proximity whether in the car or sharing intimate meals, that she began to lose all sense of there being any existence other than the one she was experiencing.

She began to fantasize that she and Erik were a couple; indeed, she found herself *wanting* them to be a couple, blindly pushing all thoughts of Jamie out of her mind

Absorbed by her unreal world, she raised no objection when he touched her arm, her cheeks, her hair, flattered by his close personal interest in her, accepting without protest his growing familiarity towards her. She offered no resistance when he kissed her with an embrace that lingered on her lips long after they had left the car and returned to their hotel. And when his attentions became tantalizingly physical and left her aching for more, she gave into temptation and surrendered herself to his overwhelming charisma.

Too late she found herself in an untenable position. Too late, Callie realized what she had done.

So too did Erik.

Sensing her complete mental acquiescence to him, he made his physical ownership of her immediate and overwhelming.

"This is what you wanted isn't it?" he said, after it was over.

"Oh yes," she murmured, rendered helpless by the rapidity and forcefulness of his actions.

"A woman, when she is like this," he said, his eyes raking her, "is at her most vulnerable. And you are particularly beguiling – submissive, trusting, someone completely open to my needs and desires."

From that moment on, Callie was in his thrall: vanquished by his sophisticated sexuality, consumed and dominated by his powerful personality.

"You belong to me now," he whispered. "You will want for nothing and I shall never let you go."

And Callie knew she was powerless to extricate herself from such all-consuming intensity and also, that she had made the biggest mistake of her life.

CHAPTER 19

"You the Prize Rat?" said Baz without preamble, squinting at Ben after Edie had introduced him and he'd said he was an architect.

Somewhat taken aback, Ben looked at Edie quizzically.

She blushed and frowned at Baz.

"Sorry. I not mean to insult you. It's just that my wife Halka and I both look out for our Edie." He smiled at Ben. "You make sure you treat her right, my friend. She nice lady. I relieved you not the Prize Rat."

"Ah, you must mean Trevor?" Ben smiled. "No, I'm definitely not him." He put his arm round her shoulder. "Of course I shall look after her. There is no question."

"Good." He turned to Edie. "Two coffees?"

"Yes please. Baz does the best coffee in the whole of London," she said, by way of explanation. "Even better than Counter Coffee."

"Really? That's saying something!"

"Ah, Mr Architect, I guarantee you will love my coffee so much that you will want to come back for more." He grinned at Ben. "And then I can keep an eye on you that you are keeping our Edie as happy as she deserves to be."

"I am absolutely sure," said Ben courteously, "that you will find nothing of which you can complain."

Edie grinned at him.

"You've been together a while now," said Baz, "and I cross with Edie for not bringing you to taste our coffee sooner. She says that you have been very busy. I very busy too, so I hope that now we can make time for each other. It is good to know that you do good at your business. I do good at mine. Make nice profit for my family so that one day, we can have bigger premises and own our own place so that we are not beholden to whims of greedy landlords."

"That sounds to me like a most worthy ambition," replied Ben. He took a sip of his coffee. "Goodness me, this *is* good. You should patent the recipe."

"There is no need, my friend," said Baz with a smile. "No one knows exactly what I do and I shall never divulge its secret to anyone except my eldest son. When it is his turn to take over the family business, then it will be up to him."

Ben knew that Jamie would never take over his 'firm' in that way. Did he mind? No, not really. His was an entirely different situation to that of Baz. But, thinking about it, some small part of him regretted that everything he had built up would not be handed down to his son. Jamie would inherit the financial gain, of course, but that was not the same thing.

Still, that continuity through the generations was something of a rarity these days he thought, trying to console himself, where the norm was for children to follow their own paths and not those of their parents. Although he had seen one or two programmes recently (ones that Edie had introduced into his life; ones that he wouldn't necessarily have considered watching before and which had now captured his interest) where children *had* followed on from their parents: third or even fourth generations carrying on the family tradition, particularly in agriculture and handcrafts.

He thought of his step brothers and sisters on Cairnmor carrying on with the work started by his grandparents; he thought of Edie's brother still working the family farm on St Nicolas – his eldest son and family already heavily involved and creating new opportunities and employing diversification on the land. Maybe, thought Ben, the ties to farming were very strong; maybe love for the land created a deeper bond than in many other professions.

However, Ben knew he had never felt an overwhelming need to remain on Cairnmor and become part of the 'family firm' as his dad called it, even though he loved the island and its beauty profoundly and its Gaelic language was part of his soul. He wondered whether Jack had ever regretted that he, Ben, had never expressed the desire to live on Cairnmor and take on some of the community responsibilities that came with hereditary ownership. If he had, he had never said. Just as Ben would never divulge to Jamie how he felt.

No, it was right that Jamie should follow his own path, just as he himself had done. Indeed, it was something that his own grandfather had positively encouraged him to do.

Ben decided he should go back and visit more often; despite his busy life, despite the long journey. Yes, that would be good, especially as his father and Grace were not getting any younger. This time, he would take Edie with him and she could meet his family. He was sure they would love her. How could they not?

The longer Jamie was on combat duty, the more difficult he was finding it. If he stopped thinking about Callie, then the overwhelming horror of what he had experienced already and the carefully suppressed anxiety about what he might experience, would begin to dominate his thoughts. He discovered that she was his protection against the unremitting uncertainty of what might happen next; against the recurrent nightmares of what had already happened.

He continued to write to her but without receiving any replies, it was a thankless task in many ways. He pictured her as they had been during that wonderful, short-lived but intensely-felt week they had spent together, especially their glorious day on horseback, galloping across the heath. The vision of this, temporarily at least, seemed to satisfy his need for contact with her. Ultimately though, it was a poor substitute. He needed *new* contact with her, to hear her voice through her letters.

While he was on duty, Jamie found he could put romantic uncertainty behind him, the need for total concentration paramount. He spent the time immersing himself in his work, in socializing with his comrades – seeking to enjoy the type of camaraderie and close bonds that existed so intensely in both shared peril and shared respite from danger.

However, he was beginning to question whether this was something he wanted to do for the rest of his life. Well, it needn't be for the rest of his life, Jamie knew that, but certainly a good proportion of it. He enjoyed the ceremonial side and loved working with horses, but being out here in Afghanistan was changing his outlook. He was good at his job, he knew that, but did anyone need to be part of conflict? He wanted his service to be the safe, ordered, ceremonial existence of home. But being in a safe, ordered environment as a member of the armed forces was a contradiction in terms – by definition, being a member of the armed forces meant being prepared to go to war.

Slowly but surely, the longer he was in Afghanistan, Jamie began to question why he was fighting in some foreign land – a land in which the British army had been involved intermittently for nearly a hundred and eighty years – involved in a war that seemed to be gaining nothing in a country from which they would be withdrawing within a year. Their withdrawal would leave a vacuum the vulnerable Afghan defence forces would be hard-pressed to fill and Jamie wondered what it was really all about and what exactly had been achieved.

Had the British won the 'hearts and minds' of the people by their presence here? He hoped so. Had they succeeded in defeating terrorism? He doubted it.

Abruptly, Jamie changed the direction of his thoughts. This was not helpful and accomplished nothing. He was here; he had signed up to be a member of the armed forces and he just had to get on with it. The time for thinking about his future would be when he got home – when eventually he did.

Looking outwards, away from his introspection, Jamie saw that an *ad hoc* football match was about to begin, so he left his deckchair and his thoughts and joined his comrades in a game that had been played by off-duty soldiers wherever they were stationed for probably as long as the British army had been involved with Afghanistan.

Sometimes Edie would wake up in the morning and look at Ben sleeping quietly beside her. She still couldn't believe her luck; she sometimes still had difficulty in believing that this attractive, intelligent, loving man should choose to be with *her* – frumpy old Edie, the dinosaur; the throwback to a bygone age. Well, she might be the latter, but she was certainly no dinosaur.

She rarely thought of Trevor these days – the ex-husband who had made her life such a misery and who had chided her in those terms. She wondered occasionally how he was faring with his new family; whether he was staying the course or whether he was reverting to type and continuing with his philandering ways. If that were the case, then she felt sorry for his new wife. But, maybe the new wife would keep Trevor's roving eye in check; maybe that, combined with his age and failing looks (Edie had heard from a former acquaintance that he was looking decidedly seedy, his carousing life-style finally catching up with him), would be the barriers that kept him faithful. However, Edie doubted it. People like Trevor would never mend their ways; they just wouldn't be able to see exactly how repulsive they had become. Did she care? No. He was not her problem any more, thank goodness.

Edie also couldn't believe that she had a new career. She didn't count working for John in the Emporium as a new career, that was essentially a job to tide her over, although she did enjoy it and felt immensely grateful and loyal to him for offering it to her. But the consultancy work with Ben's firm, which had resumed almost as soon as they got back together, was a different matter altogether. At her age, most working women would be contemplating retirement, but here she was moving in a whole new direction. And she was loving it. Every moment.

She wished, though, that she was fabulously wealthy and could afford to rescue every Victorian or Edwardian house that came up in the property auctions as being 'suitable for redevelopment'. How she would love to buy as many as she could afford and renovate them in such a way that preserved their historical integrity while enabling the people who resided in them to achieve 'modern living' without the internal destruction that usually accompanied such a desire. Perhaps if she saved her earnings really hard, she would be able to do that. But for now, it would have to remain an unrealized ambition.

She wanted to somehow change people's attitudes, to make them see that putting one's 'own stamp' on a property was not a goal which everyone should strive towards. This frame of mind brought with it an inherent waste of resources: brand new kitchens ripped out and replaced with something new and shiny that didn't reflect the character of a house; pristine, newly-decorated internal walls repainted or wall-papered. True, dilapidation needed immediate rescue and hideously bright colours replacing, but why couldn't people today wait for the other things? Why couldn't they (with their often quickly-garnered wealth) work towards something, experiencing that sense of real achievement that only comes after anticipation and working towards something special? Why did everything have to happen now, immediately?

Edie supposed it was the era in which they lived – a time of instantly-available gratification; of an all-encompassing social media; of astonishing smart phones, all in a consumer society embracing changes that gathered pace with every year that passed: a transformation unknown to previous generations.

If the Victorian and Edwardians lived through the industrial revolution then the second Elizabethans were living the technological revolution. Edie wondered whether the pace of life in earlier times had seemed as rapid as today's, or had the changes come more gradually, with time to absorb what was happening? Possibly, but who could tell? It was all relative.

Edie was certainly no slouch when it came down to using computers or smart phones – she found them an invaluable tool for research and communication – but she had not grown up with them, unlike the present generation to whom the understanding of technology and technological changes were like a second skin.

Yes, life was changing fast, as was *her* life and Edie found it remarkable that she was part of such a change; that such a remarkable transformation was happening to her.

"Do you know," said Baz to his wife, "Edie happier now than I have ever seen her. She suit her new life."

"Definitely. Just as we suit ours. Though for us it is not such a new one now, eh?" replied Halka, setting out the cakes she had just baked and adjusting the sausage rolls she had put out earlier ready for the first influx of customers.

She checked that all was to her liking on the counter and smiled contentedly to herself as she disappeared into the backroom, bringing sandwiches and wraps and placing them in the open-fronted fridge.

"We see how these new combinations of ingredients go down, yes?" she said.

"I am sure they will be appreciated, as all your expert cooking is," replied Baz, giving his wife an appreciative embrace, which made her smile.

106

"We are lucky," he continued. "We take brave decision to move to this wonderfully accepting country. My coffee and your cooking bring in many customers to a premises that is ideally placed in close community near good school with lovely flat above."

"Hm," responded Halka. "A flat that still needs work doing to it and a landlord that does nothing except charge us a lot of rent."

"But what more could we want? We have each other. We have place to live. We have worked hard over the years to make the café a success, and we have even managed to save some money. Our children do well and they are great kids."

"Most of the time."

"But that is just teenage angst. It will pass."

"They need a bigger space. Their own rooms."

"Did we have our own rooms when we were growing up?" said Baz.

"No-o."

"And we turned out alright, didn't we?" He smiled his expansive smile.

Halka's lips twitched with inner pleasure but she was not to be deflected. "They need more space upstairs to entertain their friends."

"But they bring them here to the café after school where they talk and drink lots of coffee!" countered Baz.

"And eat into our profits."

"Ah, but isn't it worth it to know they are safe and not wandering dangerous streets?"

Halka smiled, an expression that was like the sun coming out from behind a cloud. "Of course it is. I would rather they were here, where we can see them. And I am glad they are happy to bring their friends."

"Of course. But one day we shall own our own place. You'll see. It will have all the bedrooms that you, my lovely Halka, could wish for. It will have large sitting-room and a bathroom that is so lavish, I shall have job to prise you out of bath where you will soak in bubble-scented splendour!"

"That, my optimistic and eloquent husband, is, how do you say? A pipe-dream, something that we shall never have."

Baz laughed. "But I would wish this for you, my Halka. It is my dream that we should own our own place. And your brave and fearless lion has not let you down yet, has he?"

"No, that is true. You are a good husband in every way and I bless the day that we met."

"As do I."

"Well, my brave and fearless lion, this is enough sentiment for one day. You have the first customers coming into the café and I must drag our sleeping children from their beds and persuade them to go to school!"

With pleasure, Baz watched her until she had left the room and then turned his attention to a couple of early-morning businessmen.

"Two coffees, to take away, yes?" said Baz, even before they had spoken.

"How did you guess?" said one of them.

"Ah, my friends, I know people and I know I make the best coffee in London!"

"We'll have a couple of those fine-looking sausage rolls as well," said the first man, with a nod of his head towards the counter. "I suppose they're the best as well?"

Detecting a hint of sarcasm, Baz looked directly at the man and said, leaving no room for any disparagement, said, "But of course! My wife, she makes them and as she is the best, then so are they!"

And with that, Baz made their drinks and the two customers went on their way smiling, despite themselves, thinking that if the coffee was as good as the owner said it was, then they'd have their lunch here as well while they were in the area.

CHAPTER 20

Quietly, Callie let herself into Edie's house.

She needed to talk to someone.

Not Amy, who wouldn't understand; certainly not her parents, who would ask too many questions and ultimately be ashamed of her. And certainly not Erik, who was the cause of her turmoil and who, since their return from Copenhagen, had become demanding of her in a way that made her increasingly uncomfortable.

She wanted to put an end to this claustrophobic relationship. It had all been a ghastly mistake from the very beginning. How could she have become so deeply involved with him? How had she allowed herself to be seduced by Erik in the first place?

She wanted to consign him to the farthest recesses of her mind so that Jamie, the man she had promised to marry, would never know the extent of her stupidity and her unforgivable disloyalty to him.

She needed to talk to Auntie Edie. She was sensible and kind. She would listen and understand and advise her.

Callie went into the kitchen where she could hear Edie pottering around.

But Edie was not alone and Callie was surprised to find a rather good-looking man sitting at the table drinking tea from a mug.

He stood up and smiled when she came in the room, observing her with a clear and direct gaze.

"Callie!" said Edie. "How lovely to see you! You've been quite a stranger in the house these past couple of months."

Callie knew there was no hint of reprimand in her voice, just simple observation.

"I know," she looked down at the floor, ashamed. Not for being elusive but for what she had become.

Edie regarded her for a moment. "Anyway, this is Ben. He's my…"

She faltered. What was he exactly?

"…lover," finished Ben impishly, grinning at her.

Edie blushed a deep red.

He extended his hand, which Callie shook and as she looked briefly into his eyes, for some unfathomable reason, she was reminded of Jamie.

All at once, guilt and remorse at what she had been doing threatened to engulf her.

"You must be Edie's niece. I'm very pleased to meet you."

"Thank you," she replied distractedly.

Edie regarded her carefully. "Would you like some tea?"

"Yes please, Auntie."

Callie sat down at the table. She needed to talk to her aunt – she was desperate to talk to her aunt – but it was impossible with a strange man in the room. He seemed very nice and she was delighted for Edie, but she wasn't about to reveal her deepest, darkest secrets in front of someone she didn't know.

Concerned that Callie looked so pale and thin, Edie said, "Is everything alright, my dear? I hope that new boss of yours isn't working you too hard."

Her aunt's well-meaning words acted as a catalyst for Callie and all her pent-up emotions and anxieties came pouring out as she covered her face with her hands and cried as though her heart was broken.

In effect, for Callie, it was.

"I've been such a fool," she gulped. "I've made a mess of everything. Just like I always do, just like I've always done."

"I'm sure you haven't, dear Callie."

Edie went over to her and standing beside her, took her hand.

"Is it work that's going wrong again?" she asked gently.

Callie shook her head.

"Then what is it?"

"I'm engaged to a lovely man and I'm in the middle of a stifling relationship with someone else that I want to extricate myself from. But if I end it, I'm afraid of what this man might do, and if I don't end it, the man I want to marry will find out and I'll lose him forever."

Her tears came in heart-wrenching sobs. Edie was so shocked, she had to sit down. She put her arm round her niece's thin shoulders and held her close.

Callie – engaged! And, not only that, but having an affair with someone else at the same time. How could she have got herself into such a mess?

Caught up in her own emotional and working life, Edie chastised herself for being so unobservant; for not perceiving the emotional traumas her niece had obviously been going through; for not offering motherly advice.

But then, to be fair, they did all lead separate, independent lives and she had not seen Callie recently or much of Sarah her other lodger, who had been on a long spell of night shifts, only keeping in contact by exchanging occasional texts.

Ben looked at Edie in concern and made the move to go but she motioned him to stay. She might need his help with this. He was a sensitive, caring man and she knew that if she needed it, she could rely on his support.

Stroking her niece's hair, she said, "So, start at the beginning, and tell us."

"I'd only been with my boyfriend…"

Callie couldn't bear to say his name, it made him too real and her betrayal too terrible.

"…for a week…" she stopped.

"A week!" exclaimed Edie.

Callie nodded. "… when he proposed and that's all the time we had together before he had to rejoin his regiment for Afghanistan." She looked up at her aunt with tear-stained cheeks. "He's in the army, you see. He asked me to marry him in our little bistro and it was terribly romantic and I said yes straight away as I really didn't want to lose him. And now I shall because of my stupidity."

Callie started to cry again.

Ben thought of Jamie in Afghanistan. So many fine young men were being sent out there these days.

"Then what happened?" prompted Edie gently.

"My boss, Erik, took me out for a meal one day and gradually, we began to spend every evening going out after work. Then we went to Copenhagen…"

"Copenhagen?"

"Yes... for a conference. And... he... we..."

Callie didn't need to finish the sentence.

Edie tried not to be shocked or appalled.

"And you've been seeing him ever since?"

"Worse than that. I've been living with him in his apartment. He insisted I move in with him as soon as we got back from Denmark."

"And you agreed?" Edie didn't understand. How could her niece not have seen the danger signals?

Callie pictured the penthouse suite with its wrap-around terrace and panoramic views over the Thames towards Tower Bridge, recalling the impression it had made upon her; remembering how she hardly had time to absorb the spectacular view before she had no choice but to succumb to Erik yet again.

"Yes," she said, shamed by the memory.

He had told her that because she was now with him forever, he would take care of everything. She would never have to worry about anything again, he said.

Flattered and beguiled by the prospect of living a life of ease and luxury, Callie had overridden her misgivings when he selected clothes for her to wear and took her to beauty salons, instructing the hairdresser to cut her hair in a certain way that he said would suit her better.

Meekly, she complied with all his wishes and made no protest when he discouraged her from meeting her friends, afraid of his strength and determination if she did argue; fearful of what he might do if she ever made him angry and jealous.

He persuaded her to cancel her mobile phone contract, saying that she could do better, that her phone was outdated. He set up a new one for her, asking to see it (on the pretence of checking that it was working the way it should) every day for messages and calls. He restricted her use of her laptop, only allowing her to use it at work, even going so far as to monitor her emails and internet searches.

He began to take over every aspect of her life until she felt she was suffocating.

Callie recounted all these things to her aunt who by now, was totally appalled.

"Surely that's illegal," said Edie.

"No, it's not because stupidly, pathetically, I agreed to all of it." Callie shook her head. "I'm a fool to let it happen so easily, to have allowed it to happen at all. I should have just walked away from him."

That wasn't all she agreed to either. She didn't tell Edie about the relentless physical demands that Erik made upon her. She certainly didn't mention that she had responded to him willingly at first, allowing herself to become a complicit partner as their sex life aroused in Callie desires and feelings she had never known before; that initially, she had found it exciting to surrender herself to his powerful appetites.

No, she told her aunt none of those things. She was too ashamed.

Eventually though, it all became too much for her and Callie had felt trapped and stifled by Erik's constant demands; there was no let-up, no respite. Sometimes, she needed time to draw breath, time to allow her body to belong once more to her.

She spoke to him one day something of how she felt.

"No, no, no," he had said emphatically. "You are mine now. I made this clear from the beginning. You agreed to become mine from the moment we made love. And because you are mine, you must do everything that I want you to do."

"But what about me, Erik? What about what I want?"

"Do you not enjoy living in my beautiful apartment? Do I not pay you well in your job? Do you not enjoy what we do in bed?"

"You know I do, but…"

"What then?"

"Sometimes I'd like a rest, you know. Sometimes I'd just like it if we spent an ordinary evening together. Reading, watching television."

"What we do is far more exciting."

"That is true, but…"

And Erik smiled at her and put a stop to any further conversation by carrying her into the bedroom.

Callie said nothing more for a while but eventually, she began to lose all self-respect and sense of identity, subsumed by Erik's voracious needs; imprisoned by his restrictions on her personal freedom.

Eventually, she knew she had to break free from his hold over her before it was too late.

One night, wakeful yet again in her growing despair, staring at the ceiling as she lay beside him listening to his quiet and even breathing, she inadvertently said out loud, "I don't want to do this anymore."

"What?" he said sleepily, reaching out for her.

"I can't do this anymore," she faltered.

Now fully awake and alert, Erik reacted with impatience.

"How can you think that? I give you everything you want. You lack nothing."

"Ye-es." In a way that was true. "But I feel trapped sometimes." *A princess in a gilded cage*, thought Callie.

"How? I fail to understand. You are being ridiculous."

"But…"

So he had covered her mouth with his to prevent her from saying anything further and once again asserted his dominance of her.

"You must stop all this nonsense," he said, afterwards, "because you are mine forever and I will never let you go. You are mine. I want to hear you say that you belong to me for always."

"I belong to you, Erik," she'd said in a small, quiet voice, hating herself for her weakness, "for always."

The next day, she pretended she was not well enough to go to work, knowing that he had an important meeting to attend and would be unable to stay at home. As soon as he'd left the apartment, Callie packed her suitcase and fled back to the simplicity and freedom of her aunt's house.

"And so here I am," she said, at the end of her story.

"Well, you did exactly the right thing," said Edie. "If you're anxious about what he might do, you must stay close to me. Come into the shop each day while I'm at work and then in a little while, to go home to St Nicolas might be the best idea. He doesn't know your address there does he?"

Callie shook her head. "But he knows that's where I come from."

"So that wouldn't be such a good idea, then would it?" A sudden thought struck Edie. "This Erik person you've got yourself mixed up with…"

Callie squirmed with embarrassment.

"… couldn't be the stranger who kept phoning you after the piece of paper with your name and mobile number on it went missing," said Edie. "Wasn't his name Erik?"

"Yes."

"It can't be the same person, surely?"

"I did wonder that when I first met him but then I decided that it was just pure coincidence. He's never mentioned it and I'm certain he would have done."

"Well, that's something at least," said Edie. She looked at Callie as a distressing thought occurred to her, "There's no possibility of your being pregnant is there?" she asked, remembering her own experience with Trevor.

"No," said Callie.

"That's a relief."

"When does your boyfriend get back from Afghanistan?" asked Ben, thinking that this unfortunate man was going to be in for a rude awakening when he returned.

"I'm not sure."

Guiltily, Callie knew she had abandoned all communication with Jamie.

"What will you do?"

"I don't know."

"Will you break off the relationship with him?" asked Edie, thinking that this would be the honourable thing to do.

"I don't know."

And Callie burst into tears again.

Secretly, although he would be supportive of Edie as she coped with her distraught niece, Ben was glad that Jamie had never become involved with a girl as weak and foolish as this one.

Fortunately, he was far too level-headed.

When Erik returned to the apartment to find it empty and desolate and all Callie's things gone, he paced the floor of the bedroom in a state of extreme agitation; raging at her for leaving him, the nightmare of his past threatening to engulf him once again.

Determinedly, without wasting any more time, he grabbed his keys and went down to the basement garage where he collected his car and set off through the interminable rush hour traffic towards Carlton, the place he assumed Callie would have gone.

No one had ever walked out on him in this way since *she… they…* had; no one had ever been allowed to do that to him again.

No one.

He had to have Callie back. He had to be in control of both her and their life together then she would never leave him as the others had.

When Erik reached Edie's house, he found it in darkness.

He leapt out of his car and rang the door-bell, hammering on the door with such insistence, that the next-door neighbour came out to see what was going on.

"If they're not answering, they're not answering," he said grumpily. "So, do us a favour will you and come back another time?"

"Are they out?"

"I've no idea."

Abruptly the neighbour turned and went back inside his own house.

Erik hung around aimlessly for a while before climbing back into his sports car and after revving the engine in frustration, drove off in a cloud of blue smoke emitted by the burning rubber from the car's tyres.

CHAPTER 21

Jamie found himself a quiet spot in the compound and began to pen yet another letter to Callie.

He was anxious that he still hadn't heard from her, but consoled himself with the fact that the mail had been erratic where he now was – close to the front-line where insurgents tested the British and Afghan defences with disturbing regularity.

Jamie knew how difficult it was to get letters to troops out on patrol but the army did try its best and invariably there would be a huge pile waiting for all of them when they got back to Camp Bastion. Conversely, it took longer for his letters to reach home.

He had much to tell her – the usual things about what they had been doing: how he and other members of the Household Cavalry had been involved in uncovering a huge cache of home-made explosive devices, remote controls and pressure pads for triggering the deadly IEDs. How they'd even found a motorbike packed with explosives ready for use as a suicide bomb.

He told her how they and their Afghan army partners, operating alongside, had received a big pat on the back for that particular success.

Above all, he told her that he was to be promoted to Lance Corporal of Horse and that this would be his pathway to receiving a Queen's Commission – *in other words to my becoming an officer*, he wrote. *I can then either rise naturally through the ranks or take the Late Entry Officer's Course at Sandhurst, which is only four weeks. I'll probably do the latter after I've reached the rank of Corporal of Horse. Up to that rank, I'll still be able to go out regularly on ceremonial duty which, as you know, is what I enjoy most about being in the Household Cavalry. But in a few years' time, I may want to have a change and not mind only going out on the really big State occasions.*

Or, he thought, but said nothing of this to Callie, *I may come out of the army altogether*. He wondered how his dad would feel about that; or his granddad for that matter. He suspected they'd both understand and, proud as they were of him with his service record, would be relieved as well. He knew how much they naturally worried about him when he was on combat duty. He would talk to his grandfather the next time he saw him and seek his advice.

Jamie was doing well at keeping his disillusionment under wraps from his comrades and his superiors, but the uncertainty and increasing number of incidents were testing his nerve and his mettle.

He sighed. What could he write now? He was running out of ideas.

How's the job coming along? And your boss? Is he as helpful as he was at first? I hope you're still enjoying the challenges the work throws up and haven't found it too stressful.

Jamie put his pen down. Perhaps it was time to stop writing to Callie altogether. He left the letter unfinished and put his pad and paper in his pack, gathering his kit together before going out on patrol yet again.

Erik returned to the house the next morning, having spent a sleepless night tossing and turning; oscillating between anger, humiliation and a resurgence of the terrible, terrible deliberate hurt inflicted on him so long ago when *she*... no, *they*... had abandoned him to his nightmare time.

He should have gone after *her* then; he should have tried to find both of them. But he hadn't and he'd made sure that no one had ever run away from him since.

Except Callie. He felt his anger rise again: an atrocious taste, like a bitter bile in his throat. He had to find her. And bring her back. She would be his again and this time he would keep her.

A well-proportioned young woman opened the door a tiny crack in response to his ring on the bell and when she saw someone standing there, dishevelled and unshaven, she quickly put the security chain on.

"Yes?" she said brusquely.

"I'm Erik van der Waals. I *must* speak with Callie."

Sarah had been warned to expect that someone called Erik might appear on the doorstep and demand to see her fellow lodger.

"I'm afraid not," she said.

"Do you know where she is?"

"Sorry, I don't."

"What about her aunt?"

"She's not here either."

"What time will they be back?"

"I've no idea."

The man's shoulders sagged and for a moment, Sarah felt sorry for him.

"Can I take a message?" she said more kindly.

"Tell Callie..." and for some reason, as he looked into this young woman's expressive brown eyes, Erik struggled to retain his usual authority and control as an unaccustomed vulnerability took hold of him as his anger dissipated, "... that I miss her. That I want her to come home."

No, no, that was all wrong, he thought. It was much too nice. He wasn't supposed to be being *nice.* He was supposed to be decisive and in command. And outraged.

"Oh."

Sarah also was taken aback. She'd been led to believe that Callie's erstwhile lover was a monster, some kind of raving lunatic. He certainly didn't seem like that to her. In fact, it was plainly obvious that he was genuinely upset and confused.

Erik suddenly went pale, almost staggering on the threshold, and Sarah quickly opened the door and supported him for a moment.

"When did you last eat?" she asked, her duty of care overriding all other considerations.

"Yesterday lunch-time, I think."

"And did you get any sleep last night?"

"No." He looked at her, his expression bleak.

Sarah took pity on him. "Look you're in no fit state to do anything. Why don't you come inside and I'll make you a cup of tea? But don't try anything, mind. I'm an expert in self-defence," and with that unexpected snippet of information belied totally by her feminine frame, she helped Erik, who was too tired to argue, inside the house.

"Close your eyes."
They had parked the car in a street in West London.
"What?"
Edie felt Ben's hand clasp hers and carefully, he helped her out of the car and up some steps.
She heard a door creak open and then click shut behind them.
"Okay, you can look now."
Edie did so and what she saw made her eyes fill with tears.
"Oh, Ben! What a wonderful house – everything's original!" she exclaimed. "Nothing's been changed. Well, almost."
"Yep. Hasn't been touched in donkey's years. It's in need of massive TLC and developers have been crawling all over it."
"How did you find it?"
"A prospective client. Wanted to get me on board before they bought it to see how much any renovations would cost them. It's up for auction tomorrow. The bidding will be fierce."
"So is this our next project?"
"Sort of." He looked at Edie and smiled. "*You* are going to buy it."
"Buy it! What with? Monopoly money?"
Ben laughed and shook his head. "I'm a successful architect, remember? I own my house in London as well as the one in Maybury. I have all the usual outgoings of any householder and businessman but I am mortgage and debt free. I've been stashing money away for the past five years ever since the business took off. My savings are not doing anything in the bank at the moment – interest rates are practically non-existent – so I thought I'd invest the money in something useful. Like property." He smiled and kissed her forehead. "And you, my love, are going to buy this house with my money and we shall renovate it together. Just you and me. It will be truly ours as we shall own it lock, stock and barrel."
He smiled and guided a stunned Edie by the hand through each room.
"It's beautiful," said Edie.
"No, it's not. It's a wreck," said Ben, enclosing her within the circle of his arms.
"Well, it isn't to me. I can see beyond the hardboard cover-ups, the mildewed wallpaper and the lack of plaster. How much is it worth?"
"Whatever someone is willing to pay for it."
"And what am I willing to pay for it?"
Ben named the sum.
Edie looked at him askance. "Wonderful as your idea is, I can't possibly bid that much of your money. I'd never be able to pay you back. Besides, wouldn't bidding for it be unethical, given that it was prospective clients who introduced you to the property in the first place?"
"Ah, I told them I couldn't be their architect because I was already acting on someone else's behalf. Which, of course, I wasn't, but from the moment I saw the house, I was. Ours. I didn't tell them that, though."

"What did they say?"

Ben laughed. "They still wanted me to give them an estimate as to how much it would cost to renovate!"

"And did you?"

"No, I declined politely. Said it would be a conflict of interest, or something like that. So, tomorrow, darling Edie, you are going to bid for your first rescue house but with our money."

"Our money?"

He looked at her lovingly and said, quietly and sincerely, "With all my worldly goods I thee endow."

Edie's heart started to pound. "Are you... are you asking me to marry you?" she said, hardly daring to believe that such a thing might be true.

"Yes. I'd get down on one knee but the floor's in a bit of a state." He smiled and took her hand in his. "So, Eden Paignton née Anderson, one day, in the not too distant future I hope, will you do me the honour of becoming my wife, my partner, my lover, my friend?"

Her eyes filled with tears and she replied with an immediate, unequivocal, "Yes."

Ben took her into his arms and they kissed, tenderly and sweetly.

"Now, my darling, having got that out of the way, shall we continue with *our* house tour?"

Edie could only nod. She couldn't speak, her heart was too full, her happiness too great.

"What happens if I don't get the house?" she remarked later as they drove back to Carlton.

"Then the wedding's off," replied Ben impishly.

"Beast."

"Yep, it's my middle name."

"Mine's Meanie."

"Then with middle names like that, we'll be alright, won't we?"

"We'd be alright even without them."

"Oh yes," said Ben, full of buoyant confidence.

Callie was holding the fort for Edie in John's Emporium while she and Ben had gone to look at some house or other.

John didn't say a great deal to her but showed her how to work the till and if a customer started haggling over some item, then she was to fetch him immediately.

"I don't expect you to get the hang of things in one afternoon but if you work here again, it'll soon come to you. Bright girl like you."

For all my so-called intelligence, thought Callie, *I'm an expert at making a mess of things.*

She merely grunted in reply and John looked at her sharply.

"Let me guess. Man trouble?" he asked perceptively.

"Something like that."

"Thought so. It usually is when young women go quiet. You don't have to tell me anything if you don't want to. I'm not prying."

"Really?" She looked at him sceptically.

John chuckled. "You'll get over it. Give it time."

Callie shook her head. "No, I won't. I shall have to live with what I've done for the rest of my life."

"Surely it can't be that bad?"

"Oh, it is," she replied. "It's worse."

"You're not pregnant are you?"

"No, I'm not," she snapped at him, "and why is everyone so concerned about whether or not I am?"

She moved away and pretended to sort through some books to hide the tears that coursed down her cheeks.

Callie knew she had to get away. Far away. Away from all these well-meaning people who asked what was wrong and who kept trying to tell her "it will be alright soon, dear."

It wasn't and it never would be.

Seeing her distress and not quite knowing her well enough to offer comfort, John slipped out of the shop to buy two coffees from Baz.

"Edie's niece not happy, eh?" said the café owner when John came in, his expression glum.

"That's the understatement of the year," said his friend. "I've left her weeping copiously over my books. I hope they won't have disintegrated into pulp by the time I get back."

Baz laughed. "Then I make your coffees quickly." He busied himself with milk and percolator. "Is it another Rat, do you think?"

"Oh quite probably."

Baz chuckled. "It is therefore an, how you say? Infestation?"

"Yeah, and you and I are the bloody Pied Pipers," said John, as he went out of the café. "Thanks for these, mate."

"No problem, my friend, no problem."

"And Callie ran away from all this?" asked Sarah in disbelief.

She was standing in the middle of Erik's spacious, light-filled apartment, having decided to come back with him to make sure he was alright. Even after tea and toast at Edie's house, he had still looked ashen.

Sarah planned that once her errand of mercy was done, she would be able to go straight to the hospital. It was an easy journey from here, just a couple of stops on the Tube.

"This place is totally stunning! Every girl's dream."

"Thank you. I had always hoped that might be the case," he replied before adding quietly, "Callie will come back to me and live here with me again."

"Are you sure?"

"Yes. She needs me."

Sarah stared at him. "What makes you so confident?"

"I just know, that's all. She won't be able to resist what we have."

"Hm," and, unable to stem her curiosity any longer, Sarah walked out onto the terrace. "Wow! This is some view. It's fabulous! I could easily spend all day, every day out here. I find riverscapes fascinating, especially one like this over the Thames. You must have paid an absolute mint for a flat with a view like this."

"Two point two million." He was unable to keep the pride out of his voice. "The apartment itself is the best in the building."

"Two point two million! You're kidding me!" She looked at him with an admiration that held no envy or avarice. "You must be loaded!"

"I have a fair amount. My businesses do well and I have taken sound advice and made a lot of careful investments over the years."

"Really? Such as?"

It occurred to Erik that Callie had never asked him questions like this. Perhaps she hadn't been interested. Perhaps he'd never given her the chance. Perhaps that was what had been wrong. He would have to rectify that when she came back to him.

"Oh, here and there," he replied, "wheeling and dealing in stocks and shares, building up companies. I have friends in all the right places."

"While I earn a pittance and work just about every hour that God sends."

"Well, I do that too."

"Yes, but you don't earn a pittance."

"True. So tell me, Sarah Adhabi, have you always wanted to be a nurse?"

"No. I wanted to be a professional ballet dancer but I was told after my audition that my breasts were too large – I mean I know I'm a thirty-four D but I've never been able to see what that had to do with anything, nor was I prepared to get a breast reduction as some girls do. They also said that they couldn't accept me because my insteps are apparently the wrong shape, and if I did go into the profession, I'd be crippled by the time I was twenty-five. I got a second and a third opinion to rule out any prejudice, only to be told exactly the same thing. It was ballet or nothing so I became a nurse instead."

"Do you still dance?" asked Erik, surveying her body with a rapid but all-encompassing glance.

"Yes, I attend class whenever I can, at least two or three times a week. I like to keep supple." Sarah caught the increased interest in his expression. "It's no good looking at me like that, Erik van der Waals," she said, admonishing him. "You're supposed to be grieving over your lost girlfriend. Besides, I'm not one of your easy lays."

"I have never indulged in easy lays," he replied, genuinely offended. "Only serious relationships."

"Good. I'm glad to hear it. Promiscuity can be detrimental to your health."

Sarah resolved to ask Callie *exactly* what it was that had upset her so much and caused her to run away. So far, she hadn't seen anything yet to indicate any dark character traits lurking beneath this man's charismatic exterior.

On a purely professional level, Sarah was intrigued by Erik van der Waals and she decided that, if possible, she would like to know him better. He was also rich and Sarah had always been fascinated by the psychology of powerful, wealthy men. Not that she'd known many, of course. But she'd always hoped to study at least one in her life-time.

There was no intention of acquisition behind her interest – she was not a gold-digger in any way but a sensible, level-headed young woman who knew her own mind. She decided she would take a purely academic, but friendly, interest in him.

She already had her Master's, perhaps she could make the study of him into a Ph.D. if she ever had the opportunity.

CHAPTER 22

The auction house was crowded.

Edie chose a seat close to the front row where she could see the auctioneer clearly and where he could see her. She also arrived early so that she could get a feel for the proceedings.

She'd seen auctions before, of course, on television, but it was a very different proposition being here herself, about to bid on a traditional Victorian property before someone else got their destructive hands on it.

The auctioneer worked his way through the catalogue. Two houses. Three. Four. Five. A building plot; a block of flats; a nursing home...

"Now we come to lot number eighteen. A fine Victorian three-storey home in a desirable location in need of total refurbishment and modernization. Lots of potential here, folks. Flats, large family house, it's up to you. So where shall we start? Let's say three hundred and fifty thousand, shall we?"

The auctioneer looked across the room. "Thank you, sir. Three hundred and fifty-five? Thank you, madam."

And so it went on. Edie sat in her seat, her mouth dry, her palms sweating; biding her time, seeing how the auction unfolded.

She should have asked John to come with her; she should have insisted that Ben came in with her. Callie. Sarah. Baz. Anyone.

But this was something Edie knew she wanted to do by herself. Something she'd always dreamed of doing. This was her one chance. Ben had said that she should stick to their limit and that if someone else bid higher than they were prepared to go, then at least she would have done everything she could.

Edie listened and waited.

When people began to drop out of the race and the auctioneer was about to declare, "Going once", she put up her hand and bid an extra thousand. And another and another exchanging bids with her rival until they were within five hundred pounds of Ben's absolute limit.

Callie was taking Edie's place in the shop. Again.

She hated it. She hated the musty smell; the claustrophobic clutter; the depressingly old-fashioned atmosphere of the place. She kept thinking of Erik, she kept thinking of Jamie. She kept thinking of both of them until her mind was spinning and her emotions a turmoil of guilt and confusion.

Guilt for being unfaithful to Jamie whom she knew she had loved during the brief time they had been together and who had undoubtedly loved her and who didn't deserve to have been treated in such an unthinking and callous manner. Guilt that she had just walked out on Erik without any explanation. Guilty confusion and aching frustration because, having become accustomed to the level of intense physicality Erik offered her, her body yearned for its resumption.

Yet it was these constant, insatiable demands which had, ultimately, caused her to leave in the first place. There were other factors too, of course, but she put those aside for the moment.

Callie knew she was incredibly foolish to have given into temptation and become so deeply embroiled with Erik.

Regret made her cry. Again.

John looked at her. This was no good. Whatever would his customers think if they came into the shop to find his assistant weeping in the background? It wasn't good for business, it wasn't good for his reputation either. They might think him to be some kind of ogre.

He went over to her.

"I'm sorry," she gulped, looking up at him with tear-stained cheeks. "I can't help myself."

"Look," said John, in a kindly fashion because she was Edie's niece but in reality all he wanted to do was tell her that she was behaving like a stupid idiot and really ought to pull herself together, "why don't you take the rest of the day off?"

"But I'm supposed to be doing Edie's job for her."

"Well," he said, casting around in his mind for an excuse, "things are quiet this afternoon, I'll be able to manage fine on my own."

"You're sure?"

Just leave, woman, thought John. *You're even making me feel down in the mouth.*

"Absolutely. So be a good girl, will you, and go and put your feet up at home with a film, a cushion and a large box of chocolates."

Although she was grateful, but feeling somewhat insulted by what she regarded as his rather patronizing manner, Callie stepped out of the shop knowing that John's remedy would not be enough to offer her any consolation whatsoever because she needed to get away.

Right away.

To find a job somewhere in a different place where no one would find her, where she could escape from herself.

Callie had just opened the front door of Edie's house when she saw Erik leap out of his car and run across the pavement towards her. He propelled them both inside, slamming the door shut with his foot and pinning her up against the wall, covering her mouth with his.

Powerless to stop him, fearful that someone might come into the house at any moment and discover them, Callie succumbed to his desperate passion as they stumbled together into the sitting room and fell onto the settee where, once again, she found herself hurtling into certain captivity under the power and potency of his all-enveloping and inescapable embrace.

"Come back with me," he whispered afterwards, "to where you belong."

"Yes, Erik," gasped Callie, trembling and breathless; overwhelmed by his strength and ardour, realizing that once again she was lost and hating herself for her weakness.

The auctioneer banged his gavel down on the rostrum and said: "Sold – to the lady on the third row for five hundred and thirty thousand pounds. Well done, madam. Your number?"

Edie held up her paddle with shaking hands while he wrote it down. Some kind person from the auctioneer's office took her name and she went with them to pay the deposit and sign on the dotted line. Once the formalities were over, Edie walked rapidly to where they had parked the car and to where Ben was waiting for her.

"Well?" he said, seeing her flushed and happy expression, knowing that she had been successful.

"It's ours!" she said, kissing him on the cheek and hugging him. "All ours!"

"Brilliant. Well done you!"

"I was so nervous."

"You were fantastic."

She looked at him. "I just put my hand up in the right places."

"I know. And as I said, you were fantastic."

"How do you know?"

"I cheated. I watched the proceedings from the closed-circuit TV screen in the foyer. Some of the big auction houses have them so that people know when their particular lot is coming up."

"And you mean to say, that you made me go through all that on my own? Meanie!" she said good-naturedly.

Ben laughed. "I'm the beast, remember? You're the meanie! You wanted to do it on your own anyway."

"I know, but even so…"

"I wanted to see you actually do the deed."

Edie put her arm through his and laid her head on his shoulder.

"I'm really glad you did."

"So," said Ben, kissing her forehead, "now the hard work really begins."

"I'm not going to be able to oversee this project and continue to work at John's, am I?" said Edie thoughtfully.

"No."

"He's been so good to me, I'd hate to let him down."

"Perhaps Callie can take your place on a semi-permanent basis."

Edie made a wry face. "She's about as much use as a damp rag, John says."

"Ah. As I persuaded you to brave the auctioneer's den on your own, I'll talk to him for you if you like."

"Would you? Although it really ought to be me."

"We can offer him some of our business. He'll agree to anything if there's money to be made."

"Why don't we both go? This afternoon."

"What about right now? Strike while the iron's hot?" suggested Ben.

"After lunch. I need to think about what to say first."

He started the engine and they headed across London.

"Why the tears?" Erik had asked her as they travelled in the car back to his apartment.

Callie had shaken her head. "Nothing."

How could she tell him that she wanted to escape again? Now. This very moment. That she wanted him to stop the car so she could run far, far away; away from him and the life she would be living forever.

124

"I shall stay at home this week to make sure you are settled in again," he had said, "and re-establish the fact that you are once again mine. Then we shall return to work and resume our lives."

Callie had not replied but had stared silently out of the window while the tears streamed down her face.

Now, as Erik cooked the supper, she sat on the sofa and flicked aimlessly through a magazine before wandering listlessly out onto the terrace.

She envied the smiling people who strolled in such carefree fashion across Tower Bridge; she envied the happy sightseers aboard the river cruisers below who laughed and joked with such abandon.

She wanted to be one of them: free to do exactly as she wished; free from all constraints; freed from this claustrophobic liaison that was crushing her.

One day she would be free. One day. When she could muster the strength and will-power to make the final break.

Checking that Erik was absorbed in what he was doing and not looking at her, Callie went to her handbag and made sure her door keys to the flat were hidden away safely in the zipped pocket just in case he locked her in at any time during the day. She made sure that the few personal possessions she had brought back with her from Carlton were readily available, yet not conspicuously so, for when she made her final escape.

And escape she would. Soon.

Edie, with understandable trepidation, accompanied by Ben, went into John's Emporium.

John had been good to her and she didn't want him to feel that she was running out on him or leaving him in the lurch. He'd taken her on as his assistant when she'd most needed a job and she had enjoyed her time working here.

Yet somehow, she had always regarded it as a stop-gap, a temporary 'fix' after her separation from Ben; biding her time until something came along that would satisfy her creative and historical needs in the same way that working on the house in Maybury had done, even if it had been for such a short time.

And something had come along – better than anything she could have possibly imagined.

When John saw them walk into his shop, he knew that Edie and her architect were about to give him some bad news. He pre-empted Ben as he was about to speak.

"So, you purchased your house then?"

"Yes," said Edie.

"And I suppose you want lots of time off to see to the renovations."

"Yes, please."

John smiled. "Well," he said, "let's work out a compromise, shall we? I don't want to lose you in the shop, Edie, but then, neither do I want to stop you doing what it is you do best. So," he continued, "you do what you have to do with my blessing but on one condition."

Relieved, Edie smiled at him. "And what's that?"

"That you give me lots of business during the course of your refurbishment."

"That," said Ben, "goes without saying and if you like, I'll set up a means of you being able to advertise within my firm. I'll have a word with my partner and we'll see what we can do."

"Thank you. I'm much obliged to you," and he shook Ben's hand, before turning to Edie. "He's alright, this fella of yours."

"Not a Rat then?" observed Edie with a smile.

"Definitely not. I'd hang onto him if I were you."

"I intend to."

"And you, my friend, must look after her as well."

"That goes without saying."

"So, when am I going to be allowed to view this property of yours? Or should I say 'ours'? Now there's a thought," said John, becoming serious. "Perhaps we could start up a whole new property developing business between the three of us. And you, dear lady, will be able to rescue all the lost and forgotten homes from the perils of modernization to your heart's content."

"That certainly is a thought," said Ben, regarding him astutely. "Look, why don't we all go out this evening and discuss it over dinner with a bottle or two of wine?"

"Sounds an excellent idea to me. I'll shut up shop here and meet you both at Edie's house in, say, an hour?"

"That's perfect, John. And thank you," said Edie, her eyes full of genuine gratitude.

"Don't thank me – I'm only in it for the pound signs you can see in my eyes!" he quipped.

They arrived at Camp Bastion weary and dust-filled, anxious for some down-time after being out in the northern provinces where the enemy were particularly active and where the villagers were reluctant even to talk to British soldiers for fear of reprisals.

The H.C.R. had eventually won the trust of most of the villagers in the area where Jamie's unit had been operating by fighting off an incursion and by talking patiently to the elders, working hard to achieve the British army's mission of winning 'hearts and minds'.

After stripping off his combat gear and having a shower, Jamie went to the distribution office to see if he had any letters.

There was a pile of them and with anticipation, he grabbed a beer and took them outside, finding one of the deckchairs that proliferated outside his mess tent in which to sit. There were three letters from his father, two from his grandfather and Grace, a couple from university friends with whom he kept in touch but he could find no letter from Callie.

Jamie went through the pile again: slowly, carefully. Still nothing. Perhaps she had been too busy, perhaps her letters had gone astray?

All of them? he asked himself. It had been more than a couple of months now since he'd had any communication with her.

As the harsh reality he had wished to avoid seeped into his consciousness, Jamie sat staring into space, overcome by a feeling of helplessness because he couldn't just go to England and find out why he hadn't heard from her.

Quickly, he skimmed through his dad's letters. He'd found a lady-friend, he wrote, (*lucky bastard*, thought Jamie bitterly) and that they were serious about each other. Her name was Edie (*wasn't Callie's aunt called something like Edie?* Jamie couldn't remember. Callie had only said her name once and after that only ever referred to her as 'Auntie'). His dad then added that he and Edie had bought an investment house together (*this must be serious*, thought Jamie) and were going to set about restoring it.

Do I mind about Edie? thought Jamie. No. It was about time Dad found someone. He hadn't been out with anyone in years.

His grandfather wrote that he was well but hadn't done any portrait painting recently; that he was currently working on quite a nice canvas of the farmhouse; that Grace had taken lots of pictures with her new super-duper digital camera that he'd given her for her birthday. She'd teased him by saying that he should be buying her a walking stick at her age instead of a camera, which would only encourage her to go hiking (thus wearing out her hips and knees in the process and causing her ankles to swell unflatteringly), rather than leaving her to snooze comfortably by the kitchen range. *Well, we've all got to stay active, haven't we, lad?* he added, saying that they'd had a good laugh over the unlikely picture of Grace ever snoozing idly by the kitchen range.

He wrote that they'd enjoyed watching a repeat of Trooping the Colour on television and that they'd even caught what they thought was a glimpse of Jamie – *though it's quite hard to tell when the cameras spend such little time focused on their subjects these days. Doesn't give anyone time to see what anything is,*" said Jack, who concluded his letter by inviting Jamie to stay with them once he was home from his tour of duty, especially as they'd missed seeing him before he went away.

Maybe, thought Jamie, without his usual enthusiasm. Cairnmor was the last place he wanted to go the moment he got home. He needed to find Callie. He might visit his grandfather and Grace in the spring, for whatever he did when he got home would depend on Callie and what was happening with her.

Jamie knew there was no point in letting himself become worked up about Callie's lack of contact. Perhaps he'd been foolish and stupid to become involved for such a brief time knowing he was coming out here. Perhaps Callie had regretted her hastiness in accepting his proposal and had decided that such an impetuous start was not the right basis upon which to build a lasting relationship.

Maybe not, but what was a fellow to do? Having seen the girl of his dreams, he couldn't let her disappear into the ether without at least knowing something about her, could he? And six months wasn't that long to ask her to hang on and wait for him. When he got back to England, they could meet up and start again and the rather tenuous link they had established before he left could be strengthened.

Yes, that would be the best thing by far.

With that positive thought, Jamie went into the Mess tent for some supper.

CHAPTER 23

A fortnight later, Callie made her final escape.

She arrived at Edie's house to find only Sarah, who had just come off night-shift, at home.

"Hello, stranger," she said, as Callie walked into the kitchen looking pale and wan. "What's happened now?" she asked matter-of-factly.

Callie's text to Edie to say she had returned to Erik had had them all despairing. "I've left him."

Sceptically, Sarah said, "For good this time?"

"Yes, for good."

Tears of relief trickled down Callie's cheeks.

It had actually been simple. He'd had an important early morning breakfast meeting at the office and knowing he would be involved for several hours before she would be needed, Callie had picked up her lap-top and her hand bag and walked out of the office and Erik's life forever.

"Didn't he come after you?"

"He doesn't know and with any luck, he won't find out until lunch-time. I can't tell you what a relief it is to have finally left him."

Curious about Erik's treatment of Callie, Sarah wondered what he had done to make her behave like a rabbit caught in the headlights of a car. In what way was he such a heinous monster?

"He didn't lock you in your office then to keep you in his evil thrall while he was preoccupied in the meeting?"

"No"

"Did he ever threaten to do that?"

"No."

"At home?"

Callie shook her head.

"Hm." Wanting to know more about Erik's character, Sarah said, "Did he keep phoning you up to check what you were up to if you were on your own at home or keep coming into your office during the day at work?"

"I was never on my own. We were always together, even at work as my office was next to his. Every evening though, I had to show him all the calls and messages on my mobile and any emails I'd written. He didn't let me have my laptop when we were at home and he cancelled my phone contract and set up a new one with a different company."

"Didn't you object to that?"

"No."

"Why not?"

"I just didn't, that's all. It seemed simpler to just do what he said. I was too scared of what he might do. When I knew he was going to take the phone away, I managed to take out my old simcard and hide it in my handbag. So that I didn't lose all my contacts. You know. And could reinstate it at any time."

"He didn't check that it was missing when he took the phone?"

"No, obviously not."

Intrigued and appalled at the same time, Sarah asked, "Did he try to control what you thought or said?"

"No, but he wouldn't let me see my friends."

"Didn't you kick up about that?"

"I was afraid to."

I would have done, thought Sarah. *No way would I let him get away with all this. But then, I wasn't there, in Callie's position.* "Did he get angry if you didn't give into his every whim?"

"No-o. But I always did give in. Just in case. Besides, he never gave me the chance to argue the toss. I was just totally overwhelmed by him most of the time."

What a wimp this girl is, thought Sarah. "So, apart from his manipulation, what else made you want to leave?" she asked.

Callie blushed. "Too much sex."

Sarah threw her head back and laughed.

"Is that all?"

Callie looked at her. Sarah couldn't possibly understand or have known what she had endured.

"His appetite is voracious. He's incredibly demanding. You can have no idea."

Sarah found herself wanting to have an idea.

"Was he ever abusive towards you, mentally or physically, apart from the control thing?"

"No. Never."

"Violent?"

"Passionate and forceful but never violent, though I always felt there might be a dangerous, aggressive side to his character, you know, lurking just beneath the surface, ready to strike at any time."

"But he never actually hurt you?"

"No. He knew how far to go."

"Did he have weird predilections or fetishes?"

Callie shook her head. "No. He was perfectly normal."

"Did you enjoy what you and he did?"

Callie blushed again and nodded, feeling ashamed.

"So why did you leave? You had it made, girl! Rich, attentive fella and all you want to do is run away!"

"I had to leave because he was using me whenever he wanted, without any sort of consideration for what I might be feeling. I was so engulfed by him that I lost myself."

"Gordon Bennett, I've always wanted to experience a feeling like that – to be so engulfed by a man that you could lose yourself in him!"

The more she heard about Erik, the more Sarah wanted to know. She knew she was strong enough to temper his need for control; she knew she could match his appetites. In fact, she knew she would find him exciting.

At least, in her imagination she knew she would.

"Really?" Callie couldn't believe it. How could anyone want that? "And besides I felt guilty."

"Because of your briefly-met fiancé?"

"Yes."

"So what do you plan to do now?"

Callie shrugged. "Go somewhere far away. Look for another job. I still have my reference from Royal Court Chambers."

"What about money in the meanwhile?" Sarah began to wonder how practical Callie actually was.

"I've about twenty-thousand in savings. At least he didn't get his hands on my bank account. If I don't find a job and run out of money, I can always go home to my parents."

"Better to be independent, though," observed Sarah, "than have to go home and confess."

I was independent, thought Callie, *before I met Erik*. "To go home would be much too embarrassing," she said.

"Especially without any money," added Sarah, not unsympathetically.

Knowing she was right, Callie's eyes filled up with tears again.

Edie and Ben stood in the deserted house and surveyed their purchase.

"How does the state of this one compare with yours when you first bought it?" he asked.

"Worse."

Ben laughed. "Well, it's had nearly forty more years of neglect."

"Thank goodness! What that really means is that it's had forty more years without being vandalized. Fortunately, whoever lived here just boarded up everything that was regarded as being old-fashioned rather than ripping it out and changing everything beyond all recognition. It really annoys me when people buy a house because they like the character and then proceed to change everything so completely that the original internal fabric of the house – the very thing they purported to have found so attractive in the first place – is changed beyond all recognition!"

"Well, with John on board, it might be possible to start a whole new reclamation business for you."

"That would be great. I'd prefer to rent the houses out if we can afford it because if we sold them on, then some bright young couple with more money than sense will want to 'put their own stamp' on the house and wreck everything that we had lovingly restored. I saw a programme the other day about some people who'd had all these extensions and open-plan areas created inside their Victorian house and who then declared that the only remaining original room on the ground floor was their favourite place in the whole house! How ridiculous is that? They should have left things as they were."

Ben hugged Edie for her enthusiasm and concerns.

"I bet you feel pain when trees are chopped down."

"Oh, I do," said Edie, turning his slight tease into something more serious. "Real physical pain, unless it happens to be necessary because the tree is diseased or dying, of course. That's a different matter. I mean you look outside in the garden of this house – yes, it's overgrown but think how many bird's nests those bushes and trees

130

are harbouring and how much bird-song you can hear in this little haven of tranquillity in the centre of London. Who cares about decking and 'party areas' when you can enjoy the wonders of nature literally on your own doorstep, and in the middle of the city as well!" Edie smiled at him. "Anyway, that's enough of my pontificating. Let's get on. We need to have a preliminary skirmish before getting down to brass tacks."

"Oh," said Ben, "I'm all for having a preliminary skirmish!"

"Later, dear, later, especially with this floor being the way it is!"

"Well," said Sarah, ever practical, "you've got to have some idea of where you're going to go. You can't just set off without a destination in mind."

"I suppose not," said Callie, sipping dejectedly at the cup of coffee Sarah had made for her. "I hadn't thought about where, exactly, just that I had to go somewhere. Anywhere."

"Now, while I do accept that you've got to get away from here – otherwise," she observed, "Erik'll just come after you again and then, like before, you won't be able to resist his amorous embrace and find yourself back where you started. Which is no good at all." Sarah thought for a moment. "Look, finish your drink and while you go upstairs and pack, I'll have a look at Edie's travel books. Some of them are seriously out of date, but it might give you an idea or two as to where you could go. I'll bring them upstairs. You don't have to tell me what you decide if you don't want to, but at least it will give you an indication, something positive to aim for."

"Okay." Gratefully, Callie went upstairs.

She lifted her largest suitcase onto the bed and threw inside a random assortment of clothes and a few favourite personal possessions.

"Have you got your passport, bank books, insurance certificates – all that stuff, you know?" said Sarah, as she came into the bedroom looking critically at the chaotic mess of garments and papers on the floor, the bed and dangling erratically from open drawers. "He never got his grasping hands on those I hope."

Callie shook her head. "No, he didn't, fortunately. There are some in my handbag, some in the suitcase here."

The enormity of what she was about to do began to dawn on her.

"I don't think I can do this," she said feebly, flopping down onto the bed.

"Of course you can. And you must."

"What will Auntie Edie say?"

"You leave her to me, girl."

"What about my share of the rent?"

"She won't worry. Especially as she's still on the Emporium's payroll and going in for this house-purchasing lark."

"No, I suppose not. I don't want to let her down though," added Callie.

She'd let just about everyone else down, she didn't want to add her aunt to the list as well.

"Edie'll just be glad you've made the break at last and can get your life sorted out. After all, that's the object of the exercise, isn't it? I'm sure she'll hang on to your room so that it'll be there for you when you get home."

"I suppose you're right," said Callie morosely.

"Come on, pull yourself together and let's get you sorted," and Sarah began to take things out of the suitcase while she spoke, folding them in neat piles on the bed. "We need to be methodical about this otherwise you're going to find yourself with loads of flimsy dresses and no warm clothes for the worst of the winter that'll be on us all too soon." She went through Callie's wardrobe and chest of drawers and extracted suitable garments. "Now, when we've got you all packed up and hunky-dory, we'll have a look at those travel books. I've brought up a huge stack of them. A selection from just about the whole of Great Britain, I think."

"How full is my diary for the rest of the day?" asked Ben, as he came into the office later that morning after he and Edie had done all they could for the time being at the house.

"Well, you've got a meeting at eleven to discuss the starting date for that riverside project, if you remember."

"Yes. Anything else?"

"There's the Fulham development to discuss with the freeholder. She wants seven flats now instead of five."

Ben made a face. "No chance. She'll never get planning permission for that."

"That's what I told her, but she's insisting that she speaks to you about it anyway. So I set up an appointment for," Judith consulted her computer screen, "for two-thirty this afternoon."

"Well, at least I'll have some time to work on Edie's house," said Ben, going into his office.

Judith followed him.

"Do you have a moment?" she said uncertainly.

"Of course." Ben began to shuffle the papers on his desk.

Judith shut the door and sat down.

"Ever since we, you know…"

Ben looked at her sharply. He had no wish to be reminded of that particular debacle. "Yes?"

"I've been feeling uncomfortable, you know, working here."

"I thought we'd put that episode behind us and both of us were behaving in a mature, professional manner towards each other."

"Oh, we have and we are. It's not that. It's just that I feel uncomfortable. Embarrassed."

"What still?" His words came out more brusquely than he intended.

"I know it was ages ago, but I think of you often."

"Judith!"

"I think what I'm trying to say, is that I'd like to leave."

"Why?"

"Before I disgrace myself further."

Ben regarded her for a moment without speaking, his expression clear and direct. Having put the incident out of his mind totally and been completely and utterly absorbed in his own happiness with Edie, it had never occurred to him that his P.A. might be under any emotional strain.

"Especially now you'll have Edie on the payroll," she added.

"But her job is different to yours. She's an additional employee, not a replacement for you."

Judith looked at him. "But she is a replacement for me."

"I don't wish to be unkind, but there was never anything between you and me on a personal level in the first place."

Ben had work to do, he really didn't want to be having this conversation.

"I realize that now."

"Look," said Ben, "why don't you take a couple of days to think it over. You're an excellent P.A. and there's no sense in you giving up your job unless you absolutely have to. Think of your children."

"Okay, I'll think it over."

The phone rang and Judith picked it up.

"It's for you," she said, handing the receiver over to Ben, as she went out of the room.

"John here. Sorry to trouble you at work, but I've made an interesting discovery. Any chance I might pop across and see you at your office? I'm over your way this afternoon to Southey's with a view to bidding on a potential haul."

"How about lunch-time? I've a really busy day today. I presume it won't wait until this evening?"

"Nope, 'fraid not. It won't take long. One o'clock?"

"Bring your sandwiches!"

"You're on!"

"Right, so let's have a look at these," said Sarah.

Everything was packed and orderly – large suitcase on wheels completely full and zipped up; sizeable haversack containing Callie's laptop as well as food and drink for the journey and overflow toiletries; her handbag containing her immediate needs – with all the luggage ready to be taken downstairs.

They sat on the settee by the dormer window in Callie's room and sifted through the pile of books that Sarah had brought upstairs.

"How about the Channel Islands?"

"I was born there. On St Nicolas."

"So that's no good then."

"Not really. Besides, masses of relatives live there."

Sarah laid that particular guide book aside.

"How about this or this?"

Callie shook her head.

"What about somewhere in Derbyshire? *Visit the Peak District and enjoy the Great Outdoors.*"

"That's alright now but during the winter months?"

"I take your point." Sarah put the slim volume on top of the rapidly growing discard pile. "What about Wales?"

"Too wet."

"Manchester? You could lose yourself in a big metropolis like that."

"Too dreary. I went there once on a court case. Besides, I don't want to be any more lost than I already am."

Sarah laughed, pleased to see a glimmer of wry humour.

"Liverpool?"

"The same."

"Well, don't let the Scousers hear you say that! How about Norfolk?"

"Too flat."

"Not all of it. I went there for a holiday once."

"Oh. Sorry."

"Doesn't bother me."

Sarah picked up the next book. "This looks pretty remote," she said, looking at the front cover. She opened it up. "*Cairnmor, one of the Outer Isles,*" she read, "*is situated some eighty miles off the West Coast mainland of Scotland. It is a remote land, a place of great beauty and undisturbed wilderness; a haven for wildlife, a land of golden-white sandy beaches and inland fertile plains.*" She looked at Callie. "It sounds idyllic," she added. "Just the sort of place you need to get over the emotional shock to your system. Erik won't find you here."

Sarah read on. "*It is a land that opens a path through history, encompassing the Vikings, the Celts, the Stuarts, the Clans and the Christian Church together with a vibrant Gaelic culture. It has a unique sense of community, forged through common purpose and the need to survive.*" Sarah smiled. "I love these phrases. Even makes me want to go there."

"Let's see." Callie took it from Sarah as she handed it to her. "When was this written?" She looked inside the front cover. "1970. That's ages ago."

"Yes, but life doesn't change much up there I would imagine."

Callie continued to turn the pages. "The illustrations are quite beautiful and the scenery looks stunning in these photographs."

Something tugged at her heart – a yearning, inexplicable and unexpected. The potential for release and renewal. The possibility of freedom.

She showed the page to Sarah, whose eye caught the words: *It is subject to violent Atlantic storms; a land that can be isolated for weeks or even months at a time and where the islanders have to be self-reliant and self-sufficient.*

"You have to go there," she said. "This is the place. You'll be safe there. A complete escape."

"Yes. A complete escape," echoed Callie. "From Erik. From Jamie. From myself."

"From the first two, certainly, but not the third, I'm afraid. You have to come to terms with yourself, Callie, and learn to live with who you are and what you've done. You can never escape from that."

"But I could lose myself in a place like this."

"True, but really, you need to go somewhere to find yourself."

"Maybe. But this is the place."

"I agree. Now, let's see how to get you there."

They looked at the book again.

"It says here that the best way to travel is to take the night sleeper from Euston to Glasgow Central then another train to Oban where there is, apparently, *a very pleasant hotel overlooking the harbour that offers good hospitality before you board the ferry to Lochaberdale.*"

"But that was 1970," observed Callie. "Transport and accommodation must have changed since then."

"I tell you what," said Sarah, "I'll put this lot back on the shelf and have a look on the internet about travelling to Cairnmor. Why don't you bring your stuff downstairs, then you'll be all ready to go? You shouldn't hang around here for too much longer, just in case his lordship discovers you're not where you should be."

"Okay."

Callie deposited her luggage in the hallway and went back upstairs to Sarah's room.

"Do you think I should write to Erik or something? I've got his door keys here that need to be returned. He can have his phone back as well. I don't want it." She looked at Sarah. "You've been so wonderful already, you couldn't...?"

"Take the stuff back and tell him that he shouldn't try to come after you?"

"You'd do that for me?"

"Ye-es, but also," she said, without revealing that they'd already met, "I'd like to know this guy properly. I'm curious about him."

"Well, be careful. You know what they say, don't you, about curiosity?"

"Killed the cat?"

Callie smiled and nodded.

"Yes, but if I'm a cat, that also means I've got nine lives, and as far as I'm aware, I haven't lost any of them yet. Where does he work?"

Callie wrote down the address and gave Sarah the keys and mobile. "He normally leaves the office about five o'clock."

They sat down at Sarah's laptop and planned Callie's route and connections.

"It doesn't really seem to have changed much in length of journey time since 1970," observed Sarah. "Flying is quicker but by the time you've got to Heathrow and bought your ticket and checked in, you'll still be catching the same train from Glasgow to Oban and still have to stay overnight, just as you would have to do if you went all the way by train. The transfer between stations is easier by rail as well."

"I'd rather go by train. It's simpler. But I don't want to wait for the night-sleeper."

"Well, there's a train at eleven-thirty this morning. That'll get you on your way before his meeting finishes. I'll come with you to Euston and then, once I've seen you safely on board, I'll drop these things off to Erik the Terrible."

"You'd do all this for me? Today? Even though you've just come off night-shift? You must be incredibly tired."

"Yes to all those things. But," she gave a shrug of her shoulders, "I've got two days off after this so I can collapse in a heap when I get home and sleep until I go back to work if necessary."

They set off for Euston and Callie managed to secure a though ticket and seat reservation, the last one that was available.

"You see," said Sarah, "it's your destiny!"

"Thank you," said Callie gratefully, as they stood by the ticket barrier.

"Look, you've got my number. Once you've bought yourself a new pay-as-you-go phone (it'll be too hard to set up a new contract), text me if you become desperate. And text Edie to let her know when you get to Oban and every so often after that. Although we're all independent and go off doing our own thing, she does worry about both of us if we're away from home and she hasn't heard from us. You don't have to say where you are, just that you're fine and quite safe and that you need a bit of time to yourself. Your whereabouts will be our secret."

"How can I ever repay you?"

"You don't have to, so don't worry about it."

And, after giving Sarah another hug, Callie boarded her train.

CHAPTER 24

"So, what's this great discovery you've made?" said Ben, letting John into the office just after Judith had gone out for her lunch.

"Well, someone brought in a rather intriguing book which prompted me to do a bit of research on the internet. One thing led to another and I discovered that 'our'," he raised an eyebrow at Ben, "house was once owned by one Samuel Lescaut who, it would seem, was an architect and designer in the latter part of the nineteenth and early twentieth centuries."

"And?"

"Apparently, there is a story that he left some valuable merchandise somewhere within the house."

"It's not that sort of house, I wouldn't have thought. Nor the area."

"That's what I thought, so I looked up the street on Booth's 1898 London Poverty Map – you know, where the roads were colour coded as being either poor, comfortable, well-off or wealthy – it would seem that the area, which was deemed 'comfortable' on the map, underwent a reversal of fortune and descended into an undesirable area after the First World War. It's only now seeing a resurgence as an up-and-coming area."

"And you think that our house may have some buried treasure in it?"

"Well, it's worth a try at least."

"And I suppose you want to go looking."

"I think we should all go looking before you and Edie start ripping the place apart," said John with a smile.

"You know very well that's not our intention," he said, feigning indignation.

His friend chuckled. "I know."

"I wonder why he left it hidden in the house?"

"Illegal contraband, perhaps?" suggested John mischievously.

"We should be so lucky. When did he die?"

"Unfortunately, in the Great War."

"Perhaps it was his own personal nest-egg that he was saving up for when he came out of the army."

"But he never did and no one, presumably, has ever found his booty."

"Perhaps."

"It would be quite exciting if that were so, wouldn't it?"

"Yes, but even if we did discover something, Samuel Lescaut's descendants would have prior claim, wouldn't they?"

"True, but what if there are no descendants? Then the freeholders of the property, namely you and Edie, would be entitled to keep it."

Ben laughed. "I suppose you'd want a share too."

"Well, I did do the original research," observed John amiably.

On her way back from Euston, Sarah took the Tube to Erik's office.

As she came out of the station, she looked up at the glass and metal building unable to be anything but overawed by its sheer scale and, after walking through silent, smoothly revolving doors, by the light airiness of the interior. Green foliage and slender, ornamental trees abounded within the escalator-crossed, cathedral-like entrance atrium and Sarah looked on in wonder as she ascended slowly and majestically towards Erik van der Waals's suite of offices.

When she asked if she could speak to the man himself, the receptionist looked at her disdainfully and asked if she had an appointment.

"No, but please tell him I'm here." Sarah gave her name. "We have met before. If he doesn't want to see me, then I'll go away again. But I think he will appreciate it if you could tell him I am here."

The receptionist looked at her again and went on her way. She returned presently, and with surprise in her voice, said, "Mr Van der Waals will see you now. Please follow me."

Sarah was shown into his office. It was as plush and elegant as she had anticipated. This was going to be more difficult than she had first thought. She took a deep breath.

"Come in, Sarah," he said, walking over to her and extending his hand courteously. "Please do sit down. This is such an unexpected pleasure." And he indicated a chair.

It's not going to be when I tell you why I've come, she thought.

When she had, Erik went pale and sat down.

Again, just as when he had first come to the house looking for Callie, this wasn't the reaction of the evil monster Sarah had been led to expect. She wondered if he had, after all, really cared for Callie.

She observed him silently for a few moments. From the little she knew of him, he seemed, on the surface, to be a mass of contradictions – rich, good-looking, charismatic; an obvious ladies-man and definitely exuding an air of danger which bubbled beneath the surface, never quite breaking through.

Callie was right about that, she thought. *Even if she didn't like it, there are many women who find that combination exciting and irresistible. Including me.*

He was also, from what Callie had told her, controlling and manipulative but something made Sarah hope that somewhere alongside this less than acceptable character trait, he might be capable of normal, human feeling.

She wondered just how many relationships he had had before Callie and why none of the women in his life had stayed the course. And what a course that would be. It would take a strong woman to counter his desires and need to dominate.

Instinctively, Sarah knew she possessed that particular strength. A flicker of desire to find out manifested itself.

"Callie asked me to give you these," she said quickly.

She put the keys and mobile on his desk and when this elicited no reaction from him, stood up to leave.

Suddenly, appearing already to have recovered his equilibrium, he smiled at her disarmingly. "Don't go. Stay for a moment, please. I'm grateful to you. This is the second time you have shown me kindness in my hour of need."

As she sat down again, Sarah wondered how much of his true self he ever revealed, whether his charm was completely natural or a well-practised mask. She wondered whether any of his women friends had actually bothered to find out or had tried and failed before leaving in frustration (having been attracted initially by his suave manner, wealth and prestige), unable to find the every-day domestic harmony they had been hoping for with a man who was perhaps incapable of providing what they desired.

Or was it their lack of personal freedom that had eventually defeated them, just as it had Callie who was totally unsuited to him anyway, even if he had really liked her.

Or had he just used her?

"Have lunch with me," he said, watching her intently.

"No, not today," replied Sarah, caught by surprise.

She wondered also how long Erik went between the end of one relationship and the start of another. Was his grief shallow and short-lived as he moved quickly to establish a new liaison, or did he not look for someone else until the pain of the finished relationship had passed? Did he use that next relationship as a means of camouflaging hurt of the broken one?

Did he feel any pain or grief at all? Was his reaction to Callie's departure an unusual one?

"Why ever not? I could do with some company. No strings, I promise."

Sarah wondered how often he'd used that particular line.

She needed time to think about this. Having acknowledged a growing fascination for Erik van der Waals, it would be all too easy to slide into something from which it might be difficult to extricate herself later, should she need to.

She wondered how many women, Callie included, had gone through these particular thought processes before accepting Erik's undeniably tempting offer of lunch or dinner or the cinema or the theatre.

Torn between her natural sympathy and desire to help someone who had just been dealt an emotional body-blow and her wariness where Erik was concerned because of what she knew about him, Sarah sat in silent contemplation for a few moments.

It was just lunch after all. And she was curious. And it would be an opportunity to study him further.

"Alright. I accept. But I'm hardly dressed for an elegant lunch."

He smiled. "Who said it was going to be elegant?"

"Well," said Sarah, regarding him sardonically, "if it's not going to be elegant, then I shall have lunch on my own."

Erik looked at her for a moment and smiled again. "One elegant lunch it is then."

And Sarah felt her calm, sensible inner world somersault.

Callie arrived in Glasgow on time and took a taxi across to Queen Street station where, using her through ticket, she boarded the train to Oban.

Because it was late afternoon, she set off on the next leg of her journey in darkness, disappointed to find that she would be unable to enjoy any of the stunning scenery that defined Scotland.

Trying hard not to think about Jamie or Erik, deprived of anything spectacular to look at from the window and having already spent four and a half hours on a train, Callie dozed fitfully, waking up with a start when the train's announcer heralded their arrival at her destination.

It was difficult to gain her bearings as she left the station but much to her relief, Callie could see that the ferry terminal was adjacent to the station itself. She went into the building and purchased her ticket for the first sailing the following morning to Lochaberdale. She asked and was directed to the nearest hotel (expensive) and gratefully sprawled out onto the bed before venturing down to the dining room for a singularly unappetizing supper

As she returned to her room, Callie began to wonder if she should have booked ahead for the hotel in Lochaberdale. What would happen if there was nowhere for her to stay? Would she be cast out, wandering the streets? (Were there streets on Cairnmor? She had no idea). Would she be obliged to come straight back to Oban, having been unsuccessful in her quest? Perhaps she ought to get a return just in case. What happened if there were no more ferries until the next day?

Anxious now, Callie spent a restless night. It didn't occur to her to check the internet on the new phone she had purchased before leaving Glasgow and investigate possibilities.

It was almost as though she had lost all ability for coherent thought.

After work, Ben met Edie in the house and methodically, they began to search the place from top to bottom looking for John's mysterious treasure – in all the cupboards, in the cellar (sifting carefully through the rubbish that littered the floor) under the stairs, in the kitchen, scullery, sitting room, dining room, all the bedrooms – everywhere that they could think of that would constitute some kind of hiding place.

"It's too dark now to search the outbuildings in the garden and we haven't got a ladder to get up into the attic." Edie closed her eyes and held her breath while she brushed the cobwebs from her hair and the dust from her clothes. "Ugh. I shall need a bath as soon as we get home."

Ben watched her lovingly, thinking how far they had both come on their particular journeys since knowing each other.

"We'll have another foray into the delights of our neglected Victorian house at the weekend but earlier in the day when it's lighter. I think we're on a wild goose chase, personally. I reckon John made it up just so he can arrive unexpectedly and find us up to our necks in dirt and grime and have a good laugh at our expense!"

"Well, if that's the case, I shall give him a broom and a mop and he can clean the place up himself. In fact," and Edie's eyes were twinkling, "we'll suggest that when he comes with us at the weekend anyway, then he can do his own dirty work! I'm glad he's taking an interest though."

"Oh he is. He's really serious about coming in with us as a business partner and forming a property company to save lots of derelict houses."

"Goodness!"

"You see, you've had a profound effect on all of us," and Ben put his arm round Edie's shoulder. "What say we go home for a shower and some supper? Your place or mine tonight?"

"Yours. It's about time we spent some time in it. It'll be feeling neglected as we've been virtually living in mine."

"Which house shall we live in eventually do you think?"

"I don't know. That's a difficult one," replied Edie, knowing she couldn't give up her house and unwilling to allow Ben to sacrifice his wonderfully spacious town house in South Kensington, which she had come to love and appreciate. "How about we live in both? After all, isn't that what we're already doing now? It seems unnecessary to make changes to something that works so well."

Ben laughed. "An admirable compromise! One day, Jamie will need a base in London and when that time comes, then I might decamp permanently to your house because I know how attached the two of you are to each other. I'd hate to be the one to come between you and it," he added, gently teasing her.

Edie batted him gently on the arm and said, "Home please, before you spout any more of your nonsense."

"Ah," said Ben, "actually, it isn't nonsense because I'm convinced that a house comes alive when it's inhabited by people and their thoughts become imprinted on the very walls."

Edie chuckled. "I know. I wonder what stories this one could tell?"

"Lots I would imagine given the number of hearts that must have resided here. You see, I'm a great believer that home is where the heart is and for us personally, that means as long as we're together, it doesn't matter where we live."

"I understand exactly what you're saying," replied Edie earnestly. "And it's a wonderful thing to say. But I'd still be reluctant to leave my house."

Ben smiled. "Well, as both of us are happy to follow your suggestion of sharing our lives between Carlton and South Kensington, I can see no need to make any changes that would cause either of us grief."

"Even when we're married?"

"Even then. Besides, we might even decide to live in this one."

"But not at the moment."

"No, even if it is our house."

"A compromise too far, you might say, given its present state of dilapidation."

"Exactly."

Gratefully, Edie tucked her arm through Ben's and they locked the door behind them and went on their way.

That night, Sarah lay awake, unable to sleep despite her mind and body being in a state beyond tiredness – caused by her lack of sleep from being at work during the night and the surprising events of the day – recalling all that had happened during the past twelve hours.

Firstly, the haste and bustle of Callie's departure.

Secondly, she thought of Callie's email received only a couple of hours previously to say that she had arrived safely in Oban and giving the information that as she had been told there was only a dial-up internet connection on the island and an erratic mobile signal, further communication would be difficult. Writing a letter would only give away her location because of the post-mark, so Sarah would have to trust that she was alright. She sent her love to Auntie Edie and asked that

Sarah should tell her not to worry and that she, Callie, would probably be away (on business?) for a few months at least.

If I can't stand it anymore, if the loneliness and lack of creature comforts get to me, then I shall come home. In the meantime, I shall stay in Scotland and make the best of it. Love Callie x

Thirdly and most disconcertingly, Sarah thought of lunchtime.

Erik had taken her to the Savoy Grill for lunch where her flamboyant top and brightly-coloured trainers engendered a few raised eyebrows but he seemed not to notice or if he did, he made no comment nor showed any signs of embarrassment.

The staff seemed to know him well and, having got her emotions more or less under control again, Sarah had studied her surroundings trying to make the most of an opportunity she had never thought to experience.

The menu was complex but Erik, subtly and without a hint of condescension, guided her through it as she made her choices.

Apart from occasional moments of (she supposed) Callie-induced distraction, he was attentive and solicitous towards her. They chatted amicably about politics, the National Health Service, the on-going financial crisis. No one in the restaurant, had they been observing him, would have guessed, either from his words or his manner, that he had just been deserted by his lover.

Perhaps, thought Sarah, he really did feel nothing.

But she, for some reason, didn't want to believe that he was a completely heartless bastard. She wanted to believe that somewhere underneath that undoubtedly psychologically disturbed and charming persona, there beat a heart that might actually care about another human being.

She wondered how many other women had looked for that and never found it, going away at the end of their relationship with him disillusioned and heart-broken. She wondered about events in his past life which may have influenced his personality and whether, with her professional knowledge of psychology, she might be able to help him.

Whichever way she looked at it, Sarah began to realize the enormity of what it would mean to become involved with Erik. And the dangers it might pose to her own emotional well-being. It would be a challenge, certainly, and one that she would relish, but she wondered whether she wanted that kind of involvement.

When lunch was over, he had thanked her for her company and said, in words which she perceived as genuine (and the utterance of which, unfortunately, took her breath away), that he valued her company; that he felt comfortable with her; that he would like to see her again – very much.

But not just yet, he added. He hoped that Sarah would understand. He said he would call her when the time was right.

Would that be acceptable?

And Sarah had looked into his mesmerizing eyes and without any hesitation, found herself saying that of course it was alright, that she'd look forward to it.

Just before she drifted off to sleep, Sarah wondered whether he always selected his next lover in advance, waiting until he had recovered sufficiently from the previous relationship before embarking upon a new adventure.

She realized that this was what each lengthy sexual encounter was to him – an adventure. But, like all adventurers, he could be caught out, just as he appeared to have been with Callie.

Once again, Sarah wondered just how many women there had been in his life and whether, after a few months, having grown tired of his conquests he then (courteously and charmingly) dropped them.

Had she been selected as Erik's next 'victim', she wondered? She might, no doubt, find out one day soon.

If she was foolish enough.

CHAPTER 25

The next morning, Callie embarked on her five-hour crossing to Lochaberdale.

The ferry was basic but serviceable and arrived on time at two-thirty in the afternoon after an uneventful, though slightly uncomfortable, crossing.

As the boat reversed beside the jetty, Callie stood on the top deck looking out towards the land to which she had come and her heart beat rapidly with a sense of having arrived in a completely different world. She was used to island life – having grown up on St Nicolas and being familiar with the other Channel Islands – but even from the harbour this place *felt* different.

Remote. Majestic. Compelling.

For Callie, this was a step into the unknown, into the unfamiliar. She had no job, a finite amount of money, her conscience to square and, moreover, she was completely on her own, something she had never experienced before.

Throughout her life, she had always been surrounded by friends and family; had allowed herself to be organized by them; had gone along happily with the crowd, not even aware that she might be sacrificing her own desires or mind-set in preference to someone else's.

She had become a barrister because her father wanted her to use her intelligence in what he saw to be a 'noble calling'. He had always wanted to become a lawyer himself, he said, and wanted her to have the opportunities he never had. Therefore, she had duly gone to university to fulfil her father's thwarted dreams and ambitions.

Even at uni, she had been organized by her group of friends who roped her in for this and that. Her boyfriends automatically assumed that she would to go to bed with them – and she did, allowing the first to take her virginity because she was in love with him and had believed (falsely) that he was in love with her and the second, knowing she was on the rebound, had said she would find it comforting if they slept together. She didn't.

Therefore, Callie had done all these things, blown this way and that by the wishes and whims of other people; trying all the while to please everyone and ending up pleasing no one (apart from her tutors who encouraged and commended her for her academic diligence, this proving to be her one solid achievement in a sea of inconsistency) – not herself, her employers, her father (were he to find out the recent events of her life), her erstwhile fiancé because she had betrayed his trust and her lover because she had left him without so much as an explanation.

But here, now, for this one glorious moment, Callie knew no one and no one knew her. She had come to this place on the spur of the moment with only a vague notion of what it might be like from a guide-book that was over forty years out of date.

For the first time in her life, she could please herself. Completely. There would be no one to influence her; no one to advise or tell her what to do; no one to push her this way or that until she didn't know which way to turn.

She found the prospect of this daunting yet realized that if she was brave enough to take the opportunity, it could prove to be deeply empowering. Moreover, there would be no one to witness her mistakes, her insecurities, her inability to cope with life in general.

"Tell me," said John, "why am I spending my Saturday afternoon searching the grimy outbuildings of a grimy run-down dwelling looking for some improbable buried treasure?"

Ben laughed. "Because, my friend, this was your idea."

"It was, wasn't it?" said John, regretting his enthusiasm.

"How did you come across the information, anyway?" asked Edie.

"A book, in amongst a job lot that a customer sold me, chronicling the lives of local writers killed in the Great War. Belonged to his uncle apparently. And, before you two ask, no, he's not related to the chap in any way shape or form. His uncle bought the weighty tome at a jumble sale many years ago and the old man has just passed away. The family was sorting through his belongings before the house clearance people move in."

"What's happening to the house?"

"They didn't put it in the box with the stuff," quipped John.

"Watch it, otherwise I'll throw this at you," and Edie picked up an old bucket.

"Ugh. Put it down. You don't know what it may have had in it. Anyway, the son's going to live there, apparently. So there's no hope for you in that direction, ma'am."

"Buried treasure," mused Ben, not really paying attention. "Could be anything."

"Diamonds, cash, some exotic precious object from the Orient?" suggested John.

"Or a locked box," said Edie, straightening herself up after grovelling in a cupboard. "This?"

Ben and John came over to her as she put it down onto the workbench.

"Good grief!" he exclaimed, as he brushed away the years of accumulated dust and cobwebs. "It's an Ernest Stevenson!"

"A what?" said Ben.

"It's a jewellery box designed by Ernest Stevenson."

"Who?"

"Ernest Stevenson, one of the leading lights of the Arts and Crafts movement in the nineteenth-century."

"How can you tell?"

"By the design on the lid. The floral inlay is typical of his style with its use of a triple inlay of walnut and holly on the edges."

"Is it valuable?" asked Ben.

"If it's an original, then yes. Not so much if it's just one that's based on his designs."

Edie tried to open it but it was locked. Ben was about to exert a little force but John stopped him.

"There must be a key somewhere. We really don't want to damage that lock. It would detract from the value of the piece."

They hunted for a while through the shed but without success.

"I would imagine the key's been lost," said Ben, as they went back into the house

"Probably."

"What shall we do now?" asked Edie.

"I have a colleague who knows about this sort of problem," replied John. "I think I'll pay him a visit tomorrow. Or at any rate, give him a ring and see when I can go round."

Gently, he shook the jewellery box. Something inside rattled but it was difficult to discern exactly what that might be.

"So, do you reckon that this could be our buried treasure?" asked Edie.

John pursed his lips. "Only time will tell," he replied. "But in the meantime, we'll keep on looking. You never know, we might just come across that key. But whatever happens, I must leave at ten and open up the shop, I'm afraid. Can't afford to lose customers."

"Especially as we might need your money."

"I see," said John, "so that's all I'm good for. A ready supply of cash!"

He smiled and winked at Edie who laughed.

"Well, I think we all deserve a cup of tea," she said.

"You're surely not going to brew it up in this filthy place?"

Edie chuckled. "Of course not. I brought a couple of Thermos flasks."

"I should get her to marry you," said John to Ben, "before I snatch her from under your nose."

Ben and Edie looked at each other and imperceptibly, she shook her head.

She wanted to keep their decision to themselves for the time being; wanted it to remain their own personal, private secret. Not because she doubted that it would come to fruition – she didn't – but because she wasn't quite ready to broadcast it to the world in general yet. She wanted it to be a beautiful, quiet thing between herself and Ben; she didn't want a repetition of the haste and pressure that had accompanied the announcement of her engagement to Trevor.

Ben smiled at her, understanding. Edie smiled back and poured the tea.

John gave a knowing smile.

The half-dozen or so cars that had made the crossing were the first to be directed away from the ferry by several efficient but relaxed men in high-visibility jackets, followed by one lone cyclist and a couple of other foot passengers, all of whom soon disappeared to, she presumed, known destinations.

The vehicles waiting on the quayside were directed onto the ferry as the turnaround was quite tight and Callie stood uncertainly by the harbour wall with her luggage, watching the proceedings for a while, wondering what to do.

The wind tugged at her hair, sending it flying out in all directions, so she tucked it into the collar of her coat and knotted her scarf more tightly around her neck.

Finding somewhere to stay was her first priority but there seemed to be no one who was available to ask. After surveying her surroundings, she set off on an upwards sloping path in the direction of an imposing, much-extended, white-painted building that dominated the top of a hill and in front of which stood a sign proudly announcing that this was the Lochaberdale Hotel.

As she drew nearer, Callie saw from the sign that the hotel was only open from April to October. Experiencing slight panic at this piece of unhelpful information, she nevertheless tried the door and finding it unlocked, went inside to the lobby.

There was the murmur of conversation and laughter coming from a room off to the right and as she looked in, found herself standing in a bar, set with tables and chairs.

The bartender looked up as she approached.

"Can I help ye, lass?"

"Yes. I'm, er, visiting the island and I need somewhere to stay?"

"Are ye intendin' to stay long?"

"I'm not sure. A couple of weeks? A month?"

The man looked at her quizzically.

"Well, if ye're plannin' to stay any length of time that's unfortunate because, apart from the bar here, we're closed now for the winter."

"But there's nowhere else to stay," said Callie plaintively, panic rising in her chest, visions of spending long shivering nights exposed to the elements filling her mind.

"Aye, that's true enough because the season's over here now, lass, I'm afraid," he said only partially apologetic. "And I can't even help ye out in an emergency as I've arranged for a wee bit of refurbishment before the winter storms set in. Ye'll be better off goin' back to the mainland. The hotel at Oban stays open all year round. Sorry, lass."

"Oh." Callie felt as though she was about to cry.

Taking pity on her, one of the customers said, "Doesn't Marie du Laurier over at Bannockburn House do B&B occasionally out of season?"

"Aye," said another, "that she does. She charges thirty-five pounds per person per night during the high season but it might be cheaper at this time of year. She'll do an evening meal as well if ye want. Though ye'll have to pay extra."

"Aye, she does good food does Marie. Fine cook she is," muttered another of the locals from his corner.

"She'll look after ye," said the second man. "Ye won't starve, lass, nor will ye have to sleep out in the open."

"We do have bar food here," added the bartender, feeling somewhat chagrined by his earlier inhospitality. "Lunchtimes and Saturday evenings."

"There's also the café in *An t-Sràid* if ye're stuck but that closes at three o'clock in the winter," said the man in the corner.

"How do I get to Bannockburn?" asked Callie, feeling as though she'd stepped back into the past.

"I'll show ye."

The man led the way out of the hotel and gave Callie directions, telling her to keep to the path and avoid the boggy bits. The ground was fine in the summer, he said, but with all the rain they'd been having, things were a "wee bit soggy at the moment."

"Thank you," replied Callie uncertainly, wondering what sort of place she'd come to.

She followed the directions she'd been given and there, not far from a solid-looking stone church, was a substantial bungalow with a full line of washing blowing in the considerable breeze which threatened to flap the sheets from their restraining pegs.

Callie rang the door-bell and heard footsteps as someone approached.

"Mrs du Laurier?"

"Aye?"

"Hello," she said, the fear of being stranded making her speak quickly, "I'm Callie Martin and I was wondering if you had a room that I could stay in? They said at the hotel that you sometimes take visitors out of season?"

Marie contemplated the young lady before her for a few moments. "Aye, that I do," she said at length. "Come away in and we'll see what we can do."

She ushered Callie into the hallway where there was a small table in the corner on which was a display of leaflets.

"Did you come from Oban on the early ferry?"

"Yes."

"Where are you from originally?"

"London."

"Goodness, that's a long way. On holiday, are you?"

"Sort of."

Broken heart, thought Marie, seeing the sadness in Callie's expression. Well, she'd keep an eye on the poor lassie, make sure she was alright.

"Now, I'll put you in this room here. It's the largest and has the best view of any of my guest rooms on this side of the house. The front door and hallway are for our guests and we have a separate entrance and private rooms on the other side of the bungalow for the family." She smiled warmly as she led the way through the building. "We're always full during the season and do have occasional visitors the rest of the year. As it's just me and my hubby running the place, we can afford to have people staying all year round. It supplements our income from the croft and helps to pay for the things the children need now they're growing up so fast."

She opened the door and Callie was rewarded with a wonderful vista: uplifting in its breadth and beauty.

"This room has a dual aspect and you can see right down across the bay out of this window and up towards South Lochaberdale from the other. Now, I'll leave you to unpack. Here's the key to your room and one for the front door. Time was when we didn't need to lock our doors on the island, but society changes doesn't it? And not always for the better. Anyway, here on Cairnmor, I still reckon that we're luckier than most."

Marie handed the keys to Callie who thanked her.

"Do you have any idea how long you'd like to stay?"

"No. Does that matter?"

Marie smiled. She understood. "Not at all. Just make yourself at home. You're free to come and go as you please. There's a few leaflets on the table and I presume you'll be wanting supper?"

"Yes, please."

"We usually eat at six. As it's your first night, you may prefer to eat on your own in your room this evening. I don't usually allow my visitors to do that, but I'm guessing you'd prefer some time to yourself at the moment. Once you have your bearings, then you can eat in the guest dining room."

It was a statement not a question but Callie was grateful for it, nonetheless.

148

Jamie was counting the days. With any luck, he might be home before Easter.

Though, if rumours were to be believed, there was the possibility that the present H.C.R. tour of duty might be extended to nine months. In which case, it would be early summer. If he was away that long, Jamie knew he would certainly lose Callie forever.

He had by now, stopped writing to her. It was hard writing to someone who didn't respond so he kept a diary instead, recording his thoughts and feelings and military events as they unfolded in the hope that one day he would be able to share them with her.

Jamie recognized the need to have some outlet for his emotions otherwise he would go mad with the combined frustration of probably having lost her and not being able to do anything to retrieve the situation.

He assumed that she had found someone else, which was why he hadn't heard from her. The thought pained him greatly; not just from a natural grief and humiliation but, because she had agreed to marry him, it would show a worrying character flaw if she had not kept her word and reneged on their understanding without giving him any indication that her feelings and wishes had changed.

Jamie knew that no matter what the temptation, because of their engagement, he wouldn't even have considered looking at another woman until he knew once again how things stood with Callie, even if he'd been in a position to do so.

Perhaps she didn't have his sense of honour or self-discipline but even in the short time they had known each other, Jamie hadn't taken her to be the flighty, unreliable sort of girl he now preferred to avoid.

His first girlfriend had been like that. Pretty, vivacious but fickle. They had met on his first day at university and he had been instantly attracted to her. As soon as this became clear to others in his circle of friends, he'd been warned off the girl. However, Jamie had ignored this sagacious piece of advice and asked her out anyway. She had been instantly willing to go out with him and they had dated (seriously – at least on Jamie's part) for six months.

He'd learned a lot from her. Especially in bed. It would seem she was something of an expert in that particular field and as he was a complete novice, she took great delight in initiating him. However, things gradually cooled when Jamie began to despair of her unreliability and lack of consideration as she became increasingly restless (presumably needing to move onto pastures new), and they parted by mutual consent. Her new relationship also lasted six months. And the one after that. And the next. It seemed that six months was the limit that she (or her long-suffering boyfriends) could sustain.

Jamie's second girlfriend was the complete opposite – quiet, studious and totally reliable. She had never been out with anyone before and Jamie found himself in the combined roles of tutor, confidante and frustrated lover, as she was adamant that she didn't want to sleep with anyone until she was married and merely wanted a chaste relationship until she did. After two months of trying hard to contain himself, it all became too much for Jamie who, because he wasn't in love with her and didn't want to marry her, quietly dropped her. There were no hard feelings on either side and they remained friends until they left university.

His third romantic outing came in his final year and was an intense, passionate time that almost cost both him and his girlfriend dearly. They spent more time in their bedroom than at their studies and their work suffered to such an extent that about three months before Finals, they both received a wake-up call from their tutors who warned them that unless they pulled themselves together, neither of them would have anything to show for their three years of study.

Unable to cool the relationship when they were together, they agreed to part until after their final exams. Jamie moved out of their shared student flat to find different accommodation and although it was all incredibly hard at first, they threw themselves into their studies and came out with respectable, even good, results. However, when all was complete, Jamie and his girlfriend found that having made the break and been apart for all that time, they no longer wanted to be together and went their separate ways.

Although he had cared for his first two girlfriends, was involved with the third in an overwhelming way, Jamie had never been *in* love. Until he'd met Callie, of course. Then he'd fallen for her completely and utterly almost immediately.

But that hadn't got him far, had it? Because of time constraints, they'd been unable to develop the relationship properly and no matter how attracted and attached to each other he and Callie might have been before he left, they had had no time to create and build a solid and lasting basis for their relationship. Therefore, like the proverbial house built upon sand, at the first sign of an ill-wind (his posting, her attraction to someone else?) it had collapsed.

However, Jamie knew that he would never be able to forget her. Callie would always be the love of his life no matter what had happened. Although, if she had become involved with another man, he wondered if he would actually be able to forgive and forget, especially as he would have remained faithful to her if the roles had been reversed. He had naturally expected her to have done the same.

On the other hand, what if her lack of communication meant she had simply had second thoughts and hadn't known what to say, so, rather than hurting him because he was abroad, she had just stopped writing to him? That he could understand and was something that could be easily remedied when he returned home.

Whenever that might be.

In the meantime, he would just have to bide his time patiently and keep his diary so that he would have something to show her when he finished his tour of duty.

Suddenly, a siren went off to be followed almost immediately by a series of terrifying explosions coming from somewhere nearby. Instinctively, everyone threw themselves onto the ground before grabbing their weapons and helmets and rushing to the scene of the fracas.

CHAPTER 26

Callie awoke early the next morning.

Overtaken by exhaustion after the long journey and the emotional traumas of the previous months, she had gone to bed almost immediately after taking her finished supper tray into the guest dining room and returning to her room, waking briefly to turn off the light and the television.

Feeling considerably refreshed after a shower and a night of rest, she made her way downstairs. She helped herself to cereal and apple juice and when Marie came in with Callie's chosen breakfast, she asked if she had any particular plans for the day as it looked like being relatively fine.

"Not really," said Callie. "I thought I might take a look round Lochaberdale."

"Aye, that sounds like a good idea. Though as it's a Sunday, everywhere will be shut. We try to keep to the old ways when there are no tourists. Still, at least you'll be able to get your bearings and find your way around. There's a wee map on the hall table, if you've a mind to look at it, and a couple of brochures. That'll tell you where to find everything. Then perhaps on Monday, you can really see what we have on offer. Today, though, I'll leave sandwiches down here for you as there's nowhere else open on the Sabbath at this time of year. Even the hotel bar is closed today."

Callie thanked her and after breakfast, collected her coat and wandered down the hill towards Lochaberdale.

She passed the harbour where a small fleet of fishing boats and a couple of substantial winter-covered private yachts bobbed up and down on their moorings; where the empty ferry berth seemed industrial and bereft in the misty morning light.

Callie made her way along what Marie had called *An t-Sràid*, saying that in English it simply meant 'The Street', to a line of ancient cottages that over the years had been carefully extended or adapted to house a variety of businesses.

She found a tiny bank, a post office that also doubled as a gift and stationary shop and a small supermarket which, when she peered in through the window, housed just about every tinned and packaged item that one could wish for. There was a butcher's, a baker's (*a candlestick maker's* – Callie smiled at the child's fictional rhyming thought) and a doctor's surgery to which was also attached a pharmacy. Next to this, there was a spacious double-fronted building with 'Ron's Stores' displayed ostentatiously above the door and which turned out to be a ship's chandler-cum-hiking shop as well as a draper's, selling both men's and women's clothes. She passed the café, closed and deserted with its opening times and simple menu on the door.

It started to rain: a soft, gentle precipitation that was nevertheless rather wet, but Callie decided not to allow it to deter her from her exploration. She was enjoying herself in the fresh air with no pressure of work or time constraints before she was obliged to be somewhere else.

A rare feeling.

Further along *An t-Sràid*, set back from the road and up a slight incline, there were some buildings which turned out to be a library and museum and next to this, an art gallery – all surprisingly modern, yet very much in keeping with their characterful surroundings.

Callie could see that these had been designed and constructed in such a way that they didn't detract from the overall picturesque effect of *An t-Sràid*. In fact, the gallery and library managed to achieve that rare feat of blending new with old until they merged and sat comfortably together within their wider environment.

She cupped her hands round her eyes and peered in through one of the windows of the art gallery and was surprised when an elderly man looked up from what he was doing and smiled at her before getting up to open the door.

"Come in and take shelter," he said hospitably. "You'll be wet through shortly, even though the rain is not heavy. We're not open on a Sunday at this time of year, but I had some work to finish. You're welcome to take a look round – if you want to, that is."

"Thank you. I'd like that. But only if you're sure it's alright. I wouldn't want to disturb you."

Callie loved looking at paintings; finding in their world an escape into the moment of time captured by the artist.

Her heart gave a painful lurch and tears pricked her eyes as she remembered the untroubled, blissful days she and Jamie had spent together in the art galleries in London; when she had felt free and happy; before he had had to leave, before the nightmare that had been Erik wrecked her life.

Seeing a shadow pass across her face, the man wondered about her.

"You won't disturb me," he said, appraising her briefly with professional interest as she moved round the room.

Callie could see that the paintings on display were done by a number of different local artists, each with their own distinctive style. However, there was one particular set covering most of one wall that stood head and shoulders above the rest. She sat down opposite it on the long, oval-shaped, padded seat that ran along the centre of the room: drawn to vivid, life-like portraits; absorbed by the subtle hues and delicate watercolours of countryside images; uplifted by the striking palette used to depict dramatic scenery.

Unlike the other groupings of pictures, there was no name or brief biography on the wall to indicate who this person might be but there was something about this artist's style that drew her in; something that seemed familiar.

So involved was she in her contemplation of the paintings that she didn't notice the man watching her; nor did she see him put aside the wooden picture frame upon which he had been working, exchanging it for a sketch-pad upon which he drew a rapid pencil-line portrait of her.

Callie was about to stand up and have a look at the signature on the paintings when he asked her to sit for a bit longer, which she did.

"Thank you," he said, when he had finished. "I hope you didn't mind, but I couldn't resist drawing you. You have rather engaging features."

Flattered, Callie blushed. "No one's ever said that to me before! I'm supposed to be like my grandmother who still looked beautiful even in her eighties." Her cheeks took on a brighter shade of red. "Oh, I didn't mean it to sound like that."

Amused, the man merely smiled at her without replying.

152

"I mean," said Callie, "I hope I take after her when I'm as old as that."

She bit her lip. Here she was, digging herself in even deeper. Perhaps she shouldn't have mentioned age, although the old man in the art gallery did give the impression of being rather sprightly.

She looked at him again. He didn't seem to have taken offence and was regarding her with such an open and direct expression that for a fleeting moment reminded her of Jamie.

Mentally, Callie shook herself. What on earth was the matter with her? First Edie's partner and now this man. What was going on? Could it be that subconsciously she saw Jamie in every man she came across (apart from Erik, that is, who bore no resemblance whatsoever) because of her guilty conscience?

"Would you like to see the sketch?" he said.

"Yes, please."

Callie went over to him and looked at what he had done. It was an excellent likeness. And yet there was more to it than that. Much more.

"I didn't know I looked like this."

"It's your inner self; your soul, if you like. I'm afraid I tend to do that. I always see beyond the surface. I hope you don't mind."

"Of course not. That's your gift, I would imagine. I look so sad."

He looked at her astutely before saying, gently, "Perhaps you are."

Callie's eyes filled up with tears. Hastily, she blinked them back.

"Anyway," he said, "the sketch is yours, if you wish to have it. Or I can make it into a portrait if you'd care to sit for one."

"A portrait? Really? I've never had my portrait done before." It would be something new, something different; something that wouldn't remind her of the immediate past she was trying so hard to forget. It took Callie only a moment to decide. "Yes, please. I should like you to do that. Very much."

Instinctively, she trusted him. She trusted that he would portray her with honesty, without pretence; without trying to make her into someone she was not.

For Callie instinctively knew she needed help. She needed someone else to show her exactly who she was; not tell her, but *show* her so that she could see herself absolutely. Otherwise, on her own, she would never be brave enough to face the truth.

"Good." He smiled. "How long are you here for?"

"I have no idea," replied Callie honestly. "A long time, I think."

"Splendid. I'll make some more sketches over the coming days and then in a while you can sit for me. As there's no hurry, we can take our time."

He smiled again and held out his hand. "I'm Jack, by the way," he said.

"I'm Callie Martin," she replied, shaking his hand and wondering what his surname was but not liking to ask because he hadn't offered it.

"So, Callie Martin, where are you staying? At Bannockburn?"

"Yes."

"Good. I'll ring you in a week or so, if I may. Give you the opportunity to settle in and nose your way around the island, to find your bearings."

And also, so I can see how her expression alters once she's been here for a while, thought Jack. In the meantime, he would make preparatory sketches without his subject; his visual memory still sharp, his capacity to recreate that image still intact.

"If you should change your mind, please don't hesitate to say. It might be that you would rather be a free agent without any ties while you're here."

"No, it's fine," said Callie. "It would be a real privilege. Thank you for suggesting it."

Jack gave a wry smile. "You may not thank me so much when you have a crick in your neck from sitting still for hours on end. Especially as I'm not as quick as I once was."

"I'm sure I'll be alright."

"I'll give you a ring at Marie's."

"I'll look forward to it."

Callie left the building with a lightness in her step, looking back at the gallery and wondering about her surprise encounter.

As the clouds of dust and debris gradually settled, it was revealed that the insurgents had launched a mortar attack on the outer perimeter wall, reducing a huge section of it to rubble. Jamie, as one of the first to arrive on the scene, was directed, along with half-a-dozen men, to search the immediate vicinity for any casualties and unexploded shells and bombs.

Cautiously, they fanned out, moving slowly, carefully; each step measured, each survey deliberate and thorough. Almost immediately, they were joined by the bomb disposal experts with metal detectors and after some hours of intense scrutiny, Jamie was able to report that there was no ordnance and no casualties.

Eventually, the all-clear sounded once it became apparent that the camp was not going to be subjected to subsequent rocket attacks from the air or follow-up assaults from the ground.

The Royal Engineers had already set about re-building the shattered section of wall and Camp Bastion remained on full alert for twelve hours. Jamie knew that incidents such as this were never usually isolated and the lives and safety of thousands of men and their equipment were at stake. The defence of the military base was paramount and the next day, Jamie went out on a dangerous patrol with his regiment, searching for those who had perpetrated the attack.

"Marie?"

"Dad! How are you?"

"Fine, fine."

"The children are coming over tomorrow afternoon, did Mum say?"

"Yes, and we're looking forward to it. Look, can I pick your brains? I'd like a bit of background info if you've got any to give."

"You mean on Callie?"

"Yep. So, how is your guest? As she's now been here for a while, has she revealed any deep, dark secrets to you yet?"

"No. Like I said to you a couple of days ago, she's very quiet but she seems quite content, though occasionally her eyes are a bit red. After shedding a few tears, I'd guess."

"I'm going to do her portrait."

"Yes, so Mum said. And she's delighted because she's been worried that you'd sort of stopped painting since you did the farmhouse."

Jack chuckled. "Not intentionally. It's just that it takes a lot of effort these days and it has to be a subject I find particularly intriguing."

"Well, Callie certainly has lovely features and it is all a bit mysterious as to why she's come here. But I'm not going to pry."

"I might."

Marie could hear the mischievous tone in his voice. "Well, don't scare her away. Do you need any help on the creative side?"

"Not on this occasion, but thank you, my artistic daughter, for the offer. I'll ring you up if I need you to mix my paints or wash my brushes for me."

Marie chuckled. "Okay."

"So, could you tell Callie that Grace will come and collect her tomorrow about eleven?"

"Don't overdo it," said Marie.

"Nah. You know me."

"Exactly." She smiled. "See you tomorrow, Dad."

"Yes, my dear."

Sarah decided, after much deliberation, that she was not going to wait for Erik to contact her. She was going to be the one to take the initiative rather than passively waiting for him to do so, thus placing her on the back foot. She felt more in control if she made the first move.

She had no thoughts other than a sensible friendship; a helping hand to hasten his recovery (did someone like Erik need to recover?) from Callie's abrupt departure. She had some holiday due to her so, on the first day, Sarah took a deep breath and travelled to the City.

After ascertaining that he was free, the snooty receptionist showed her into Erik's office. He looked up from his laptop as Sarah was shown into the room.

"This is a pleasant surprise," he said. "To what do I owe the pleasure?"

"I thought I would pre-empt your wish to see me again and present myself on your doorstep."

Erik regarded her with interest.

"Really?" he said smoothly. "Well, I'm glad that you did. I was on the point of contacting you."

"Really?" replied Sarah equally smoothly.

Erik smiled. "Yes, really," he said softly.

Sarah took a deep breath. "How are you, anyway?"

"I'm fine. All the better for seeing you."

"That sounds remarkably like a line from a fairy tale."

"Little Red Riding Hood, you mean?" He laughed. "Well, as long as I don't turn out to be your grandmother, I shall be quite happy."

"I'll do my best, Mr Wolf."

Erik opened his eyes wide, not quite sure how to respond. Was she being insulting or was it part of the repartee? He decided it was the latter.

"So, what brings you to my office?"

"I thought we could have lunch together," she said.

"Interesting. I'd like that. Very much."

Sarah smiled and Erik regarded her with unconcealed admiration. Against her better judgement and a rapidly beating heart, she allowed him to do so without comment.

They left the office immediately and took a taxi to the Dorchester where the waiter showed them to a private booth that Sarah had pre-booked in Erik's name.

"You did that?" He was genuinely surprised.

"Yes. I knew I wouldn't have been able to get a reservation in my name, so I said I was your P.A. And so, here we are."

Erik smiled at her, picked up her hand and kissed the palm.

At his touch, Sarah became aware of her own vulnerability.

What is it with this man, she thought, *that I can't help myself? Are his pheromones so strong that every woman to whom he pays the slightest attention loses all common sense and rolls over like some obedient dog?* She reprimanded herself sternly. *Well, if he is coming onto me, it's my own stupid fault. What did I expect asking someone like Erik van der Waals out to lunch?*

Gathering her thoughts, she said decidedly, "This is strictly friendship, Erik."

"But, of course." He smiled at her. "Yet you could not wait any longer to be in touch with me."

"Yes. No." Sarah found herself blushing. "Stop it, will you?" she said, admonishing him good-naturedly.

Erik shrugged his shoulders apologetically. "When I am free and single, I can't seem to help myself."

Sarah gave him a direct look. "That much is obvious."

"I never make a move on another woman while I am in a relationship," he said defensively.

"I'm glad to hear it. So tell me, Romeo, how many women have you wined and dined and taken back to your apartment to live in splendid, unmarried bliss?"

"This is not a question that any woman has ever asked me before."

"We're friends, remember? Therefore, I can ask you any question I like."

"Within reason."

"Possibly."

"You are sure you wish to know?"

Did she? Sarah took a deep breath. "Why not?"

Erik leaned across the table and whispered in Sarah's ear. Her cheeks grew warm at his proximity to her and her mouth dropped open in amazement at the number.

"Have you ever had yourself checked out?" she asked, stunned by his revelation.

"Of course," he said with dignity. "I go to a discreet private clinic in Harley Street. I am very careful and very clean. Every woman that I might wish to take into my bed is first 'checked out', as you so elegantly phrased it."

"What about Callie?"

"She was clear."

Sarah sat in shocked silence, her stomach tight.

"You did ask," said Erik, observing her reaction.

"Yes," replied Sarah, wishing she hadn't.

Silently, they selected their dishes from the menu and handed the large, elegant bill of fare back to the waiter.

"Do you mind if I ask you some more questions?"

"Only if you're prepared to cope with the answers and when you've finished allow me to do the same to you."

"That's fair. Will you answer my questions honestly?"

"Of course. Will you answer mine in the same way?"

"I'll try." Sarah took another deep breath. "Have you ever been in love?"

"Once. A long time ago."

"But not since then?"

"No."

"While you're in one of your 'committed' relationships, have you ever been unfaithful to that woman?"

"No, never."

"Who usually ends your relationships?"

"I do."

Sarah's heart beat faster as she found the courage to speak the words that had plagued her ever since she had first talked with Callie about Erik.

"Did you find Callie's name and mobile number on a piece of paper blowing along the pavement?"

"Yes," he replied. "I did."

CHAPTER 27

Grace collected Callie from *Bannockburn* in her ancient Morris Traveller and they drove along the steeply upwards-winding narrow road to the farmhouse where she parked the car and took Callie round to the studio.

"Thank you for agreeing to do this," said Grace. "It means a great deal to Jack, you know, to find a subject. He loves landscapes and details of the natural world but portraiture has become something of a speciality for him over the years. It's been a while since he's painted anyone."

Proud as she was of her husband's achievements, she didn't give Callie any indication of just how famous Jack was in the art world, not wishing to make their young guest feel overawed and self-conscious, as Jack had said he wanted Callie's sitting to be as natural as possible.

"Really?" she ventured, not quite knowing how to respond. "I must admit, it's a completely new experience for me. I hope I can do his request justice."

Grace smiled at the hint of bewildered modesty in her manner.

"I'm sure you'll be just fine." She pointed to the building just beyond the farmhouse. "You'll find Jack in there. I'll bring in some tea later. Do you take sugar?"

"No, just milk, please."

Callie contemplated her surroundings for a few moments after Grace had left. It was beautiful up here, even more so than Lochaberdale in many ways and that was quite something as the scenery around and beyond the harbour was stunning in itself.

Unexpectedly, from behind its grey cloak of cloud, the sun emerged, taking Callie's breath away as the vibrant colours of the land came alive within its mantle of light. She remained still, absorbed in the sudden change wrought by its radiance; knowing that just as the colours changed with the light, she herself was slowly, imperceptibly, being changed by her sojourn on the island, in small things as well the profound.

She had begun to stop worrying about her hair style and make-up. She had ceased fretting about her appearance or how much she weighed (she had no scales). As there was nowhere for her to have a manicure, she had cut her nails short and no longer bothered about using nail varnish. She thought she might even stop shaving her legs.

Following her encounter with Jack in the art gallery and wanting to experience more and travel further over the island while she was waiting for him to contact her, Callie had paid a visit to Ron's Stores, purchasing a pair of walking boots, thick socks, a small haversack and substantial waterproof leggings and jacket. The shopkeeper, who told her his name was Roland and that he was the original proprietor's grandson, threw in a woolly hat for free as she had spent so much money in one go, and was impressed by the way that she listened to his advice.

"Not many tourists do that these days," he'd said to his wife that evening. "She'll be alright, this one."

So, despite the intermittent rain, Callie had explored beyond *An t-Sràid*, which she now knew how to pronounce correctly, and discovered the Great Hall (*Talla Mòr* – which was actually quite straightforward to say) where a regular ceilidh was held each Saturday. She walked past the primary school, housed in a beautifully preserved Victorian building that she knew would have made Auntie Edie's pulse race with joy and, further on, she found a thriving boat-yard complete with a characterful boatshed where Callie had stood for a long time, observing the process of traditional boat building and repair.

She could see it had been sited carefully – near to the harbour yet far enough away from the school and village for its industry not to be intrusive; perfectly positioned so that the prevailing wind took the occasional clamour up and away over the hillside.

Callie had walked as far as the road would take her until she came to the head of a loch close to which was a thatched-roof cottage, much extended and enlarged, where chickens clucked in the farmyard and sheep foraged on the grass that surrounded the small-holding and where cows ambled down to drink at the water's edge.

A young woman, gathering in her washing as the rain began to fall, took the time to wave to Callie, calling out a cheery greeting in Gaelic which the latter couldn't understand but nevertheless responded with a hesitant, "Good morning."

After this, Callie began to spend each day in outdoor exploration, saving up the library and museum for the really inclement weather which, she was assured, would inevitably arrive. She didn't bother with television, even as the late afternoons gradually darkened.

Tired out with fresh air and exercise; her hunger satisfied by the nourishing home-made food with which she was being provided, she occupied herself by transferring and cataloguing the increasing number of photographs she was taking with her phone onto her laptop.

When the bad weather did come in all its attendant fury, Callie still eschewed the library, venturing further and further afield in her exploration of the precipitous eastern side of the island where she gave herself up to the elements: to the wind and the rain; to the spectacular, mist-shrouded cliffs where, clinging on tenaciously in the driving gale, she found sheltered places in which to hide, safe from the teeth of the wind.

Even with all these adventures, coming to the studio with Grace was her first foray across to the far shore of the island. And, as she stood in contemplation, with the beauty of Cairnmor manifesting itself all around her in even greater measure, its vistas expanded until Callie could scarcely breathe with the wonder of it all.

"Why did you keep phoning her?" asked Sarah, as something of Callie's irrational fears encroached on her mind.

"I was curious, intrigued." Erik looked at her. "At the time, it seemed to me a novel way of getting to know someone, especially as I was looking for a new relationship. When she wasn't willing to respond on the second occasion I phoned her," he shrugged, "I let it go."

"Did you know she became a bit paranoid about the whole thing? She changed her number and moved out of her flat, afraid that you were going to come after her."

"Really?"

His surprise seemed genuine and Sarah was glad.

"Did you try to find out where she worked?"

"I looked up her name on the internet, certainly, when I first found the piece of paper but as there were a couple of women with the same name living in London and even more outside the area and, as I had no idea of her profession, I did not pursue the matter further. I wasn't about to contact every Callie Martin that I came across. There were other women out there for me to find."

"How come you traced her via her friend?"

"That was pure coincidence. You know, one of those mysterious things that happens from time to time. One of my businesses is a book publishing firm. One of our authors was having legal difficulties. As I take a close personal interest in the legal side of things, I rang this author's agent to keep her informed of the situation and quite spontaneously, after my having said that I would be seeking legal representation for the client, Amy recommended Callie. So, of course, because the name was the same as that on the piece of paper, I accepted her recommendation immediately, even though I had no notion that it might be the same person." Erik looked at her and smiled. "Alright?"

Sarah nodded. "Thank you," she said, knowing that this coincided with exactly what Callie had told her.

She could see how things had happened now. Erik was not turning out to be some kind of perverted fiend after all but a reasonable, sane man and the initial irrational fears had all been in Callie's mind. She felt immensely relieved by this knowledge.

Their first course arrived.

"So, Sarah Adhabi," said Erik, "I have been frank in answering your questions, now it is your turn." He smiled at her. "How many men have you been to bed with?"

Sarah opened her eyes wide in fear at this and Erik laughed. Her heart beat quickly with embarrassment.

"None," she said, defiantly seeing his expression change to one of deepening curiosity. "I had a strict upbringing and as I had no wish to be married to the person my parents had chosen for me, I chose to have no one."

"I see." He smiled. "How old are you?"

"Twenty-four," she muttered, feeling mortified by her age and lack of sexual experience – a hindrance and source of humiliation that she had hitherto kept concealed from the outer world.

Exposed and stripped of her protective outer layer of self-assurance and objectivity by her admission, Sarah looked down at her plate to hide her naked vulnerability, afraid that someone as sophisticated and experienced as Erik would laugh at her.

However, he didn't, merely tilting her chin upwards so that she couldn't avoid his gaze.

"Don't be ashamed," he said gently, without any hint of mockery, after feeling her react to his touch, "for it is a rare and precious jewel that you have. Treasure and protect it until the right man comes along." Even as he spoke, Erik found his own heart beating faster in anticipation of where *he* could take this woman. "Promise me that, having at last revealed your secret, you will not do anything rash just so that you can say to the world, 'I have lost my virginity' as though to do so is some kind of achievement. Believe me, it is not."

Held captive within the depths of his penetrating gaze, Sarah made him that promise and as she did so, Erik lifted up her left hand and placed his lips upon her fingers.

Later, as she travelled back to Carlton and he had returned to his office, despite his words, despite his absolute and convincing sincerity, a niggling thought at the back of her mind made her doubt him and wonder if, having revealed her naïveté, he would now see her as some kind of challenge, a trophy of innocence to add to his collection of conquests.

She hoped not because she really didn't want it to be that way. She wanted him to want her because he truly cared for her, just as she knew that, from the moment she had made her promise to him, she had wanted him. Completely and utterly.

And that was definitely not what the doctor ordered.

Callie stood uncertainly in the middle of the floor of the light-filled, high-ceilinged studio; its wall of picture windows giving stunning views out over the Atlantic Ocean.

"Where do you want me to sit?" she asked hesitantly.

She had expected him to tell her what to do: how he would like her to pose; where the best light was. But he only contemplated her silently for what seemed like an eternity.

"I'd like you to make that decision," he said after a while.

"I've never been particularly good at making decisions."

"But you've been making quite a few since you arrived on the island."

That was actually true. Without her even being aware of it. And, what was more, it had seemed perfectly natural to do so.

"How do you know that?" she asked.

Jack smiled. "You're the only visitor in Lochaberdale at the moment."

"So everything I do is noticed?" And she had been so blissfully unaware.

Suddenly, she felt self-conscious, as though everyone had been watching her, staring at her.

Seeing her frown, he said, "It's alright. You don't have to be concerned by it. It's just friendly observation. We are a close community here and unobtrusively look out for each other, so it's a natural thing. Different from London." He smiled at her.

"Oh."

"Now, take your time to find a place to perch. There's no rush."

She looked around the room, filled with indecision. Where would be the best light for the artist? If she sat somewhere inconvenient, would he think that she was a complete idiot?

"The important thing is for you to feel comfortable and relaxed," said Jack. "Wander around the studio for a while if you like; get a feel for its dimensions, for its atmosphere. Get to know it. Don't worry about me. I shall still be able to work whatever you're doing, so it really doesn't matter."

Callie looked at him feeling vulnerable. He seemed to be able to read her mind.

The sadness in her eyes is going, thought Jack, *but she still doesn't know who she is*.

"Just be yourself," he said.

Affected by his words, Callie unexpectedly had to blink back the tears.

"I don't really know who I am," she blurted out.

"Then perhaps being here will help you to discover that," he suggested gently.

She wanted to look out of the window while he painted her; to see the wild ocean and watch the gulls as they wheeled and called, buffeted by the wind, free in the sky.

She moved a chair towards the light. Jack adjusted the position of his easel accordingly and as she sat there quietly, he began to paint.

CHAPTER 28

"Sarah?"

"Erik!"

"Will you have dinner with me this evening?"

Her heart started to do somersaults. "Yes, of course," she replied without hesitation.

They had been out together every day since their lunch-time question and answer session at the Dorchester – for lunch, to the theatre; eating cosy suppers in candle-lit wine bars; talking closely, getting to know each other.

After her revelation, Sarah quickly regained her outward composure and Erik seemed content to allow their relationship to evolve naturally. He had made no physical demands upon her and for this, Sarah was grateful despite her growing desire for him; a desire that conflicted with the fact that she did not wish to become just one more acquisition in his lengthy line of women. She had too much self-esteem to allow herself to fall into that sort of trap, no matter what she felt.

Or had she reached the stage when it really didn't matter anymore?

"I'll collect you about six," he said.

"Okay. But I only have one day left of my two weeks' holiday."

"I know." He paused for a moment. "I've been thinking about you."

Sarah had been thinking about him as well. All the time.

"Have you?" she said, trying to keep the joy out of her voice.

"Yes."

He sounded unexpectedly vulnerable. Or was that just part of his seduction technique?

"I've been thinking about you too," she heard herself say.

Sarah could almost feel him smile at the other end of the phone. A smile of triumph? The certainty of conquest following the subtle change he had now instigated in their relationship by declaring that she had been on his mind?

"Until six, then."

"Yes."

"Tell me about your grandparents."

After two weeks of sitting for Jack, Callie had begun to feel completely at ease.

"My grandparents?" The question caught her by surprise.

The rain lashed down outside and the wind rattled at the skylights and windows but the studio remained a warm sanctuary from the elements raging outside. Callie now felt at home within its airy spaciousness and was enjoying the process of sitting, of just 'being' while Jack created his painting.

He said she was a natural model and she had felt her confidence rise by his praise.

"Yes." He came over to her and made a slight adjustment to the angle of her head before returning to his easel.

Callie was becoming used to this now. Sometimes, he made verbal suggestions; sometimes he made the minute adjustments himself. He was professional and considerate and Callie trusted his judgement implicitly.

"Why do you want to know?"

"I'm curious because the first day we met you said you resembled your grandmother."

Callie remembered. "I did, didn't I?"

There was nothing wrong with Jack's memory then. Not for the first time did she wonder how old he was.

She thought for a moment.

"My grandparents were called Robert and Sophie and they had a wonderful rambling farm on St Nicolas that my grandmother inherited. They both loved horses and spoke fluent French and German. Granddad was going to become a teacher after the war but became involved with the farm, which he grew to love. Grandma wanted to stay, so it was an easy decision for him, as they *had* to be together."

Jack thought of himself and Grace: how, even after forty-three years of marriage, they still couldn't bear to be apart. He thought of Katherine and Alastair, her parents, who had shared the same devotion, and his chest constricted with grief for their passing but also with deep affection and gratitude for the legacy and love they had bequeathed.

He wondered how many couples these days could claim that kind of constancy.

Quickly, to hide his emotions, he rinsed his brush.

"Do you know what your grandfather did during the war?" he said, after a lengthy pause, resuming the conversation once he could trust himself to speak again.

Jack contemplated the light around Callie's eyes and made a minute alteration on the canvas.

"A little. I know that he became a P.O.W. but managed escape back to England. I don't know anything much after that except that he worked for British military intelligence alongside my great-uncle who was in the Royal Navy."

"Really? I was in the Royal Navy during the war," said Jack. "And for many years afterwards."

He added some white to his palette.

"I wonder if you ever met?"

"What was his name?"

"Richard Langley. I remember him talking about being in a destroyer and going on North Atlantic convoys before he went into the secret service."

Jack shook his head. "I don't recall ever meeting anyone of that name. The Royal Navy was an enormous organization during the war and my duties took me elsewhere. What about your grandmother? How did she spend the war years?"

"After the German occupation of the Channel Islands she was deported to Germany – to the very same camp, would you believe, where Granddad had been a P.O.W."

Jack smiled and fell silent for a moment, concentrating on his work.

"Are they still alive?"

Callie shook her head regretfully.

"Were you close to them?"

"Yes. We all were. They were wonderful people and the whole family adored them."

"How many children did they have?"

164

"Four, well five really. Two sons and two daughters. My uncles Adam and Edward; my mother, Meg, Auntie Edie, with whom I've been living in London, and my half-aunt Gabrielle, who's the eldest in the family."

"Who runs the farm now?"

"Uncle Adam and his family."

"What about your parents and your own childhood?"

"My parents are interpreters working for the EU. They're based in Brussels at the moment. The happiest times of my childhood were on St Nicolas with my grandparents."

"In what way?"

"Everything felt so safe and secure. They were always *there*. I didn't have that kind of consistency with my parents. Until they secured their jobs in Brussels, they were always going off here there and everywhere, wherever the work was. My life was unsettled and disrupted and full of the uncertainties created by the constant moving around. I had no choice but to be swept along in their wake." She shrugged. "I had no roots except on St Nicolas."

That would explain an awful lot, thought Jack.

"Do you speak any languages?"

"Not now. I learned French at school, but that was it. I was obliged to, as I mostly went to International Schools, and didn't stay long in any of those. I'm the only one in my family who isn't fluent in another language. Which used to be embarrassing because my cousins all speak either German or French, or both, fluently."

"Did you go to university?"

"Yes. My studies and my grandparents were the two great constants in my life, even though the places where I studied changed frequently."

"Why did you become a barrister?"

"Because my dad thought it would be a good career for me. So I went into it to please him. But I'm useless at it."

Just one more thing in a line of hopelessness, thought Callie.

Seeing the downward turn of her mouth and the sourness in her expression, Jack changed the subject.

"How are you finding Cairnmor?" he asked.

Callie smiled and it was as though the sun had come out from behind a dark cloud. Quickly, Jack caught the moment on canvas.

"Oh, I love it," she said. "I absolutely love it!"

They drove to a hotel overlooking the River Thames on the outskirts of London which he said served the best food of any restaurant in which he had ever been.

As it was a hotel, Sarah began to wonder what he had planned for the rest of the evening. Nervousness caused her to be quiet and withdrawn during the meal. Because of this, Erik found it increasingly hard to instigate their usual genuine and lively conversation. He had realized a long time ago that charming urbanity went nowhere with Sarah.

He kept glancing at her until eventually, after coffee was served, he said, "What's up?"

She shook her head. "Nothing."

He looked at her and smiled.

"When a woman is troubled, she will always say 'nothing'," he said gently.

"And you would know all about that, wouldn't you?" Sarah blurted out.

She saw him wince as her words struck home.

"I cannot change my past," he said quietly, "nor can I help if it bothers you."

"I know. I'm sorry. That was unfair. I don't know why I said that."

Of course she knew. She was jealous of the other women. And suddenly fearful for her own virtue, knowing she was in grave danger of giving in should he suggest they went to bed together that night.

She mustn't let it happen, though. Not tonight. It was too soon, she wasn't prepared. She would be taking a huge gamble, a real risk.

"Are you sure?" he persisted.

"No."

"What is it then?"

He took her hands in his and her eyes filled with tears.

Unable to help herself, she said, "Dammit, Erik. I've gone and fallen for you, haven't I?"

There she had done it. Made the classic mistake. Told a man that she was in love with him and someone like Erik would not hesitate to take advantage of or respond to that.

This was not how it should be happening. Not now, not tonight.

"Is that such a crime?"

She felt herself melting as he slowly kissed the palm of her hand.

"I don't want to be just another one of your conquests," she said bravely.

"What if I said that I have fallen for you?" He paused and looked directly into her eyes.

"I wouldn't believe you."

"Why not? I believe you when you say it."

"Because... because..."

"You think that this is one of the ploys I use to get a woman to go to bed with me?"

Embarrassed, Sarah nodded.

"I have never used those exact words to any woman before."

She looked up at him. "Really?"

"Really." He kissed each fingertip, not taking his eyes away from hers. "So, please believe me when I say I have fallen for you. This means that you and I are both in uncharted territory."

Sarah slowly began to trust in his sincerity. "And therefore, that makes us equals," she said, allowing relief to supersede her anxiety over the consequences of what was about to happen.

"In a manner of speaking, yes."

Erik stood up and took her by the hand, leading her to the room he had pre-booked for them and where, skilfully and painlessly, he claimed her as his own.

And Sarah, lost in her ecstasy, put all thoughts of anything else out of her mind.

CHAPTER 29

"Ben, I think there's something stuffed behind the skirting board."

"Really?" Visions of some rare document leapt into Ben's mind. "Where?"

"I was hacking out this chunk of rotten wood and could see it sticking out."

He came over to where Edie was squatting.

"We'll have to take out that bit as well," he said, pointing to the next section.

"But there's nothing wrong with it."

"Nothing that isn't getting in the way of our path to fortune."

Edie laughed. "Just because John's Art Deco jewellery box turned out to be full of nails and 'in the style of' rather than the real thing – for which he'll still make a tidy sum in his shop I might add – you two have become obsessed with discovering Samuel Lescaut's hidden treasure. I'm beginning to think that it doesn't even exist. And that we're on a wild goose-chase. And that we're wasting valuable time looking for it when we should be getting on with the renovation."

"How about we keep looking for it until the weekend and if we don't find anything by then, we'll get the chaps in to start on the electrics. Deal?"

"Deal!"

"So, I'll help you lever away this skirting board. Now, where did I leave my hammer and chisel?"

And Ben went off into the kitchen for his tool-box.

When he came back, they tugged and pulled until eventually, the flattened roll of paper slid out from the skirting board.

"What is it?" said Edie.

"I'm not sure."

Carefully, Ben unrolled the document.

"It's very old."

"Looks like a newssheet of some kind."

"Oh." Ben couldn't keep the disappointment out of his voice.

"It could still be interesting, though," said Edie. "What's the date?"

"20th July, 1837."

"Goodness! That's the year Queen Victoria came to the throne. How fascinating! But the house isn't that old."

"According to the Deeds, it was built in 1890."

"The paper's in remarkable condition, though."

"Preserved for posterity in a skirting board."

"Do you think this is Samuel Lescaut's buried treasure?"

"I've no idea. It's certainly not what one would call a conventional heirloom."

"Is there some connection to him inside the paper, I wonder?"

"Look," said Ben. "I've got to get back to the office. Why don't you take it home and have a look?" He kissed Edie on the cheek. "Where are we tonight?"

"My house."

"What if we ever forgot to ask?" he smiled.

"Then we'd spend the whole evening going round and round London looking for each other."

"I couldn't bear it if I couldn't find you."

"Nor me."

They held onto each other tightly.

"Perhaps we ought to make this house our home, then we wouldn't have to worry about where we were going to sleep. After all, it is *our* house. We did buy it together," he said.

"It is in a lovely area and the park is just opposite," observed Edie thoughtfully.

Could she leave her house? Could she leave behind all the things she had lovingly restored over the years? Could she bear to let go of its personality?

"It has a generous garden for London. Overgrown, just the way you like it." He was teasing her now and she tickled him.

"We could renovate it to suit us, even though we're sort of doing that anyway," he added.

She didn't mind now being away from her house for a couple of weeks at a time. She loved Ben's house too – its elegance, the generous green spaces outside and being able to hear the wind rustling through the leaves in the private garden square opposite. It made her spirits lift when she approached the house and also when she opened the front door and could see right through to the French windows and the garden beyond.

She loved the light airiness of it as well as the warm, cosy feeling it gave, just like Ben's house in Maybury, redolent of the people who had once lived there, who still lived there.

Edie liked the house they had just bought, but she didn't love it, not the way she loved her own house or Ben's.

He stood watching her for a while.

"Penny for them."

"I was just thinking that I like your house better than this one. Even though this is ours."

"Really? Would you consider moving there?"

"I might."

Ben was delighted but slightly sceptical. "Would you really leave your house?"

"If I knew it would be cared for, perhaps." Grief tugged at her heart. Could she actually bring herself to do that? The merest thought of leaving it for good seemed at this moment still too great for her to cope with. "Maybe. One day."

He sensed the downward inflection in her voice and knew that she wasn't quite ready to wean herself away. Perhaps she might never be, but maybe one day, their feelings for each other would be stronger than the profound attachment she held for some bricks and mortar that somehow held the key to her soul. Ben really didn't mind as he knew he could live anywhere as long as they were together.

On the other hand, as he considered the reality of it, could he leave his house that easily?

Maybe one day they would live together in their own house. One day.

Grace left a message with Marie to say that Jack had gone down with a cold and wouldn't be painting for a few days.

"He's alright, though, isn't he, Mum?" said their daughter, naturally concerned.

"Yes, he's fine, but I think he may have overdone it a bit in the last week or so, although I have to say that it's been wonderful to see him so absorbed again by his work."

"Have you seen the painting yet?"

"No. I did ask, but he says he wants it to be a surprise."

"Does he seem pleased with it?"

"Yes, I think so. In his usual quiet, secretive sort of way."

"Well, I'll let Callie know. I think all this has done her good as well."

"Really? She still seems quite remote. I wonder what happened to her to make her so sad?"

"I've no idea. She hasn't said and I haven't asked. I'm just letting Cairnmor work its magic."

Grace laughed. "It always does," she said.

Jamie could see the end in sight. He could actually count the number of days left on the calendar and know that he would be home before Easter.

Everyone due to go home was making preparations: thinking of the presents they would buy for their families, their girlfriends or wives; for their children.

The atmosphere amongst the H.C.R. contingent changed accordingly. There was the same vigilance, the same close attention to security and the task in hand but for those who would be returning to England, it somehow lightened and became more bearable.

Jamie checked his weapons, talked to his men; made sure the vehicles of which he was now in charge had been well-prepared and re-armed ready for their next patrol. He wanted to leave nothing to chance, nothing that would spoil his or his comrades' chance of going home.

Above all, he wanted to find Callie.

And find her, he would. He knew where she was working – in the high-rise, glass building in the City she had described in one of her early letters. He knew the name of the company and the address, both of which she had provided for him.

He would walk in one day and surprise her. He would sweep her off her feet and take her out to a friendly restaurant where they would start their relationship all over again.

But try as he might, Jamie couldn't feel close to her. It was as though there was a void between them; a great, yawning gap. Not just in terms of physical miles but a mental one that no amount of positive thinking and hopeful daydreams could bridge.

He put his book to one side – he hadn't read anything of it anyway – put on his flak jacket and went for a restless walk around the compound.

He'd had a letter from his dad to say that Granddad was busy painting again and Grace was worried in case he might overdo it, but that he seemed to be doing well, so far, although she hadn't seen the painting. Apparently, Grace hadn't said who or what Grandpa's subject was, just that it was good to see him take an interest again in portraiture after such a long time.

His dad went on to say that he and Edie were thinking of getting married but they had decided to wait until Jamie came home, so that he could be at their wedding.

Jamie wondered how he felt about this. For his dad to have a girlfriend was one thing; to marry someone other than his mother was a completely different ball game. He wondered what she was like. For his dad's sake, he hoped she was genuinely a nice person. But how did he really feel about having a step-mother?

If he was honest, not so good. She would be an interloper into his and his dad's private world. On the other hand, to think such a thing was ridiculous. Jamie was independent, his own man. He wasn't beholden to his father in the same way that he had been when he was a child. It would have been far, far worse had Dad decided to remarry while Jamie had still been at school or even university.

What, then, if this Edie didn't like him? Jamie smiled to himself. He decided that for his father's sake, he would get to know her and hopefully, be able to genuinely get on well with her. After all, he couldn't imagine his father choosing anyone who was unsuitable.

For the first time, he wondered what his dad would make of Callie. Not a lot, given her present unreliability, he thought. He was glad he'd kept his involvement and his hasty engagement quiet given their present lack of communication. At least he wouldn't have to put up with anyone, no matter how tactfully expressed, saying, 'I told you so'.

When he and Callie were properly established as a couple, then that would be the time to take her home and reveal to the world that this was the woman he was going to marry.

With no sitting that day, Callie wandered down *An t-Sràid*.

Seeing it was open, she went into the little library and museum. It was surprisingly spacious inside and housed a good range of books. There were one or two other people browsing the shelves and not sure whether she would be allowed to borrow a book, Callie approached the librarian, an elderly woman with silver hair.

"Hello," she said.

"Hello."

"I'm just visiting the island and I was wondering if I would be able to borrow a book."

"Are ye the lass staying up at Marie's? The girl in Jack's portrait?"

Did everyone know about her? And was that how she was known? The Girl in Jack's Portrait?

"Yes."

"Will ye still be with us for a while?"

"That's the plan, anyway."

"Well, then, that'll be fine. If ye just fill in name and address and date of birth just here."

"Home address?"

"Aye, and where ye're staying."

Callie duly completed the card, using Edie's address as well as Marie's, and the librarian issued her with six tickets.

"We do things the old way," she said. "Jack and Grace won't have the automatic machines like they have in the libraries in Glasgow and Edinburgh or even down south in England. I did suggest it, but they said it was too impersonal."

"How is it their decision?" Callie didn't quite understand.

"Och, ye don't know?"

"Know what?"

"They own the island."

"The island?" said Callie, in disbelief.

"Oh aye. They own Cairnmor."

"Really? It's privately owned?"

"Aye. A lot of Scottish islands are."

"Do you know them well?" asked Callie, wishing she hadn't said that as everyone seemed to know everyone else here.

"Jack and Grace? Aye, I know them well." She smiled. "My name's Fiona du Laurier. I'm Marie's mother-in-law."

"And?"

"Marie is their daughter. She's married to my son Paul. Did she not tell ye?"

Callie shook her head.

Fiona smiled. "She will when she's a mind to it."

"Du Laurier isn't exactly what you would call a traditional Scottish name, is it?" observed Callie.

"No. My husband, Léon, is French and came to live here in the late Sixties. We have six children," she added with pride.

"Does everyone have large families here on the island?"

Fiona laughed. "Bless you, no, but we did. The average family size is three or four."

"Large enough," observed Callie.

"Aye, but it keeps the population healthy. And without people, the island would lose its life-blood."

"I suppose so."

Callie thought of St Nicolas. It was brimming with people these days, especially now the building restrictions had been lifted. Yet the same fate hadn't befallen Cairnmor. It still seemed spacious and remote.

"Aye. We have a thriving community. Léon is keen on that."

"How so?"

"He chairs the Island Council."

"What about jobs?"

"There's enough to keep people here. Just. The boatyard is expanding now and the tourist industry continues to thrive. There's a livery stable…"

"A livery stable?" Callie's interest was sparked.

"Oh aye. We offer pony trekking during the summer season."

"I thought I'd explored most of *An t-Sràid* and up along the eastern seaboard – the accessible parts anyway. I haven't come across any stables."

"Och, it's beyond *An t-Sràid*. On David and Beth Stewart's farm. Down by the loch. Ye can't miss it – it's right by the water's edge where the road ends."

Callie remembered. The place where the woman was collecting in the washing.

"Are ye interested in horses?"

"Oh yes. My grandparents loved horses and were expert riders. They kept thoroughbreds and sold them. My grandfather used to play polo as well when he was younger and he taught me to ride."

"Well, you could pay them a visit. Granger Farm, it's called. I'll give Bethie a ring and tell her to expect you sometime."

"Thank you. That's very kind."

Callie still couldn't believe the consideration she was encountering.

"There's the Outdoor Centre as well, if you're interested. That's run by Jack and Grace's daughter Sandy. She's the wildlife ranger for the island. At the Centre, they do climbing expeditions and extended walks and offer pony trekking in conjunction with Beth and David."

"And these are only open during the season?"

"Mostly, though we do get a few keen weekender's – intrepid retired couples and so on who come for the peace and quiet as well as ornithologists who study the migrant birds that flock here each winter."

"Where do all these people stay if the hotel is closed?"

"Bless you. There's not that many. But those who do venture this far out stay with Marie and the other B&Bs dotted over the island. And some crofters take in paying guests. That helps their income from the farming or fishing. To survive on an island like this, especially in this day and age, you have to turn your hand to all sorts of different things."

"Do you?"

"Aye. Now that one of our sons and his family is working our croft, I'm free to do the bookings for the Great Hall and look after the museum and library. I have help, of course, and I don't get paid for it but it keeps me busy and I enjoy seeing people."

"What else goes on?"

"Let's see, who else does what? Mike, Marie's brother, organizes the Classic FolkArts Festival that's held every August. Cairnmor is absolutely packed then, as well as during the Cairnmor Games. Everyone puts somebody up for both of these weeks. Then there's a holiday camp site for touring caravans and tents. Oh, and Donald runs the buses for the island."

"There's a bus?"

"Oh aye. There are three. Have ye not seen them?"

Callie shook her head.

"He has two for the school run and a smaller one that circles the whole island during the day and will stop to pick people up from anywhere as long as they stand in the road and stick out their hand. He operates a regular timetable and it's a popular service. It keeps the number of cars down on the road, especially as all fuel has to be imported from the mainland. Most people have a car of some description, of course. You can't get by if you haven't these days. But they like the bus because it's a cheap and friendly way to travel."

"I had no idea that any of this went on."

Cairnmor had seemed to Callie to be a quiet, sleepy sort of place.

"Well, if ye want to know more about the island, then ye need to read the guide book. It's pretty comprehensive."

"My Auntie has an old copy from nineteen-seventy – a first edition, I think. It's what brought me here. I'd never heard of Cairnmor before that."

"Well, if it is a first edition, then she should hang onto it. They're quite rare and, like its original counterpart, *Mrs Gilgarry's Herbal Remedies*, as the two were published together, worth a great deal of money."

"Why?"

"Why? Because they have original illustrations by Jack of course."

"Jack?"

"Yes. Jack. The man who's painting your portrait. The artist Jack Rutherford, R.A. Didn't you realize who he was?" Fiona was amazed.

Callie went a deep shade of red. "No, I didn't. I had no idea. He only introduced himself as Jack, you see, and when I was at home, I only skimmed through the guide book, so I never realized."

"You have heard of him though? Surely you must have heard of him?"

Callie swallowed hard. Had she? "Well, sort of," she said diplomatically.

Fiona looked at her. "Well, you're quite young. He's very well-known amongst those in the know. He's now a Senior Academician."

"Oh." Callie bit her lip. "Is there anything about him in the library?"

Fiona laughed. "Ye'll find something. But the best place to learn all about him – unless you ask Jack himself, of course – not that he'll tell you much – is in the Art Gallery. It'll be open on Saturday."

Callie thought again. Jack Rutherford? Had she heard of him? She couldn't be sure. She must have come across his paintings if he was as famous as Fiona was suggesting. She knew that it was only eminent artists who'd had their work exhibited at the Royal Academy in London that were entitled to put 'R.A.' after their names but…?

A sudden panic set in. Jamie's surname was Rutherford.

"Is Rutherford a common Scottish name?" she asked.

"Oh, aye. It's common enough."

"Like MacDonald or Stewart or MacKellar?" Callie was anxious to know.

"As common as those. Why?"

Callie smiled, relieved. "Oh, I just wondered, that's all," she said.

"So, would you like to see the guide books?"

"Yes, please."

"I can show you all of them. We have every edition, right from the original to the present day. Grace does a new edition every two years as we usually sell out all over the island during the season and things also change. Here ye are," and Fiona led the way to one of the tables. "I'll bring all of them to ye, then ye can see the progression. When you're done with that, there's the history of Cairnmor and the Herbal Remedies book. They've been reprinted several times as well. It'll take you a while as the library copies are for reference only and ye cannae take them home."

"That's alright. I'm in no hurry." And Callie sat down and began to read.

CHAPTER 30

Sarah moved in with Erik almost immediately. He saw no point in waiting and she agreed. She didn't tell her parents exactly what she was doing, otherwise they would have been upset and humiliated by her actions. They were simple, devout people and proud of her achievements and she was unwilling to hurt them unnecessarily. She didn't lie to them about her new life but nor did she reveal the whole truth, only giving them the bare essentials – the details of her new address and saying she had found a fantastic flat in a good location at a reasonable rate. Sarah also felt strongly that at her age, she had earned the right to live her own life in the way that she chose, carefully putting aside any misgivings she may have had about the way in which this choice went against everything she had been brought up to believe.

She gave notice to Edie, who was naturally disappointed but who said generously that if Sarah ever needed a room again, then there would always be her old one waiting for her and she would be welcome to return at any time. Edie didn't ask where she was going to live nor did Sarah say, other than she had found a really nice flat near the hospital.

She thought it best and less complicated if she didn't mention Erik.

There was no need. Having made her decision, Sarah put all her doubts behind her. She was so happy and confident in her new life that she believed it would last forever. Also, having had that long conversation with Callie before she had left for Cairnmor, Sarah was primed as to what Erik might insist upon and therefore had taken the time to prepare herself and her strategy.

In the light of this, when Erik suggested that she give up nursing and come to work for him, she was adamant in her refusal – explaining that she wanted to go on helping people and to do some good in the world. When he became insistent and difficult, Sarah said she would not allow him to make love to her until he agreed and surprisingly, eventually, after giving her a chilling, dangerous look, and being thoroughly bad-tempered for a day or so, he gave in.

They argued volubly over her continuing to see her friends. Sarah maintained that she should still be able to; that she enjoyed their company; that she should have that freedom.

"Why do you need them when you have me?" he'd said. "Am I not everything to you?"

"Yes, darling," she'd replied disarmingly. "But I have other friends as well. You don't. I wasn't thinking of going off on some flippant social whirl every night. I'm not that type. Most of my friends are married and I go round to see them at their homes and have staid dinners. Why don't we meet up with them together? You and I?"

"Are you going to refuse to sleep with me if I don't say yes to this as well?" he'd asked, slightly sulkily.

Sarah laughed. "No, darling. But why not come with me? You never know, you might enjoy yourself. If you don't, then I'll think again. That's fair isn't it? But remember, I'll be able to tell if you pretend you're not having a good time."

Erik had regarded her with a straight look, to which Sarah responded by leading him into the bedroom.

So, they met occasionally with Sarah's friends and surprisingly, Erik discovered that he did enjoy himself. He found it something of a novelty to be sociable in a situation other than business lunches or while trying to entice a woman into his bed.

After that, he bowed to Sarah's wish to keep her own hairstyle and choose her own clothes. However, to keep him happy, she sought his opinion and often involved him in the process of shopping, listening to him when he made suggestions, most of which she usually adopted in the end because she felt they were *right*. Erik knew more about clothes and style than she did and seemed to have the uncanny knack of selecting items that suited her. Wisely, she accepted this, using his previous experience with other women to her advantage and praising him for his taste.

For his part, Erik found he could cope with her refusal to acquiesce to all his demands because he knew that Sarah belonged to him in a way that no other woman had ever done before, even Callie. She came without previous sexual experience or expectations; no other man had tarnished or influenced her responses by their touch and she became his creation in the place where it mattered most to him – the bedroom.

Erik shaped her to his physical desires, to his needs; he took complete possession of her body and because he knew she was in love with him, he presumed (incorrectly) that he owned her, body and soul. She was feisty in bed and out of it and he relished the way that she matched his ardour and adventurousness with an abandonment and willingness that allowed him to express himself to his heart's content.

Sarah couldn't believe that this passionate, captivating man was the same sex fiend and stifling, overbearing ogre that Callie had described. He could be difficult and autocratic, certainly; demanding, insatiable and controlling but it was nothing she couldn't handle. She wasn't afraid to stand up to him and she worked hard at their relationship, using her knowledge of psychology in guiding and helping this flawed man, with whom she knew she had fallen completely and utterly in love, into becoming a more relaxed and rational human being.

She decided she would take her time in trying to uncover the events in his life that had led to his patterns of behaviour but even more than this, Sarah knew she was also biding her time to reveal the life-changing secret she carried within her and had done so virtually ever since the beginning of their relationship.

It would not be wise to tell him too soon. To do so, might be disastrous.

"What do you do, Callie," asked Jack, "when you're not posing for decrepit artists or exploring the wilds of Cairnmor or reading up on me in the library and the art gallery?"

He had resumed his work after a week of rest; his cold gone, his energy restored.

Unfazed now by the fact that he knew everything that she was doing, she replied, "I'm a barrister."

"Successful?"

"No. Spectacularly unsuccessful."

"Is that why you're running away?"

"Who said I was running away?"

"Well, you are, aren't you?"

Callie sighed. "Yes, I suppose I am. That's not the reason though."

Jack paused with his brush in mid-air. "What is the reason?" He smiled at her gently. "You don't have to tell me if you don't want to."

She wondered if now was the right time to talk about what had happened to her, whether she was strong enough; whether she knew Jack (whom she was coming to regard as some kind of surrogate grandfather) well enough to trust him with her embarrassing mistakes.

It was odd, this sitting for a portrait, she thought. There was both an intimacy and objectivity within which she felt secure yet simultaneously vulnerable. Her very soul was laid bare before the artist, beholden to his technical skill and his interpretation of her character.

She wondered what he could see. Even she didn't know what was going on in her innermost self. Jack had not yet allowed her to look at the painting and, even after having gained an understanding of his range, she had no idea what style he might now be employing. She might emerge as some grotesque cubist vision with one eye in one corner of the painting and the other across the page. If she had any eyes at all, that is.

Callie smiled and Jack caught the moment.

Not that he's ever done anything like that, she thought. *His paintings are real, heart-breakingly real, sometimes.*

She sat in silence for a long time, thinking, contemplating; wondering whether it was right to say anything. If no one knew her past, then it would be easier for her to continue to wipe the slate clean, making a fresh start. On the other hand, she knew that what she had done still troubled her; that it still played on her conscience and there was a danger that one day she might blurt it all out at some hideously inopportune moment.

"If I do tell you," she said at length, "please promise me that you won't repeat it to anyone. I'm beginning to know what this place is like. Everyone seems to know everything about everyone else."

"Actually they don't. At least I don't, nor my family. People on Cairnmor might say what someone has been doing and make an observation about them, but generally they don't pry. However, if you don't mind, I shall tell Grace because she and I have absolutely no secrets from each other. She will respect your wish for confidentiality."

Callie watched the terns wheeling and dipping; heard the honking geese as they flew overhead; saw the ocean waves crashing silently against the shoreline way below them.

She took a deep breath.

"To put it simply, I met a special young man who asked me to marry him. I accepted. A couple of weeks later, he went off to Afghanistan and soon after he left, I allowed myself to be seduced by another man with whom I had a torrid affair and from whom I eventually ran away. To here."

Callie looked up at Jack: exposed and afraid, hastily wiping away the rogue tear that trickled down her cheek and threatened to open the floodgates of remorse that she had thought she was beginning to master.

Sympathetically, Jack looked at her and then smiled at Grace who had come into the studio with a pot of tea and some cake on a tray.

He raised his eyebrows at his wife, as though to say, "*Did you hear any of that?*"

Grace nodded. "Yes," she said. "I came in at the point at which you said you have no secrets from me."

They smiled at each other, perfectly at ease. Jack also felt a sense of relief that she had heard Callie's confession.

"Would you like some emotional assistance?"

Jack smiled again and Grace kissed his forehead.

She went over to Callie, drew up a high stool and sat beside her, still and quiet. Callie looked at her in surprise. Deep in her own emotional world, she hadn't even heard Grace come into the room. However, now that she knew she was there, Callie accepted her presence and responded to her as though it was the most natural thing in the world.

"What was he like, this man from whom you ran away?" asked Grace.

"A horrible monster," said Callie, trembling uncontrollably in her effort to contain her emotions.

"And your fiancé?"

"A wonderfully kind and considerate man. I betrayed him by being stupid."

And unable to help herself, she burst into tears.

"I'm so sorry," she gulped between sobs. "I didn't think I'd do this. I thought I was recovering."

"You've only been here a few weeks. It takes longer than that to get over something like this. There's the emotional trauma, the guilt; the feeling of having let everyone down – your fiancé, your family, your friends. Yourself."

"Oh yes." And Callie leaned towards Grace, instinctively seeking the proffered human comfort and understanding.

Jack took up his sketch-pad and began to draw – Callie, upheld by Grace, his beloved wife, his muse, whose form and character came as easily to him as his own breath: the younger woman leaning against the older one in perfect symmetry, the afternoon's golden light behind them, their heads touching. Not that he regarded Grace as being old by any means. To him, she would always be the beautiful young woman he had known all her life, with whom he had shared the very best of his life.

"Yes. It takes a long, long time," continued Grace, her stance changing minutely, knowing exactly what Jack was doing.

She had always loved being sketched by him. Instinctively, she had always known how to sit, how to stand; how to *be*. Even when she was a little girl.

"Have you written to your fiancé recently?" she asked.

"No. I stopped."

"Is he still writing to you?"

With a guilty start, Callie realized she hadn't considered this. What if he was?

"I don't know," she said uncertainly. "I suppose he might be." What if his letters were piling up on the hall table at Edie's house? "Only my friend Sarah knows I'm here."

"What about your aunt?"

"She knows I'm safe. So do my parents. They all think I'm on holiday. Which in effect, I am. But they don't know exactly where I am."

"What about the man you left?"

Callie's eyes filled with tears again. She didn't want to think about Erik.

"Was he married?"

"No."

"At least that's something positive then. And I presume you're not pregnant?"

"No. I just couldn't stay with him any longer," she blurted out. "I felt I was losing my…"

"Identity?"

"Yes." She hesitated. "I was living with him, you see. In his apartment. I tried to leave him once before but he came after me. It was dreadful, terrible."

Callie hung her head in shame and Jack and Grace exchanged a momentary expression of shock.

"Was he violent towards you? Did he hurt you physically in any way? Or force himself upon you without your consent?" asked Jack.

Callie shook her head, her eyes cast down. Then she looked at him. "No."

Realizing she spoke the truth, Jack breathed a sigh of relief. "Well, that's something, anyway."

"But you knew you had to break free," said Grace.

"Yes, before it was too late. So, I came here," she continued. "To escape. To leave this man who took over my life and rediscover who I am. Not that I've ever truly known," she added sadly.

For a moment, Grace was silent. She was not insensitive to Callie's obvious distress in what she had been through or her desire to overcome her stupidity, but somewhere at the back of her mind, she also had to fight her own disapproval of Callie's perfidiousness towards her fiancé and her apparent inability to pull herself together even after several weeks of trying.

Still, she thought, not everyone was blessed with great strength of character. It took some people a long time to be comfortable with who they were and learn to cope with life. However, Grace knew that her innate compassion was stronger than any slight prejudice she might be feeling. Besides, Callie was not the first young woman to be taken in by a powerful, overbearing man.

"Perhaps you should look at it this way," she said at length, "that, by acknowledging the need to escape and then taking the decision to finally leave, you made a brave and courageous choice."

Callie had not thought of it in that way before.

"I expect you've spent a long time berating yourself for being cowardly, a terrible person," said Grace.

"Yes," she replied, looking down at the floor. "Every minute of every day, nearly. I was so ashamed of what I'd done, of what I'd allowed myself to become. He was sexually very… demanding, you see."

178

"Well, given everything you've said, it sounds to me as though you did exactly the right thing in leaving. Did you love him?"

"No. I found him compelling, addictive, overwhelming; while the wonderfully kind young man with whom I'd fallen instantly in love went off to war, which makes it even worse."

"Do you want to see your fiancé again?"

"Yes. No. Maybe. Perhaps. I don't know." Her tears spilled over once more. Hastily, Callie wiped her eyes. "I'm not worthy of him now. I've let him down. Betrayed his trust. How can I ever face him again?"

The honesty of her guilt and transparency of her remorse was so heart-felt that Grace put her arm round Callie's shoulders and Callie clung to her and wept as though her heart would break.

"I'm so sorry," she apologized, after a while, wiping her eyes. Again.

"Don't be. To finally and completely let go is exactly the right thing to do."

And Jack smiled to himself as he continued to sketch, although, had she looked, Callie would have been surprised see that the drawing contained neither tears nor anguish but the radiance of a soul cleansed by redemptive confession within the security of trust.

CHAPTER 31

"So, Edie woman, what is in the newspaper?" said Baz. "I grateful you bring it in to show me. I curious to see it. It must be fragile."

"Fairly, though if I'm careful, it should be fine. It's all about Queen Victoria becoming queen and settling into her new home at Buckingham Palace."

"Ah, she was a great queen. I read about her in history book I get out of the library. My children laugh at me and say that I should get e-book version. But what would I do with e-book on e-reader? I like to have the weight of *real* book between my hands not some flimsy plastic oblong that has no character. I love to turn the pages, to see the whole thing, to have books in my house. I love smell and feel of a book. It is a real thing and each one has its own character just as each book has its own story to tell."

Edie was impressed. "Goodness, Baz, that's so lyrical!"

"Lyrical?"

"Eloquent, expressive."

"Ah," he said, still not quite understanding.

"But I agree, absolutely. And e-books are in danger of making real books and bookshops obsolete and if that were ever to happen it would be a real tragedy. I think there is a place for both but the internet organizations that sell them should make sure that both are promoted equally; that it shouldn't just be about profit but about culture and tradition as well."

Edie knew she was getting on her soap box, but she couldn't help herself because she felt so passionately about it.

"A world without real books or the shops that sell them would be a much poorer place," she added.

"Absolutely I agree." Baz put more coffee in the percolator. "So, what will you do with this newspaper?" he asked.

"Keep it for a rainy day, I think, much to John's disapproval, who wanted me to give it to him to sell. Or I could take it to the British Library to see if has any intrinsic value."

Baz laughed. "It is probably most valuable but much better for you to keep in case you need funds. So, what other history does it teach us?"

"Er," said Edie, scanning the pages, "Brunel's S.S. *Great Western* being launched at Bristol and the opening of the brand-new Euston Station, complete with huge stone portico and great hall. I'd love to have seen it as it was before the philistines knocked it down in the Sixties. What they built in its place is a monstrosity, a travesty without a soul."

She stopped herself before she launched into yet another rant and ended up sounding like the grumpy old women on that television programme a few years back.

"Ah, Edie, the whole modern world is lacking in soul. Except here. I find lots of soul come into my café every day."

"That's because you are here," she replied.

"Thank you, dear lady," he said expansively and quickly wiped the counter to hide his emotion.

Jamie's commanding officer asked to see him.

"Do come in, Jamie. I've some bad news, I'm afraid, with regard to our present tour of duty. We're going to be here for another three months, I'm afraid. Rather hard on everyone."

Hiding his shock and disappointment, Jamie said, magnanimously, "It's not so bad for me, sir, as a single bloke, but it's pretty tough on the guys who have families."

"I realize that. But, if all goes according to plan, no one will have to come out here at all after the withdrawal, just a few military advisors."

"True, sir. Do you think it will work, us Brits coming home and leaving the country to its own devices?"

The C.O. looked at Jamie and sighed. "I certainly hope so otherwise we've been wasting our time for the last ten years, haven't we?"

"A lot of the lads feel the same as that, sir." *Including me*, thought Jamie.

"But at the end of the day, it's better that the Afghan people should take responsibility for their own security."

"Let's hope they can withstand the insurgents and not be intimidated by the threats."

"Well, we're doing all we can to train the Afghan army to take over from us. And we're continuing to try to win the hearts and minds of the local people wherever we've been sent in Helmand Province. You've done well in that particular department, Lance-Corporal."

"Thank you, sir."

"Pass the orders on to your men, will you? Soften the blow a bit in advance of the official announcement this evening. Here's a list of those who will be required to stay and the official blurb. Pin it up somewhere prominent so the men are forewarned."

"Thank you, sir."

With a heavy heart after carrying out his orders, Jamie returned to his accommodation tent and penned a letter to his dad.

With sadness in his heart, he knew that he really would lose Callie now.

"Well, Callie," said Jack. "I think that's about it for now. Thank you," he smiled, "you really are good at this."

"At what?" she asked in amazement.

"Being an artist's model. You're a natural. You should sit for some art classes at the secondary school, if you'd like to do that. Our son is the headteacher. I could speak to him."

"I wouldn't want to do any life classes."

Callie looked up anxiously. She had no wish to pose in the nude.

Jack laughed. "No, you'll be able to keep your clothes on, I promise. I doubt that nakedness is allowed in school art these days, in any case. And more's the pity as kids will grow up without any appreciation and true acceptance of the human form.

I believe that the beauty of the human body in all its shapes and sizes should be celebrated and accepted. By everyone." He smiled again. "So, you have no need to worry, you'll be quite safe."

Callie smiled back. "Perhaps I might go and see the school."

At last, she had found something at which she was good.

"I'll let my son know."

"And thank you for asking me to do this. I've really enjoyed it." And she had. "When do I get to see the portrait?"

"When they're finished. There's two, you see."

"Two?"

"Yes. The one of you on your own and the other of you and Grace."

Callie looked at him aghast, imagining herself looking red and blotchy. "But I was crying."

"That won't be in the painting." He grinned at her. "It took on a life of its own."

"Oh."

Before visiting the school, the next day, Callie found her way to Granger Farm which was situated, as Fiona had said, at the end of the narrow road that led from Lochaberdale to the head of a loch.

She knocked at the door of the farmhouse and a man opened the door.

"Hello," she said. "I'm Callie Martin? Fiona said she would telephone you and let you know I might be coming?"

"Ah, yes. You're the visitor who rides." He smiled. "I'm David Stewart, by the way. What was it exactly that you were wanting? My wife took the call but she's out at the moment taking the children to school, so I don't know any details. I'm afraid that the new season hasn't started yet, so we're not doing any pony treks until April now, if that's what you were interested in."

"Yes, I know." Callie bit her lip. Was she being presumptuous by coming here? "I was wondering if you needed any help? Mucking out, exercising the horses?"

David smiled. "We could always do with help in that direction. I can't afford to pay you yet, though. Feeding the horses during the winter months takes most of our spare income until we're able to earn again during the season."

"Oh, I don't want money or anything. But I'd love it if I could just work with the horses."

"What experience have you had?"

"I more or less grew up with them, certainly during the school holidays. My grandparents kept thoroughbreds and they taught me how to ride."

Being around horses was something Callie *knew* she was good at.

"Okay, let's go and see what you can do. Do you have a hat or any riding gear?"

"Not with me, I'm afraid."

"Well, I'll lend you a hat and you can buy some boots and trousers from Ron's Stores in *An t-Sràid*." Quickly, he assessed her size. "Swallow should suit you to start with. She's nice and gentle and highly adaptable. I'll show you where the tack room is and you can saddle up. Then we'll go out for a ride. Okay?"

"Okay."

They trotted round the *ménage* for several turns and once David could see that she knew exactly what she was doing, they set off along the road beside the loch.

Confident and relaxed, Callie enjoyed herself and David was sufficiently impressed to offer her the unpaid job.

At the end of April, Edie made the momentous decision to move in permanently with Ben at his house in South Kensington.

After weeks of agonizing, in the end, the decision seemed an obvious one and Edie wondered why she had taken so long to arrive at it. They had finally, both of them, had enough of their peripatetic existence and knew it was time for one of them to make the move. Together, they discussed the advantages and disadvantages of both houses, as well the one they were currently renovating, and came to the conclusion that Ben's house was where they would make their permanent home.

Ben, naturally, was very happy with this suggestion. He had never lived in this house with his wife – only Jamie – therefore, it would be easy for them to make it their home.

Edie decided that she would rent out her house, fully furnished, to carefully selected tenants: people who would appreciate its worth and its unique character; tenants who would care for the interior, who would act as custodians of its unique Victoriana; tenants who also didn't mind Callie continuing to rent her room at the top of what would now be their house or keeping her things there.

After rejecting several applicants, she accepted an older couple – a professor of history and his curator wife – recently retired and looking for somewhere central that would enable them to continue with their extensive hobbies, which for him seemed to involve post-graduate lectures at King's College, London, and for her, lengthy research at the Victoria and Albert Museum and occasional consultancy work at stately homes around the country.

"There you are, Edie, you have found the perfect people to live in your beloved house," said Baz, when she went to see him the day before she was due to move. "They will love and cherish its quaintness and idiosyncrasies."

He gave her a cup of coffee, refusing payment, saying it was "on the house."

"Ah, but my beloved Halka and I will miss you now you have joined the architect in his posh palace." He sighed.

"Oh, but I shall come back. Often. How could I ever forget my friends?"

And Edie meant it. Every word.

It was harder and yet easier to leave than she thought. She packed up her books, her clothes, her ornaments, her computer and printer, her favourite mugs, cooking utensils and dinner service, her bed linen and table cloths. She boxed away her precious photographs, videos, VHS tapes, DVDs, CD and LP collections ready for the removal van. She donated her elderly television and DVD player to Baz's son but kept her video player as they were like gold-dust, John told her, and that she should hang onto it.

Edie sorted through nearly forty years of accumulated baggage, discarding or recycling an awful lot of unnecessary clutter hoarded in the attic or under the stairs in case it ever proved useful – finally throwing out the things that Trevor had left behind or other equally useless stuff from their marriage with which she had never done anything.

She allowed John to have free access to anything she didn't want to take with her or leave behind and he went away happily with sundry items that Edie knew were not of any special significance either to herself or the house but which would no doubt make several of John's clients happy and his pocket considerably heavier.

Yet, after the removal men had deposited her considerable belongings at Ben's house, to Edie, they looked strangely lost; out of place in this spacious, elegant house with its warm and comfortable atmosphere.

"They'll get used to being here," said Ben, coming home to find her sitting disconsolately in the middle of the first floor sitting room surrounded by half-unpacked boxes, the contents of which were strewn haphazardly across the floor. "Look, why don't we take some of my books out from this side of the fireplace. Then you can make that yours. In fact," he added, as a further idea struck him, "even better than that, if I take half of my books off both sides, then you can utilize the spaces, which is much more symmetrical and satisfying. Our books will be together then."

Ben went to peruse the shelves thinking that it was about time he had a good sort out anyway.

"And, I tell you what," he said, taking Edie's hand, "as you unpack your books, I'll use the same boxes to put mine in. And because the bookcases here are in the same situation as at your house," (he was careful not to use the phrase, your *old* house) "they'll have the same appearance, the same feeling."

Edie nodded, close to tears, as the enormity of what she was doing in leaving her house behind suddenly struck at her heart. "Yes, I'd like that. Very much."

So, they followed Ben's suggestion, arranging her books and his on the shelves on either side of the fireplace, placing them together until it was almost impossible to tell where Ben's ended and hers began. Over the weekend, they rearranged the house from attic to cellar (apart from Jamie's rooms in the basement), integrating Edie's possessions until it became truly theirs. And when Edie returned to Carlton to collect her last few remaining items, she was struck by how dark her old home seemed by comparison.

Yet, despite this, she still felt its protective, all-enveloping personality. Or was it, Edie wondered, her own imagination being reflected back to her – nearly forty years of her thoughts and feelings embedded into the very fabric of the walls?

How much of herself was she leaving behind? How lost and alone might she be without its atmosphere to cosset her? How much of that atmosphere would she be able to take with her to sustain her in her new life? How much would she actually need?

What if the house changed with someone else's personality? Could she bear it if it did change? She knew how the ambience had lightened after Trevor had left – or was that just her own relief at his going?

Edie could answer none of these questions but she knew that she could talk about them with Ben. Of all the people that she had ever known, he was the one who would understand, the one who felt the same as she did.

"I'm not far away," she told the house as she stood in the hallway for a long time before finally leaving. "I still own you, you are still mine. I shall always look after you."

Satisfied that her house understood, Edie closed the front door behind her and looked outwards to a new chapter in her life, bravely coping with the pain of leaving the old one behind.

At the end of April, Sarah decided to tell Erik that she was expecting a baby. She had begun to show and knew he would notice her rounding stomach sooner or later.

She realized she had been lucky to keep it from him for this long. Her morning sickness had been no more than a slight queasiness and the tiny life-form inside her seemed to have coped with their energetic sessions in the bedroom. She was fit and active, her body was supple and strong so she hadn't seen any reason why her pregnancy should curtail their activities

In the event, she prevaricated for a further fortnight, anxious as to how he might react; knowing that, like his relationship with her, this really was uncharted territory.

So she supposed. She hoped he hadn't any other offspring tucked away anywhere.

Eventually, she knew she could not keep it from him any longer and decided to tell him one evening when he came home from work.

She prepared a special supper and put it in the oven, knowing that as soon as he walked in the door, he would take her with him into the shower or the bath and then into the bedroom or whichever part of the flat took his fancy on that particular evening.

Usually, she looked forward to his homecoming, relishing the intimacy and variety of their life together. However, tonight she felt nervous. How he might react was beyond her preparation and control. Repeatedly, she told herself that she had no need to worry, either about the baby or her relationship.

Erik went pale after she told him.

"I thought you were on the Pill," he said, his voice ominously quiet.

"No, I never was," she said, suddenly feeling afraid.

"Do you mean to tell me that in all the time we've been together, you haven't been using any contraception?"

"No."

Sarah wished the floor would open up and swallow her, while Erik was so dumbfounded, he had to sit down.

"How could you do this to us? To *me*!"

"You caught me on the hop that first time we slept together. I wasn't really expecting it to happen so soon but I took a chance because I wanted you so much, just as you wanted me. And by the time I'd got myself organized, it was too late. I found I was already pregnant."

"You fell pregnant after our first time?"

"More or less."

He took a deep breath. "How far gone are you?"

"Five months."

"Five months!" His face became contorted and he banged his fist down onto the arm of the sofa. "Why in God's name didn't you tell me as soon as you found out?"

Erik knew that had she done so, he would have dropped her like a ton of bricks ending the relationship before he'd become so involved with her, before he'd begun to care for her almost as much as he'd cared for…

Quickly, he shut his mind to the girl who had once been the passionate love of his early life and who, just like his mother when he was seven, had walked out on him without explanation or a backwards glance, leaving him completely devastated and a solitary, depressive shadow for months. It had been a time of terrible withdrawal from normality for him, the grim power of this traumatizing abandonment dominating his thoughts until he could bear it no longer.

Eventually, Erik had found his way back into the world, vowing to get even with womankind in every relationship that he would ever have: to so control and dominate every aspect of a woman's life that not one of them could spring any destructive surprises on him and leave him without warning. If the woman got hurt in the process after he had asked her to leave, which he would do when he felt the urge to move on to someone else, then so be it.

However, after going from relationship to short-term relationship, he discovered an enduring passion for the company of women that he made no attempt to resist or curtail; a passion that grew as his liaisons gradually lengthened, making his jurisdiction over the successive lovers in his life more complete, his control over them more radical and profound; his ability to hurt them even greater.

"I didn't want to cramp your style," said Sarah, wondering what he was thinking. "Besides, I felt so secure in our relationship that it didn't seem to matter."

"Didn't matter!" He stood up and began to pace around the room. "Of course it matters! How could it not matter to discuss every aspect of our relationship? How could not telling me about a baby not *matter*?" He glared at her, his mind still set on how the whole disaster had come about, trying to stop old vulnerabilities from surfacing. "This is all your fault. With you being in the medical profession and knowledgeable about anatomy, I had assumed you were already using some form of birth control before we went to bed together."

"Well, while we're apportioning blame," retorted Sarah, "for your part, you didn't bother to check up that I was on the Pill before we spent our first night together, did you? With your track record, you of all people should have known better." She felt her own anger rising. "I sincerely hope you haven't always been so negligent."

"I've always been as meticulous about that as all the other things," said Erik defensively, realizing that what she had said was true, remembering that he had been so keen to get the virginal Sarah into bed, that he hadn't given it a thought.

"I'm glad to hear it. In any case, why should contraception be just a matter for the woman?"

"Because the Pill gives me the most freedom and the most security."

"But it isn't fool-proof."

He couldn't answer that.

"When I've had *our* baby," she said pointedly, "then I'll go on the Pill. Alright?" She was challenging him, pushing him.

"It's too late."

"Too late for what?" For a brief moment, Sarah experienced a sense of panic.

"Just... just too late. I do not want to have children."

"Why not?"

Erik looked thunderously at Sarah, as memories of his lost love surfaced.

She had left him, hadn't she? He'd wanted marriage and children with *her* more than anything and by leaving, *she*'d taken away all his joyful possibilities. So, he had resolved never to have any children with anyone.

Ever.

"They ruin everything," he said lamely, unable to express the buried truth. "Curtail my freedom, wreck my sex life. I've seen it at the office. Men who come into work looking haggard and drawn after being up all night with their children; complaining that they never have sex any more with their wives or girlfriends because they're too tired or too frazzled or just not interested. The women are so wrapped up in the new little life that the men feel like outcasts."

Sarah's gathering fear dissipated and she threw back her head and laughed.

Erik looked aggrieved. "What's so funny?"

"You are, my darling." Sarah smiled and ran her hand over his body which leapt into life at her touch. "Has it made the slightest bit of difference so far?"

Erik closed his eyes in ecstasy. "No-o," he managed to say.

"I can assure you here and now that it won't. I shall not allow our offspring to interfere with our sex life, apart from the obvious consideration of our privacy. I shall also make sure that you will be the one male in all of fatherdom who will not go into the office looking haggard and drawn because you feel deprived or neglected."

"I hope so," he said quietly, moving carefully on top of her.

Afterwards, when Sarah had fallen asleep, Erik lay awake beside her contemplating the difficult and surprisingly heart-rending decision he would have to make.

And it would have to be soon. Before he became any more involved than he already was.

At the end of April, in reply to a long-standing invitation from the Royal Academy to display some of his work at the annual summer exhibition, Jack decided to accept their offer this time and chose the two paintings he wished to display: *The Girl in Jack's Portrait* (as the painting had become known colloquially by those who came to view it in the Cairnmor gallery and which had subsequently been adopted as its official title) together with its smaller companion piece, *The Girl and Jack's Muse*.

As a Senior Academician, he was entitled to exhibit six paintings altogether so Grace persuaded him to offer four more, none of which would be for sale, and in lieu of this Jack would make his usual donation to sponsor the next generation of up and coming artists who normally benefited from any paintings sold at the Academy summer exhibition.

That particular year also would see, in the general exhibition, a series of paintings by nonagenarian artists.

"In which case," Grace had told him, "you've got to show you're still around and working."

Jack had sold many, many paintings over the years but because they rarely came back onto the commercial market, they were all the more prized and sought after by collectors and aficionados of his work, and commanded high prices at prestigious auction houses in the United Kingdom and abroad.

Through her reading at the library and at the art gallery, Callie had begun to realize just how well-known Jack was and how inextricably his fame was linked to Cairnmor itself.

So, she continued to study the island itself, working her way chronologically through the entire selection of guide books, tracing the gradual changes made over time; gaining insight into the archipelago's unique character.

She read the history books too, about the ancient settlements and wild landscapes that were first tamed by the Vikings and the Celts and ruled by the Clans. She came to understand the resilient character of Mrs Gilgarry and others like her: how they lived and worked, how they survived in a remote and often hostile environment.

She learned about crofting and fishing; the clearances and forced emigration; she learned about the cultivation of a rugged and fertile landscape by a tenacious community that refused to be exiled from the land of their forebears; she read with especial interest about the historic House of Lords Appeal in 1937 that preserved for all time the islander's right to live as they chose.

Steadily, Callie read all the books until she knew just about everything there was to know about Cairnmor; about the inestimable legacy of Katherine and Alastair Stewart; how the money from the former's inheritance and the sale of Mathieson's Shipyard on the Clyde funded the cottage hospital and the secondary school; how, together, they worked and planned for future generations, enabling Cairnmor to become the thriving island community it was today; how that task was continued by their daughter Grace, her husband Jack and their family.

And by reading about them, these people whom she had never met became as real to Callie as anyone she knew. Katherine and Alastair seemed to reach out, to speak to her across the generations and she could do nothing but carry their personalities with her in her imagination.

She talked to Jack about them – when the weather was fine, taking short strolls with him along the beach near the studio or, when it was not, sitting in the gallery snug and warm while the wind howled around outside and great spumes of white water flung themselves over the harbour wall. She listened with wrapped fascination to the stories he told, drawing ever closer to both Jack and Grace who always accompanied him and sat quietly with her tapestry, pausing to look up at her beloved husband while he spoke, adding her own reminiscences to his words.

By the end of April, Callie had integrated herself fully into island life. She sat for art classes at the school, took her turn in the library and art gallery and worked at the stables.

With the improvement in the weather and the increased daylight, Callie took the horses further afield for their exercise: roaming across the flat, fertile grassy plain of the machair, galloping across the white-gold sands or carefully picking her way along the treacherous, narrow track that led to Mrs Gilgarry's cottage, which she discovered had been left exactly as it always was – a testament to the old lady and a way of life long since gone but which still resonated with the crofting present.

Filled with an inexpressible energy and sense of renewal, Callie experienced a profound release in her new life. Here, it didn't matter anymore what she had been: her uselessness, her mistakes and her weakness.

It was who she was now that mattered the most and with this knowledge came the beginning of an inner confidence and independence of mind that she had never before experienced.

At the beginning of May, Jamie began to cross off the days on his calendar until the time when he would be coming home.

His father wrote in his latest letter that he and Edie were now living together permanently in Cornwallis Gardens and he hoped that Jamie wouldn't mind. When he came home on leave, his rooms in the basement would still be there waiting for him and he would always have his own space. He added that Edie's children were grown up, two of them with families of their own and one who was single. They had mostly been pleased for their mother, he said, but had yet to express a desire to meet him and had so far avoided making any direct contact.

Ben said he knew that Jamie would behave better than that.

Of course I shall, Dad, thought Jamie and tactfully said as much in his reply.

He wanted to meet Edie. His father had said so much about her; was obviously happy and content and if his dad felt that way, then who was Jamie to spoil his peace of mind by being churlish? Besides, Jamie felt no resentment of the unknown Edie. He genuinely wanted to like her for herself but especially for his dad's sake, who had supported him through everything and who Jamie counted as one of the most influential people in his life as well as his best friend.

No, he would never let his dad down. He would always strive never to disappoint him. His dad deserved all the happiness that he could get.

At the beginning of May, John paid a visit to Ben's office, only to find him not there.

He chatted for a while to Ben's well-endowed secretary and then stayed on to chat some more over a cup of tea, with Judith chatting back happily. They were still talking away when Ben returned, so absorbed they didn't see him arrive.

At the conclusion of his business with Ben, John came out of his office and immediately asked Judith out on a date. As it was a Wednesday, she accepted.

They met at a restaurant in the West End and spent the whole of the evening chatting away. They didn't stop talking during their date the following weekend nor the Wednesday after that either. They continued to talk when Judith invited John to meet her children and they talked when they all went out to the park together, after which, John treated them all to burger and chips in a fast-food restaurant.

The next weekend, he brought his children with him to Judith's house and the four offspring, after an initial wariness and teenage dragging of sulky feet, gradually began to find a great deal in common.

"Video games and pop music are good talking points," remarked John, sitting with his arm round Judith on the settee, while from above came the sound of laughter and intermittent thumps and bangs and snatches of loud music.

He looked at her ample curves and began to kiss her.

Up to that moment, their courtship had been completely circumspect. Judith had been badly burned by her encounter with Ben and had forsaken her hitherto somewhat promiscuous life-style. John just hadn't met anyone that he fancied enough to take to bed with him for a long time.

He fancied Judith, though, and said so the following Wednesday and again the Sunday after that.

"Your place or mine?" she said, eventually. She fancied him too.

"Yours?" he ventured, thinking of the messy clutter in his bedroom.

"Mine it is, then," she said.

And hers it was. Every Wednesday and alternate weekends.

CHAPTER 32

Jamie was home. At last.

He had completed his final tour of duty in Afghanistan without major incident or mishap – apart from the usual skirmishes and the constant, exhausting need for vigilance while out on patrol. If he was absolutely honest, he'd had enough of the sand and dust and of being away from home.

He knew he was lucky. Despite witnessing some horrific incidents, which he was still trying to put out of his mind, he had survived more or less without the physical or mental scars that afflicted so many of his comrades after being in Afghanistan.

He had nightmares, of course, but accepted these as part and parcel of what had happened to him while operating in a war zone. Millions of men in the armed forces had been through conflict and coped. Thousands hadn't, but Jamie knew that unless things changed drastically, he was one of the fortunate ones who would manage to cope.

Besides, he had six weeks leave – six weeks in which to find Callie and hopefully re-establish their relationship. That would give him focus and take his mind off the strangeness and sense of euphoric disbelief at being back in England.

Afghanistan had been his reality for the past eight months; he had made the adjustment to being there and he knew he would have to make a similar one to being at home. He was also keenly aware that it would take him a while to settle and even longer to decide upon his future.

So, when he arrived at Cornwallis Gardens, Jamie was relieved to find that the deep familiarity of the house was unchanged; that it possessed the same welcoming atmosphere he had always treasured, the same feeling of 'home' that he had experienced as a soon as he and his dad had moved in after his mother had died and the house became available.

"It's a fresh start, son," his dad had said. "For both of us."

And it had been. Jamie had loved it from the first moment they'd stepped over the threshold and now, as he moved through the interior drinking in the blessèd unreality of being at home, he began to notice subtle changes.

The furniture was arranged differently; there were new easy chairs and unfamiliar books on the shelves in the sitting room. The kitchen had acquired additional culinary items; the dining room had table lamps, as well as occasional tables and chairs that he didn't recognize; even the garden had additional plants in it – the actuality, he supposed of his father living with someone else. However, he found none of the changes distasteful or jarring, nor did they detract from the ambience of the house. In fact, he had to admit, they enhanced its homeliness and, if such a thing were possible, the house felt 'content' in a way that it hadn't done before, or not that he'd noticed, certainly.

Jamie took his kit downstairs, confident he would find his basement flat unchanged. He went from room to room, relieved and delighted to be back in his own space, grateful that his father and Edie respected his world and would not alter anything without his permission.

But, he thought briskly, enough of wandering around the house. Knowing he wanted to find Callie as quickly as possible now that he was home, he quickly showered and changed out of his uniform before leaving the house and travelling to his father's office.

"Jamie!" exclaimed Judith as he walked in through the door.

"Hi Judith."

At least he assumed it was Judith – he'd remembered his father's P.A. as being a rather brassy, peroxide blonde – this version had dyed her hair a more natural colour and her clothes were less blatant, both of which suited her.

"Your dad's not here at the moment. We were expecting you tomorrow," she said, smiling at him.

"I know. I'm a day early."

"He'll be so glad to see you!"

"Where is he?"

"Oh, he, John and Edie have gone to an auction. They're hoping to buy another house. That'll bring their property portfolio to three now."

Property portfolio? His dad hadn't mentioned anything like that in his letters. And who was John?

"When will they be back? And who's John?"

"I've no idea what time. It depends on when their particular lot comes up in the auction room. John, by the way," she said proudly, "is my boyfriend."

"Oh. Right."

Jamie didn't want to hang around and chat idly. He needed to get on and find Callie. He'd catch up with his dad later after he'd finished work.

First he travelled to her house in Carlton. If her aunt was in, then she'd be able to tell him where she was and that would make his life simple.

With mounting anticipation tinged with trepidation, Jamie rang the doorbell.

An elderly lady with silver-grey hair answered the door.

"Yes?" she said.

"Would it be possible to speak to Callie?" he asked, assuming this was her aunt.

"Callie?" The woman looked puzzled for a moment.

Didn't she know her own niece? thought Jamie.

Then her expression cleared. "Oh Callie! Yes, of course."

Jamie's heart skipped several beats as he expected to be ushered into the hallway and to see Callie running down the stairs after her aunt had called her.

"I'm afraid she's not here at the moment."

His spirits plummeted. Was nobody in? Had everyone that he wanted to see disappeared off the face of the earth?

"Do you know when she'll be back?"

"I have no idea. You see, she's supposed to rent the room upstairs but we haven't ever met her."

"Never met her? But I thought…"

"We're only tenants, I'm afraid," she said, with an apologetic smile.

"Tenants?"

"Yes."

Where was Callie's aunt?

"Would Callie's aunt know where she is?"

"I'm afraid I have no idea."

"Could you tell me where I could get in touch with her aunt?"

The woman hesitated. "Does she know you?"

"No, we've never actually met."

"Then I'm afraid I can't. She's rather protective of her privacy."

Stymied, for a moment, Jamie didn't know what to do.

"Look, have you got something I could write on? If I give you my contact details, please could you give that to Callie's aunt and ask her to contact me? It is really rather important."

"Of course. Please wait here a moment."

She returned almost immediately and handed Jamie a piece of paper and a pencil.

He wrote down his name and mobile number. "Please do give this to her aunt. It's so important," he reiterated.

"Of course, my dear," said the woman affably, who after Jamie had gone, put it on the hall table, alongside the piles of letters and advertising literature dumped with increasing regularity through the letterbox, and promptly forgot about it.

Jamie went down the steps into the street where he dialled Callie's number for the umpteenth time since arriving back in the country but heard only the annoying tones of the voice stating that this number was no longer available. Again.

There was no point in trying to leave messages.

Needing a coffee and some lunch, he found a café just around the corner and went inside. Perhaps someone there might know where Callie was. If they didn't, he'd go across to where she worked.

He was bound to find her there.

Edie, Ben and John sat in the auction room. The atmosphere was tense.

A rival property developer, who they knew specialized in complete (destructive) renovations, was bidding against them. The price kept going up and up.

"We're going to reach our limit soon," muttered John under his breath.

He really wanted this house. He had his eye on it for himself and Judith one day. It was close to the Emporium and near enough to Ben's office for Judith's commute not to be too arduous. It was far, far better than her tiny flat and his pokey rooms above the shop.

"Best not to go over the figure we agreed," cautioned Ben.

"Has this guy got bottomless pockets?" said John in frustration, as his bids were matched and raised.

He put his hand up. And again.

"Must have," replied Edie.

Another five-hundred. John was over their limit. In desperation, he raised his hand and made one more bid.

Their rival shook his head.

"Yes!" said John in triumph as the hammer came down on the podium.

"Well done, sir," said the auctioneer, "You really wanted that one, didn't you?"

John nodded and held up his number.

The three of them left the auction room, completed the formalities outside and after collecting the keys from the estate agent, went straight to their new purchase.

"Needs a lot of work," observed John.

"Well, we knew that right from the beginning when we first came to view the property," said Edie.

"It's a bit dark and damp," said Ben.

"Only at the moment and I'm sure that you and your trusty building team will work your usual magic," John replied.

"We'll certainly try our best," said Edie.

"I'd quite like to live here one day. With Judith."

Edie smiled. "Really?"

"Does Judith know that yet?" asked Ben. "Let alone the fact that you've bought her a house?"

John shook his head. "No, not yet. I want it to be a surprise when it's all finished."

"What happens if it's not to her taste?"

Supposing Judith was the open-plan type? thought Edie. She wouldn't be too happy with Victorian interiors and smaller rooms.

"Well, I'll talk her round. She'll love it once she's seen it."

Edie and Ben exchanged a quick glance.

"I hope you're right," she said.

While they were in the vicinity, they called in to see Baz and to tell him of their success.

"It is nice house, that one," he said. "Though very dirty and dingy."

"We'll soon brighten it up," said John. "Besides, the garden's south-facing so it'll have lots of light during the day."

Baz gave them their coffees.

"I been thinking," he said. "I have spare money put aside for a rainy day. It does nothing in the bank and I have no wish to line greedy banker's pockets further. My tax money already bail them out when the government give them a helping hand and I have no wish to give them another penny. I wish to keep my money for myself, for my family." He leant across the counter meaningfully. "I wish to come in with you. Form, how you say?" He thought for a moment. "A syndicate!"

Edie smiled at him. "It takes a lot of courage to do that."

"Courage is not a problem for me. I leave the country of my birth and start new life with my family in England. I have courage."

"You do indeed," said Edie.

"There are risks involved," said Ben.

"Ah, but I shall turn to you, my friends, for guidance and advice. I will not do anything without consulting you first. But if we work together, then I shall be safe."

It was an awesome responsibility if they were to agree, thought Ben. "We can't always be sure that things will work out smoothly. No matter how careful one is, things can always go wrong. A house can easily throw up a few expensive surprises."

"It can also turn up healthy profit, as well," said Baz, passing them their coffees, "so one can make a decent living and provide for the family and have pension in old age."

"And making a profit is the name of the game, my friends, isn't it?" observed John, viewing his long-standing acquaintance in a new light.

"Up to a point, and then only to be able to finance the renovations or the next purchase," said Edie, anxious that the motivation behind their purchases remained pure and unmaterialistic.

They stayed for a while discussing the new house until they'd finished their drinks and after Baz had finished serving a new batch of customers, they came over to the counter to say goodbye.

"Oh yes," he said. "I nearly forget! My Halka say there was a rather handsome young man in here earlier looking for your niece, Edie. Said he was her fiancé."

"Goodness me!" Edie exchanged a look of consternation with Ben. They were all too aware of Callie's misdemeanours. When this poor chap, whoever he was, finally caught up with her errant niece, he was in for a real shock. "Did he leave his name or a contact number?"

"No."

"Did Halka give him my name and telephone number?"

"No. She said as she didn't know him, he could have been anybody, a Rat, even. We both respect your privacy."

Edie smiled. "I appreciate that, Baz, and thank you. Well, even if you had given him my details, I wouldn't have been able to tell him where she is anyway, as I have no idea. I had another email from her a few weeks ago, so I know she's alright, but I still worry about her. So does her mother; she's only had a few emails as well. I hope he wasn't too disappointed," said Edie.

"Apparently, he just shrugged his shoulders and thanked my Halka for the coffee. Said it was the best coffee he'd ever tasted," he added proudly.

Ben smiled at their friend. "Well, this young man obviously has good taste." *In coffee*, he thought, *but not in girlfriends*. "Perhaps he'll come back for another one sometime and we'll find out who this mysterious fiancé is."

"Don't forget my proposal," called out Baz as they left the café.

"No, we won't," said Edie.

"Would you like to come?" asked Marie. "We're having a bit of a party on Saturday up at the farmhouse to celebrate my Dad's birthday. He'll be ninety-two."

So that's how old he is, thought Callie. "Are you sure I wouldn't be intruding?"

"Not at all. Mum feels a bit guilty, I think, that she has never invited you into the house, especially as you spent all that time sitting for Dad's portrait."

"I didn't give that a thought, actually. I didn't do much and besides, I hardly knew anyone back then. I mean I just sat there. And I did so willingly. It was Jack who did the hard work."

"Aye, but he said you were the perfect model and the portrait wouldn't have been as good without that being so."

"Well, that's nice of him and yes, I'd love to come. If you're sure I wouldn't be intruding."

"Of course not. Jack would want you to be there. And although it's just a family 'do', there'll be so many of us that you'll be able to blend in with the crowd just fine." Marie smiled. "Even I find it hard to keep up sometimes!"

Later, Callie wandered along *An t-Sràid* wondering what she could purchase for Jack as a present. What did one buy a ninety-two-year-old man who owned an island and was a wonderful artist?

She was by now fully conversant with his artistic style and background, after both reading up on him and having gone on a trip with Jack and Grace to Glasgow a few weeks previously, where they had paid a visit to the Kelvingrove Art Gallery, the city's most famous and prestigious gallery, to discuss with the curators a possible retrospective of Jack's work. It would bring together his best-loved paintings and original illustrations gathered from private collectors and galleries around the world, as well as from his own personal collection.

News that two major new Jack Rutherford portraits were to be hung at the Royal Academy in the summer had become a serious talking point in the art world and Scotland was first to claim the privilege of a retrospective. As Callie was the subject of both paintings, not forgetting Grace, she had accompanied them on the trip. She had felt both shy and honoured, but by remaining quietly in the background, had truly enjoyed every moment.

With a wifi connection readily available, Callie had emailed her mother and aunt again and sent a text to Sarah, who responded a few hours later but only to say she was glad that all was well and it was good to hear from her. Callie was puzzled by its brevity and the fact that Sarah had given none of her own news, sensing, with her new-found awareness, a reticence on the part of her friend to do so. Or maybe it was merely her own imagination? She wondered if there was something that Sarah didn't want her to know about or maybe it was just that Sarah didn't want to continue their friendship, which after all, had been quite brief.

Like Jamie's.

Resolutely, Callie stopped her thoughts from going down that particular path.

Searching for Jack's present, she looked in the post office without success before going to the museum gift shop, but that was no good either. If only she was in London, she thought, or had the internet. She'd find something online without any trouble at all.

She wandered into Ron's Stores and rummaged through various things.

"Can I help?" said Roland. "Oh, it's you! The Girl in Jack's Portrait. Sorry, I mean, Callie. It's how you've become known, you see, in Lochaberdale."

Callie smiled. "I don't mind. In fact, I take it as a compliment."

"And so you should. Especially as yere portrait is going to be displayed in London and now Glasgow as well, we hear. So, what can I do for ye today?"

"It's Jack's birthday on Saturday and I need to buy him a present. I have no idea what he'd like."

"Why don't you ask Grace or Marie?"

Callie blushed. "I'm too embarrassed and besides, I wanted to find something for myself."

"But ye'll ask me," teased Roland.

"You don't count," retorted Callie.

"Thanks."

They smiled at each other.

"Well, my wife always gives me socks but that's probably not what ye had in mind."

Callie shook her head.

"How about a tie? Jack's rather partial to ties or cravats. It's his Royal Navy background, I reckon. You never see him out and about unless he's properly dressed."

"Okay, so what have you got?"

Roland brought out a large selection. "Some of these go back to the nineteen-sixties and seventies, I reckon."

"They're a bit outdated," said Callie.

"Oh," he said morosely, fingering his stock with nostalgic fondness. "I ought to get rid of them in that case. No one'll buy them."

Seeing his crestfallen expression, Callie said, "Don't do that! Lots of people like retro things and I bet if you displayed these to the tourists, they'd snap them up. You could market them as being indigenous to Cairnmor, or something."

"Do ye think so?"

"Definitely."

"I hadn't thought of doing that." His expression brightened.

"I'm going to take this one," said Callie, selecting a rather lovely tie that reflected the subtle shades and colours of some of Jack's landscapes. "This is perfect." It was the sort of thing that she could see him wearing.

And it was just the sort of thing that Callie would have chosen for her own grandfather, although the colours would have been different as Robert's eyes had been brown whereas Jack's were blue.

Very blue. Just like Jamie's.

Not for the first time did a flicker of familiarity chime within the recesses of her mind; not for the first time did she sense some kind of resonance. After all, she'd had plenty of opportunity to study Jack while he had been making a study of her.

But then, lots of people had blue eyes, didn't they? Just as lots of people in Scotland had the surname Rutherford.

She tried to remember what Erik's eyes had been like but their precise colour, like his face, were blurred and faded around the edges whereas the image of Jamie, the longer she was on Cairnmor, was inexplicably sharpening into focus.

And that only served to increase her guilt.

CHAPTER 33

Sarah was insistent that Erik accompany her when she went to ante-natal classes and to the hospital for her scans.

Reluctantly, he had agreed, delaying the inevitable moment when he knew he would have to end their relationship. He needed to be in charge of his life and those around him. Once a baby arrived, he would have no control; in fact, a child would dominate everything and he would lose his freedom.

Above all else, Erik prized his freedom. It was his protection from emotional pain.

He would support the baby, of course, making sure that Sarah and the child would never want for anything financially or materially. However, he had no wish to have any contact with the infant after it was born (even though it would be part of him) and the relationship with its mother had ended.

Yet, it was with this that he had an enormous problem. He cared for Sarah. He hated to admit it. Somehow, she had managed to break through the protecting wall he had built around himself after *she... they...* had left him.

True, he found Sarah demanding and difficult at times but at the same time he admired her fiery spirit. Especially in the bedroom. Overcoming the challenges with which she presented him in their domestic life meant that their time together was never dull or mundane but always held that edge of excitement and danger his damaged soul craved.

Often, though, he would think of Callie, remembering her complete and absolute acquiescence to him, her total surrender. There were moments when he thought he had found in Callie his replacement woman for *her...* the one he had lost so long ago; the one who, like his mother before, had abandoned him, leaving him with a drunken and disillusioned father.

He should never have allowed Callie to escape so easily. He should have pursued her again after she had left him for the second time. Sometimes he even wished that Sarah was Callie, then he could have the chance to hurt her the way *she* had hurt him by leaving.

On the other hand, perhaps he didn't want that in his relationship with Sarah. Sarah didn't make him think of revenge. She was different; a balm for his troubled spirit. She seemed to understand him, to soothe him.

Callie, for all her submissiveness, had come to him with a previous track record whereas because of her innocence, he had been able to mould Sarah completely to his tastes and desires. Besides, physically, she was the most supple of any woman he'd ever known.

As he pictured Sarah in his mind and visually covered everything he had planned for them to do when he reached home, he became so alive with desire and longing that it was an enormous effort to drag his attention back to the contract of which he was supposed to be giving approval.

The intercom buzzed and he jumped.

"There's a man out here wanting to speak to Callie, Mr van der Waals. What shall I tell him?" said his P.A.

Someone to speak to Callie? Funny that he should have been thinking about her only a moment or two ago.

"Show him up here, please," said Erik, intrigued.

"You have the revue meeting at two o'clock."

"I haven't forgotten. I've a few minutes yet."

He stood up as Jamie came into the office and extended his hand towards his visitor.

"Hello, my name is Erik van der Waals."

"I'm Jamie Rutherford."

"Please do sit down. Would you like a coffee?"

"No, thank you. I've only just had one."

"Do you mind if I do?"

"No, by all means, go ahead."

"Now, what brings you here?" he said, as he sat down, placing the cup and saucer carefully on his desk.

"I'd like to speak to Callie Martin, if I may. She's one of your employees?"

Erik regarded him for a moment. "Why have you come here to see her and not contacted her outside of the workplace?"

"I've been trying but she appears to be..." he searched for the right words "...somewhat elusive at the moment."

"So you thought you'd find her here?"

"Yes."

"I see. When you do find her, will she want to see you, do you think?"

"I certainly hope so."

"Why?"

"Because I'm her fiancé."

"Her fiancé!" exclaimed Erik, caught by surprise. "I had no idea she was engaged. She never said. How long?"

"Ten months."

"Ten months!"

He looked sharply at Jamie.

Callie – engaged to someone else all the time he was making love to her. He smiled. That had been *his* triumph, then. Not that he usually went in for that sort of thing. If a woman was already engaged or married, he didn't usually pursue her, unless she was particularly irresistible and her previous relationship was coming to an end.

"Have you seen her recently?"

"No. I've been in Afghanistan. I'm in the army."

"And you're on leave now?"

"Yes."

"Well, Mr Rutherford, I hate to disappoint you, but I'm afraid she no longer works for me."

Jamie was taken aback. He had been so sure that he would find her here.

"When did she leave?" he asked.

"About six months ago."

"Six months!"

"You seem surprised."

"I am."

He tried to remember how long ago it was that Callie had stopped writing to him, but couldn't. He'd have to look at her last letter again.

"Did she not say she was leaving my employ or where she was going?" asked Erik, deciding that he would not reveal that Callie had been spectacularly unfaithful to this young man; that he, Erik, had enjoyed a passionate and no-holds-barred relationship with the missing fiancée.

And, thought Erik, *when this man does eventually find out, as he inevitably will because Callie will be moved to confess everything, then he'll probably end their relationship. And Callie will be distraught.*

And that, from his perspective, would be revenge enough, wouldn't it, for Callie having walked out on him?

Erik wondered how he and the fiancé compared in bed. He looked Jamie up and down and decided there was no contest.

Something about Erik van der Waal's manner – an underlying projection of superiority, a gut feeling that this man knew far more than he was letting on – made Jamie wary.

"How long did she work here?" he asked.

"A while," replied Erik evasively. He smiled again. "She was an excellent employee." *In every sense of the word*, he thought. *Until she left.*

For some obscure reason, Jamie wanted to punch him on the nose. He kept his clenched fist hidden under the table.

"Do you have any idea where she might be now?"

"I'm afraid not." He looked at Jamie intently, as a sudden idea struck him. "However, she may have gone to St Nicolas. After all, she more or less grew up there, and where better than to hide away than in your home environment?"

Why didn't that occur to me before? thought Erik. *Dammit, I should have gone there after her.*

Jamie spotted the older man's momentary annoyance and wondered what had prompted it. However, whatever the cause, Erik van der Waals had given him something of a lead. St Nicolas was a very good option. If Callie wasn't in London, then she was most likely in the place where she had spent much of her childhood. It would, as Erik had just said, be a good place in which to hide away.

But why should Callie feel the need to hide? Who was she hiding from or what? Himself? Her former employer? And if so, why?

What on earth had been going on?

If Callie was not working here anymore, Jamie saw no point in prolonging this uncomfortable encounter, so he thanked Erik for his time and went on his way.

Much as he wanted to see his dad and meet Edie, Jamie knew he had to act immediately and decisively in order to sort things out as soon as possible. Then at least, whatever had happened, he would know where he stood.

On reaching Cornwallis Gardens, he scribbled an apologetic note to his father saying that something had come up (he didn't specify what) and that he'd be back in a few days' time. He packed clean clothes, checked ferry departure points and availability online, booked a ticket on the overnight ferry, collected his car from the garage and set off for St Nicolas via Portsmouth.

The first thing that struck Callie when she was shown into the sitting room was the huge portrait of three children that hung above the fireplace.

"Who are they?" she asked Jack.

"That's Grace, Anna and Rupert when they were little."

"Anna and Rupert?"

"My brother and sister," said Grace, exchanging a quick glance with Jack. "Although the relationship is rather more complex than that."

When she didn't elaborate further and moved off to greet other members of the family just arriving, Callie asked, "Where are they now?"

"Rupert and his wife Rose live just outside Glasgow and were professional musicians before they retired – their son is the David Stewart who runs the stables here and organizes the music side of the Classic FolkArts Fest."

"Really?" Callie looked closely at the portrait again and could see something of a resemblance between the little boy in the picture and his now mature offspring for whom she worked. Or was that only because of the information she had just been given?

"David's sister is a professional cellist with the Northern Sinfonia," added Jack.

"What about Anna?"

"She's an actress and pianist. Or at least she was. Lives in New York."

"An actress?"

"Yes, Anna Stewart. Have you heard of her? She's probably a bit before your time."

"I'm afraid I haven't."

"She was reasonably well-known on television during the sixties and seventies. She was my first wife."

"Oh." Callie was surprised. She hadn't imagined Jack being married before; he and Grace seemed as though they had always belonged together.

"We had a son, Ben, who's an architect and lives in London."

A shiver of apprehension travelled down Callie's spine.

Auntie Edie's friend was called Ben – she had never known his surname but he was the one who was there in the kitchen when Callie had come home so distraught that day. She remembered being reminded of Jamie, just as she had again that first day when she walked into the gallery on Cairnmor and saw Jack.

However, like Jamie's surname of Rutherford, Ben was a pretty common first name, and once again, Callie dismissed any possible connection from her mind.

"So he inherited your artistic talent then?" she said.

"Yes, rather like Marie here, whose paintings adorn the walls of our little gallery and who has a degree in fine art."

Callie turned to Marie admiringly. "I had no idea!"

"I didn't think to say anything. I suppose I assume that everybody knows."

With a modest smile, Marie went into the kitchen to help Grace.

"You have a talented family."

"So do you."

"Apart from me."

"You do yourself a disservice," said Jack. "You just haven't found what it is you want yet."

"No," said Callie, "not quite yet. But I have found a place where I can be myself; amongst people who have accepted me for who I am, not for who they think I ought to be or what I should be."

Jack smiled. "And if you understand that, then you have come far indeed. For that, Callie, more than anything else other than being with the person or people you love more than anything, is what is most important in this life. The rest follows on from that."

"Thank you," she said, looking at him with gratitude, and wondering about Jamie. Was he the person she loved most? Could she have been so unfaithful to him if he was?

However, Callie knew that Jack, above anyone else, had helped her to find confidence in herself. In many ways, with his calm philosophical ways and vivid story-telling, he reminded her of her grandfather and yet as people, they were very different. She was certain they would have got on well with each other, though.

Tea was served in the kitchen and presents given amid affectionate hugs and blown kisses.

Jack was delighted with his tie.

"Where did you unearth this from?" he said to Callie, admiring the subtle hues and design. "It's really rather special."

"From Ron's Stores, would you believe! I thought the colours reflected the shading in some of your landscapes."

"They match your eyes perfectly," said Grace.

"When we go to London for the summer exhibition, I shall wear it," declared Jack. "And I shall say that it was a birthday present from The Girl in Jack's Portrait and who, because she sat so still while I daubed her in paint and because she listened so carefully to my boring old stories, from this moment has just become an honorary granddaughter."

Callie didn't quite know where to look and blushed a deep shade of red.

"Welcome to the family," said Grace and kissed her warmly on the cheek.

"When would you like to go to Cairnmor and meet my folks?" said Ben, as they lay in bed that night.

Edie hesitated. "This latest house is going to take up a lot of time and we still haven't finished the other one yet. Then there's your clients and that lease to sort out..." She cast around trying to find reasons to delay such an ordeal.

Ben smiled, sensing her nervousness, putting his arms around her.

"All those things can wait. They'll all still be there when we get home."

"Do you think they'll like me?"

"They'll love you."

"Just because you do, it doesn't necessarily follow that they will."

She could recall how Trevor's family had hated her.

"Of course they will. They're very astute."

"Oh dear, that means they'll see into my soul."

202

"Well, if they do, they'll discover a beautiful person."

"You're prejudiced."

"True. And proud of it."

"Do you think they'll wish I was younger so that you and I could provide them with more grandchildren?"

Ben threw his head back and laughed. "Not for a moment. There are already so many grandchildren and great-grandchildren, even I can't keep up with it. We're a highly proliferating family. I'll have to show you the family tree when we're there. You'll be amazed."

"What if I don't like them?"

Edie knew that would be a catastrophe. She hadn't liked Trevor's family at all but, for the sake of the children, had made the effort to get along with them.

"I can't imagine you not liking them because they're your sort of people. However, we'll cross that bridge if and when it arises and," he kissed the tip of her nose, "don't worry about it in the meantime."

Reassured, Edie returned his kiss. "Perhaps we should wait until Jamie gets back from whatever it is that he's doing and we can all go together? After all, I haven't even met him yet."

"I think that's a lovely idea. He hasn't seen my dad and Grace in over a year. But I am rather cross with him for rushing off as soon as he gets back from Afghanistan though. He could have waited to see us before disappearing. Whatever it was can't have been that urgent."

"It might have been on his mind for a while. From his note, he sounds like a decisive young man and it was obviously important to him."

Ben didn't say he hoped that Jamie wasn't resentful over Edie; that he had come home and seen the changes to his home and felt he couldn't stay.

Knowing that Jamie had too much generosity of spirit to react in that way, Ben dismissed the thought from his mind and brought Edie into his arms where she responded to him with joyful confidence and a total lack of inhibition.

CHAPTER 34

If Jamie imagined that Port le Bac would be anything like Lochaberdale, then he was quickly disillusioned. It was a bustling, busy tourist destination, thronging with people and cars jostling for position on the narrow road beside the harbour, where cafés and souvenir shops spilled onto the pavements.

If Lochaberdale remained a haven of peace and tranquillity despite its expansion over the years, then Port le Bac had sacrificed its serenity a long time ago to the thousands of travellers drawn by the warmth of the climate and cosmopolitan yet staunchly British feel of St Nicolas, one of the larger Channel Islands, making it into one of the most popular holiday destinations anywhere in the United Kingdom.

So this is where her family come from, he thought, as he looked around him, *and Callie too*, he supposed, although he had no idea where she was actually born. All he knew was that her grandparents had settled here after the war and that numerous uncles, aunts and cousins still lived on the island.

Without difficulty, Jamie found his hotel, set back from the noisy sea-front up a slight hill, and booked into his room where, exhausted from constant travelling – Afghanistan to London and London to St Nicolas with hardly time to draw breath – he undressed, lay down on his bed and promptly fell asleep, waking confused and disorientated some eight hours later.

He had been dreaming, vividly. Not a nightmare exactly but he found himself back on patrol in the dust and the heat; every yard a potential death-trap; every bump in the road making his pulses race.

He was in a Scimitar – the light, rapid, manoeuvrable tank of the H.C.R. – racing over the desert, covering the ground with ease, their mission unknown, their target invisible.

He woke up, his body damp with sweat and he calmed his rapidly beating heart with several deep breaths.

Inordinately thirsty, he drank several glasses of water before taking a long, settling shower and going in search of food – his next immediate priority. After consuming an all-day breakfast in a delightfully old-fashioned little place called Mabel's Café on the sea-front, he headed straight for the Tourist Information Centre to obtain a map of the island and anything else that might help him: focusing on his search, determinedly using it to push Afghanistan out of his mind and acclimatize himself to the increasingly strange reality of being back on British soil and alone without his mates in a shared situation.

Jamie decided he would look first for small coves situated not far from farmhouses – Callie had spoken often of a secret cave on a little beach where she used to play as a child and which her grandparents always regarded as being their special place.

It was to here, he decided, that she was most likely to flee.

Standing in the information building, he studied the map and noted a number of likely locations.

He felt frustrated by the fact that they had only talked in general terms about their childhoods and never in specifics. He realized that he knew marginally more about St Nicolas than Callie certainly did about Cairnmor (and that in itself was little enough) but he was now acutely aware of the fact that he had not even said its name – merely referring to it as 'the island where his father had grown up.'

It was ridiculous that they had not mentioned names – their, he realized now, stupid idea of not letting family ties or relatives impinge upon their new-found togetherness was a real hindrance in an unprecedented situation like this. Jamie needed all the help he could get and he wished now that they had been more precise; that he had asked more questions, that Callie had asked more questions.

He asked the girl at the desk if there was such a thing as a local telephone directory. The internet search on his phone had not revealed anything of use and he was relieved when she produced one for him.

"Were you looking for anyone in particular?" she asked helpfully.

"Yes. Someone called Callie Martin? Or the Martin family? I don't suppose you'd happen to know her or them by any remote possibility?"

The girl shook her head. "Sorry. I haven't been here long. I would imagine there are a lot of Martins in the directory. It's quite a common name."

"Yes." Jamie sighed.

"Are you a relative?"

"Not exactly. A friend. We haven't seen each other in a while."

"Oh, I see."

Once again, just as it had been when Callie had first appeared in his life and he tried to find her, it was like looking for a needle in a haystack.

Jamie scanned the list again. If only he knew the Christian names of Callie's parents or even their occupations, that would be something at least. But then, on the other hand, he had only mentioned to her in passing that his dad was an architect. Why on earth had they been so spectacularly un-curious?

He thanked the assistant, gave her back the directory and then perused the shelves, picking up several leaflets he hoped would be helpful as well as a detailed guide to the island. He decided that as he was here, he might as well make a holiday of it and escape from his thoughts, while at the same time searching single-mindedly for his errant fiancée.

The latest scan that Sarah had had done was slightly indistinct but clear enough to discern the form of the baby she was carrying. Once again, she insisted that Erik accompany her and he had been surprised at his own reaction to the blurred but discernible image of the little child.

His child.

All at once, it became personal to him. This little form was his creation, a living breathing human. It belonged to him and Sarah; a joining of both of them – the intimate result of their intimacy.

It took him a while to assimilate this, to realize its significance, but still it did not make him wish for the life of shared, restrictive domesticity that a baby would bring. However, he did think that he would visit Sarah and the child from time to time rather than severing all personal ties, just to see how it was developing and to make sure that Sarah had everything she needed.

At work, Erik often found himself thinking of the baby. He would stare out of the window at the street far below wondering how many of the people he could see had children at home; how many of them managed to juggle home and business, freedom and constraint.

He knew he would find all that difficult; his freedom from emotional ties a precious commodity, one that he wished to protect at all costs. His overriding reluctance to relinquish this aspect of his personal life was almost stronger than anything else.

He would never put himself in such a position where he could be hurt again as he had been by the two women he had loved the most all those years ago. That was a given.

Besides, he needed the variety that his ever-changing relationships brought; he needed the space to do exactly what he wanted, when he wanted. He knew he was a man of enormous appetites, something that was both a blessing and a curse, his sex life needing to be constant and without interruption – except when he was between women, of course, but this only served to give him time to recharge his batteries and seek out his next conquest.

In fact, since learning of Sarah's pregnancy, he'd begun to look around discreetly at other women for the one who would take her place. He needed to plan in advance as he didn't want to be left high and dry without the thought of anyone to entice into his bed.

He took several desirable women out over a period of time for discreet, platonic lunches but none matched his criteria nor did they possess the same appeal as they would have done before he had met Sarah or, he had to admit, even Callie.

He felt no urge to charm these potential acquisitions; he made no effort to ensnare them. He found their conversation spurious and shallow and the thought of making love to them unappealing and wearisome even though the women he selected were obviously beautiful and overtly sensuous. And vulnerable.

He dismissed the thought that there was something wrong with him as he had no desire to pursue them and experience what they had to offer. He dismissed the thought that he no longer had the inclination to go out with someone then leave them just as he had been left.

On the contrary, he began to realize just how eager he was to get home at the end of the working day to be with Sarah and take her to bed with him, knowing that it was she and only she whom his body now craved. There was nothing amiss with his libido, he concluded, he just wasn't ready yet to move onto someone else or leave Sarah behind.

True to her word, Sarah continued to place no restrictions on their love-life and apart from his own consideration for her and the safety of their child, they continued in much the same way as they had before. Erik relished this, absorbing himself in her body by constantly reaffirming and deepening his connection to this woman who was sharing his home life in every possible way.

And that really was taking him into territory in which he had vowed he would never stray again. It also increased his dilemma as to what he should do once the baby was born – the prospect of a planned separation becoming far more difficult and unappealing than he had first thought.

Callie, Jack and Grace were studying the family tree which consisted of several large, comprehensive documents, each stretching back to the early seventeen-hundreds.

"I did tell you that we were a proliferating family," said Jack, with a wry smile. "Each branch seems to have mostly gone in for large families."

"I think that mine comes pretty close," replied Callie, finding herself thoroughly absorbed as she looked at the documents, recognizing many of the names from her studies of the island. "It must have taken someone an enormous amount of time and patience to compile this."

Jack and Grace smiled at each other.

"It's taken us years," said Grace. "My father, Alastair, started the process and we continued from where he left off. It's as much a legacy of Cairnmor as the history books and the guide books are as it chronicles the lives of those who have affected the island's recent past and its present stability. Also, it tells of everything the family did before Cairnmor came into their lives and how what happened to them had a direct consequence for the island."

"Is it finished yet?" asked Callie.

"Is any family tree ever finished?" replied Grace.

"No, I suppose not, unless the whole line is particularly unfortunate. There's usually a new generation to take over."

"And that's important," said Jack. "The future is vital to the success and furtherance of any family." Carefully, he extracted the final sheet of paper. "There's just one more to see and that's Grace's and my little contribution to continuity."

Callie looked on with interest once more at the lines that converged and the miniature histories of each person underneath their dates.

"... and this is my son, Ben, the architect, and my grandson, Jamie. Jamie's in the Household Cavalry and should be coming home from Afghanistan any day now. We're all terribly proud of him," said Jack.

Callie suddenly felt sick and faint and had to sit down.

Concerned at her unexpected pallor, Grace said, "Are you alright? Can I get you some water?"

She shook her head. "I just felt a little dizzy for a moment, that's all."

Callie took in nothing more, her mind racing haphazardly with disastrous realizations.

Grace gathered up the papers, returning each roll to its container, while Jack quietly and astutely observed Callie as she sat in stunned silence, staring out of the window but seeing nothing.

Edie was fully occupied organizing builders and carpenters. There was a great deal of re-building to do in this, their latest acquisition.

After the renovations had been completed, their other two properties had rented easily and two families were enjoying Victorian-style living combined with covert modern conveniences.

Edie loved to visit her houses and meet her tenants when she went to check, like any good landlord should, that all was well. The rent was paid by direct transfer into a bank account that she and Ben had set up especially for that purpose, so she didn't have to worry about collecting cash or cheques.

She relished her new work. Not only was she overseeing their existing properties, which she found most satisfying, but she was also acting as an occasional consultant for Ben's architectural practice. She had never been as busy in her life, nor had she ever felt as fulfilled.

Edie scoured the auction catalogues avidly, researching those Victorian, Edwardian or nineteen-thirties properties that had been left either intact or derelict. Some had been partially refurbished already and she considered these carefully, but if too many original features had been removed or walls knocked down and it was too late or too expensive to restore the fabric of the buildings, then reluctantly, she had to let them go.

With John's involvement and his extra injection of cash that served to finance the houses they really did want to keep, they had bought and sold a couple more properties of no particular merit that hadn't needed much renovation other than a basic face-lift, making a tidy profit in the process and ensuring the syndicate as a business venture was progressing well.

Baz kept reminding them that he wanted to join the organization, but once Ben had had his firm's accountant look into the café owner's finances, he dragged his feet on this, reluctant to use Baz's hard-earned cash in a venture that, despite their current success, might one day lose them money.

"You need your money as a safe-guard for a rainy day," he'd told their friend. "My accountant says that you don't have quite enough surplus to act as a cushion for your existing business and buy other property."

"But can I not just invest a little amount, as much as I can afford?" said Baz disappointed.

Ben had shaken his head. "No, it's better to wait. Keep doing well with the café and we'll have another look a year or so down the road. Your eldest will be off to university soon, so he'll need all the help you can give him."

"Well, I'll keep selling my coffees and my lunches and try to make as much profit as I can, then soon I join the syndicate and work with my friends."

"You do that, Baz. It'll all pan out, you'll see."

CHAPTER 35

Callie was in the grip of a terrible dilemma.

What should she do? Go or stay?

She didn't want to go – she had come to love Cairnmor and the life she had made for herself on the island. Truly happy and content for the first time, she knew that deep down, she wanted to stay. Yet, once Jack discovered that Jamie, *his* grandson, was the fiancée to whom she had been so unfaithful, surely he, and by default Grace, would want nothing more to do with her?

Could she keep it from them? Could she maintain such a deception with two people she had come to care about yet still feel free to be herself with them? And Callie knew that above all, she was herself with them. Particularly Jack, who had seen into her soul and had revealed it to her through his portrait.

Freed from all constraints and obligations of her former life, during her time on Cairnmor, Callie had at last come to terms with who she was and what she wanted to do more than anything: to stay on the island and make some sort of independent living for herself, just as she was doing now.

It was ironic that, at the very moment she knew what she needed, Fate, or whatever people wanted to call it, had intervened. Faced with such an impossibly difficult, unforeseen situation as her past caught up with her, all Callie's former doubts and insecurities came flooding back until she couldn't see anything clearly.

Should she talk to Jack? To Marie? To Beth and David? To Grace?

Instinctively, she knew she couldn't talk to Grace because for all her acceptance (tolerance?) of her, Callie somehow felt that Grace vaguely disapproved of her and this would inevitably become more marked if she knew the truth; indeed, Callie couldn't be sure that Grace had really approved of Jack's desire to paint her portrait in the first place, although she would never have said anything and naturally supported her husband in all his endeavours.

Callie knew she wasn't close enough to any of the others except Jack. He was the one person she could confide in but he was the one person she shouldn't. Could she actually talk to him? Would he understand? Would *he* disapprove and would she lose her position as honorary granddaughter, something she really didn't want to happen?

She gave a wry smile at the irony of it all. If she hadn't been so stupid, then Jack would have become her real (by marriage) grandfather. And Callie knew she would have liked that – very much.

She sat down in the dunes, not far from an old tarred hut that Jack told her had been there for over a hundred years and which she knew featured in several of his paintings of South Lochaberdale, the old place having become something of a tourist attraction over the years as a result.

She found comfort beside its venerable wooden form and looked out over the ocean, drinking in the beauty of the scenery and trying to face up to the inevitability that she would have to leave. Silently, the tears fell as the thought tugged at her heart.

Callie knew she couldn't bear to go just yet, to tear herself away from such a place as this. She'd try and stay for as long as she could, for as long as she could maintain the deception.

But wasn't that her being dishonourable? Again.

Jamie explored every single cove he could find on St Nicolas.

It was a beautiful place, he decided, and once away from the bustle of Port le Bac, the rural nature of the scenery held great charm. He drove past farms and fields where cows and sheep munched contentedly on lush pasture; where greenhouses and walled gardens proliferated; where narrow fragrant lanes wound steeply up hills that gave panoramic views towards France or out across the Atlantic Ocean.

He passed ugly concrete fortifications, a dominating legacy from the German occupation of the islands during the second World War, exploring those that were open to the public, seeing at first-hand what it must have been like for both civilian and occupier alike, taking a professional interest in the turrets and empty gun-emplacements.

He walked down steeply sloping paths to tiny secluded beaches away from the tourist hot-spots but failed to find any that held hidden caves resembling those that Callie had described.

He visited the museum in the town and saw artefacts dating back to prehistoric times; learned about the early sailors who travelled between the islands in frail looking craft – the ancient fishermen who, like their present-day counterparts, earned a precarious living from the sea – and he saw how and why the tourist industry came into being.

He discovered another museum dedicated to life under the occupation as well as the fate of those who were deported from St Nicolas to Seeblick and other internment camps in Germany – reading first-hand accounts, looking at photographs and studying the faces and listening to personal recollections of the people who had been subjected to forced removal from their homes and livelihoods.

There were also written records from German soldiers in the occupying force, including several who had returned to the island to marry local girls whom they had met during that time or others who had struck up a romantic attachment at the end of the war.

Remarkably, there had also been many exchange visits between the internees and the villagers of Seeblick who had befriended each other during the time of the incarceration.

Jamie sifted through photograph albums and displays and listened to audio recordings – a living history of the invasion and the deportations, compiled from as many people as possible who had lived through it before it was too late, before there was no one left who could recount exactly what it had been like.

He sat spellbound watching films of personal recollections made at fifty, sixty and again at seventy years after the events of the Second World War. And his jaw dropped in total surprise when he saw Callie speaking to the camera of her experiences – well, it wasn't Callie, but it was someone who, as a much younger woman, had looked remarkably like her.

Or was it just his mind playing tricks? Anxious to see this particular film again, he pressed the button and re-started it.

He listened and studied Sophie Langley – an English-born woman marooned on the Channel Islands at the outbreak of war and later deported to Seeblick – as she spoke of her life during the occupation and afterwards.

At the end of the conflict, she married a man called Robert Anderson, a former British soldier, who earlier had been a P.O.W. in the same camp in which she had been interned, before he joined British military intelligence and became involved in covert operations on the island during the war.

Robert's recollections were also recorded for posterity and Jamie watched in fascination as he saw progressively older versions of Sophie and Robert speaking and smiling before his eyes; a couple devotedly in love, their individual and collective memories clear and vivid.

There were differences between Sophie and Callie, of course, but the similarities in appearance and gesture were striking and unmistakable, nonetheless.

Jamie remembered that Callie's grandfather had had a distinguished war service record. As he studied Robert's war service, he realized that this could be him.

Robert spoke of a privately-owned cove where he and his Royal Navy comrade had hidden canoes to facilitate their arrival and departure from the island during their secret mission.

Sophie spoke of her two aunts with whom she had lived in an old rambling farmhouse before her internment and how one of them had married the first *Kommandant* of the island when he came back at the end of the war. She spoke of how he found acceptance by the islanders because he had been wise and kind during his time as *Kommandant*.

The camera then showed lengthy shots of the cove with its secret grotto as well as the farmhouse in which, Robert revealed, he and Sophie still lived.

At last, Jamie knew he had positive evidence in his quest to find Callie's relatives.

At the end of the film and without waiting to explore the museum further, he leapt into his car and headed across the other side of the island to pay a visit to the farmhouse, wondering if Robert and Sophie were still alive and, if not, whether the farmhouse still belonged to their family.

Would he find Callie? Would this be the place in which she had chosen to hide away?

"I receive letter from my landlord today," said Baz.

"Oh?" replied Edie, seeing his anxious expression. "Good or bad?"

"Bad. Very bad. He is selling the freehold to the shop and our flat. He putting it all up for auction."

"For auction!" exclaimed Edie. "Do you know when?"

"Next week." Baz shook his head. "It is terrible news. The new landlord will probably put up rent and we won't be able to afford to live here. Or we might be given notice and have to leave because he no longer want café here. And we will never be able to afford somewhere else."

Edie's mind was in a whirl. This couldn't be happening to her friend Baz. After all his hard work, he mustn't be allowed to lose his home and his business.

She said nothing to Baz for the moment, other than offering him sympathy but for the rest of the day she gave considerable thought to the problem. That evening she invited John round for supper and put her idea to both him and Ben.

"We have to bid for it," she said. "We *have* to get it. This really is something that Baz can put his money into. It means he would have a part-share in his own building and it would be the ideal investment for him. In fact, the more I think about it, the more perfect it seems. How much do we have in the pot?"

John drew in a deep breath. "I don't have that much."

"Nor I. We've just about used up every spare penny," said Ben.

"Then we must re-mortgage one of our houses to use as collateral if the bank shows any reluctance to give us a loan on this latest potential purchase."

"Re-mortgaging is far too expensive," said Ben. "However," and he paused for a moment looking at Edie, "your original house has no mortgage on it at all."

Edie busied herself by filling the kettle and switching it on, her heart pounding. To raise finance against a house they had bought was one thing; to take that risk with her own was a completely different matter.

"How much would we need?" she said quietly.

"What's the guide price?"

"Three hundred and fifty thousand."

"For a going concern? For a three-bedroomed flat and shop in Carlton? That seems incredibly cheap," observed John.

"Presumably, the landlord wants to arouse interest by setting the guide price low. Developers are going to be crawling all over the place. It's in a prime location."

"How long is the lease?" asked Ben.

"There's only ten years left, but that's irrelevant as he's put the freehold up for sale so the whole thing will be available," said Edie. "I went along to the auction house and picked up a catalogue and studied the legal pack as soon as Baz told me what was happening. What do you reckon it will go for?"

Ben named a sum – well in excess of what they could afford between them and that was including Baz's possible share.

"Well," he said, "with John's, mine and Baz's contribution, that'll mean a mortgage of…" and Ben tapped out the figures on his phone and showed it to the other two. "It's not too excessive. It should work."

"It has to work!" said Edie determinedly.

For Baz's sake. For the sake of her beloved house.

Sarah came to the conclusion – and this was something of a momentous change for her – that it would be too much for her to continue to work after the baby was born and look after their child in the way that she would wish while keeping her needy lover satisfied. Her hours were too long, the demands of the job too great to do all three successfully and above all, she wanted to do all three successfully.

She didn't want to arrive home from the hospital tired out and frazzled, unable to fulfil her stimulating domestic duties in the way that she would like for the person (and soon to be two people) she loved the most; nor did she want someone else to bring up her child. Besides, she didn't need to work from a financial standpoint – Erik was wealthy enough to support them both and would in fact prefer it if she was at home. Sarah might even be able to study for her Ph.D. once the baby was old enough, something she had always wanted to do and never been able to because of the pressures of having to earn a living.

She was also aware that blissful domesticity with a child would not be Erik's forte. With his nature, she could see he might feel trapped and hemmed in. However, she was glad that he was, as yet, showing no signs of restlessness but she was under no illusion that as soon as the baby was born, he might find it all too much and leave. He would ensure that she and the baby were looked after financially and materially, of that she had no doubts, but Sarah wanted *him*. She loved him and, despite his domineering tendencies which she had become adept at mitigating, they were making a good life together.

Therefore, in order to keep him with her after the baby was born, Sarah knew she would have to play something of a canny game.

She made sure that Erik wanted for nothing, that he continued to be gratified in the way that was most important to him. Her one certainty was the knowledge that for all his varied and colourful love-life in the past, based on what he had told her, he would remain faithful to her all the time they were together. She also knew that if he were planning to leave after the baby was born, he would already be quietly looking around for her replacement.

This thought would have made a less grounded woman feel insecure and anxious but Sarah felt confident in the strength of their relationship and her own ability to draw him to her and keep him by her side – without him being aware of what she was doing.

She also made sure that he had no time for any other female company except herself. If he went away on business, she accompanied him; if he entertained clients at a restaurant in the evening, she went with him, swapping her shifts if necessary. (As she was going to leave the hospital anyway, she no longer felt obliged to tread carefully with the management).

Charmingly and lovingly, Sarah involved him in shopping expeditions for the baby, happily allowing him to choose the cot, high-chair and baby-buggy; making judicious, practical suggestions only where necessary. She drew his attention to the attractiveness and cute-factor of the tiny clothes and soft toys that their baby would need and discovered that for all his sophistication, after an initial period of reluctance, Erik soon began to show an unanticipated responsiveness and involvement in the baby's material needs: enjoying taking control in choosing and deciding the best possible options, with money, of course, being no object.

Sarah's reward was the joy she felt in seeing that beneath the debonair exterior and flawed internal character of her lover, there beat the heart of a potentially caring father.

Of course, it could all be an illusion – Erik's clever and tactful way of remaining faithful to her and hiding his real feelings – after all, he was as skilled at playing the psychological game as she was, but Sarah knew him well and all the while she was able to remain objective (which was often quite difficult being pregnant) she knew she could keep him.

Sarah realized that she was Erik's match and if he was aware of her feminine wiles and subtle possessiveness, he didn't run away from it or feel entrapped by it;

on the contrary, together with his own need for control, it locked them together in such a way that both found deeply satisfying.

All she had to do was to make sure it stayed that way.

CHAPTER 36

"Can I help you?"

A man's voice coming from behind him made Jamie jump.

"Ah, er, I was wondering if I might find Callie Martin here. I gather that her grandparents lived here or might still live here?"

"They did until they passed away five years ago."

"I am sorry."

The man looked at him slightly suspiciously. "And who might you be?"

"Oh," Jamie moved forward and extended his hand. "Forgive me. I'm Jamie Rutherford. I'm a friend of Callie's and as I was... on holiday here, I thought I might see if she was around. On the off-chance, you know."

For some reason, he felt as though he was a naughty school-boy; a miscreant, caught committing some heinous crime.

"Well," the man replied without introducing himself or shaking Jamie's hand, "we haven't seen Callie for some time. Nor heard from her. My sister, that's her mother, has been really worried. Two emails and a couple of text messages in the last eight months or so that's all she's had. Apparently, Callie's not living in London any more but she says she's alright so we've all had to be content with that."

"She's not on St Nicolas, then?" Jamie tried hard to keep the abject disappointment he felt out of his voice.

"'Fraid not, old son," he said, giving Jamie an astute look. "We've none of us any idea where she is, so I can't help you there. Known her long, have you?"

"We met just under a year ago and got to know each other... quite well. I've been abroad, so I haven't seen her recently either."

"Well, she's an elusive young lady, that's for sure. Have you come far?" he asked.

"Quite far, I suppose you could say. Afghanistan via London."

"You're in the army then?"

"Yes. Household Cavalry."

"Wow!" The man's manner changed from suspicion to openness. "That must be quite something – all that ceremonial stuff. I never miss Trooping the Colour and my wife loves all the Royal pageantry. Do you wear the full uniform when you're on duty? That breastplate, what's it called?"

"Cuirass."

"Boots, sword and helmet?"

"Yes, the full regalia."

"And you like horses?"

"Love them."

The man smiled suddenly, his brown eyes warm and welcoming. "I'm Adam, by the way. Adam Anderson, Callie's uncle." He extended his hand this time which Jamie took. "Would you like a cup of tea? Seems the least we can do for you after you've had such a wasted journey. Afghanistan to St Nicolas is a hell of a distance."

"That's one way of looking at it."

Grateful and intrigued, Jamie followed Adam into the farmhouse.

"Your father was called Robert?" he ventured.

Adam smiled again. "Yes, he was. Have you seen the films up at the museum?"

"They're what led me here. Your dad must have had quite a career during the war."

"He was awarded the Victoria Cross during the Battle for France in 1940."

"He didn't mention that in the film."

"No, he wouldn't. A copy of the citation and medal is in the museum but he was always secretive about the exact details to everyone except Mum. We knew he was proud to have received it but he didn't speak about it much and donated the real V.C. to the Royal Welch Fusiliers Museum at Caernarfon Castle. Said that's where it belonged with all the others, that he wasn't the only one to have received that honour."

"So the R.W.F. was his regiment?"

"Yep. He was proud of them too, as well as all the secret service stuff he got involved with. Anyway, park yourself on that chair and I'll make that tea. The wife's out at the moment. She's taken the girls off to some fête or other in Port le Bac. Rob, that's our eldest – he was named for his grandpa – is somewhere out and about on the farm seeing to the horses. Dead keen, he is. Wants to take over the farm when I retire, which is a blessing in this day and age when so many youngsters want to go off and do their own thing. He'll make a go of it as well."

Adam placed the kettle on the range and while they waited for it to boil, he asked, "Would you like to see the horses?"

"I'd love to."

"Okay, we'll do that once we've had our tea."

"Do Callie's parents live on the island?"

"Not as a rule, although they have a house here. Her dad's just got a new job with NATO, so they're off to New York. You'd think that at their age, they'd want to slow down a bit, but no. Been on the island for two months and that's as much as they can stand. Always did have the restless bug. Used to feel sorry for Callie because as a child she was always being dragged from pillar to post with no time to settle or please herself. But she seemed adaptable and accommodating, accepting that she didn't have much say in anything. She loved being with my mum and dad most though so they used to have her here every school holiday. Gave her the stability she needed. But I expect you know that about her."

Jamie half-nodded in acknowledgement, thinking it best not to disclose that he didn't. "She told me a great deal about her love of horses," he said.

"Yes. You definitely have that in common. Callie would ride all day if she had the chance. And sit in a library and read. She's so like my mother, Sophie, who was content as long as she could follow her heart. And to follow her heart meant being with Dad or with us children and having time to read her books and ride. She was so happy with Dad, just as he was with her, and together, they made a fantastic team in bringing us up and looking after the farm. I only hope I've done as well with my brood and again with the grand-kids."

They drank their tea and Adam led the way out into the stable-yard.

"So, what do you reckon, then Baz?" said John, as they gathered in the café one evening after it had closed and they had told him of their plans.

"I cannot believe that you would do such a thing for me and my family! It is a great thing you do. But it is too much. Much too much." Baz hung his head, humbled by their offer; by the depth of their friendship.

"But it's not just us trying to help – it's the perfect investment for you," declared Edie. "I mean, what better way to use your own money than in a part share of your own business premises?"

"I will pay you back," he blurted, his voice thick with emotion. "Every penny. I will get out mortgage myself."

"Perhaps one day but for the moment, look on it as a joint investment, your initiation into the syndicate, if you like."

"Thank you, my friends; thank you so much. My Halka and I do not know how we will ever repay you for your kindness. We shall be forever in your debt."

Baz's eyes were becoming moist and in order to deflect the possibility of too much sentiment and save his friend from embarrassment, Ben suggested that he make them some coffee.

"To celebrate," said Baz.

"That is yet to come," said John. "We've got to secure the property first. How are the finances?"

"Shaping up," replied Ben. "The bank have agreed a loan in principle using Edie's house as collateral and will assess the building for a mortgage when we've bought it. We have more than enough for a deposit, so it's all coming together rather well."

"We just need to get to that auction," said Edie, "and do the deed."

"Or rather, get the Deeds," said Ben, smiling at her.

"Let's hope there is not much interest from other people," observed Baz nervously.

"At its guide price – unlikely. But we've a great deal of experience so I am optimistic," said Ben.

"It has not been nice having people look at my private house. Halka make things neat and tidy. I go round and untidy them. She get cross with me but I say that the worse it look, the more the people will be put off."

"Not necessarily," said Ben, "but anything is worth a try."

"What time do we meet in the morning?"

"Nine o'clock at the auction house. Do you know where it is, Baz?" asked Edie.

"John, he bring me. I think I shall be nervous."

"I think we shall all be nervous," said Edie.

They raised their coffee cups.

"Until tomorrow," said Ben.

"Until tomorrow," they all responded.

"I have a business meeting in Manchester," said Erik, one evening after coming home from the office. "It will be difficult for you to come with me."

"Why?"

"Because I have to go on my own."

217

"Why?"

"Because I do. Please accept my word on this and do not question me."

Sarah's heart began to pound and she stopped herself from saying anything other than a sardonic: "I see."

She looked at him. For the past week or so, he had seemed moody and less demanding physically. There were times when he would go off by himself into his study or the home cinema room and not come out for hours on end.

And now this.

They talked as much as they always did, but he often seemed distracted and distant – the classic symptoms of a man having an affair, Sarah tried not to say to herself.

She trusted him, didn't she? She knew he would not stray from his usual pattern of fidelity while he was in a relationship. Yet something made her uneasy. Just as she was beginning to think that her strategy was working, Erik proposed this trip.

"How long will you be gone?" she asked. "You can tell me that much at least."

"A week."

"How long is a week? Five days? Seven?"

"Seven."

"When do you go?"

"In the morning. Early."

"Oh."

Erik looked at her face, so downcast, so miserable and an unaccustomed pain gripped his chest. This was to have been the start of his graduated separation from Sarah; the beginning of the end. But it was hard, very hard. He would hurt her terribly if he went through with it and that doubled his distress.

Erik had never held that consideration for any of his women before; love 'em, leave 'em and hurt 'em had been his philosophy – treat all women in the way that he had been treated. So he did, with barely a backwards glance. Except for Callie and now, with even greater difficulty, Sarah.

The train journey up to Manchester was a lonely one for Erik, as was his sojourn in the city. After checking in at his hotel, he went about his business meetings: contacting clients, signing contracts; keeping himself busy and not allowing himself time to think or feel. In the evenings, he returned to his hotel room, aimlessly flicking through the satellite television channels or trying to read the documents he had brought with him.

But all he could think about was Sarah. He missed her; he missed her so terribly that, by the third evening, he could stand the loneliness no longer and went down to the hotel bar where he ordered himself a whisky.

"So, what's an attractive man like you doing all alone in a place like this?" said a voice behind him.

Erik turned and exclaimed. "Lucy! What on earth are you doing here?"

They kissed – formally, a peck on each cheek.

"I'm on assignment. All highly mysterious and hush-hush. My editor made me promise not to reveal this particular piece of investigative journalism to a living soul. Until it's finished, of course. Then it'll be explosive! Look, why don't we go over there," and she indicated a vacant table in the corner of the plush lounge-bar.

218

"So how are you?" she asked once they had sat down.

"Fine," said Erik.

"As busy as ever?"

"Busier, if that were possible."

"Really? When we were together, you were always off here there and everywhere as it was," she said without rancour. "We had a good time though didn't we?" she asked.

Erik smiled evasively. "We did."

"I've always been sorry it didn't last."

"Have you?" he replied noncommittally, unable to remember the manner in which he had dismissed her or what she'd been like in his bed.

"Yes. I've always sort of felt that I'd do things differently if we had our time over again."

"Really?" His interest underwent a minute change. Because he couldn't recall the details, re-discovery might prove to be quite exciting. "Is there anyone special in your life at the moment?"

"No," said Lucy, "I haven't ever found anyone else who can match your... capabilities."

"Ah," said Erik, flattered by her praise.

"What about you? It's unusual to see you without some beautiful woman on your arm. If you are free, then I'm available."

Erik hesitated for a moment, aware that if he told her about Sarah, Lucy would know that because he was with someone else, he would not contemplate sleeping with her; on the other hand, if he denied his current liaison, then he would be free to take up with Lucy again.

Somewhere at the back of his mind was the vague memory that she'd been mildly entertaining. She might make the ideal transitional relationship to ease him away from Sarah.

And Erik realized he could begin that process straight away with the nature of his reply. To purport to be free and engage in a casual encounter would be an unusual approach for him, but then again, he was in real physical need.

"So if you're not with anyone at the moment," continued Lucy, not waiting for him to reply, assuming his silence represented a singular state, "and although I realize this is not your usual scene, how about we spend the night together? You know, just for old times' sake?"

Erik regarded Lucy dispassionately and considered his options.

"I had a letter from Ben this morning," said Jack to Callie as she sat in the kitchen of the farmhouse drinking tea after riding up to South Lochaberdale from Granger Farm.

"Your son."

Jamie's father.

Callie felt her world spinning out of control again.

"That's right. He's coming up for a week or so and bringing his partner with him so that we can meet her." Jack looked over the top of his glasses at Callie, noting her pallor but not remarking upon it. "I didn't tell you, did I? After all these years of being on his own, he's finally found someone who has been able to take the place of his wife." He glanced at the letter again. "They're hoping to come up in a couple of weeks' time. Apparently, they have some house purchasing business to sort out first and are waiting for Jamie to come back from wherever it is he's gone on holiday to – Ben doesn't say – before setting off. They're hoping to stay for a while, which is excellent news. He says he's all agog to see my latest paintings and is longing to know who the mysterious girl is in the portrait." Jack chuckled. "I've left it as a bit of an unknown quantity on purpose so that I can reveal your identity when they see the painting!"

Callie felt sick.

Jamie. Jack's grandson – coming here to Cairnmor. His son Ben – the architect and what was more, bringing her aunt. It had to be. A picture of the man with Jamie's eyes sitting at Edie's kitchen table leapt into her mind.

"What's she called, your son's partner?" She had to know for certain.

"Edie. She's the same age as him, apparently, and," he looked over the rim of his glasses at her again, "has a barrister niece the same age as Jamie."

"Yes," said Callie, almost inaudibly.

"But you knew that, didn't you?" said Jack softly.

"Yes." She hung her head in shame. "You see, Edie is my aunt and… and Jamie is my fiancé."

"Of course they are," said Jack, taking her hand in his.

CHAPTER 37

The auction room as usual, was crowded.

Ben, Edie and Baz waited with growing nervousness while successive lots were offered and despatched; while people came and went; while the auctioneer's hammer banged against his lectern; while delighted new owners showed their paddle numbers before disappearing with a member of the auction house to claim their prize.

They had positioned themselves on the front row, in direct line of sight of the auctioneer, so that there could be no mistake when they made their move. They had their maximum carefully worked out yet had allowed themselves a little leeway in case a few hundred pounds was all that was needed to clinch the deal.

Edie was to do the bidding and as the time for Baz's café came nearer, she ran the palms of her hands along the legs of her jeans.

"You'll be fine," whispered Ben. "Remember, I'm here every step of the way. You're not doing this by yourself."

Edie smiled. "It feels like it though."

"I know." He squeezed her hand. "Would you rather I bid?"

She shook her head. "No, I want to do this. It's funny, but no matter how much experience you have at bidding, it never gets any easier. And with this one, more than any other, there's so much at stake."

"We come to lot number twenty-five," said the auctioneer as a picture of Baz's familiar café came up on the large television screen to the left of the podium. "A fine opportunity this. Business premises with a three-bedroomed flat above. Who'll start the bidding at three-hundred thousand? I shan't begin any lower." The auctioneer scanned the room. "Thank you, sir," he said as someone at the back of the room raised their hand. "Do I have three-ten anywhere?" He looked to his right. "I have three-ten. Thank you, madam. Three-twenty? Back with you, sir. Three-thirty do I see? To my right at three-thirty."

The bidding was brisk and the price kept going up and up until it had surpassed the guide by a long margin. Still Edie kept her hand down, still she waited; watching and listening, waiting for the right moment.

"Five-hundred thousand," said the auctioneer. "If there are no other bids." He paused. "Going once at five-hundred thousand…"

Edie put up her hand. "Five-ten," she said.

The auctioneer looked at her and smiled. "A new place at the front. Just in time, madam."

"Do I see five-fifteen? Five-fifteen, sir, thank you. Five-twenty?"

"Five-sixteen," mouthed Edie.

"Five-sixteen at the front. Five seventeen at the back. It's against you, madam."

"Five-eighteen," said Edie.

"Twenty."

"Twenty-one."

Two. Three. Four. Five. Six. Seven.

"At five hundred and twenty-seven with the lady in the front row. Sir?"

The man at the back shook his head.

"Are we all done then at five twenty-seven?" The auctioneer paused. "Going once... going twice... Yes, sir. A new bidder. Five-thirty, thank you, sir."

Edie's heart sank and she looked at Ben and then at Baz and saw his face go pale; beads of sweat on his forehead, his eyes wide and staring.

She knew they had reached their limit. Yet she couldn't stop now. They were so close. They had sufficient money for a deposit if they went a bit higher. They'd raise the rest of the money somehow.

Ben winked at her and smiled, knowing what she was thinking.

Then just as she was about to raise her hand for one final bid, Baz stood up and said loudly and clearly, "Five hundred and thirty-five thousand."

The auctioneer's lips twitched. "Thank you, sir," he said kindly. "Five hundred and thirty-five thousand. Madam?"

"We're together," said Edie, trying not laugh.

"That's a relief," said the auctioneer. He turned to his audience. "Are we all done then, ladies and gentlemen, at five hundred and thirty-five thousand pounds?"

No one else raised their hand or offered another bid.

"At five hundred and thirty-five thousand, then. For the first time... for the second... for the third and final time... are we all done now?" He banged his gavel on the lectern. "Sold to the lady and gentleman on the front row for five hundred and thirty-five thousand pounds. Well done."

Baz leapt up and hugged Edie and Ben, much to the amusement of the people around them as well as the auctioneer and his staff, and shook their hands, pumping them up and down in gratitude and relief.

"Thank you, my friends, thank you so much. I shall never forget your kindness."

Ben smiled and put his hand on Baz's shoulder.

"Don't mention it. Just remember that you have your money invested in this property as well."

"And it feels good! I like this bidding at auction."

Edie and Ben exchanged a smile.

The three of them went with the auctioneer's assistant to complete the legal formalities and as they left the room, they were approached by a man, who rushed over to them in a state of hurried agitation.

"I should have been here for lot twenty-five," he said, clearly out of breath, "but I got stuck in traffic and my phone's run out of battery so I couldn't phone the auction house to get them to bid on my behalf. The lot I was after is the one you've just bought. What did you pay for it in the end?"

Ben named the sum.

"I'm prepared to offer you seven-hundred thousand for it. Right now."

"What?" chorused Edie, Ben and Baz together.

It was a great deal of money.

"Why would you offer us that much?"

"I own the rest of the properties in that block. I want to convert them all into flats. To have the property you've just purchased, will make the project financially viable and turn in a healthy profit for me. Hence my offer to you of seven-hundred thousand."

If they were to accept, Edie knew that for her it would mean that she didn't have to put a mortgage on her house. For Ben and John it would mean more money for further investment and underpin their businesses. For Baz, it would mean better premises and something of a financial cushion.

Or would it? Would seven-hundred thousand be enough to make it worthwhile for all of them? They looked at each other. Not quite.

"Make it a million and we have a deal," said Baz unexpectedly.

They all stared at him open-mouthed.

Sarah was worried. She had been unable to reach Erik on his mobile early that morning and when she phoned the hotel and asked them to ring his room, they said he had already left for the day.

Frantic with anxiety and suspicion, she called in sick at the hospital, packed an overnight bag and headed to Manchester on the train.

The two-hour journey from Euston seemed interminable and the baby kicking and squirming inside her only added to her discomfort. It was as though the infant could sense her extreme disquiet.

Sarah took a taxi to the hotel, ascertained that Erik was indeed staying there and booked into a separate room without revealing her identity. After all, she still had her credit card and debit card in her own name – she had been adamant in her refusal when, at the start of their relationship, he had said that he would open a new bank account for her in his name and she could close the others as she would not have need of them.

Now, finding herself in this situation, she was glad she had firmly declined his suggestion.

Sarah unpacked the few things she had brought with her and set out to wait for him to come back, positioning herself in the lobby so that she could observe the revolving entrance door unnoticed, having no idea of where he might be or when he might return.

About four o'clock he appeared and was immediately met by an attractive woman who kissed him on the cheek and tucked her arm into his in a way that shouted of familiarity. They disappeared together into the lift and the bottom fell out of Sarah's world.

Despite the doubts and fears that had prompted her precipitous flight to Manchester, she had been so certain that Erik would remain faithful to her; that she would find him lonely and bereft and that he would welcome her sudden and unexpected appearance with open arms.

From what she had just seen, it was obvious that this scenario would be unlikely.

Not to be deterred, Sarah went over to the lift and from the number display saw that it had stopped on the third floor, so she got into a second lift and headed in the same direction.

As the doors opened, she cautiously peered out and saw them disappear into a room some way along the corridor.

What should she do? Burst in and catch them *in flagrante*?

Could she cope with that?

Yet she had to know what he was up to. She had to know if the father of her child was the womanizing bastard his reputation had always suggested that he was.

Yet, simultaneously, Sarah had always been convinced that their relationship had the power to offer him the stability and longevity he obviously craved, knowing what she did now about his past, having contacted his cousin (whose email address she happened to find on Erik's computer), and getting in touch via a friend's laptop at the hospital (so that Erik would never know what she had been up to) and having a lengthy phone conversation.

After learning about his trials and tribulations and his reaction to them, Sarah was more convinced than ever that with her, he had found something different; that he had found the thing he'd subconsciously been searching for; that she was the one important catalyst that would reconcile him to his past and make him stay with her and only her.

She wondered how many other women had felt that way only to lose him anyway. But then, they may not have known what she now knew.

Taking a deep breath, Sarah made her way cautiously and reluctantly along the corridor towards Erik's door, on the other side of which hung her fate and the continuation of her relationship with the man whom she knew was the only love she would ever know.

Callie sat on the window seat in her room, staring out across the wind-tossed harbour recalling the vital, pivotal conversation she had had with Jack the previous day.

"How did you know?" she had asked, looking at him in amazement.

Jack had smiled. "I know many things," he said. "I knew for certain when you went so pale and almost fainted when we were looking at the family tree."

"Oh."

Callie had gone quiet then, not quite knowing what to say.

"You don't have to leave because Jamie is coming here," Jack had said carefully.

"How did you know that's what I was thinking?"

"I painted your soul, remember?"

Callie had looked at him then with tears in her eyes and nodded.

"You could make a fresh start with Jamie. Really get to know him properly this time."

"Perhaps."

"Do you want to get to know him properly?" Jack's question was gentle, kindly expressed, yet Callie knew there was much, much more behind his words.

"Yes, but…"

"You're afraid that if you do allow yourself to have that thought and then find he can't forgive you, the pain and embarrassment would be unbearable and all the good that being here has done you would be undone in a moment."

"Something like that."

"Or, are you afraid to get to know him because you haven't forgiven yourself yet, therefore you can't see how anyone else could possibly forgive you?"

Callie nodded.

224

"Well, only time will solve that one." Jack regarded her for a moment, wishing they were in his studio so that he could capture her expression. "However, there's one burning question I haven't asked."

"What's that?"

"Are you in love with Jamie?"

Callie hesitated. "I thought I was, otherwise I wouldn't have agreed to marry him. On the other hand, I can't be because I allowed myself to be seduced by another man."

"There is that, of course. But, having transgressed, the only way to find the answer to that question, is to meet with Jamie and be absolutely honest. Then see what happens; see what his reaction is; see how you really feel about him once you have brought your mistakes out into the open. Could you do that?"

"I wouldn't want to hurt him in such a blatant manner. Besides, I don't know that I'm brave enough."

"Not brave enough!" exclaimed Jack. "You who can still the most skittish of horses? You who have been seen out on the eastern seaboard battered and soaked by the wind and the rain? Come on Callie, I thought you had more mettle than to be afraid of seeing Jamie."

Did she?

"What about you?" she asked, partly to avoid the issue and partly because she needed to know.

"What about me?"

"Can you forgive me?"

"I'm not the fiancé to whom you were unfaithful," he said pointedly.

"I know that," she said quietly. "But I need to know because..."

"Don't worry, I'm not going to reject you as a granddaughter, if that's what you're afraid of." He took her hand and looked at her tenderly. "What happened, happened and you have to deal with it. Otherwise, you'll beat yourself up about it for the rest of your life and that, Girl in Jack's Portrait, is not a course of action I would recommend to anyone."

Ruefully, Callie had smiled at him.

"Thank you," she said. "That is what I wanted to know."

"Just do whatever it is you still have to do to sort yourself out," said Jack, "then I shall be as proud as if you really were my granddaughter."

Callie had hugged him then and Jack had smiled suddenly, his expression one of affection tinged with slight regret, almost as though he knew what it was she was going to do even before she did.

Now, sitting in her room at the guest house, she looked up the hill to South Lochaberdale and tears filled her eyes as she came to the inevitable conclusion.

"Would you like to go riding?" asked Callie's uncle.

At Adam's hospitable insistence, Jamie had visited the farmhouse on several further occasions, he and Adam having developed something of a rapport.

That first day, he had been shown photographs and memorabilia, book collections and had, at Adam's invitation, subsequently spent much time on the little beach in the private cove, enjoying the peace and quiet, relishing the amazing fecundity of the grotto and the *au naturel* bathing opportunities presented by the secluded pool.

"Really? You'd trust me with one of your thoroughbreds?" Jamie was incredulous. "I'm still a virtual stranger. I might be anyone."

Callie's uncle smiled, a twinkle in his eye. "True, but if you're not who you say you are, even with our burgeoning friendship, this'll really sort you out. Besides, I think I'm a pretty good judge of character and if you haven't manifested your true colours by now, I would know, believe me!"

Jamie chuckled. "Okay."

They made their way to the stables where half a dozen horses poked their heads out of the open upper-half of the stable doors and greeted the new arrivals with expectant shaking of heads and manes.

"This lot are the thoroughbreds," said Adam. "My parents started this breeding programme – my dad was an expert polo player and saw a niche for that particularly lucrative market. We have three Suffolk Punch horses as well – two mares and a stallion – and that's my contribution. They're something of a rare breed these days and I'm keen to see the line continue."

"Expensive though," observed Jamie.

"Oh, they earn their keep," replied Adam. "There is still a profitable sphere for polo ponies and I use the Suffolks in the fields. One of our farm workers is an absolute nut and would rather plough fields the old-fashioned way. Can't be doing with 'these-'ere new-fangled tractors', he says. So, as we keep the fields small, it works well. He's way past retirement age but he's still spry, so the Suffolks are his pets and he looks after them for me and keeps them busy."

Jamie smiled. He liked that; he liked this man's consideration towards a fellow human being. After the things that he'd witnessed in Afghanistan, it was like a balm to his soul, a restoration of his faith in man's humanity to his fellow man.

It was a small thing, but it meant the world to Jamie.

He also decided that as he had been getting on so well with Adam and was now having the opportunity to ride, if his new-found friend really was agreeable to his staying at the farmhouse, as had been warmly hinted at, he would extend his sojourn on St Nicolas.

That would give him more than enough time, surely, to reacclimatize himself to home territory, to recover from the stress and strain of combat; to re-familiarize himself with normality and decide on his future before finally going home and being with his family.

Yes. It would do him good. And he would find out an awful lot more about Callie in the process.

CHAPTER 38

The door of Erik's room opened and Sarah hid herself behind an adjoining corner, listening intently, wondering what bombshell was going to be delivered into her mind and body.

She expected that he and this woman would emerge together with a promise to meet later; she anticipated that she would overhear phrases of appreciation for the night they had spent together with the delicious prospect of more to come.

Her mood darkened and all she wanted to do was scream and run away. No, not run away. She wanted to confront them and demand that the woman leave because Erik belonged to *her* and only her and that this interloper, this *harridan* should get the hell out of there.

"Thank you for supper last night," said the woman's voice.

(*Was 'supper' their euphemism for something else?* wondered Sarah).

"It was my pleasure," said Erik smoothly.

(*Bastard*, thought Sarah).

"Next time you're in London, you must look us up," he continued.

(*Us? Which us? Us at the office?*). Sarah could almost hear the woman smile with pleasurable anticipation at his words.

"Thank you, that's very kind of you, darling. But perhaps not. I'm sure that your current…"

(*Current?*)

"…partner wouldn't want some ex-girlfriend appearing unexpectedly on her doorstep. I know I wouldn't."

(*What!*)

It took a moment or two for Sarah to absorb the significance of the woman's words. Still not quite believing what had just been said, she then heard a small sound.

A kiss? Where? On the lips? On the cheek?

"You're a lucky man, you know," continued the woman. "She must be someone special if you were able to resist the temptation I put your way last night to re-kindle the passion we once had together."

Sarah's heart did a somersault of joyful surprise.

"Yes, she is. Very special."

Erik wished that Sarah was here. Now. At this very moment.

"Well, all I can say is that she must have cast some sort of spell over you, Erik. What you seem to have with her is what I always wanted when we were together, but somehow it didn't quite work out in that way, did it?"

A small silence.

He's thinking about what to say, thought Sarah. *How to reply tactfully without overtly causing offence or insulting her*.

"I did enjoy our evening yesterday after running into you so unexpectedly. It was good to see you again."

"It was good to see you too, Erik. I think."

Sarah heard her sigh.

"God, I was a fool to let you go. Not that I had any choice in the matter," added the woman ruefully. "You really hurt me, you know, the way you more or less threw me out."

Sarah could hear a tinge of bitterness in her voice.

"It was just one of those things, I guess. Well, look after yourself, Lucy."

"And you. And good luck with the baby."

There was a small sound again. But it went on for longer this time.

"I'm sorry that you wouldn't sleep with me last night, even for old times' sake, you know."

"I've never been like that."

"I know and it's what puts you above other lotharios." She saw Erik wince at the label. "Well, be seeing you. Thanks for letting me collect my scarf from your room."

The woman walked past Sarah, her eyes cast down, unseeing, and got into the lift. Sarah walked out into the corridor and approached Erik as he stood in the doorway.

He looked at her in shocked surprise for a moment.

"I didn't..." he stammered, experiencing a genuine moment of anxiety in case Sarah had misinterpreted what had just taken place.

"I know," she said, smiling at him, her expression full of love, trust and certainty. "I overheard. Everything."

"You did?"

"Oh yes. And I'm so, so glad."

Unable to wait a moment longer, Erik pulled her into the bedroom and locked the door.

How she came to be there was another conversation. But that could wait. Right now, at this moment, all he wanted was her. He was desperate for her and given the way she was responding to him as well, he could see she was just as desperate for him.

That morning after breakfast, Callie said to Marie that she had come to the end of her time on Cairnmor but that she would be sorry to leave.

"Will you come back, one day, do you think?"

"Oh yes," said Callie, "I do hope so," trying to avoid the regret and disappointment in the kind woman's voice.

David and Beth were also sad that she was leaving, but thanked her for all her help with the horses.

"There's a job waiting for you if ever you decide to come back and settle permanently on the island," said David.

"I might just take you up on that," said Callie, as she patted each horse by way of farewell.

Fiona said that she would miss her company in the museum and art gallery.

"You've become quite an expert on Cairnmor," she said appreciatively. "You would make a highly informed guide, if you wanted."

"Thank you," Callie replied. "That's something I might consider doing one day."

She went to see Roland and thanked him for all his help in supplying her with such good-quality equipment.

"We aim to please," he said amiably. "We'll miss ye, lassie," he added, giving her a brotherly hug.

However, saying goodbye to Jack was one of the hardest things she had ever done in her life. It was like breaking a bond so deep that she almost hesitated in her resolve.

"Am I doing the right thing?" she said.

"Only you can answer that particular question," he said, as they walked slowly together along the white-gold sands of Cairnmor.

Callie nodded. "Yes, I know." She looked up at him earnestly. "But I shall come back. I promise you that."

"Thank you. And will you make one more promise to me?"

"Of course!" she said without waiting to find out what it was. "How could I possibly refuse after all you've done for me?"

Jack smiled.

Once he had said what it was he wanted her to do, Callie had fallen silent. What he asked of her was hard, very hard. Yet she had to do it. There was no choice.

They walked on until they came to the tarred wooden hut where they sat down in the dunes, looking out to sea. Jack took her hand and Callie rested her head on his shoulder, her eyes full of tears, her heart full of pain, understanding the significance of what he was asking of her.

"Yes," she said at length. "I promise."

"Good girl," he said.

Edie, Ben, John and Baz sat in the little café in stunned silence.

"I can't believe he agreed," remarked John after a while. "It was a preposterous suggestion."

"I know," said Ben, chuckling. "I never thought he'd swallow it."

"He must have been desperate," observed Edie, "to go for something like that."

"No, my friends. He will make a vast profit, I assure you," said Baz, "and that is the only thing what drives him forward."

"I never knew you had it in you," said Ben. "What you did was pretty audacious."

"Ah, I have the eye for business opportunity," replied Baz. "It was gamble but we had nothing to lose. We had secured the purchase and if someone was foolish enough to offer us more money, then why should we refuse? Seven hundred thousand sounds great deal, but it would not have gone far."

"That's true. You can move to bigger premises now," said Edie.

"And you can save many properties for, how you say?"

"Posterity," said Ben.

"Ah, yes. Posterity."

"I wish I'd been there," said John. "I'd love to have seen everyone's faces in the auction room and that bloke as well when Baz did his stuff."

"They were absolute pictures," said Edie. "The house staff couldn't believe it when Baz asked the guy for a million and got it."

Baz chuckled. "I have found a talent for this property thing and London is *the* place in which to do it. One day, I shall be rich developer driving a Lotus and wearing gold watch."

229

"With delusions of grandeur more like and head too big to go out of door," said Halka, coming to join them.

"There speaks voice of reason and common sense," said Baz, putting his arm around his wife's waist. "We need to find bigger café. And better flat for all of us; perhaps even house with small garden."

"We can find you just the place," said Edie.

"At next auction. I come with you. We pick up another bargain and make another profit."

"Only if we're lucky. This sort of thing is a once in a lifetime thing. You need to exercise caution," observed Ben.

"Ah, my friend, caution is for the cowardly. I am brave lion." Baz tapped his chest with his fist.

"Well, my brave lion," said Halka, "we have customers to serve and everyone else have work to go to. We are meeting tonight at Ben's house? Yes?"

"Yes," replied Ben.

"And there we can discuss percentages and how we divide up the money," said John.

"Makes us sound like bank robbers," said Edie.

"Now there's a thought…" said Baz, who received a gentle slap round the back of his head from his wife.

"Back to reality, my husband."

"*Tak, moja miłość!* Yes, my love."

Edie, Ben and John left the café and went their separate ways – John to the Emporium and Ben and Edie to Cornwallis Gardens.

"Do you have to go into the office today?" asked Edie.

"No. I shall work from home I think. It hardly seems worth the journey now."

"Well, at least you were able to keep the day free from clients, thankfully."

"True."

"Shall we walk via my house to the Tube station?" said Edie.

Ben put his arm round her shoulders. "If you'd like to. Do you want to call in?"

"No. I just want to see it and then go home."

Ben looked at her astutely. "Time was when that was your home."

"It still is in a way, and always will be. I'll always carry it with me somewhere in my heart, if that makes any sense."

"It makes perfect sense. Though perhaps only I can understand what you mean. You feel it's part of you and you know now that wherever you go, you'll never lose that feeling."

"Exactly." Edie felt warmed by his perception. "I was afraid when I first moved out that I would lose something of myself, leave a part of me behind as well as the house. But I haven't."

Ben nodded. "Whatever we bring to somewhere or something we happen to be doing, we get back as much as we give. Just as it is with the people we love."

He took her hand in his.

"The more you give, the more you get in return," she mused softly, echoing his words, turning towards him.

They stopped outside Edie's former house and stood on the pavement.

230

"And Cornwallis Gardens?"

"Ah," said Edie, looking up at him and smiling, "that is where my heart now lives because you are there."

Ben took her into his arms and kissed her, there and then, in the street, in front of the house where she had spent so many years longing for a better life.

Jamie leant against the railings of the ferry, his extended sojourn on St Nicolas at an end.

He had spent the past week staying at the farmhouse with Adam and his family; grateful for their generous hospitality, for their acceptance of him. He had ridden along quiet lanes lined with high-banked hedgerows, finding peace and tranquillity among the heady fragrance of the May blossom and the timelessness of the patchwork fields and quiet hamlets. He had heard the stories of Callie's family and met several of them, had seen photographs and learned of her ancestry.

He had not found Callie herself but he had learned much about her, so many things he didn't know before. Jamie had felt at home with her family and hoped they liked him as much as he liked them.

He had talked at length with Adam of his involvement during his tour of duty and by being open about it with someone who in turn had talked deeply with his own father and whose understanding was instinctive, the experiences and occasional terrors of Afghanistan began to fade: his survivor's guilt aired and discussed, his feelings about combat and conflict put into their proper perspective.

It began for him the process of adjusting to a different reality than the one he had known for the past eight months and helped to facilitate his return to everyday normality.

Jamie came to the decision that once his leave was over, he would enquire about selection for officer training at Sandhurst and after this, investigate the possibility of a permanent posting in London with the H.C.M.R. training horses. If that wasn't possible, he would look at his options for coming out of the army, though he knew that would be something of a wrench.

Working with horses was what he wanted more than anything and he now knew from what he had been told of her childhood that, should he find Callie and should they resume their relationship, she would understand and be comfortable with this.

Although he knew he had proved himself to be totally capable, being in an armoured regiment was not what he wanted to be part of. His heart really did lie in the ceremonial side of things.

So, his energies restored and his spirit calmed by his holiday, Jamie found the capacity and courage to look ahead.

His priority was still to find Callie, and Adam had promised to get in touch with him as soon as he knew anything. He had apologized for his niece's erratic communication skills and said that she had always been the same. Adam supposed it came from her peripatetic upbringing – he assumed she had never been in one place long enough to put down roots or be able to keep properly in contact with anyone.

However, Jamie knew that before he resumed his search for Callie, he would go with his father to Cairnmor and visit his grandfather and Grace. It had been too long since he had seen them and Jamie was all too aware that his granddad was not getting any younger, although from what his dad had said in his last letter, he was busy painting portraits again, something he had neglected during the past few years.

Jamie leant against the railings watching the Isle of Wight and then Portsmouth come ever closer, contemplating the inevitable meeting with Edie. He hoped he liked her. He hoped that she made his dad as happy as he said she did; as happy as Jamie wondered if he would ever make Callie.

But, in order to do that, he had to find her first.

CHAPTER 39

"So he turned out to be bogus?" said Grace.

They were sitting – Edie, Ben, Jamie, Grace and Jack – round the kitchen table in the farmhouse on Cairnmor after supper a week after Jamie's return from St Nicolas.

"Yes," said Ben. "It turns out he wasn't a developer at all, but someone who goes round the auction houses trying to persuade people to relinquish their purchases there and then and allow him to walk away with the property with no more than a promise of financial recompense at some later date."

"I hope you didn't do that?" said Grace, appalled.

"Of course not! We said we would arrange everything through our solicitors. In the meantime, our purchase of the property would go ahead in the normal way. We said he could buy it from us after that," replied Edie.

She liked Ben's family, she felt at home with them. She had taken to them from the moment they had been greeted by Grace and Jack when they arrived at the farmhouse that afternoon. She liked Cairnmor too, the little she'd seen of it, even though it was completely different from St Nicolas, although the farmhouse, with its same feeling of warmth and welcome, reminded her so much of her parent's home.

She thought that Jamie was a fine young man and hoped that he liked her, although he had been very quiet ever since he had returned from his mysterious mission. She hoped his reluctance to communicate wasn't because of her. Even though Ben had assured her that it wasn't; that he thought there was something else on Jamie's mind and that he would speak of it when he was ready, Edie remained anxious. She so wanted to be accepted by him.

"Anyway," continued Ben, "we duly got in touch with his supposed solicitors, who incidentally, had never heard of him."

"Goodness!" exclaimed Grace. "What did you do then?"

"Called the police," said Edie, "and then the next thing we knew, a couple of detectives from the Fraud Squad, or whatever they call it these days, paid us a visit."

"What did they do?"

"They questioned us about this man – exactly what he had said and what he looked like."

"Apparently, they'd been on his trail for a while," said Ben.

Jack sat listening quietly to the conversation but only half taking it in, observing both his son and Edie together.

He liked Edie. She and Ben were comfortable with each other and he had never seen his son so relaxed and happy; far more so than when he had been with Jamie's mother, who had been lovely but who had always exuded a feeling of restlessness as though she was anxious to be elsewhere. Edie suited Ben, he could see she was absolutely right for him.

Callie's aunt.

He wondered if Jamie had realized exactly who Edie was. To Jack, the resemblance was striking and obvious, but then he had studied Callie's features in intimate detail and spent an inordinate amount of time with her.

More than Jamie had, he supposed, from what Callie had told him.

Edie and Ben; Callie and Jamie. He could see how the chemistry was working. It was a fascinating juxtaposition.

He wondered how Edie would react once she knew that her niece was engaged to Ben's son. Some people were funny about connections like that. Jack knew that neither Jamie nor Ben would have a problem – after all, Ben's grandmother had married her former father-in-law.

Jack smiled. How intriguing it all was. He was curious to see how it would all unfold.

"Anyway, the detectives stayed for a couple hours asking us this and that and then we had to go down to their headquarters and look at mug-shots," said Ben.

"Did you identify him?" asked Grace.

"There was no one who really resembled him, although we identified two possibilities."

"It was rather nerve-racking," said Edie, "but the detectives were kind and helpful."

"It seems that he's quite elusive," said Ben, "and has been operating all over the country. They were surprised that he was chancing his luck back in London again."

"I wonder what his success rate is?" asked Jamie.

"Not good, I imagine, otherwise he would have made a fortune by now and retired on the proceeds," said Ben. "He's got a nerve though."

"It must have been hard to give up the dream of a million pounds," observed Grace, getting up from the table to put the kettle on the stove.

Edie eyed the range with a knowledgeable appreciation.

Ben chuckled. "Oh definitely. Edie had dreams of saving masses of houses from destructive modernization."

"Our colleague John had visions of a luxurious retirement," said Edie.

"Baz wanted to move to bigger premises and had ambitions to establish a whole chain of cafés, making a fortune in the process."

Edie and Ben looked at each other and smiled.

"Well, it did seem rather too good to be true," she said, "so we've all been pretty philosophical about it, actually."

"Except Baz, who is still angry as he thought he had secured this fantastic deal for all of us and feels he's let us down and is disgusted that such a thing could happen in his adopted country."

"But we tried to tell him that no one can evict him now; that his café and flat are secure and that he has a part share in his own premises."

"How did you finance the purchase?" asked Jack.

"I mortgaged my old house, Ben and our business partner John put in some money and Baz contributed all his savings." Edie smiled at Jack. "We wanted to do it for Baz and his family. We couldn't bear to see them lose their home, you see."

"How many houses do you own altogether?"

234

"We have five that we've renovated and rented out including my house. So with the café and flat, that makes six."

Jack smiled to himself. It would be interesting to paint both Callie and Edie together. Just as he had done with Grace and her mother, Katherine. If he had a photo of Sophie, he could add her to the portrait as well – three generations exhibiting genetic similarity. Perhaps he could also paint Callie's grandfather and grandmother together, just as he had done with Katherine and Alastair. Except that had been from real life.

He must ask Callie if she had any photographs. On the other hand, perhaps he should ask Edie – Robert and Sophie were her parents, after all.

Suddenly, Jack felt excited and energized by the prospect and the familial connections.

Catching his expression and feeling his energy surge, Grace looked across at him and they smiled at each other.

"After the exhibition," she whispered in his ear as she gave him his tea. "That would be the best time to start on a new portrait."

How well she knew him; how well they had always been able to read each other.

"I could make a start before we go," he said, looking up at her.

"You could," she said, "but there'll be a great deal of work to do before London."

"That's true. But even so…"

With her hand on her husband's shoulder, Grace turned to the assembled group and spoke of Jack's involvement in the summer exhibition at the Royal Academy.

"I do hope you'll all be able to come," she said.

"Just try and keep us away!" said Ben. "Which paintings do you plan to show, Dad?"

"They're in our little gallery at the moment. We'll all go down there in the morning and I'll show you."

Jack's eyes held a mischievous twinkle and Grace smiled at him knowingly. She would let him reveal everything, aware that he would handle things tactfully and carefully but that he would also enjoy the moment of revelation.

"How exciting!" said Edie. "The summer exhibition at the Royal Academy is quite something."

"It will be this year," said Jack enigmatically.

Jamie stood before the covered portrait on the easel.

"Well, Granddad," he said amiably, "don't keep me in suspense especially as you've brought me down here on my own before everyone else is even out of bed."

They had come to the little gallery just after dawn.

Always an early riser – a legacy he supposed of his days in the Royal Navy – Jack had encountered Jamie already up and dressed and seated at the kitchen table drinking tea and eating toast while reading the previous day's newspaper. After eating his own breakfast – a scant bowl of cereal – he had persuaded his grandson to take him down to the gallery in the car straight away.

Jack went over to the painting and carefully observing Jamie, he lifted off the cover.

Jamie went pale with shock.

"My God! Callie!" There was no doubting the likeness. He looked at his grandfather. "It is her, isn't it?"

"Yes, Jamie, it is," replied Jack quietly.

"She was here? On Cairnmor?" He could scarcely believe it.

"Yes."

"How long did she stay?"

"Six months."

"Six months!"

Why hadn't she told him where she was; why hadn't she written to him and said that she had met his relatives? And what on earth had led her to Cairnmor of all places?

"I suppose she confided in you?"

"Yes."

"Did she tell you that I asked her to marry me?"

"Yes."

"Did she tell you that she stopped writing to me?"

"Yes."

"Do you know why?"

"Yes."

Jamie regarded his grandfather with a mixture of despair and frustration.

"Why didn't you let me know that she was here?"

"Because she made me promise not to tell anyone. Apart from Grace, whom she knew I would tell anyway."

"Grace knew?" Jamie was angry now. "And you both kept it from me?"

"Yes. Although to be fair, we didn't know the connection until a few weeks before she left."

It then occurred to Jack that he hadn't considered contacting Jamie to let him know that Callie was on Cairnmor. He had been so wrapped up in her wish to keep her whereabouts secret, that he hadn't given it a thought. It was remiss of him from Jamie's perspective, yet it was right from Callie's.

With a flash of insight, Jack realized he was the intermediary – was that the right word? Did it convey exactly what he was? He was the catalyst, a broker; an inadvertent link in their tenuous chain.

To a certain extent, he held their fate in his hands. But only to a certain extent, most of it would be up to them.

"I'm sorry, Jamie. It never crossed my mind."

Jamie threw his grandfather a look of pained despair.

"Have you any idea how long I've spent searching for her? Both before we met and since I got back from Afghanistan?" He began to pace the floor.

"No, I didn't, though to do something like that would be in your nature."

"How much do you know?"

Would Callie want him to tell Jamie, wondered Jack? Was it better that Jamie should know before he encountered Callie again?

"Everything."

"And do you care to tell me?"

"Only if you want to hear."

236

Did he? Jamie's inner self was in turmoil. What had happened to make Callie run away?

"Go on, then."

"She ran away from you Jamie and stopped writing to you not because she had stopped loving you, at least that's how I read it, but because she did something very stupid that made her feel ashamed."

Jamie remained silent.

"She had an affair."

Jack wished Grace was there beside him, to be supportive; to soften the impact of the truth.

"Do you know who with?" asked Jamie, his voice ominously quiet.

Jack hesitated. This was a young man, he thought, who'd just returned from a tour of duty fighting a hostile enemy. *Lord knows what he's witnessed, what he's seen, what he's had to do.*

Jack knew only too well the effect of combat on someone's psyche. Many men thought they were dealing with the stress of war, in whatever form the latter had taken for them, only to have it, at the slightest hint of emotional stress, trigger all kinds of extreme reactions that would normally be completely out of character.

Therefore, he hesitated, wondering whether or not to reveal the man's identity.

"If you know, for God's sake, tell me!" said Jamie, his voice urgent, his manner insistent.

"It was her boss."

"Her boss!" Jamie was furious. "That smooth-talking bastard, Erik van der Waals? I'll kill him."

"That would be stupid," said Jack, "and would solve nothing."

Jamie took several deep breaths.

"Do you know him?"

"I met him once when I went looking for Callie at her office." A nerve began to twitch in his cheek.

"Did she love him?"

"Not as far as I can gather. But she allowed herself to be seduced by him."

Jamie clenched his fists, exerting enormous self-control not to smash the portrait of this perfidious girl with his fist.

Jack observed him closely.

"It happens," he said.

"Unfortunately. But not to me."

Jamie began to pace the room. He stopped abruptly and turned back to his grandfather.

"There's more, isn't there?" he said. "Was it just the once?"

"No, it wasn't, I'm afraid," replied Jack, as gently as he could. He was finding this hard, much harder than he imagined it would be.

Perhaps he should have left Callie to explain and confess her own actions and accept the immediate consequences of what she had done. On the other hand, his natural inclination was to protect her, knowing how fragile she was emotionally and how much she needed to build up her inner strength. Until she was able to do that, she would be no use to Jamie or to anyone.

Also, when they did eventually meet again, and he felt certain that they would, Jamie would have had time to come to terms with the situation. With Callie having finally (hopefully) recovered her equilibrium, they would meet in the same place – figuratively, if not literally, speaking – and be better able to decide their future.

Yes, this was the right way to do things, thought Jack. But goodness knows what Jamie must be going through at this moment.

But then he, Jack, knew, didn't he? Anna, Ben's mother, had been unfaithful to him, hadn't she? Jack remembered his physical reaction and anger towards the man he'd found in bed with his then wife; how he had punched him on the jaw before propelling him naked down the stairs and out onto the street.

"I see. So tell me," said Jamie.

"She lived with him for a couple of months."

"Lived with him? For a couple of months!"

Perhaps Callie wasn't for him after all, thought Jamie. Perhaps he's made some terrible, dreadful mistake. Perhaps he'd been a complete and utter fool.

Jack watched his grandson storm out of the gallery, slamming the door behind him, knowing it would do Jamie good to be on his own for a while.

Later that morning, Edie and Ben stood in front of the portrait.

"Why it's Callie! It's my niece!" exclaimed Edie. "It must be. It's just like her."

"Is it Callie?" asked Ben, thinking of Edie's idiot niece who had appeared at the house in floods of tears.

"Yes," replied Jack.

"She came here?"

"Yes."

Here we go. Round two, thought Jack, catching Ben's expression of disapproval and seeing Jamie standing in the open doorway, knowing he must have overheard Edie's statement. *If real people's emotions weren't involved, it would be like some sort of French farce.*

"Callie's your niece?" exclaimed Jamie.

"Yes," said Edie, turning towards the new arrival.

"You know her?" Ben was confused. "How?"

"She's my fiancée."

"Callie is your fiancée?"

How could his sensible, level-headed son have become involved with a girl as flighty and irresponsible, even if she was Edie's niece? Surely there must be some mistake.

"Yes," replied Jamie.

"And she was here? On Cairnmor?" said Ben, still in the throes of disbelief.

"So it would seem."

"You do know she had an affair with her boss?" he said bluntly, the emotional knowledge of the way his real mother had treated his father making Ben's observational question far more brutal than he would normally have been.

He did not want Jamie to be hurt in the same way his father, Jack, had been; in the way he himself had been by his absent mother's faithlessness.

"Ben!" exclaimed Edie, looking at Jamie in consternation, distressed by the older man's lack of tact. "Supposing Jamie doesn't know? How can you be so thoughtless?"

Does everyone know except me? thought Jamie as Ben fell silent.

"I do know, Dad," he said, with a shuddering breath. "Granddad told me earlier this morning."

Edie laid her hand on Jamie's arm. "She came to us after she had left him, you see," she said gently, "dreadfully upset because she knew she'd behaved despicably towards you, hating herself for what she'd done. She was very brave to have left her boss. He was a brute of a man, by all accounts."

Jamie shook his arm free. "I'll get him for that," he said murderously.

"Think of the consequences," said Jack. "It's not worth wrecking your life over something you cannot change."

Jamie took some more deep breaths. "No, you're right. But it's a hell of a mess. And now, more than ever, I need to find Callie and hear her side of things."

"Really?" said Ben, still unhappy with the situation. "Perhaps, given the circumstances, you're well shot of her! She's certainly not someone I'd prefer to have as my future daughter-in-law!"

Seeing Edie go pale, Grace went over to Jack and took his hand. Wearily, he rested his head against her, knowing that this was not at all how it was meant to be.

CHAPTER 40

Jack regarded the assembled group carefully.

They had returned to the farmhouse from the gallery at his suggestion in order to try and break the tension but, even now, they were sitting round the table in an emotionally charged silence.

Edie's mind was in a whirl.

How had Callie allowed something to happen that could wreck her future with this lovely young man? Whatever was she thinking of? What kind of emotional aberration had overtaken her?

For Edie knew that Callie was not a Rat like Trevor; she was just a young woman who had made one stupid mistake and would never do anything like that again.

She hoped that Jamie could forgive her. It seemed obvious to her that they had loved each other. But if they were to be married, that raised a potentially awkward situation for herself and Ben.

How could *she* possibly marry Ben if his son wanted to marry her niece? It wasn't right. The family connections would be too close. If it turned out that Callie and Jamie did find each other again and all went well, then she wouldn't want to stand in their way. They could have children, whereas she and Ben could not, and it was important for every young couple to have children if they could.

Edie saw in Jamie the right man for her niece. Although she didn't know him well, he seemed honest and kind. He was certainly good-looking, though that wasn't a prime consideration. He had mostly dealt in a mature manner with what must have been a considerable shock and shown the inner strength that she knew Callie needed in the man she was to marry.

Her eyes filled with tears and a terrible pain gripped her chest as she even remotely contemplated a future without Ben. She just couldn't do it, it was impossible. She couldn't let him go or be without him. It really would break her heart and her spirit if they were to separate.

So that self-sacrificing consideration on her part was out of the question.

Perhaps Jamie and Callie wouldn't get together. That would leave her and Ben free to marry. Edie immediately chastised herself for the thought. How could she be so selfish and deny two young people in love – and she liked to think that despite present circumstances, they really had been in love – the chance to be happy?

Much as she was upset with Ben's opinion of her niece, she acknowledged that Callie had behaved like a silly girl but then, from what Jack had said, she realized she had and seemed to be going through some sort of penance.

"She's genuinely upset and full of remorse," he'd said, before they'd left the gallery. "She's trying to get herself and her back life together."

"She really does regret what she did," added Grace.

Sitting quietly at the table, Edie wondered where Callie was now and what had precipitated yet another disappearance.

Their imminent arrival, probably.

Ben looked at Edie, knowing she was holding back the tears, guessing at some of the thoughts that were going through her mind.

He had no problem, from a purely familial perspective (putting any moral considerations of Callie's character aside) with himself and Edie, Jamie and Callie being together. After all, his grandmother had married her former father-in-law, and his own father had married Grace, his mother's younger sister. There could be no closer legal ties than those. No, for him, that was not a problem. Neither would it be for Jamie, who understood their family's convoluted history.

Besides, under no circumstances would he ever allow anything to come between himself and Edie. He couldn't bear to be without her and would not even allow himself, or her, to contemplate any such possibility.

However, Ben knew that in other ways he did have a problem with his own son marrying Callie. She was not the steady, honest girl he had envisaged for Jamie. She seemed flighty and unreliable, weak and deceitful. Ben regretted his tactlessness in expressing his opinion about Callie's suitability as his son's future wife but he was just being honest. And he had apologized afterwards to Edie and Jamie.

He wondered whether Edie saw any similarity in Callie's treacherous behaviour with Trevor's towards her? Probably not, as Callie was her niece and he knew that Edie had put Trevor out of her mind. Also, Grace had been at great pains to point out her contrition.

If Jamie should persist in this stupid engagement, then there wasn't a great deal that he, Ben, could do. If Jamie managed to forgive Callie and really wanted to be with her because they were truly in love, Ben knew he would have to put his own ambivalent feelings towards Callie aside. He didn't want them to become a bone of contention, a barrier coming between himself and Jamie; between himself and Edie. Ben had no desire to poison the atmosphere when they were all together or wreck the close relationship he had with his son.

He tried to think of some good points about Callie but was unsuccessful. He accepted that he had only met her once in distressed circumstances and didn't really know her, but what he did know was enough for him to make up his mind.

He had to admit that she was attractive-looking, anyone could see that (including her boss, unfortunately) and his father's portrait was certainly striking. But for Ben, looks were only a surface indicator; it was underneath that surface where true character lay and from what he knew about her, Callie had not so far demonstrated any depth.

"Study her portrait for a while, son," Jack had said to Ben, before they'd left the gallery. "Callie said I'd painted her soul."

"You always do in any of your portraits, Dad," he'd replied, glancing briefly at the portrait and thinking he would come back later for a closer look.

Jack had smiled and shrugged his shoulders.

"I just do what I do," he'd said. Then, he'd put his hand on Ben's arm. "For all her faults, and she has many, Callie is a lovely person inside, trust me on this."

"But what if she hurts Jamie even more later on?"

"That's an emotional risk any of us take when we embark on a relationship, isn't it?"

Unwilling to answer or admit that his father might be right, Ben had remained silent. He didn't want his own son to be damaged emotionally by reactivating an ill-judged relationship.

"Look," said Jack, "if Jamie does decide to marry her, accept it. If he's willing to take the risk, then be there for him if he ever needs you. Get to know Callie for his sake at least, even if you do disapprove of what she's done. He's a grown man but he would still want to have your blessing should he decide to go ahead with what would be the most important decision of his life."

And sitting at the table with his family, Ben thought that perhaps he would be able to do that; perhaps he would try for Jamie's sake, for his father's sake, who had obviously become fond of Callie. But that would be difficult because The Girl in Jack's Portrait was no longer on Cairnmor.

She'd run away.

Again.

Jamie's thoughts oscillated between despair and anger, between humiliation and an intense need to see Callie; to speak to her, to hear her side of the story. To hold her in his arms.

Like her boss had done. Frequently.

Jamie now understood Erik van der bloody Waal's superior attitude; why he, Jamie, had felt so uncomfortable the day he went to Callie's office to find her. The thought of that bastard in bed with Callie made Jamie feel sick and he wanted to knock him to the ground. Perhaps he would when they all went back to London.

Would the army forgive him if he became involved in a fight no matter what the justification?

No. It would wreck any career he might wish for.

In any case, van der Waals would probably sue him for assault and that would be the end of that. He would heed his grandfather's advice and stay out of trouble. The bastard wasn't worth it.

Had Callie been seduced? Had van der Waals forced himself upon her? Or had she felt a genuine attraction and willingly gone to bed with him?

It was this latter thought that upset Jamie the most. How could she have done it? How could she, knowing she was engaged to be married, allowed another man to…

He left the sentence unfinished, unable to bear its completion.

Jamie stood up and went over to the range, intending to refill his cup from the coffee jug. But he just needed to get away from the table, to distance himself from the close proximity of prying eyes and family disapproval or concern.

Perhaps this was why Callie had disappeared again; perhaps this was why she had needed to be on her own – so she could nurse her hurt and her guilt (*had she felt guilty?*) in peace away from public scrutiny.

If so, then he could understand that.

When they'd been together, they had wanted to avoid family interference or observations about their relationship.

Well, that now existed in spades, with every family member present knowing the sordid details of Callie's errant behaviour and forming their own opinion as to the suitability (or not) of his choice and which, no doubt, would be expressed at some stage, tactfully and diplomatically in front of him but with brutal honesty behind his back, all of which would hurt and reflect upon his own judgement as well as Callie's

And Jamie would be obliged to listen to them. He didn't want to do that. He didn't want to stand there while they gave him advice, he didn't even want to pretend he was listening. He wanted to make up his own mind; reach his own conclusions; make his own mistakes.

He wanted Callie. Still. Even after all she had done.

Or did he? Was it wise? Would she be unfaithful to him again several years down the road, too weak to resist the advances of an attractive, persuasive man (and Jamie had no doubt that Erik van der Waals could be and had been highly persuasive)?

He hoped not; he hoped she would learn from all of this and ultimately become a better person.

What a load of crap, thought Jamie, suddenly. *How bloody idealistic. She's behaved like a slut and deserves to be left alone.* He wouldn't be looking for her again, that was certain. He hoped she disappeared off the face of the earth.

No, he didn't. Of course, he didn't. He wanted to take her in his arms and kiss her and by doing so, magic away the pain she had caused him; the pain she had brought on herself; that she had brought on both of them. He wanted to tell her that he still loved her; that he would always love her; that what she had done didn't matter as long as they were together again.

But at the moment, he couldn't tell her anything, could he?

Because once again, no one knew where the hell she was.

"I've got tickets for the opening of the Summer Exhibition at the Royal Academy," said Erik triumphantly as he came through the door of the apartment.

"You have?" said Sarah, laying down her book and adjusting her position as she rested with her feet up on the sofa.

Erik came over to her and kissed the top of her head before sitting down beside her. He'd become used to not making love as soon as he came home; he'd trained himself to wait until she felt able which, as she had promised him, was very often indeed.

In fact, rather than feeling resentful and deprived by their current circumstances, Erik had to admit he was rather lucky. From what he could gather, he was far better off than most men who discussed, in embarrassing detail in the men's rest room, how their pregnant wives couldn't cope with sex. Silently listening to their conversation, he knew Sarah could and did and he was strangely grateful to her because of it.

"They're like gold dust. We're incredibly lucky," he said, producing the tickets from his wallet. "Jack Rutherford is unveiling two new portraits in the main exhibition as well as some other paintings in the nonagenarian event which I'd like to see. Have you ever come across him before?"

Sarah shook her head.

"He's an amazing artist, I've always admired his stuff, particularly as he's more or less self-taught. I had no idea he was still alive, let alone painting. He does wonderful landscapes as well."

He kissed Sarah's cheek, his manner light-hearted and boyish.

"So is that alright? Are you happy to go?"

Sarah smiled. "Absolutely. You know I love it when we go to exhibitions. When is this exactly?"

"Second week of June."

"That's only a few days before the baby's due. I hope I'll be able to manage."

Erik's high spirits dissipated.

Reality. A baby to cramp their style.

Two weeks left before he left.

He'd forgotten that. He'd been thinking forever in his mind, forgetting that he would be gone by then. Sarah wouldn't need the tickets and he wouldn't be ready to take someone else. He'd wasted his effort.

He stared dejectedly at the floor.

"Perhaps the baby will come early," she said optimistically, sensing the downward turn in his mood. "After all, it's only a week or so away. I'm sure it will all be fine."

A week or two away. Erik looked at her with intense anguish in his eyes.

For a moment Sarah was puzzled and then her expression changed as an appalling reality began to dawn on her.

"My God! You're thinking of leaving as soon as the baby's born, aren't you?" she said, moving away from him, her heart and mind in a state of sudden, terrible shock. "How can you do that? How can you even think about deliberately wrecking what we have together? How can you desert me and your child like your mother did you? But that's what you do, isn't it, you heartless bastard? You punish the people who might actually have feelings for you by meting out the same treatment you had."

Dumbstruck, Erik looked at her in amazement.

"That's surprised you, hasn't it? That I know? I can see it in your face. I did some digging into your past, Erik van der Waals. I had to know what has made you the way you are. I had to know whether it was some mental aberration or chemical malfunction in your brain. Or whether it was triggered by some traumatic event in your childhood. I had to know, you see, so I could make some kind of objective diagnosis of the stupid man I'm stupidly in love with."

She glared at him.

"Yes, your mother left you. You're not the first child to ever experience that. Yes, your first girlfriend left you. You're not the only teenage boy ever to have a broken romance. But because you were hurt so badly twice, somewhere in that subsequently damaged, convoluted mind of yours, you decided to get your own back for your mother's and girlfriend's desertions by hurting every woman you had a relationship with. Well, I'm not just any woman. I'm the woman that's going to have *your* baby. *Your* baby, do you hear me? Do you really want *your* baby growing up without knowing one of its parents, just like you did? Do you want it growing up thinking of you in the same way you think of your mother? Would you really punish your own child, your own flesh and blood, because your mother walked out on *you*, leaving you in the not-so-loving arms of your drunken father?"

Erik sat staring at her, shocked into silence by her outburst; groping for words that would not come; hardly able to breathe in his anguish and confusion.

Sarah's body began to respond to her extreme distress and a sudden pain gripped her abdomen.

"No!" she said, putting her hands below her stomach. "No! The baby can't come now. It's too early."

Erik began to panic. He was out of his depth and disturbed at having been the cause of this possible catastrophe

"What shall I do?" he asked, finding himself in a situation beyond his control.

"Call my midwife," gasped Sarah, as the contractions began to come with increasing power. "Tell her what's happening and then get the car out and take me to the hospital, you stupid bastard."

Meekly, Erik did as he was told and within half an hour, he and Sarah were on their way to the room which he had booked in advance in the best private clinic his money could buy.

For a while, the contractions lessened but began again with even greater force almost as soon as she was taken to the maternity suite. Erik held her hand and bathed her forehead and Sarah accepted his ministrations, trying to stem her anger and distress, knowing that to allow his imminent desertion to dominate her thoughts would make the birth more difficult and endanger both her and the child.

With great presence of mind, she put his callous perfidiousness aside and focused on the most important thing – giving birth safely to their baby. Perhaps, by some stroke of remote good fortune, he would become so besotted with the infant that he couldn't bear to leave. Not now. Not in two weeks or whenever it was he had planned.

Not ever.

It was the one small ray of hope that Sarah held onto; the one thing that helped her concentrate on the birth and allowed her, through all the pain and the effort, to enjoy the wonderful feeling of achievement and satisfaction as she pushed and sweated while Erik stayed close by her side and encouraged her, unable to stop himself from becoming profoundly moved by the miraculous appearance of the new life that he had created with this amazing woman.

After it was all over and mother and baby settled and happy, Erik decided he would give the tickets to a colleague at work.

He had no use for them now as Sarah would not be ready to traipse round looking at paintings. They could go next year or the year after that. It didn't matter when. But right now and forever, all Erik wanted was to be with his baby son and the woman who, as soon as she was well enough, he would make his wife.

And, unlike his own mother and the former love of his life, he would never walk out on her – this clever and voluptuous woman who had taught him, finally, about the possibility of allowing himself to love again; of being *able* to love again and who he knew would guide him through the uncharted territory that stretched before them, helping him reach once and for all beyond the confines and destructive grief of his past.

Royal Academy of Art
Summer Exhibition
London

They gathered – Edie, Ben and Jamie together with Jack and Grace around *The Girl in Jack's Portrait*.

They stood admiringly – well, not Jack, who was inundated by the press wanting to photograph him in this position or that position; asking questions about how it felt to be back at the Royal Academy after all these years; trying to ascertain who the mysterious girl was in a portrait that had caused a considerable stir in the art world for its fine detail and infinite depth.

He parried their enquiries courteously, tactfully, graciously, sitting upon a high stool to conserve his energy; wondering when all this nonsense would finish and he could slip away quietly and be with his family again.

The portrait was admired and regret expressed that it was not going to be sold; that *The Girl and Jack's Muse* was not next to it in this, the main gallery, where it should have been, but had been placed in the Nonagenarian Exhibition instead.

Jack said he was happy as long as people were able to see both of them and the others that were on display; that as long as it had a place, that it was the picture itself that mattered the most, not where it was positioned.

People arrived and departed, crowding round, curious and intent: dissecting the brush strokes, the light, the use of colour; the shape of the Girl's eyes, her nose, her mouth; discussing in minute detail the perspective, the position of the subject within the setting; speculating upon the identity of the Girl and her relationship to the artist.

They spoke of all these things in mounting excitement and, amid the well-meaning mêlée, Callie quietly appeared at the back of the room.

Jack saw her immediately and smiled. She smiled back, her demeanour poised yet wary.

"If you uphold your promise, which I know you will," he'd said to her that last day on Cairnmor, "to come to the exhibition because you are the subject of the painting, then you will have to be prepared to face a confusing circus of people all firing questions at you from different directions. As well as Jamie."

"Yes," she'd replied bravely. "I know."

She'd dreamed, that last night on Cairnmor, that she would arrive and Jamie would turn and see her as she stood by the doorway and come across to her and take her into his arms.

And she would lie to him and tell him that she couldn't be with him; that she was married to someone else, an ex-boyfriend from university with whom she'd met up.

And that would be the end of it and she wouldn't have to worry about embarrassing herself or his family ever again in case he didn't forgive her or she found she didn't love him anymore.

At that moment, Jamie turned and saw her and went across the room towards her. But he didn't take her in his arms as she had imagined he would.

They stood looking at each other in silence for what seemed an eternity before he took her hand, guiding her out of the crowd to a quiet place where they could be alone.

"Why?" he said, the simplicity of the word belying a whole world of emotional distress and deliberation.

She should have pulled away from him at that moment and regarded him with regret in her eyes, the facial expression she had practised so often in front of a mirror.

"I can't be with you," she should have said: the words she had repeated to herself over and over again; the words she should be saying now.

But Callie found that she couldn't say any of them, that she couldn't say the lie. She couldn't deny that in the intervening weeks between leaving Cairnmor and the exhibition as she roamed the lonely moors of Northumberland, she had known with absolute clarity that she wanted to be with Jamie; that she was desperate to be with Jamie; for him to forgive her; for them to recapture the untroubled, carefree romance they had known in those few brief, heady days before he went away.

Above all else, Callie knew that to tell such a lie would be letting Jack down and in doing so, he would know, just as she now did, that she would be denying the person that she really was; that as herself, putting all other considerations aside, she was indeed in love with Jamie.

"I'm sorry," was all she managed to say. "Forgive me."

"What for?" said Jamie. *For running away? Sleeping with another man? Hurting me? Hurting us? Not that there ever was much of an 'us'.*

But now was neither the time nor the place to air those things.

Eyes forward. Look neither left nor right. Let the future unfold.

There would be time enough for dissection, for analysis; for the inevitable confession, moments of recrimination and ultimate forgiveness. There would be time enough for rebuilding and strengthening, time in which to grow closer.

"For everything," she said.

"Yes, in time," he said simply, bringing her to him.

He stroked her hair and she closed her eyes, responding to the lightness and gentleness of his touch, unable to bear the pain that emanated from him.

"Perhaps," he said softly, "we have both grown stronger because of it."

"But it needn't have happened."

"No," he swallowed hard, "but it did and as we can't change that, we'll just have to learn to live with it as best we can. Both of us. Together. I still want you for my wife, Callie."

"Despite what happened?"

"Despite that."

Freedom and blessed relief filled her soul.

"Oh, Jamie."

He lifted her left hand in his and kissed the empty ring finger.

"Can we start again?" she said. "From the place we left off?"

It was all and everything she knew she wanted; it was all and everything she hoped that Jamie wanted.

"Yes. I'd like that. Very much."

The clamour from inside the room began to reach them.

"Unfortunately, though," he said ruefully, "for the moment, we have to go back in there and face the music of your new-found fame and our combined, curious families."

He smiled at Callie and she smiled back. Softly, he touched her cheek.

"We'll have to save everything else for later," he said, regarding her carefully. "We have a lot of making up to do."

"Yes," said Callie, her spirits soaring.

And Jamie led her by the hand towards their waiting relatives and the waiting press.

Eyes forward. Look neither left nor right. Let the future unfold.
Remain in the still, calm centre of love.

OTHER PUBLICATIONS FROM
ŌZARU BOOKS

The Call of Cairnmor
Sally Aviss

Book One of the Cairnmor Trilogy

The Scottish Isle of Cairnmor is a place of great beauty and undisturbed wilderness, a haven for wildlife, a land of white sandy beaches and inland fertile plains, a land where awe-inspiring mountains connect precipitously with the sea.

To this remote island comes a stranger, Alexander Stewart, on a quest to solve the mysterious disappearance of two people and their unborn child; a missing family who are now heirs to a vast fortune. He enlists the help of local schoolteacher, Katherine MacDonald, and together they seek the answers to this enigma: a deeply personal journey that takes them from Cairnmor to the historic splendour of London and the industrial heartland of Glasgow.

Covering the years 1936-1937 and infused with period colour and detail, The Call of Cairnmor is about unexpected discovery and profound attachment which, from its gentle opening, gradually gathers momentum and complexity until all the strands come together to give life-changing revelations.

"really enjoyed reading this – loved the plot... Read it in just two sittings as I couldn't stop reading." (P. Green – amazon.co.uk)

"exciting plot, not a book you want to put down, although I tried not to rush it so as to fully enjoy escaping to the world skilfully created by the author. A most enjoyable read." (Liz Green – amazon.co.uk)

"an excellent read. I cannot wait for the next part of the trilogy from this talented author. You will not want to put it down" (B. Burchell – amazon.co.uk)

ISBN: 978-0-9559219-9-5

Changing Tides, Changing Times
Sally Aviss

Book Two of the Cairnmor Trilogy

In the dense jungle of Malaya in 1942, Doctor Rachel Curtis stumbles across a mysterious, unidentifiable stranger, badly injured and close to death.

Four years earlier in 1938 in London, Katherine Stewart and her husband Alex come into conflict with their differing needs while Alex's father, Alastair, knows he must keep his deeper feelings hidden from the woman he loves; a woman to whom he must never reveal the full extent of that love.

Covering a broad canvas and meticulously researched, Changing Times, Changing Tides follows the interwoven journey of well-loved characters from The Call of Cairnmor, as well as introducing new personalities, in a unique combination of novel and history that tells a story of love, loss, friendship and heroism; absorbing the reader in the characters' lives as they are shaped and changed by the ebb and flow of events before, during and after the Second World War.

"I enjoyed the twists and turns of this book ... particularly liked the gutsy Dr Rachel who is a reminder to the reader that these are dark days for the world. Love triumphs but not in the way we thought it would and our heroine, Katherine, learns that the path to true love is certainly not a smooth one." (MDW – amazon.co.uk)

"Even better than the first book! A moving and touching story well told." (P. Green – amazon.co.uk)

"One of the best reads this year ... can't wait for the next one." (Mr C. Brownett – amazon.co.uk)

"One of my favourite books - and I have shelves of them in the house! Sally Aviss is a masterful storyteller [... She] has obviously done a tremendous amount of research, judging by all the fascinating and in-depth historical detail woven into the storyline." ('Inverneill' – amazon.co.uk)

ISBN: 978-0-9931587-0-4

Where Gloom and Brightness Meet
Sally Aviss

Book Three of the Cairnmor Trilogy

When Anna Stewart begins a relationship with journalist Marcus Kendrick, the ramifications are felt from New York all the way across the Atlantic to the remote and beautiful Scottish island of Cairnmor, where her family live. Yet even as she and Marcus draw closer, Anna cannot forget her estranged husband whom she has not seen for many years.

When tragedy strikes, for some, Cairnmor becomes a refuge, a place of solace to ease the troubled spirit and an escape from painful reality; for others, it becomes a place of enterprise and adventure – a place in which to dream of an unfettered future.

This third book in the *Cairnmor Trilogy*, takes the action forward into the late nineteen-sixties as well as recalling familiar characters' lives from the intervening years. *Where Gloom and Brightness Meet* is a story of heartbreak and redemptive love; of long-dead passion remembered and retained in isolation; of unfaltering loyalty and steadfast devotion. It is a story that juxtaposes the old and the new; a story that reflects the conflicting attitudes, problems and joys of a liberating era.

"the last book in Sally Aviss's trilogy and it did not disappoint ... what a wonderful journey this has been ... cleverly written with an enormous amount of research" (B. Burchell – amazon.co.uk)

"I loved this third book in the series ... the characters were believable and events unfolded in a beguiling way ... not too happy ending for everyone but a satisfying conclusion to the saga" (P. Green – amazon.co.uk)

ISBN: 978-0-9931587-1-1

Message from Captivity
Sally Aviss

When diplomat's daughter Sophie Langley is sent on an errand of mercy to the Channel Island of St Nicolas in order to care for her two elderly aunts, she finds herself trapped in an unenviable position following the German invasion.

In the Battle for France, linguist and poet Robert Anderson, a lieutenant in the Royal Welch Fusiliers, finds himself embroiled in an impossible military situation from which there seems to be no escape.

From the beautiful Channel Islands to the very heart of Nazi-occupied Europe, the epic, meticulously researched tale "Message From Captivity" realistically captures the atmosphere of life under enemy control, together with the struggle of participants on all sides to 'do the right thing', even in the impossible circumstances of war. It weaves factual authenticity into the fabric of a narrative where the twists and turns of captivity, freedom and dangerous pursuit have unforeseen consequences, where integrity is tested to the limit, and great inner strength is needed to cope with the decisions and challenges faced. Espionage, malice and romance combine in a story that will lift the spirits and wrench the heart.

"If you like a good read you will love this book! The structure of the book takes you between the main protagonists and weaves their lives together as the story unfolds, add to that authentic research on the events of the period and you have a great story which keeps you guessing to the end." (P. Green – amazon.co.uk)

ISBN: 978-0-9931587-5-9

Reflections in an Oval Mirror
Memories of East Prussia, 1923-45
Anneli Jones

8th May 1945 – VE Day – was Anneliese Wiemer's twenty-second birthday. Although she did not know it then, it marked the end of her flight to the West, and the start of a new life in England.

These illustrated memoirs, based on a diary kept during the Third Reich and letters rediscovered many decades later, depict the momentous changes occurring in Europe against a backcloth of everyday farm life in East Prussia (now the north-western corner of Russia, sandwiched between Lithuania and Poland).

The political developments of the 1930s (including the Hitler Youth, 'Kristallnacht', political education, labour service, war service, and interrogation) are all the more poignant for being told from the viewpoint of a romantic young girl. In lighter moments she also describes student life in Vienna and Prague, and her friendship with Belgian and Soviet prisoners of war. Finally, however, the approach of the Red Army forces her to abandon her home and flee across the frozen countryside, encountering en route a cross-section of society ranging from a 'lady of the manor', worried about her family silver, to some concentration camp inmates

"couldn't put it down... delightful... very detailed descriptions of the farm and the arrival of war... interesting history and personal account" ('Rosie', amazon.com)

ISBN: 978-0-9559219-0-2

Carpe Diem
Moving on from East Prussia
Anneli Jones

This sequel to "Reflections in an Oval Mirror" details Anneli's post-war life. The scene changes from life in Northern 'West Germany' as a refugee, reporter and military interpreter, to parties with the Russian Authorities in Berlin, boating in the Lake District with the original 'Swallows and Amazons', weekends with the Astors at Cliveden, then the beginnings of a new family in the small Kentish village of St Nicholas-at-Wade. Finally, after the fall of the Iron Curtain, Anneli is able to revisit her first home once more.

ISBN: 978-0-9931587-3-5

Skating at the Edge of the Wood
Memories of East Prussia, 1931-1945… 1993
Marlene Yeo

In 1944, the twelve-year old East Prussian girl Marlene Wiemer embarked on a horrific trek to the West, to escape the advancing Red Army. Her cousin Jutta was left behind the Iron Curtain, which severed the family bonds that had made the two so close.

This book contains dramatic depictions of Marlene's flight, recreated from her letters to Jutta during the last year of the war, and contrasted with joyful memories of the innocence that preceded them.

Nearly fifty years later, the advent of perestroika meant that Marlene and Jutta were finally able to revisit their childhood home, after a lifetime of growing up under diametrically opposed societies, and the book closes with a final chapter revealing what they find.

Despite depicting the same time and circumstances as "Reflections in an Oval Mirror", an account written by Marlene's elder sister, Anneli, and its sequel "Carpe Diem", this work stands in stark contrast partly owing to the age gap between the two girls, but above all because of their dramatically different characters.

ISBN: 978-0-9931587-2-8

Ichigensan
– The Newcomer –
David Zoppetti

Translated from the Japanese by Takuma Sminkey

Ichigensan is a novel which can be enjoyed on many levels – as a delicate, sensual love story, as a depiction of the refined society in Japan's cultural capital Kyoto, and as an exploration of the themes of alienation and prejudice common to many environments, regardless of the boundaries of time and place.

Unusually, it shows Japan from the eyes of both an outsider and an 'internal' outcast, and even more unusually, it originally achieved this through sensuous prose carefully crafted by a non-native speaker of Japanese. The fact that this best-selling novella then won the Subaru Prize, one of Japan's top literary awards, and was also nominated for the Akutagawa Prize is a testament to its unique narrative power.

The story is by no means chained to Japan, however, and this new translation by Takuma Sminkey will allow readers world-wide to enjoy the multitude of sensations engendered by life and love in an alien culture.

"A beautiful love story" (Japan Times)

"Sophisticated... subtle... sensuous... delicate... memorable... vivid depictions" (Asahi Evening News)

"Striking... fascinating..." (Japan PEN Club)

"Refined and sensual" (Kyoto Shimbun)

"quiet, yet very compelling... subtle mixture of humour and sensuality...the insights that the novel gives about Japanese society are both intriguing and exotic" (Nicholas Greenman, amazon.com)

ISBN: 978-0-9559219-4-0

Sunflowers
– Le Soleil –
Shimako Murai

A play in one act
Translated from the Japanese by Ben Jones

Hiroshima is synonymous with the first hostile use of an atomic bomb. Many people think of this occurrence as one terrible event in the past, which is studied from history books.

Shimako Murai and other 'Women of Hiroshima' believe otherwise: for them, the bomb had after-effects which affected countless people for decades, effects that were all the more menacing for their unpredictability – and often, invisibility.

This is a tale of two such people: on the surface successful modern women, yet each bearing underneath hidden scars as horrific as the keloids that disfigured Hibakusha on the days following the bomb.

"a great story and a glimpse into the lives of the people who lived during the time of the war and how the bomb affected their lives, even after all these years" (Wendy Pierce, goodreads.com)

ISBN: 978-0-9559219-3-3

The Body as a Vessel
Approaching the Methodology of
Hijikata Tatsumi's Ankoku Butō
MIKAMI Kayo

An analysis of the modern dance form
Translated from the Japanese by Rosa van Hensbergen

When Hijikata Tatsumi's "Butō" appeared in 1959, it revolutionized not only Japanese dance but also the concept of performance art worldwide. It has however proved notoriously difficult to define or tie down. Mikami was a disciple of Hijikata for three years, and in this book, partly based on her graduate and doctoral theses, she combines insights from these years with earlier notes from other dancers to decode the ideas and processes behind butō.

ISBN: 978-0-9931587-4-2

Turner's Margate Through Contemporary Eyes
The Viney Letters
Stephen Channing

Margate in the early 19th Century was an exciting town, where smugglers and 'preventive men' fought to outwit each other, while artists such as JMW Turner came to paint the glorious sunsets over the sea. One of the young men growing up in this environment decided to set out for Australia to make his fortune in the Bendigo gold rush.

Half a century later, having become a pillar of the community, he began writing a series of letters and articles for Keble's Gazette, a publication based in his home town. In these, he described Margate with great familiarity (and tremendous powers of recall), while at the same time introducing his English readers to the "latitudinarian democracy" of a new, "young Britain".

Viney's interests covered a huge range of topics, from Thanet folk customs such as Hoodening, through diatribes on the perils of assigning intelligence to dogs, to geological theories including suggestions for the removal of sandbanks off the English coast "in obedience to the sovereign will and intelligence of man".

His writing is clearly that of a well-educated man, albeit with certain Victorian prejudices about the colonies that may make those with modern sensibilities wince a little. Yet above all, it is interesting because of the light it throws on life in a British seaside town some 180 years ago.

This book also contains numerous contemporary illustrations.

"profusely illustrated... draws together a series of interesting articles and letters... recommended" (Margate Civic Society)

ISBN: 978-0-9559219-2-6

The Margate Tales
Stephen Channing

Chaucer's Canterbury Tales is without doubt one of the best ways of getting a feel for what the people of England in the Middle Ages were like. In the modern world, one might instead try to learn how different people behave and think from television or the internet.

However, to get a feel for what it was like to be in Margate as it gradually changed from a small fishing village into one of Britain's most popular holiday resorts, one needs to investigate contemporary sources such as newspaper reports and journals.

Stephen Channing has saved us this work, by trawling through thousands of such documents to select the most illuminating and entertaining accounts of Thanet in the 18th and early to mid 19th centuries. With content ranging from furious battles in the letters pages, to hilarious pastiches, witty poems and astonishing factual reports, illustrated with over 70 drawings from the time, The Margate Tales brings the society of the time to life, and as with Chaucer, demonstrates how in many areas, surprisingly little has changed.

"substantial and fascinating volume... meticulously researched... an absorbing read" (Margate Civic Society)

"a page turner... I enjoyed looking at the pictures/illustrations. This book will be kept on my library shelf... Highly recommended for anyone who has either had fond memories of Margate or would be interested in the history" (Jeanette Styles, goodreads.com)

ISBN: 978-0-9559219-5-7

A Victorian Cyclist
Rambling through Kent in 1886
Stephen & Shirley Channing

Bicycles are so much a part of everyday life nowadays, it can be surprising to realize that for the late Victorians these "velocipedes" were a novelty disparaged as being unhealthy and unsafe – and that indeed tricycles were for a time seen as the format more likely to succeed.

Some people however adopted the newfangled devices with alacrity, embarking on adventurous tours throughout the countryside. One of them documented his 'rambles' around East Kent in such detail that it is still possible to follow his routes on modern cycles, and compare the fauna and flora (and pubs!) with those he vividly described.

In addition to providing today's cyclists with new historical routes to explore, and both naturalists and social historians with plenty of material for research, this fascinating book contains a special chapter on Lady Cyclists in the era before female emancipation, and an unintentionally humorous section instructing young gentlemen how to make their cycle and then ride it.

A Victorian Cyclist features over 200 illustrations, and is complemented by a fully updated website.

"Lovely... wonderfully written... terrific" (Everything Bicycles)

"Rare and insightful" (Kent on Sunday)

"Interesting... informative... detailed historical insights" (BikeBiz)

"Unique and fascinating book... quality is very good... of considerable interest" (Veteran-Cycle Club)

"Superb... illuminating... well detailed... The easy flowing prose, which has a cadence like cycling itself, carries the reader along as if freewheeling with a hind wind" (Forty Plus Cycling Club)

"a fascinating book with both vivid descriptions and a number of hitherto-unseen photos of the area" ('Pedalling Pensioner', amazon.co.uk)

ISBN: 978-0-9559219-7-1

Bicycle Beginnings
Stephen Channing

It is difficult to imagine that a little over a century ago many regarded cycling as reprehensible, revolting, or indeed revolutionary. The best way to get a feel for what early 'velocipedists' encountered is to read the words of the times, and this book gathers into one volume the most enlightening, entertaining and extraordinary insights from contemporary sources. Stephen Channing's earlier tome "The Victorian Cyclist" focused on one of the sport's pioneers and garnered universal praise for its wonderful writing and meticulous detail. Bicycle Beginnings now plays the spotlight over a wider domain, excerpting hundreds of 19th century newspaper reports and letters to convey the atmosphere in which the first cyclists found themselves.

The mammoth work (over 190,000 words, covering the period 1779 to 1912) contains race reports, legal developments, technical innovations and inventions, records, advertisements, acrobatics, clothing, poems, arguments for and against the new-fangled vehicles, debates over women cyclists, and a long travelogue, "Berlin to Budapest on a Bicycle" capturing the excitement of a forgotten age of adventure on two wheels.

Not all the inventions were two-wheeled, however. This book also reveals the numerous variations that came into being before makers standardized on the shapes we commonly see nowadays: tricycles, ice velocipedes, water-paddle hobby-horses... These are explained with the aid of numerous illustrations, covering the gamut from cartoons to technical drawings and photographs. Even the race reports demonstrate far more variety than we are accustomed to seeing: 'ordinaries' (penny farthings) versus 'safety' bicycles versus tandems, monocycles, dwarf cycles, tricycles, double tricycles, four-wheel velocipedes, horses, ice skaters, steamships...

Rather than a single narrative to be read in one go, it is an anthology of fascinating glimpses into cycling's 'golden age', providing a new understanding of a bygone age of experimentation and much amusement, whenever the reader dips into it.

ISBN: 978-1-5210-8632-2

Also available on Kindle. Note: the paperback edition includes several indices not present in the Kindle version.

Lightning Source UK Ltd.
Milton Keynes UK
UKOW04f0247250118
316773UK00003B/165/P